Murder... in a Small Town

Alan E Losure

Alan E Losure

© Copyright 2017, Alan E Losure

All Rights Reserved

No part of this book may be reproduced, stored in a retrieval system, or transmitted by any means, electronic, mechanical, photocopying, recording, or otherwise, without written permission from the author

ISBN: 978-1-946977-81-6

Prologue

Whether one believes in the scientific approach to the creation of the earth, along with all forms of life within, or the creationist's view point that God created our planet 6,000 plus years ago, doesn't really matter as far as this book is concerned. Either way, the simple fact is that a huge body of natural gas was formed deep within the ground of what eventually became East Central Indiana. Experts tell us that this was caused by the natural decomposition of plant and animal life seeping into the surface of the ground. Intense heat and pressure, from the earth itself, caused the chemical reaction break down that produced natural gas. This process either took millions of years to complete or 6,000 plus. For the sake of this novel, the length of time involved is left entirely up to you, the reader.

We are also told that the Chinese were the first people to use natural gas about 500 BCE. Apparently, they discovered a pocket of it seeping from the earth and used hollow bamboo wooden poles to form a primitive piping system to boil salt water to extract valuable salt. A very ingenious people indeed.

We may also be certain that the native Indian tribes that once inhabited East Central Indiana, as well as the early settlers that followed, had no idea that this valuable resource lay beneath their feet 1,000 to 1,200 feet below. It would take the beginning of the early industrial age to release this natural treasure from its underground captivity and put it to industrial work in ways never conceived before.

Please note that this is not a book that centers on the Gas Boom itself but rather uses it, as well as the small towns it helped to create, as the background for this fictional story. I will, from time to time, introduce the names of a few real historical people that carved out their place within the local wilderness and of actual historical events that did in fact take place, but its the fictional characters I hope will assist in balancing the book into a realistic story. I have chosen the time period of 1893 as a historical starting point for this story but I have no intention of boring the reader with a geography lesson of Gas City, Indiana only to introduce to you an interesting small town into which the story shall revolve.

It is said that people take their health for granted until it is gone and that is certainly what happened to the Natural Gas Boom of this period. Here today...gone tomorrow.

Acknowledgments

I sincerely wish to thank the following members of the Gas City Historical Society for their assistance in many of the historical specifications of this novel. They are: Mrs. Patty Chapman, Mrs. Lana Pattison, Mr. Frank Wayman, and Mr. David Huffman. I am positive they were tempted to lock the front doors of our wonderful Gas City Historical Museum each time they saw me coming their way, asking many questions, and becoming a real pest.

Any historical inaccuracies within this novel are entirely of my own doing to ensure a workable story line is presented to you, the reader.

I also want to thank and dedicate this book to my wonderful wife, Susan, for her support of my efforts.

Through my research, I have taken a few actual interesting historical quotes and news events from people of this time period and blended them into the story line without changing their historical nature. If you are interested in learning more about Gas City, Indiana, please visit their Web site at www.gascitymuseum.com

Alan E. Losure

Chapter 1

March 28, 1893

Justin Blake felt he simply had taken enough. It was not working outdoors that bothered him. Growing up South of Cleveland, Ohio on a family farm, Justin was well accustomed to working outdoors in all types of weather. He discovered early on that farming was not to his liking. His younger brothers, Travis and Franklin, seemed happy with that lifestyle as they wished him luck working in the big city of Cleveland. It was not his job itself that bothered him. Being a dock worker loading and unloading cargo from incoming and outgoing commercial shipping on Lake Erie was hard work, but working on his family farm for twenty-two years has made Justin Blake strong and healthy. Standing six foot tall and weighing 170 pounds, Justin was solid muscle and fully capable of performing his required work load of twelve hours a day, six days a week with no complaint.

No, it was what happened every Saturday evening once each dock worker lined up to receive his pay envelope that really bothered him. Being forced to pay one dollar tribute to the Sicilian Gang. That was the last straw.

It wasn't only Justin that had to fork over his hard earned payment each week, but every dock worker who worked along the piers. As soon as the men lined up in front of the paymaster's window, groups of large, and, yes, armed thugs from the gang stood off the property waiting for the men and their earnings to come their way. The Sicilian gang even had a list of the dock workers' names and would check off each name once payment was received. Pretty ruthless but efficient.

It was quite normal for a new man, who didn't know the rules, to laugh in the faces of these thugs or refuse payment when approached. A severe beating quickly changed his mind and kept the other workers fearful but in line. One could not earn a paycheck with a broken arm, a knife blade stuck in the ribs or a crushed foot. Nobody working along the docks spoke about this gang's practice, knowing that any loose talk might prove fatal if word got back to them. All new workers would have to find out "the rules" of the game on their own the hard way.

Justin remembered the young fellow who tried to organize his fellow dock workers into refusing to pay up, saying there was safety in numbers. Right, his number was soon up as his lifeless body, wrapped in a section of carpet, washed up a week later after he had gone missing. That alone was proof that these thugs meant business. Better to just pay up and live to see another payday.

It was said, in hushed voices, that the Sicilian Gang also had their fingers in the pockets of the ship owners. No ship's cargo was loaded or unloaded without the owners paying what the gang demanded. If not, well, cargo had been known to accidentally drop into the water, catch on fire, go missing, or become damaged in other ways. The owners now considered it the price one had to pay in order to stay in business and added the extra expense onto the final products being shipped or received.

Many of the dock workers, after paying their weekly tribute, met for a drink or more at the nearby Warf Bar. Justin did not fall into that category. He had nothing against an occasional drink but Justin had other plans for his money. He was planning on leaving the Cleveland docks and the Sicilian Gang once and for all. Looking back now it was funny how all of that transpired.

It was on a cold and bitter January day, three months ago, that Justin found himself inside a local restaurant one evening. With the winter snow furiously blowing outside, he was in no hurry to leave the mostly empty restaurant and sat drinking a cup of coffee while considering his future options.

At a table next to him sat three businessmen talking about the future of their glass company. It was impossible not to hear every word they were saying as the fat man, who appeared to be their leader, spoke loudly and seemed to enjoy the power he held over the other two. Justin noticed the fat man reaching into his satchel and extracting three sheets of paper, which he handed out to the other two businessmen, keeping one for his own references.

"As you can see here, gentlemen, by moving our glass producing factory over to nearby Indiana we can save a small fortune on our costs. Imagine what profits we will earn not having the expense of buying coal for our furnaces. Two of our competitors are in the process of relocation there as we speak. Gentlemen, we must do the same to remain competitive and I am asking for your support at the Monday afternoon executive board meeting. Can I count on your vote?" Each of the businessmen nodded their approval, and soon, the group departed.

Justin finished his coffee, stood up to put on his heavy coat, and laid his payment for the meal upon the table. As he was preparing to walk away he noticed that one of the businessmen had left his copy of the paper on the table. Out of curiosity, Justin picked it up, glanced at it, and folded it up placing it into his coat pocket. Something to look at when he returned to his dinky one-room flat in town.

Upon arriving there, he removed his coat and lit his candle as the evening darkness was soon approaching. Sitting down upon the single wooden chair Justin removed the paper from his coat pocket and began to read it closely.

It was an advertisement from a group called the Gas City Land Company. **"Free Fuel! Free Land! Free Water! Paved main street, brick schoolhouse, well-paying jobs, a perfect place to relocate factories, or open your business. We are close to completion of the Mississinewa brick hotel and an opera house for your cultural entertainment. The Pennsylvania Railroad provides daily rail service to and from all points of locality making the shipment of your finished products very convenient. An endless supply of Natural Gas enables homes and businesses to be heated for free. Main Street to be lit up by gas light very soon. Come to experience the Gas Boom that has made Grant County, Indiana the talk of the industrialized nation."**

Laying the paper down upon his table, Justin considered the possibilities. *This sounds like a place where I can make a new start*, he thought. Since that day three months ago, he had tried to save every penny he could for the train fare to Gas City. Of course just getting there would just be the start as he would need additional funds for food and lodging until he could acquire work. Checking with the railroad ticket agent, he learned a second-class ticket from Cleveland to

Gas City would cost $12.50. Justin also sold his old shotgun to a friend for additional funds.

He figured by early April he would be ready for his first trip by rail. He was told by a frequent Pennsylvania Railroad traveler that the old "Pennsy" Pacific Locomotive could hit speeds up to a staggering 50 mph. He collected his final week's pay, informed the paymaster he was quitting, forked over his dollar tribute to the gang, picked up his travel bag, and headed to the railway depot station for what he hoped would be a life-changing relocation. Arriving early, he purchased his ticket and took a seat in the waiting area. The ticket agent informed him that he would travel west to Chicago then pick up a southbound train to his destination. That sounded just fine to Justin.

Sitting several seats away on a different bench, a middle aged man was explaining the new features now being offered in modern transportation to another bewildered passenger who had the look that he wished to be sitting anywhere except next to this talkative know-it-all.

"Yes sir, the Pennsylvania Railroad offers the best that can be offered in modern transportation," he told his weary fellow passenger. "These new vestibule passenger cars are the latest thing. No more going outside to step over into another moving car with only a small safety chain to prevent you from falling off. No sirree, these enclosed passageways protects the traveler from the swaying cars and exposure to rain, or soot and red-hot cinders. Why, I remember one time I was traveling between Boston and Philadelphia when...."

Just then an announcement was made by the ticket agent of the arrival of his westbound train. Rising from his seat, Justin glanced back to see if the big-mouth talker would be entering his second-class railroad car. Thank goodness the man and the unlucky traveler were both destined for first class.

Justin couldn't help but smile at his good fortune and, upon entering the passenger car, took an unoccupied seat. His new life was soon to begin, and he would truly be surprised if he had any idea what fate had in store for him.

Chapter 2

Justin found traveling by train most exciting as he continued along mile after mile seeing beautiful farms and the ever-changing countryside. He noted that every few miles large loads of cut wood were stacked neatly for much needed fuel to power any steam locomotive finding itself running short. *This Pennsylvania Railroad thinks of everything*, he thought. After short stops in small towns, boys came aboard the train trying to sell sandwiches, newspapers and such. Justin purchased a ham sandwich from a boy who couldn't have been more than eight years old. Due to the soot being discharged from the engine's smoke stack, experienced travelers knew to keep their windows closed while the train was in motion. With the beautiful April evening and the sun beaming through his window, Justin found himself getting a little sleepy. Leaning against the side of the passenger car, he allowed himself to drift off to the gentle movement of the rail car.

Arriving later that night in Chicago, Justin had some time to kill before the southbound train arrived. Stepping outside of the huge railroad terminal, he was taken back by the magnitude of the modern-day city. *If things don't work out in Indiana, perhaps I might return here*, he thought. Finally, morning arrived and it was time to board his new train for the southward journey. Justin had purchased a magazine inside the terminal and started skimming through it to help kill time, as he still had a long way to go.

"Fort Wayne," the conductor finally shouted, "Next stop Fort Wayne and a thirty-minute lay over for fuel. Here's your chance to stretch your legs. If you depart the car, please ensure you have your boarding ticket with you."

Justin was unsure just how long he had dozed off during the night but felt completely refreshed now. He thought he might as well go ahead and get off the train for a few minutes too. Leaving his traveling bag in his seat, he stood up and stepped off out of the car. It felt good to be walking around again but Justin felt a little uneasy on his feet like he was still moving. *Quite odd,* he thought. About twenty minutes later he re-boarded for the final journey to Gas City. As he approached his seat he noticed an old man with a heavy beard had taken a seat directly in front of him. The man wore a broken-down hat and was dressed like a poor farmer. Thinking nothing more about it, Justin settled back into his traveling mode for his final destination.

The old man leaned back against the window and looked up at Justin. "Afternoon young man," he said. "You travelin' to Gas City or Indianapolis?" The thought of the know-it-all first-class passenger quickly passed through his mind before he replied. "Getting off at the Gas City stop." The old man smiled and Justin knew he was about to experience a long discussion with a total stranger. Still, there was something about the old man that intrigued him. "You ever been there?" Justin asked him. The man replied, "Lived there or around there all my life. When I was born, only a few white people lived there in parts at a small tradin' post. My pappy fought with Lieutenant Colonel Campbell against the Miami Injuns back in 1812 at what's come to be known as The Battle of Mississinewa, so it makes me a native I reckon'. You just passin' through or fixin' ta stay a spell?"

Justin immediately took a liking to the old man so he felt comfortable in discussing his future plans. "Here's a flyer I found that tells of jobs to be found in Gas City." He handed it to the old man who stared at it then turned it sidewise before handing it back. "Can't read, Sonny, never felt it important enough ta learn it. By the way, name's Zeke Miller but folks just call me Zeke." Justin offered his hand. "My name is Justin Blake and I'm looking for employment and maybe a place to settle down for awhile."

"Well," Zeke replied, "guess it's as good as any place to do that in. Plenty of jobs now that the factories are a movin' in. Payin' good too, fer seventy hours of work a fella can make close ta ten dollars a week if he's skilled labor in one of dem factories. I heard we got twenty-five drinkin' saloons, seven or eight hotels, and all kinds of stores and such all lit up day and night by them there gas street lights. Probably so bright at night it blinds the bats flyn' overhead! Gettin' a mite too big for me though, buildin' up and so many folks driftin' in, no offense intended."

Smiling to show none was taken, Justin asked, "So, Zeke, what do I need to know about the town?"

"Two towns actually on both sides of the Mississinewa River. I grew up ah callin' um Harrisburg and Darlington, but now they're bein' called Gas City and Jonesboro. The river is named after an injun word meanin' *it lies on a slope*. With the Natural Gas boom now takin's place, many factories and stores are movin' in. A strong, healthy young man such as yourself ain't gonna have no trouble ah gettin' a job there."

"You mentioned Indians, is there a large reservation of them there?"

"Nope, not many left anymore. The treaty of 1854 changed all that. About fifteen years ago Injuns were required to start payin' taxes on their land. That pretty much drove um away. But I remember' um com'un around ta traden an such. Shucks, old man Conner used to trade with um he told um the man who made Cambric needles died and charged them a dollars' worth of furs for every needle while his supplies lasted. Injun's never did catch on! I'll tell ya one thing true about um though if you visited with um and they gave you sugar or an egg, that's a sign that they like and respect ya. But let um get their hands on whiskey and they're just as soon ta lift your hair."

Sitting two rows back on the other side of the car was a man that Justin had presumed earlier to be a traveling salesman. "Now come on Zeke," the man said while lifting his hat over his eyes. "You're going to give this young man the wrong impression of our thriving little community." Looking back Zeke smiled, "I didn't see ya sittin' there, reverend. Why don't ya cum up and take a seat and jaw-jack with us sum." "I don't mind if I do," he replied with a smile, "if it's not interfering with your wild Indian tales."

"Young man, my name is Reverend Clarence Stokes of the Gas City Friends Church." Rising up to offer his hand, Justin Blake introduced himself and encouraged the Reverend to sit down beside him. "Zeke," the Reverend exclaimed "I am somewhat surprised to see you riding on a modern-day locomotive. I have heard you say many times that you would never get caught riding an iron horse," laughing as he said it.

Sheepishly, Zeke in an almost whispering voice replied, "Shucks, Reverend, my old bones don't ride a horse like they use ta. I would take it kindly if ya forget ta seein' me on this here train. Wanted ta visit my sister in Fort Wayne while I felt up ta it."

Smiling, reverend Stokes told Zeke his secret was safe with him. Justin liked the way the reverend handled the old man's feelings without embarrassing him. "I, too, have a small confession to make," the reverend said. "I was called to Fort Wayne last week to visit with a dying member of my original church's congregation who was living her final days with her daughter. She passed this week and I found myself having to travel on the Lord's Day in order to get home for this evening's services. I, too, feel uneasy about being seen traveling on a Sunday. Luckily, I had arranged for another person to take over my church duties while I was away."

"Gas City," the conductor bellowed walking through the car. "Next stop is Gas City for a twenty-minute stop over. Anyone traveling on to Indianapolis, please ensure you have your boarding pass with you, should you choose to leave the train."

Zeke stood up and grabbed his carpet bag, "You fellers gotta forgive me but I feel the need ta slide off the back of this train so folks ain't gonna notice me a gettin' off." Once the car had stopped, Justin stood and followed the Reverend Stokes out of the car. Finally, he had arrived and it was a truly beautiful day also. *So this is Gas City*, he thought. He could clearly make out several natural gas derricks in the distance in what he presumed to be the industrial area. Across from the depot on the other side of the train was a wooden structure with a sign on its front, Panhandle Hotel and Restaurant.

Justin and the Reverend had hardly traveled more than fifteen feet when both men noticed a large crowd of people rushing past, in front of the engine. The train station agent saw Reverend Stokes and quickly moved to his location. "I think you better go down to the river, reverend, they're pulling a body out of it." "Thanks, Matt, I'll go to offer prayer. You might as well come along, too, young man," he said to Justin.

Together, they walked the quarter-mile distance down to the river where a crowd of people had gathered. Strange how people seemed to want to see death and destruction right up close. Looking out into the river, Justin could see that the April rains had produced a high and swift water current. About twenty feet out from the shore was a small wooden boat with two men in it. The front of the boat was tied off to a rope that several other men on shore were attempting to hold in place, while its occupants frantically used their paddles to try to keep it from spinning around. There, beside the boat, was a whitish floating mass that Justin knew in an instant was the remains of a human being several days in the water. The men in the boat were trying to slip a rope around the body so they could then pull it up to shore.

"Back, everybody, please step back and give the men room to work," spoke Marshal Kenneth Brewster. He was a big man probably in his fifties and perhaps a little old for the job required of him. His stomach hung over his beltline, and he was always seen wearing a Remington Model 1875 single action 44-40 revolver. Many people laughed privately that the old town marshal probably couldn't hit the wide side of a barn with it anyway. Still, the aged man was willing to do the job that most would not. Seeing that the men were struggling, Brewster gave directions to the men in the boat who, after three attempts to rope the body, finally succeeded and pulled it toward them.

North of the train depot was a small, low-cost, newly constructed housing addition that many of the railroad employees, saloon keepers, and factory workers lived in. Small, four room framed houses built for a working man's family. Mrs. Edith Small, the wife of a tin plate factory worker, was one of the occupants and at that minute was outside hanging her laundry out on the rear clothesline to dry. One had to hang the laundry between trains or expect to find soot covering whatever you had spent hours washing. Her eight-year- old daughter Emily had observed that something was going on down at the river bank but, due to the large crowd, the child could not get close enough to see.

Probably out of boredom or simple frustration, Emily started splashing a stick into the raging river's edge for enjoyment, but due to the wet river banking her solid footing let loose tumbling her into the rapidly flowing river. She managed to scream once before being sucked under, bobbing to the surface as the muddy current pulled her steadily toward the group of people standing on the bank. Most stood there in total shock as the child was quickly moving downstream. It was happening so quickly.

Suddenly someone from the group made a mad dash to the river's edge and dove into the muddy waters. He surfaced to see the child about twelve feet in front of him and he knew he had but one chance to grab onto her or she would be swept away and lost forever.

Fighting the heavy current, Justin managed to catch the edge of the child's dress and jerked her into his arms. He had her now and despite her fear and struggling managed to keep her head above water. Now the problem was, who would save them? Luckily the men in the boat realized what was happening and using a boat oar managed to reach Justin's outreaching hand and pulled him and the child safely towards their boat. Soon, everyone had been pulled to the shore as Justin shielded the child's eyes from viewing the floating corpse. Still, there was no shielding anyone from the terrible odor and the assembled crowd soon had enough of the dead person but joined in congratulating Justin's bravery. Someone had gone and brought the child's frantic mother to the scene who, amid tears of joy, was eternally thankful for saving her daughter's life.

Having only arrived in Gas City less than twenty minutes before, Justin found himself a town hero. Everyone kept asking him questions, "Who are you?" "Did you know the girl?" "Where do you work?" It was enough to make his soggy head start to spin. Finally, Marshal Brewster shooed most of the people away saying, "Please, folks, give the young man some room. Can somebody bring him a towel?" Apparently, a man had already thought about it and a towel from the depot soon arrived. Gratefully, Justin took the towel and wiped the dripping water off of his face and head. "Son," Marshal Brewster said, "that was a mighty brave thing you just did. I don't recognize you. Exactly who are you anyway?"

"My name is Justin Blake, and I just arrived a few minutes ago on the train from Cleveland."

Alvin Jensen, a reporter from the Gas City Journal who happened to witness the entire ordeal spoke up, "Mr. Blake, that was quite an entrance you just made into our fair city. If you don't already have lodging acquired, my paper would be pleased to put you up overnight at our brand-new brick Mississinewa Hotel. I'm sure you would like to get cleaned up and put on a dry set of clothes. Of course, I will need to interview you for our paper."

Justin was not one to take charity but figured the newspaper interview would more than cover his overnight lodgings so he readily agreed. "Let me retrieve my travel bag from the depot and I'm ready to go." Someone brought the reporter's carriage around, he was then driven down Main Street, getting the twenty-five cent tour of the city along the way.

Back at the drowning location most of the assembled people had already left for home. Doctor Baxter had already made his preliminary examination of the body. The man was quite dead indeed. "A couple of you men haul this body to my office for me," Doctor Baxter directed. Reverend Stokes completed his silent prayer and, knowing he could do nothing more, congratulated Justin for his fine work and said he hoped to see him again very soon.

As the body was lifted up, one could easily see that the poor man's hands were clearly tied behind his back. This was certainly no drowning accident. "Doctor," Brewster said, "I'll be down later to see what you have discovered. I have something I need to do first. Thanks again for your assistance. I know it will not be a pleasant examination for you."

Doctor Baxter looked up, "Yes, these things are never pleasant. Give me a couple of hours and I'll probably have something for you by then."

Earlier, Marshal Brewster had been sitting in his office, if you could call it an office, inside a combination jail and city fire barn. He had been looking at paperwork when a citizen barged in saying he witnessed a body floating down the Mississinewa River. For convenience, Brewster then jumped into the seat of the man's wagon as they responded together. Now that his job was finished, he was walking back towards his office but, first, stopped by the Western Union Telegraph office. Walking inside, the operator peppered him with questions about the drowning which Brewster quickly waved off. "I have a telegram I want you to send to Cleveland, Ohio, asking for any information they might have on a young man known as Justin Blake."

Chapter 3

Justin Blake had just finished cleaning up, using the water basin in his room, and was dressing when there was a knock on his hotel room door. It was the local reporter, Alvin Jensen. "Mind if I interview you over lunch?" he asked. "No problem," Justin told him "Give me a couple of minutes and I'll meet you down stairs." Upon entering the dining room, Justin saw that the reporter already had a table for them and took his seat opposite the man.

"By the way, the pork chops are delicious here. I suggest you try them," the reporter offered. "Lunch is on us, too."

"So tell me," Justin asked as he leaned closer so as to keep his voice quiet, "why is a reporter like you working on a Sunday anyway?"

"The news doesn't stop just because it's a weekend and you, my new young friend, are the second half of my story. I can see the headlines now: "*Newcomer Saves Drowning Local Girl*." It'll make a great reading in tomorrow's edition of the Gas City Journal. Then after I leave you, I will be checking with our local authorities on the identity of the dead man in the river. I'm sure my editor will give me some time off later on...he's my uncle." After a few questions, Jensen had completed his interview and was on his way while, Justin decided it was time to walk the town to get a general idea of its layout. Tomorrow his job search would begin, as well as locating other lodgings. The hotel was fantastic but a little expensive for an unemployed worker.

Marshal Brewster felt enough time had probably elapsed, so he walked over to Doc Baxter's office and found him sitting at his desk recording notes of his medical findings. "Got anything yet, Doc?" Removing his wire spectacles and rubbing his eyes, Doc Baxter motioned for the Marshal to have a seat. "Yes, it's old Joe Three-Toes and he was severely beaten before he died by drowning." Brewster removed a notebook from his left shirt pocket and was ready to take notes, saying "I was pretty sure he was the old rummy who worked and lived as a swamper in the backroom of the White Dog Saloon. I didn't want to speculate about it in front of that crowd of people or that nosy reporter. That man is like a bee to honey, always turns up when a story breaks. So tell me what you have discovered."

Doc Baxter put his spectacles back on and began to read out loud, "Severe trauma to the face and skull, fifteen burn marks on the torso, probably from a person or persons holding a lit match to his skin, hands bound behind his back by a thin coarse rope, and knotted with a five foot long piece of the same type of rope tied around his left ankle. The end of that rope was frayed. I'm guessing that end was tied off to something heavy that was used to submerge the body in the river with the current dragging the weight along the bottom, finally breaking free. By the condition of the body, I would say it had been in the river for about thirty-six to forty-eight hours."

"Then he was probably taken a couple miles upriver and dumped sometime the night before last or even later. I just sent the body over to L.C. Frank's funeral home," replied Brewster. "Thanks for your help, Doc. I'll see that the city plants him tomorrow in a proper pauper's grave."

Marshal Brewster walked back to his small office in the fire barn to find three visitors there waiting for him. "Afternoon, gents, and what brings all of you out on a Sunday afternoon?" The two shorter men looked up at the tallest middle-aged man, waiting for him to speak for them. "Marshal, you know full well why we are here. It's about that killing...that makes the second one since the beginning of the year and don't forget the beatings that also took place. As three of our town's leading citizens, we feel it's our duty to find out what you are going to do about finding the killer or killers." The speaker was Mr. Matthew Brooks, one of the town's barbers. His companions were Mr. Timothy

Morgan of the Morgan Grocery and C.H. Rothinghouse, of Rothinghouse Brothers Drugstore.

"Gentlemen," the Marshal replied, "I appreciate your concern but I am only beginning my investigation on this recent incident. As to the caning of the Negro and the man dragged to death behind a horse, those cases are still open but I do have some ideas and, if you will give me a little more time..."

Mr. Brooks interrupted, "Marshal, I got to tell you that almost every man who comes into my barber shop says the same thing. It's the White Caps that's behind all of this madness."

The marshal leaned back in his chair, "What made you come to that conclusion, gentlemen? The vigilante group known as White Cappers are a mostly Southern Indiana group. What makes you think they have spread this far north and are operating in our area?"

Mr. Morgan cleared his throat. "Sir, it fits their pattern. A group of vigilantes who feel justice has not been properly served or the law is helpless to punish the guilty, then don flour sacks over their heads at night and take it upon themselves to punish the transgressors as they see fit. They target lazy drunks, wife beaters, wayward women, and more. They feel they are the moral police of society, but I call them thugs and no-good murdering hooligans who must all be brought to justice." Both of his friends nodded in full agreement with the grocer.

"Well," the marshal replied, "I can see where you get that idea but I need facts to go on, not just local opinions. I also require names. I appreciate your visit, gentlemen, but I must get back to work. Please enjoy what's left of your Sunday afternoon. Good day."

Leaning back again in his swivel chair, Marshal Brewster considered what they had suggested. The thought had already entered his mind prior to this latest crime. He had tried to obtain information from the frightened Negro after Doc Baxter had treated his severely beaten body. He was simply too frightened to answer questions and soon left the area. The man who was dragged to death by his horse had his leg tied tightly to the stirrup. It was no accident. The poor man's head was severely bashed to pieces. It was also an open secret that the married factory worker who was beaten half senseless was seen frequently visiting a local house of ill repute. Perhaps it was some form of punishment from the wife's kin folks? If all of this was the works of the White Caps, they were becoming braver and braver coming up into central Indiana.

~~~~~~~~~~~~~~~~~~~~~~
~~~~~~~~~~~~~~~~~~~~~~

Having completed his interview with the new arrival, reporter Alvin Jensen was en route to the marshal's office when he noticed the three townsmen exiting the fire barn. Sensing a possible story, he approached them. "Good afternoon gentlemen, I couldn't help but notice you all leaving Marshal Brewster's office. Any new leads on the body pulled from the river?" The druggist, Mr. Rothinghouse, replied, "Murdered sir, and it is our combined opinion the work of the White Caps. Good day to you, sir." Reporter Jensen smiled broadly as he thought of tomorrow's banner headlines.

Shortly after returning from his sight-seeing adventure, Justin Blake stopped at the front desk of the Mississinewa Hotel and inquired as to where the Reverend Stokes' church was located. *I might as well drop by tonight*, he thought to himself.

The church turned out to be only a short walk from his hotel on the corner of North B and Second Street. Upon entering, he noticed an empty pew up near the front of the church and took a seat. Many of the parishioners were visiting with a new mother and her bawling baby, the noise of which nobody seemed to mind at all. He then noticed Reverend Stokes enter the church, making eye contact with many of his friends and shaking a few hands as he approached the pulpit. When his eyes fell upon Justin, he quickly recognized the young man and walked over to greet him. "Mr. Blake, wasn't it? I am very happy to welcome you to tonight's service."

"Thank you Reverend, it's a pleasure to be here," was his reply, as everyone became quiet for the services to begin.

"My friends, before I begin my prepared service for this evening, I would like to introduce and publically welcome a young man, who in the first twenty minutes of being a new citizen of our city, saved the life of a precious little girl down at the river. Without a moment's thought of his own safety, he leaped into the rushing muddy waters of the rain-swollen Mississinewa River to save the life of a total stranger. I had the privilege of riding into town with him only moments before, and I must tell you that God himself must have directed him to our shores. This young man seeks no publicity or gratitude for what he has done, only the chance to live and work within our community. I now ask each and every one of you to help me welcome Mr. Justin Blake to our services tonight."

There was much applause as folks seemed to line up to shake his hand or pat him on the back. All this attention simply made Justin feel uneasy, "Anyone would have done the same thing," he told all his well-wishers.

"Hello, Mr. Blake, I'm Mrs. Ruth Stokes, the reverend's wife and this young lady is our daughter, Samantha. Clarence has told us all about what you did and we would like to invite you to accompany us home after services and share our dinner."

"I wouldn't want to impose," Justin said as he smiled at Miss Samantha. She appeared to be about nineteen or twenty with long brown hair and large green eyes. Justin was a bit smitten but tried his best not to let it show.

"It's no bother at all and in fact it's our honor to have you. Nothing fancy," Mrs. Stokes modestly told him, "Just a pot of stew that Samantha helped me prepare this afternoon." Justin readily agreed and soon the services began.

After the services ended and hands were shaken, the family began walking home which gave Justin the chance to walk beside pretty Samantha Stokes. After a period of awkward quietness, Justin whispered, "I would like to learn more about you, Miss Stokes." "Please, call me Samantha," she replied with a beautiful smile. "I get enough of hearing *Miss Stokes* all day long. You see, I teach school children their ABC's and other whatnots." "That's a wonderful occupation for a bright and talented young lady," he replied. Justin thought he saw a slight blush in Samantha's cheeks. He was very happy he decided to attend services tonight!

Chapter 4

Arriving at the Stokes' family home, Reverend Stokes invited Justin into his study. "Let's just relax until the ladies call for us, shall we?" he suggested. "So tell me, what are your impressions of our fair city?"

"Well sir, everyone seems so nice and friendly. Tomorrow, I will begin my search for a place to live and seek out employment." The reverend said, "You might try Ma Richards Boarding House. She does require references so please feel free to use my name as she runs a clean, respectable and affordable establishment. The reference also applies to any employer within our community."

"Thanks, very kind of you, Reverend. I think I'm going to like it here very much." Samantha then appeared at the doorway and called the men to dinner. After grace, the normal family table talk occurred which helped Justin to relax and feel right at home.

"This is delicious, Mrs. Stokes, it reminds me of my own mother's cooking back in Ohio," Justin informed her. "Are you originally from this area?" he casually asked of her.

"Yes," she replied, "my grandparents were Quakers and operated one of the local underground railroads for escaping slaves. I remember one time when I was a little girl when a group of Kentucky planters came here looking for their runaway slaves. Grandpa encouraged the Negro men and women to return peacefully to their masters. After the group had left, grandpa got on his pony and rode to the near-by Indian village to ask the Indians for their assistance. Soon the Indians had caught up with the slave owners and their human property on the other side of Jonesboro. Their party was surrounded by the Indians bellowing war-whoops, and completely terrifying the slave owners who abandoned the Negros and made a quick getaway back to Kentucky. (chuckling) Grandpa helped many escape to freedom in Canada. Once slavery was abolished here, several Negros returned to live here due to the kindness he had shown them."

"That's funny," Justin told her. "I bet the Indians enjoyed getting to play Indian one more time." Samantha, who had remained quite still during the meal spoke up, "Mother, please recite to our guest the old slave poem you say they used to sing together. I cannot remember how it begins..."

"Well, if you think it appropriate and if our guest is interested," she casually replied to her daughter. "Yes, please do," Justin said. Clearing her throat, Mrs. Stokes began:

"I'm on my way to Canada, that cold and dreary land-
The dire effects of Slavery, I can no longer stand.
I served my master all my days, without a dime's reward-
But now I'm forced to run away, to flee the lash abhorred.

Oh, righteous Father, wilt thou pity me,
And aid me on to Canada, where Colored Men are free.
I heard old Massey pray last night, I heard him pray for me,
That God would come and in the night from sin, and Satan set me free.

The hounds are baying on my tracks; the Master's just behind,
Resolved that he will bring me back before I cross the line-
Farewell old Massa, that's enough for me, I'm on my way to Canada,
Where Colored Men are free."

"That was wonderful," Justin told her, "I cannot imagine what it was like to be a slave...or a slave master."

Soon, the evening had ended, and Justin, thanking his hosts for a wonderful evening, returned to his hotel room. Tomorrow would be a busy day for him.

~~~~~~~~~~~~~~~~~~~~~~

On Monday morning, a very grateful Justin Blake checked out of the Mississinewa Hotel and sought out the location of Ma Richard's Boarding House. Ma was a pleasant older woman, short and very round with thick spectacles. After introducing himself and mentioning his new association with Reverend Stokes, Ma perked up and welcomed him into her home.

"Nothing fancy here, young man, but I do run a clean and respectable boarding house," she told him. "I had to ask the last gentleman to leave as I caught him trying to sneak a painted hussy in," saying it with a twinkle in her eyes. It was a simple room but a great deal nicer than his old one in Cleveland, with solid comfortable furniture and nice curtains.

"The rent is $2.25 per week." Justin was pleased with its layout and paid a week's rent, saying he would then pay monthly once he landed a job.
~~~~~~~~~~~~~~~~~~~~~~

~~~~~~~~~~~~~~~~~~~~~~

If not for the discovery of natural gas and the initial investment by the Pennsylvania Railroad, there was no doubt Gas City would still be wheat fields and forests instead of the small industrial powerhouse town it was. Now many factories were in place providing jobs for the local community. The main ones were: The Tin Plate Works (largest in the world), American Window Glass Plant, Thompson Green and Amber Glass Bottling Company, Gas City Bottling Company, American Glass Works, Grant Iron and Steel Works, and the United States Glass Company. In addition, there were various mills and others companies under construction such as the Gas City Strawband Company, Chicago Edged Tool Company, J.M. Frazee Box Factory and the E.P. Chapman Company. There was no doubt why Indiana ranked third in manufacturing among the other states.

The Thompson Green and Amber Glass Bottling Company was another successful example of the businesses who now considered Gas City home. Take its shop foreman, Mr. William Dorsey, for example. He was a man who worked very hard and improved his position in life. Starting as a boy working within one of the seven-man mold-blowing shop teams, Bill advanced to a skilled gaffer worker before finally being recognized and advancing into management as a shop foreman, a rare achievement in these days. He
~~~~~~~~~~~~~~~~~~~~~~

knew the bottling business inside and out as his company made all kinds of glass bottles and jars for its customers. It didn't matter if the job called for glass bottles for beer, wine, whiskey, medicine, tonic, bitters, or fruit jars, they had the know-how to produce a fine product.

There were several steps involved in the production of a bitters bottle, for example. A skilled blower (gaffer) would dip his blowing pipe into a pot of molten glass, roll, and partially blow the glass before placing the end inside an open two or three piece mold. A boy, who sat at the blower's feet, would then close the mold. Then the blower would force the glass into the mold until he met resistance, indicating the mold was filled.

His blowers pipe was then snapped off while the unfinished bottle was taken by another boy to the skilled finisher, who would work the pliable glass top into shape using his tools. With a crew of two blowers and one finisher, many bottles could be produced quickly. Then when cooled, boys and sometimes girls would pack them into wooden crates with packing materials for shipping by railroad to each customer.

That is how the process was supposed to work, but lately, things had not been running smoothly. As shop foreman, William Dorsey knew he would be held responsible for correcting the difficulties with his men. It was close to 8 a.m.

when he entered the private office of Frank Livingston, the plant manager.

"Good morning Frank," replied Mr. Dorsey as he entered and closed the door behind him.

"Morning Bill, how is your wife feeling these days?"

"Thanks for asking," He sadly replied. "Betty has her good and bad days but the doctor isn't too optimistic. Cancer of the breast is untreatable you know. I'm thankful her sister will stay with her while I am working." Hearing his friend say it out loud, again, always produced a lump in the throat of Mr. Livingston. He thanked God daily for the health and safety of his own family.

"I am so sorry to hear all this, Bill, and if there is anything I can do, please don't hesitate to call upon me day or night," replied the plant manager.

Regaining his business composure, Mr. Dorsey addressed the issue for which the meeting was called. "I have looked into the scuffle that took place last Friday and it was another example of two intoxicated workers. I can understand why the men frequent the nearby White Dog Saloon, with its cheap drinks and free lunch counter, but several skilled workers have lately returned to work highly intoxicated. This has led to fights, breakage, and unsafe working conditions that have affected overall production. Believe me when I tell you I have talked to the men until I am blue in the face but it doesn't seem to help. I have even threatened to have some of the offending skilled glass blowers fired, just to set an example, but they know their skills are in great demand and they don't fear being fired as another glass producer will quickly pick them up."

Sitting quietly at his desk, Frank Livingston drummed his fingers and contemplated the decision he would have to make. "With this new law that holds employers responsible for the behavior of their workers, I see no other alternative but to go ahead with the petition idea to have this nearby White Dog Saloon closed," he reluctantly said.

"The men will have a fit. A five-cent beer, free pretzels, rye bread, smoked herring, salted peanuts, and dill pickles make up the bulk of a working man's lunch," offered Dorsey.

"I feel at this point we have no other choice, both for our own good and of course the local community. Our warnings to the men have gone unanswered. We must do this." Handing the prepared petition to his shop foreman, Livingston instructed him to go into town and get as many signatures as possible from prominent people. "I have explained our difficulties to Mayor Huffman and he'll see that it gets voted on tonight at their city council meeting. I may just attend and present it myself."

"I fear there may be violence from the men, Frank."

"If so, then we must fire every agitator involved, no matter how much it hurts our business. Then the rest of the men will fall in line. Please see me when you are finished getting signatures and good luck."

~~~~~~~~~~~~~~~~~~~~~~~

Justin's first instinct was to apply for an eighteen cent per hour job at one of the glass-producing factories but quickly changed his mind when he saw how hot that working inside one of those factories would be, especially in the summer. He found out he would have to start as an unskilled worker in a "boy" position, called that despite any age, at eleven cents per hour. Justin felt he should look elsewhere for now. The lumber yard had an opening but the boss who did the hiring was away on another job. Justin was told to return in a day or two if he was still interested in the position.

He stopped by a job site where workmen were constructing another brick building along Main Street. He was told a job would be available tomorrow morning as a brick mason's helper for 23 cents per hour, if he was interested and came to work on time sober. At this point, that sounded like a good job possibility and hard physical work was no stranger to Justin Blake.

By that afternoon, Marshal Brewster got his reply by Western Union. Mr. Justin Blake had no outstanding warrants or past criminal exploits as far as the Cleveland Police were aware of. As Brewster was beginning his regular
~~~~~~~~~~~~~~~~~~~~~~~

morning rounds, he heard his name being called. "Marshal Brewster, a word with you, if you please. Any further updates concerning the body in the river?" It was that pesky reporter, Jensen, again. *Well,* he thought, *I guess it's all right to provide a name. Power of the press and all.*

"The man has been identified as the old swamper who worked and lived in the back room of the White Dog Saloon. He was known locally as Joe Three Toes."

"Joe Three Toes," repeated the reporter as he made entries into his pocket writing tablet. "Any idea why he was called that?"

"Well, Old Joe seemed to be a frequent guest in the town's jail. Liked the bottle a little too much, if you know what I mean. I do remember him once saying something about being a woodcutter in his youth. You can probably figure out the rest for yourself."

"Any leads on who killed him and why?" the reporter asked.

"Sorry, I cannot comment on an ongoing open investigation. That's all that I have for you. Excuse me, but I need to get going." With that Marshal Brewster continued his patrol, eventually finding himself outside the town's barber shop. Reaching up and feeling his three-day old beard growth, he entered and found it void of customers. The marshal then took a seat in the stuffed barber chair. "Just a shave this morning, Matthew."

Barber Matthew Brooks placed a barber's cape around his neck, "How goes your investigation, Marshal?"

Brewster was quick to reply, "It would go a lot faster if you boys in the city council would vote to allow me to hire another deputy. This town is growing fast, and I can't be everywhere at once. I've got two guys working the night shift just to handle the drunks and petty disturbances while I try to hold the fort during the daytime all by myself."

"That topic is on the council's agenda tonight and I promise I will vote for it, but who can tell with Mayor Huffman and the other three. Huffman's goal is to become the next Indiana governor anyway, so every decision he makes is political." At that, both men chuckled. As Brewster settled back and enjoyed the shaving lather being applied to his course old stubbles, the door to the shop opened.

"Gentlemen, my name is William Dorsey and I am the shop foreman down at the Thompson Bottling Company. We are circulating a petition asking the city council to revoke the liquor license of the White Dog Saloon, a cheap little dump of a shack that sets within easy walking distance to our plant. Our workers continue to visit it during their lunch time and their inebriated condition is affecting the quality of our work and creating a dangerous situation. You gentlemen are leaders within the community and your signatures will be very beneficial in our effort."

"Closing down the saloon seems a little harsh to me," the barber said, "Can't you just instruct your men not to go there?"

"That has been tried often enough with no effect as we have had almost constant problems developing within the last few months. Marshal, you have been called down to break up fights and trouble several times. You know what we are up against."

"Yes," Brewster replied, "closing that saloon would be one less headache for me," He reached for the petition and signed it. He then handed it to the barber who shook his head no. "That just doesn't set well with me, count me out. You also know that "Big Jim" Malone won't like it one little bit."

Everyone knew that Big Jim was the owner of several little shacks he called saloons that catered strictly to the tastes of the poor working man. Big Jim had purchased several of the cheaper, less desirable $200 plots of land that the Gas City Land Company had offered for sale. They were located within the industrial area and not properly suited for building a house but perfect for a tumble-down cheap saloon. Big Jim then hired men to construct the buildings and hired some of his own thugs to manage his saloons for him. A man named Kruger managed the White Dog Saloon, named after a stray white mutt that had wandered in for shelter and a free handout.

The petition soon found its way to most of the local businesses in town skipping, of course, any drinking establishment. Wherever he went, Dorsey stressed the financial rewards gained by keeping the Thompson Bottling Company in town and overall how little the White Dog Saloon provided to the community. As per his final instructions, he obtained the mayor's signature before beginning the walk back to the plant to present it to Mr. Livingston in person.

Chapter 5

Factory foreman William Dorsey was pleased with the quantity of names signed on his petition and was looking forward to presenting it to his supervisor when his pathway was suddenly blocked by three rough-looking men. "You the guy tryin' ta close down a workin' man's saloon? Ain't gonna happen," he said as he poked his index finger hard into the foreman's chest.

"Let me pass gentlemen, I don't wish any trouble as I am only doing my job," Dorsey replied as he tried to sidestep the men. It didn't work. The brute of a man called Kruger grabbed the petition swiftly out of the startled man's hand.

"You ain't gonna need des here papers, Mr. Big Shot." A determined William Dorsey attempted to retrieve his paperwork when a swift punch to the jaw landed him flat on his back. Startled at the turn of events, Dorsey could only attempt to cover his face as blow after blow and a few kicks to the head turned daylight into darkness.

It was late afternoon when William Dorsey was finally able to stagger to his feet, finding his petition torn into many little pieces and scattered around him. The vision in his left eye was blurred and blood was seeping from inside his ears and nose. With all the energy he could muster, Dorsey made his way the best he could, finally entering his supervisor's office where in front of a startled Mr. Livingston, he collapsed on the floor.

With the day of looking for a job behind him, Justin thought back on a conversation he had with Samantha before he left her home.

"Drop by the schoolhouse at 4 p.m. someday and you can walk me home. That is if you would care to do so," she had teasingly told him. He had grinned ear to ear saying he would love to do so, providing any new job would not prevent him from doing so. *Perhaps*, he thought to himself, *I should do it today while I am still free*. Justin picked up his stride and headed toward the two-story brick schoolhouse.

The Martin brothers, Todd and Kevin, were well-known local hoodlums known for theft, assaults, drunkenness, and just about everything in between. Most people quickly stepped to the other side of the street when they appeared in public. Both were destined for either prison or the rope. Take your choice. Sunday had provided a bonanza for the young thugs, having robbed at knife point a garment drummer over in Jonesboro. Feeling safe and secure from identification, the pair had spent all day Monday celebrating their good fortunes by drinking heavily in their favorite low-end saloon. Nobody asked them where they had gotten their money. To do so would result in a severe beating...or worse to the curious person. Shots of whiskey and beer chasers had left the pair very intoxicated and looking for a fight with anyone stupid enough to get in their way.

Todd Martin pulled out the pocket watch he had stolen from the salesman yesterday and was barely able to read it as 3:45 p.m. "I'm feelin' lonely fer female company!"

"What ya wanna do about it?" his brother replied, grinning like a possum at the very thoughts going through his dirty mind. "I knows, let's go pay our respects ta that fancy schoolmarm. Schools fixin' ta let out and she's bound ta be lonely fer company!" Finishing up their drinks, the Martin Brothers staggered out of the saloon and on to the direction of the brink schoolhouse.

"Class dismissed," their teacher said. "Please don't forget to study for our geography examination tomorrow morning."

"I'll be ready Miss Stokes," little Martha replied. "You make learning fun!" Almost all of the children had already left for home as the little girl always liked to walk out of the school building with her teacher. Before Samantha could lock up, the Martin Brothers arrived at the open doorway.

"Hey Teacher," one of them shouted, "let us learn' you somethin' fun, you gonna like it lots."

Startled by the intrusion of these men and fearful for her safety as well as little Martha, Samantha replied, "Gentlemen, please leave at once. You are not welcome here." Both brothers, smiling with a sick look of lust on their faces, started to approach her. Turning quickly to the little girl, she whispered "Go get help," as the child dashed out of the door.

Samantha backed towards the safety of her desk but felt pinned in as the brothers slowly approached. Little Martha was hardly out of the doorway when she started screaming, "Help! Help! Bad men are going to hurt Miss Stokes!" Hearing this, Justin in a bolt of sudden energy sprinted past the little girl and literally exploded into the room. There he could quickly see both men had Samantha pinned between them, as the terrified woman tried to push away their oncoming and unwanted advances.

Swiftly, Justin reached the nearest brother, and with all his might, punched him hard in the kidneys. Kevin screamed in pain, as he fell to the schoolroom floor. Todd, startled at first with the newcomer's intrusion, reacted to his brother's attacker with rage and charged him like a wild bull. Justin sidestepped the oncoming man and grabbing his head, slammed it hard in a downward thrust upon the wooden desk top. While all of this was taking place, Samantha had vacated the building and was standing outside in the safety of a crowd of the curious who also heard the child's screams for help.

Justin grabbed both men up by their rear collars and frog marched them outside to the wild applause of those who were assembled. "Oh, Justin, what you just did saved me from certain harm. I shall always be in your debt."

"Are you all right?" He asked, "Did they touch you?"

"I am a little shaken up but physically unharmed, thanks to you."

"You should thank the little girl, as it was her screams that alerted me. Please allow me to walk you safely home."

"I cannot help but feel our Lord guided your hand today as He did for that poor little child who was drowning." By now most of the crowd had dissipated except three strong men, who said they would personally deliver the brothers safely into the hands of Marshal Brewster. "I must first lock up the school, then we may leave," she told him.

"Have those men bothered you before?" he asked her.

Thinking back, she told him she didn't think so. "I do know for a fact they do not attend father's church," she replied, as the couple walked away. "Did you find a place to live and employment today?" she asked.

"Ma Richards took me in, thanks to your father's recommendation," he replied. "I'm still looking for the right job." Anyone observing the young couple would quickly note that Spring, and possibly early love, was in the air. Walking her to the door of her house, Justin was taken by surprise as Samantha kissed him quickly on his cheek in gratitude and ran hurriedly inside her home. Reaching up to touch the spot where her tender lips had just touched him, Justin knew he would gladly fight five more men for the chance at another kiss from the lovely Miss Samantha. *I guess I better go see the marshal now in case he has any questions as to what happened*, he thought.

Word of the drunken near assault had just reached the ears of Reverend and Mrs. Stokes as they hugged their daughter in great relief when she entered their home. Most fathers would have sought vengeance upon the attackers of their daughter, but Reverend Stokes simply thanked God for her safe return. He would make no formal complaint against the boys, hoping that they might learn a lesson and profit by it. Two years ago he witnessed them breaking a window in his church by throwing a rock through it. He had done nothing at all about it then, and had hired a man to replace the glass. *Maybe if I had, these boys might have changed to become productive citizens?* he thought.

Walking past the tiny white-framed post office, Justin made a mental note that he needed to stop by soon to see if he had a letter from his parents. He had earlier met Postmaster Harris, who was often seen on a bicycle picking up four mail pouches daily from the Pennsylvania Railroad. Harris had told him that the majority of the incoming and outgoing mail was for the Gas City Land Company but to drop by the post office anytime a crowd of people assemble. That was when names were called and letters passed out to townspeople. It sounded like a good system to Justin. *That's a job I would like*, he thought. *Let people come for their own mail*.

He then found himself stopping in front of Morgan's Grocery. In the window were advertising signs for Indiana Flour and loaves of bread for five cents. Justin had no idea if this price was reasonable or not.

Walking up to the fire barn/city jail building, Justin noticed a familiar face, old-bearded Zeke Miller working inside the adjoining fire barn. "What are you doing in there, Zeke?" The old man was busy cleaning up after one of the fire horses, "I hang out here sum, helpin' the firemen and takin' care of Old Betsy and Prince Albert. They're great fire horses, strong, brave, and always a rearn' ta go. I heard what ya did down at the river, nice job!

Entering the Marshal's office, Justin noticed the two Martin Brother inside the single cell. Seeing him enter, both brothers stood up and stared at him with pure hatred. "Marshal Brewster, I thought you might need a statement about my tangling with those two idiots."

One of the brothers pointed a finger his way, "Mister, your dead meat the minute we get out of here."

"Shut up, Todd," the marshal scolded him, "you ain't gonna be going anywhere for a while." Smiling up at Justin, he asked him to pull up a seat and Justin filled him in from start to finish on what had just transpired. "I'm glad you came by Mr. Blake," he said. "I was gonna look you up anyway. You have made quite an impression on our little community since your recent arrival. That was a fine job you did coming to the reverend's daughter's aid like that."

"Anyone would have done the same, Marshal. I just happened to get there first."

"That was also a solid descriptive report you just provided to me. You seem to handle yourself quite well in bad situations. Have you, by chance, any experience with firearms?" "Yes," he replied. "Growing up on a farm and hunting with all types of weapons."

"What are your future plans, Mr. Blake?"

"Well, I'm staying at Ma Richards Boarding House, and at the moment, I'm searching for a job." The marshal leaning back in his chair said, "I must confess I did a little checking up on you from the Cleveland police, just to be safe and all." Surprised, Justin simply nodded in bewilderment. "Have you ever considered a position in law enforcement?"

"No, I guess I never thought much about it. Why, Marshal?"

"Well, I have submitted a request to the mayor and city council to hire another deputy. I just wondered if you might be interested in working daytime with me for the town. I got two nighttime deputies, but daytime's becomin' pretty active. The council votes on it tonight so I hope to hear something by tomorrow morning. If you think you might be interested, please check back with me. Think on this tonight, son."

Overhearing the entire conversation, the other Martin brother shouted at Justin as he departed, "Tin Star ain't gonna save you from what's you got comin' ta you, boy."

Chapter 6

At 7 p.m. that evening, the city council conducted their monthly public meeting in room number 5 inside the elegant Brick First National Bank Building. On hand to present his request to close down the White Dog Saloon was plant manager Frank Livingston. Also present to cover the public forum was reporter Alvin Jensen. Since the council's vote would in fact allow Justin to be offered a deputy marshal position, he also attended and sat in the back of the room right beside Marshal Brewster, who seemed pleased he was interested enough to show up. *A good sign*, Brewster thought.

After the normal city business procedures were covered, Mayor Huffman asked that the Plant Manager, Mr. Livingston, present his petition and explain his reasoning for asking for the saloon license to be revoked. Livingston then stood up from his seat and explained the difficulties the Thompson Green and Amber Glass Bottling Company were having from highly intoxicated employees who frequented the White Dog Saloon during their lunch break. He was repeatedly interrupted by Big Jim Malone, the owner of the saloon as well as many other shady establishments in and around town. Each time, Mayor Huffman struck his gavel and instructed Malone to wait his turn before speaking. Feeling the time was right, Livingston said, "Ladies and gentlemen, I have someone I would like to introduce to you." With that signal, in walked a bloodied and bandaged William Dorsey to the gasps of the audience in attendance.

"My good friend and shop foreman, Mr. William Dorsey, was savagely beaten this afternoon by thugs as he was returning with the signatures of many distinguished citizens. Hoodlums beat him senseless and destroyed the petition that many of you signed earlier today. I ask you, shall we have mob rule within our town? Will we allow paid thugs to dictate what they feel is in their own selfish interests?" At that point, Big Jim leaped to his feet and shouted, "You can't prove I hired those three men!"

With a slight smile on his face, Livingston replied, "I didn't say there were three attackers but it's odd that you had knowledge of that very fact." With a look of having stuck his foot inside his own mouth, Big Jim sat back down in his wooden seat and remained silent for the rest of the meeting. He knew firsthand that closing one saloon would only drive his many customers to some of his other ones and in the end, no revenues would actually be lost. His display of anger and outrage was all for show at that point anyway.

Finally, with no one speaking out against the measure, the council voted three to two in suspending the liquor license of the White Dog Saloon effective immediately. Big Jim acted like nothing had happened as he left the public meeting. He had other plans in the making that would ultimately make him one of the most powerful and richest men in the state.

Reporter Alvin Jensen attempted to obtain a statement from Big Jim but was pushed aside by Malone's men. Frank Livingston walked over to his injured friend and shook his hand. "Very kind of you to show up tonight, Bill. How's the vision in the left eye?"

"Good enough to see that Malone's thugs are the ones that beat me up." Livingston quickly approached Marshal Brewster as he was about to leave.

"Marshal, I wish to prefer charges against those three Malone men for the beating of Mr. Dorsey. Bill has identified them as his assailants."

Brewster looked over at the men who were standing next to Big Jim, "All right, I'll arrest them. Come by the office and sign the complaint." Marshal Brewster approached Big Jim and told him, "I'll have to arrest your three men on charges of assault and battery." The largest of the men, the one people called Kruger, snarled at the marshal, "There are three of us and only one of you, old man."

From behind Brewster, a voice interrupted, "Two of us, you mean." It was Justin Blake giving Kruger the meanest look he could possibly muster. "Go with the marshal boys," Big Jim told them. "Clearly, a mistake has been made. You won't be behind bars for very long." With that, all four men began to laugh. Brewster appreciated the display of backup support from young Justin Blake. *I am now positive I want this man for my deputy*, he thought. Within the hour, Justin Blake was sworn in as the new deputy marshal of Gas City.

It was well after midnight when the group of four met inside the darkened storage barn one-half mile north of town. Each arrived quietly knowing that new business was at hand that would require swift justice. No names were ever spoken though the identity of everyone was known but never discussed. A barn lantern was lit and the evening activities discussed. They met not to represent the local law enforcement community but to avenge the guilty and the transgressors as they saw fit to do whether Negro, a white man, or woman. Justice would be served this night.

The woman known locally only as Kate had sat earlier in the evening at her kitchen table trying to cover that ugly scar across her right cheek with thick face powder. A trembling voice interrupted her thoughts. "Momma, we are hungry," a small boy spoke, standing next to his little sister. Each had different fathers but Kate claimed she didn't remember their names when they often asked about them. "Shut up you stinkin', whinin' little brats and get back to bed. Mommas gotta go out ta make a little money." Kate was well-known in the lower class bars, arriving late in the evening, conning a few drinks out of unsuspecting working men and then offering them special services upon payment.

Nobody knew any of Kate's history. Perhaps long ago she was a useful member of society, a lady men tipped their hats to when meeting her on the sidewalk. Certainly not anymore. Like a cockroach, Kate only came out in the darkness of the night.

Kate had just completed one of her special services out in a darkened alley and was now alone smoking a cigar butt she had found earlier in the evening. Suddenly, she sensed a movement behind her and felt a knife blade sticking at the edge of her neck. She was instructed to quietly walk where she was directed and, if she shouted or made any fuss, the blade would find its way home. In total fear, even in her drunken state of mind, Kate obeyed the voice and continued to walk. She was being led out of town and into a darkened wooded area, away from houses and businesses. Seeing a dim light up just ahead, the man with the knife pointed her in that direction. Soon, Kate found herself inside a clearing with a dimmed barn lantern setting next to a large elm tree. Her arms were then painfully placed around the tree and her hands bound tightly with a rope. Kate was now in total fear for her life and was about to scream when a cloth gag was violently shoved into her mouth.

Kate saw movement behind her but could not see who it was, as all four people had hooded flour sacks over their heads and no words were being spoken. Suddenly, the back of her dirty, cheap dress was ripped open and a voice spoke from beyond the darkness. "You have been judged guilty of being a woman of ill repute and a scourge against society by the White Caps, with punishment to commence now." Kate's eyes bulged wide. *I know that voice...where have I heard that voice?* she thought as a painful whip tore into her back over and over again.

Early morning two days later, a group of young boys out mushroom hunting, stumbled upon her gruesome remains still tied to the tree. Within thirty minutes, a runner had located the marshal along with his new deputy as they waited for Doc Baxter's initial examination. Word of another killing had spread like wildfire throughout the town and a large group of people had assembled there for their own sick curiosity. Reporter Alvin Jensen and an artist illustrator were on hand to make a printable image of the murder site. Gruesome images meant sold newspapers. Today a lot of newspapers would be sold. Alvin's uncle would be very happy.

Jensen motioned for Blake to come over to him, away from the gathering public. "I hear you been a courting my gal, deputy." Justin looked at him with mild surprise.

"Are you telling me there is an arrangement between you and Miss Stokes?" Justin asked. Pausing slightly, Alvin replied, "Well no, not exactly, but I do intend for it to become so one day soon."

Justin was relieved to hear that Samantha was not serious about the reporter. "Well, Alvin, all I can say is, may the better man win!"

Standing next to Dr. Baxter, Justin commented quietly to Brewster, "Same type of sailor's knot as was used to tie up Joe Three Toes. I saw a million of them used on the shipping docks in Cleveland. Guess we are either looking for a sailor, someone who runs boats up and down the Mississinewa River, or someone is being coy trying to lead us in other directions."

The town barber, Matthew Brooks, approached the two officers and said, "No need to keep the shop open with everyone down here looking. I still say this is the work of White Cappers." With his loud comment, many in the group started to verbally agree and demand the police do something to stop them.

Doc Baxter ordered the body to be taken to his office and approached the two policemen. "I'll drop by your office once I'm finished with my examination. Too many eager ears here." Some of the men in the crowd were visibly disappointed as they wanted to hear all the juicy facts so they could discuss them over a beer later that evening. Doc's comment also seemed to momentarily anger the reporter. “Sir, the press has a right to know.” Dr. Baxter simply ignored the comment and walked off.

Looking down at the tracks on the ground, Marshal Brewster mentioned that too many people had trampled over the crime scene to determine how many were involved in the murder. “I guess it’s time I contact the Grant County Sheriff. Maybe he can figure things out.” As the men headed back to their office, Justin posed a question, “I’ve been meaning to ask somebody, was Grant County named after President Grant?” “Nope,” replied the marshal, “named after a pair of brothers, Samuel and Moses Grant. They were settlers here who were killed by the Indians.”

“Speaking of Indians, since these deaths are rather barbaric in nature, think there is any chance one of the few remaining Indians could be behind this?” Justin speculated. Brewster was quick to point out that Indians probably don’t tie a rope with sailor’s knots.

Shaking his head, Justin replied, “No, I guess not. Anyway, from what you have told me about them this is looking more and more like the work of the White Caps.”

Returning to their office, old Zeke Miller followed them in. “Zeke,” Marshal Brewster replied, “You’re the only person in town not out at the murder scene today.” Zeke, shook his head, “Seen enough bloody bodies during the Injun raids to last a lifetime.” Brewster moved over to the pot stove and picked up their always present coffee pot, motioning to Zeke.

"Don't mind if I do, thanks" he replied as coffee was poured into a cup and handed to him. "Say Zeke, my new deputy here was asking questions about early settlers and Indians. Got any stories to tell him?" Brewster knew full well that, with only a bit of coaxing, Zeke Miller loved to gab and tell old- time stories.

"Yep, Injuns used ta leave their pony's inside the old McClure barn lot stockade in Marion and enter through the rear door of the McClure store. They liked ta barter good using the Injun tongue. Old Chief Me-sin-gha-me-ha was a frequent guest there lots of times. Ya know, some Injuns did live civilized though, even had cabins with curtains and such fixins'." Taking a gulp from his coffee cup, Zeke went on with his tales. "Injuns used ta trade for firewater, get drunk un make a big racket, but we just tied um up till the firewater wore off. Even a few of the squaws got drunk," as he chuckled at the thought.

"So you don't think leftover Indians are behind any of these killings?" Justin asked him.

"Naw, not Injuns...White Cappers. Plain as the nose on your face, young man! Everyone knows it but gonna be hard to catch um. Very secretive, that bunch. Don't do a lot of talkin'. Gotta catch um in the act of killin' someone."

Looking at the empty jail cell, Zeke asked, "Guess Big Jim sprung his men, huh?"

Marshal Brewster, with a look of disgust, replied, "Bail was made. The judge will try them next week."

Zeke looked straight at Justin, "Deputy, you gotta watch your back around them two. They're after you." Justin noticed that Zeke's comment had Brewster also looking at him. "I can handle myself just fine," he said as he patted his own Remington 44-40 pistol.

"Well, boys, I best be a goin'. Tornadoes comin' tonight so best be prepared and see that things get tied down proper and all." Zeke gave them a wave and left the office.

"Tornado? What's that all about?"

Brewster walked over to the window and looked out with some concern at the sky, "Old Zeke is known around here for telling the weather. If he says a tornado is coming, count on it happening. Says he can feel a wind storm in his bones. He even predicted the flood of '83." That evening, April 26, a destructive tornado tore up parts of Southwest Grant County. After that, Justin started believing all of Zeke's wild old tales.

Chapter 7

Since the Reverend Stokes had preferred no charges against the Martin Brothers, Marshal Brewster was forced to release them after twenty-four hours. Within a few days, the brothers were back in town celebrating another *discovery* of money, but far more likely, it came from the pocket of another unlucky traveler. The boys had arrived early in the day and were still drinking heavily in one of the low-end saloons, a place that welcomed their company and their money, honestly earned or not. And, like most brothers, soon words and accusations began. "It's all your fault we got beat up and jailed over the stuck-up schoolmarm, Todd."

Older brother, Todd, had heard this statement for the umpteenth time that day and had had enough of his younger brother, Kevin's big mouth and accusations. "If you had fought like a man not like a baby we would ah whoop' that man!" With that statement, a punch was thrown. The bar crowd was hoping to see a fight between these two as tension and anger had been brewing up all day, and now the fun was to begin. Tables and chairs were soon flying, and two wild poll cats were scrapping, tearing the saloon, and each other apart.

After about ten minutes the fight was pretty much over. Kevin lay flat on his back on the floor while Todd, in a wave of success, tossed down another shot before staggering out of the bar. Through blurred double vision, Todd reached for the reins of his horse and with a not so graceful effort, managed to saddle up. On the spur of the moment and out of pure meanness, he grabbed the reins of his younger brother's horse also and bolted down the street, leaving Kevin to walk home. *Serves um right, walkin's good for um*, Todd managed to think to himself.

Inside the saloon, the patrons slowly approached the sleeping body of Kevin Martin. Him lying there all day wouldn't do, wouldn't do at all. So the bartender picked up the slop bucket used to mop up spills and dumped it on Kevin's face, who came up a swinging to the delight of all those present. Slowly, he began to move toward the doorway and grimaced at the bright sunlight blinding his eyes. He staggered out into the street to mount his horse only to find it gone. Looking around he noticed a local man on horseback slowly coming down the street. Kevin positioned himself in front of the moving horse, grabbed the leg of the startled rider, pitched him onto the ground, mounted the man's horse and was soon galloping at high speed down the dirt street, out of town shouting and cursing with wild laughter.

The startled man picked himself up off the ground and began brushing the dirt off his clothing. Quickly, a crowd of people circled him and were pointing which way his horse and the rider went. As a group, they marched over to the Marshal's Office to report the crime they had all witnessed: horse theft.

Inside the office was Deputy Justin Blake going over some paperwork. Upon hearing of what happened, who did it and which way the horse was heading, Justin was about to go down the street to obtain a horse from the local blacksmith shop. *I'm going to need to buy my own horse and saddle soon,* he thought. He asked Old Zeke Miller to tell the marshal he was going after a horse thief. Shaking his head in dismay, Zeke suggested he better talk to the marshal first just as Marshal Brewster entered the fire barn. "Justin, I need you to go down to the barbershop of Matthew Brooks and tell him what happened," he explained. Justin was clearly confused but, orders were orders, and he made his way down to the barber shop.

Inside, Barber Brooks was cutting a man's hair, with another customer waiting and reading the daily newspaper. Justin cleared his throat, "Matthew, Marshal Brewster told me to tell you that Kevin Martin just stole a horse and rode east out of town." The barber seemed both startled and pleased at the same time by the news, and quickly stopped cutting the customer's hair.

"Gotta go. I'll finish this up in the morning." With that Matthew reached over into his cash box, retrieved something metallic, and pinned it on his shirt. It was some sort of odd-looking badge. "The boys and I will get right on it, Deputy," he said practically running out the door. Justin was clearly puzzled and proceeded back to find Marshal Brewster for an explanation as to what had just taken place.

Entering the office, Marshal Brewster smiled at the look of puzzlement and suggested that Justin pour himself a cup of coffee, take a seat, and he would explain the whole thing. "We got us a Grant County National Horse Thief Detective Association here. Started up about twenty years ago when there wasn't much law in these parts," he explained. "For only the cost of one dollar per year a member is protected by the association against horse theft. If your horse is stolen, the association dons their official badges and hunts down the thief. Got a pretty good record of catching them, too. I hear about 500 paid members all total in this county. In the old days they often strung up the thief to everyone's satisfaction but today our boys are good about bringing um in alive. Yep, Kevin Martin should be sitting in that jail cell before the night is over."

~~~~~~~~~~~~~~~~~~~~
~~~~~~~~~~~~~~~~~~~~

"Here's your prisoner, Marshal," a jubilant Matthew Brooks stated as he pushed a confused Kevin Martin through the doorway. Brewster stood up and motioned for Martin to get inside the cell while locking it. "Have much trouble finding him, Matthew?" A smiling Brooks shook his head no, "Darn fool was too drunk to stay on the horse. Found him about a half mile out of town lying on the ground sound asleep. The horse has already been returned to its owner." From the jail cell came a pleading demand to be let out. "He's been a crying and a begging since we picked him up. Score another one for our detective association!" As Brooks was leaving the office, Marshal Brewster told him to tell the boys that the first round of drinks was on him, flipping a silver dollar into Brook's outstretched hand. Justice had been served this night.

~~~~~~~~~~~~~~~~~~~~~

The traveling circuit judge from Marion, Leo McKinsey, was scheduled to appear in Gas City the following Monday to hear the case against the three men charged with assault and battery upon William Dorsey. The trial was set for 9 a.m. Now the judge would hear the case against Kevin Martin for horse theft, too. Marshal Brewster expected the three Malone men would receive a stiff fine and a little probation, as that was pretty much the norm in physical disputes of
~~~~~~~~~~~~~~~~~~~~~

these kinds. The Martin case caused him a little concern with Kevin as well as his brother being pretty much despised by the community. He would not be surprised if a hanging was in the making. *If it did come down to that, how would older brother, Todd, react to his brother's execution*? he wondered.

Judge McKinsey arrived by the Marion-Gas City Traction Line a little after 3 p.m. and walked the short distance to the marshal's office inside the fire barn. "I'm here, Marshal," he announced, glancing over at the prisoner inside the jail cell. "Let's talk as we walk. Your office smells too much like a horse stable." Brewster knew the judge to be a fair man and personally liked his company.

"Welcome back, Judge," Brewster said as he offered to carry the man's overnight bag. "It's not heavy, I can carry it," replied the judge. "I got you a room on the second floor in the Mississinewa Hotel. Should be quieter for working. I thought we might have a late lunch first," the marshal told him.

"Good idea, my late breakfast just didn't do it for me this morning and I want some time to go over the two cases to be brought before me," the judge replied. "Has legal counsel been appointed?" Marshal Brewster nodded affirmatively.

"The three men in the assault case say they will defend themselves and the horse thief has hired counsel."

The Judge added softly, "Presumed horse thief, Marshal, innocent until proven guilty." "I stand corrected, Your

Honor," Brewster replied. As they arrived at the hotel, Brewster mentioned his new deputy, his youthful age, but his grit and determination when confronted with a difficult situation. The judge replied, "I hope he works out well for you as we both know our better days are behind us and we must look to the youth to carry on our work." Once entering the lobby, the judge's bag was quickly taken up to room number 22 while both men proceeded into the dining room. "I hope they have those great tasting pork chops on the menu today," the judge casually mentioned with a hungry smile.

~~~~~~~~~~~~~~~~~~~~~~

Todd Martin had a plan. He was not about to allow these town folks to lynch his brother. Lynching was what they planned; he knew it to be a huge mistake to trust the law while feeling tremendous guilt for the joke he had played on his brother by taking his horse. It was all just a stupid mistake. *Why can't folks see it as clearly as I can? It's nutton' but revenge, that's what it is, revenge! I'll show' um, I'll show' um all!*

Todd's plan seemed simple enough. He would sneak into town this evening when it was starting to get dark, tie up his and Kevin's horses behind the hotel, go up the rear stairs, figure out which room the judge was in, and kidnap him at gunpoint. Then together they would ride out of town and
~~~~~~~~~~~~~~~~~~~~~~

commence hiding at an old hideout the boys had used before, some sort of trade would then be worked out. The judge's safe return for his brother. Sure, they would then have to ride out of the state to live, maybe to Kentucky to live, but it seemed the only plan that would work. He had no doubt that a hanging was being planned, and he just couldn't take that chance. It was now or never as far as Todd was concerned. He packed both saddle bags with grub and provisions for the long trip south. They would ride the horses into the ground if need be, then would steal more mounts somewhere else and do the same to them. Maybe even, in time, the Martin Brothers would become famous outlaws and more popular than the James gang.

~~~~~~~~~~~~~~~~~~~~~

Judge McKinsey had completed his review of both cases and was considering going downstairs for a drink, but prudently thought otherwise about it. Wouldn't do at all if folks were to say the judge was seen drinking before a trial. Still, he made a mental note to bring a small travel flask the next time he traveled out of Marion. With his boots off and dress coat over the back of his chair, McKinsey sat back in the rocking chair and contemplated his life. A successful lawyer at a young age, he had married well and felt he had nothing in life to hold him back.
~~~~~~~~~~~~~~~~~~~~~

Then she lost the baby and their world simply started falling apart. Things were never quite the same between them after that and he knew he used his new position as a judge in order to stay busy and, yes, keep away from his depressed wife who had become a total recluse. *Twenty years have passed by so quickly*, he thought, *sometimes life isn't fair at all...* He was suddenly startled back into reality by a knock upon his hotel room door. McKinsey realized he wasn't dressed for visitors but reached for the door knob anyway. Upon opening it, he found himself staring straight into the barrel of a large pistol.

As he had just gone off duty, Deputy Marshal Justin Blake found himself standing in front of the Mississinewa Hotel. Earlier, Brewster had suggested that he go over and introduce himself to the judge before the trials began in the morning. Walking into the hotel lobby, Justin asked the night clerk if the judge was in. Upon seeing that the room key was not hanging on its hotel peg, he answered, "Yes you can find him upstairs in room number 22." Justin started climbing the beautifully decorated stairs to the second floor. As he reached it, a shot rang out. The bullet that had been fired had struck the paneling about two inches above his head. Thinking quickly, Justin automatically pulled out his Remington 44-40 and began looking for the shooter. Standing at the end of the hallway was Todd Martin holding a pistol to the head of an older man he presumed to be Judge McKinsey.

"Give it up, Martin," he shouted to the gunman from cover. "You'll never get away with this. Let the judge go."

This was not how Todd's plan was to work. Here he was trapped in the hotel hallway with the old man. While using the judge for cover, he maneuvered closer and closer to the rear stairway. "I got your judge and you got my brother. Bring my brother to the back of this here hotel and we will make a trade."

Concern for the judge became paramount to Justin at this point so he shouted out to him. "Are you all right, Your Honor, has he harmed you?"

"I'm fine but don't give into his demands, Deputy." With that said, Todd Martin panicked and began randomly firing in the direction of the officer. Justin had counted a total of three shots already fired as he considered his options. Making quick eye contact with the judge, he used the barrel of his gun to signal for the older man to try to drop down. *Please, Judge, notice what I'm signaling to you*, he thought to himself.

The judge had figured out what was being signaled to him and suddenly dropped down to knee level, catching Martin completely off guard. The gunman realized too late the trick that had been played on him and got off another wild shot before Justin's bullet struck home into Martin's chest. A few seconds of quiet emerged as the smoke began to clear and a few brave heads peaked out of their doors to see what was taking place. Justin ran up to the judge, who was lying prone upon the floor. "Your Honor, are you alright?"

"Yes," came the reply. "Please give me a hand up, young man." The judge was helped to his stocking feet. "Your arrival was in the nick of time, Deputy, and I am forever in your debt," the judge told him while shaking his hand. Justin made a quick check to see if Todd would cause any more trouble. He would not. "Marshal Brewster told me he had hired a good young deputy, and I see that he was not exaggerating one little bit. If you will excuse me now, I'm going downstairs and have a drink, maybe two drinks, and I don't care what people may think!" Justin simply smiled and told the judge to have one for him as he now had an evening of official reports to look forward to completing.

~~~~~~~~~~~~~~~~~~~~~~

A much larger than expected crowd filed into the First National Bank meeting room for the two trials. At 8:45 a.m., the officers had the first three defendants in place awaiting Judge McKinsey, who seemed unaffected by the attempt on his life (or he was just good at hiding his emotions). At 9:00 a.m. everyone was called to rise as Judge Leo McKinsey entered the room and preceded to the bench. All three defendants entered a plea of not guilty. The prosecution called for William Dorsey to take the stand and relate what
~~~~~~~~~~~~~~~~~~~~~~

had happened the day he was attacked. He then pointed out the three men standing trial as his attackers. The defendants produced no witnesses, claiming they were all out of town on business that morning. In the end, Judge McKinsey found all three guilty and sentenced them to a $200 fine each and six month's probation. He warned them that if they ever appeared before him again that they could expect a long prison sentence. Big Jim paid their fines and the group left the courtroom.

Over in the jail, Kevin Martin had not slept at all the night before. Hearing that his brother had attempted to kidnap the judge to barter for his freedom, and hearing that the new deputy had killed him for it, made him feel he had no chance before the hanging judge today. By 10 a.m., Martin and his court-appointed lawyer were in discussion before the plea of not guilty was entered. This time, his attorney had many witnesses called to the stand. Each was inside the bar the day they had witnessed the brothers fighting, knew each brother to be completely inebriated and, upon following Kevin Martin outside, saw him commandeer the horse and ride away. Each was asked the following question, "Do you believe Kevin Martin was so drunk he didn't know what he was doing?" Most agreed he was stewed to the gills, with one man saying he didn't think Martin really intended to steal the horse but had only "borrowed it" for a short time.

That brought heavy laughter to the courtroom. In the end, Judge McKinsey was inclined to give Kevin Martin the benefit of the doubt that he didn't know what he was doing, and the fact that he was found later lying on the ground having fallen off the animal. His final sentence was a $100 fine and thirty days in jail. Case dismissed. The verdict went over well with some and not so well with the majority. Kevin Martin had cheated the hangman...at least for now.

Chapter 8

The following day an announcement was posted on the entry doors of the Thompson Green and Amber Glass Bottling Works:

Notice to all Employees:

Due to the frequent lunchtime problems encountered by a few of our employees, the White Dog Saloon has been ordered closed by the Gas City Council.

Signed,
Frank Livingston, Plant Manager

"They got no right to tell us we can't have a drink and a free lunch during our noon lunch break," one worker yelled out to the assembled men reading the notice. "You're right, fellas, they ain't got no business a controllin' what we're eatin' and drinkin'." A loud murmur of voices indicated that many of the plant's workers felt the same way, that management was treating them like a bunch of kids rather than the responsible, hardworking adults they were. Something had to be done was the general feeling, and each looked to the other for guidance. Reluctantly, the men set about their work knowing that only a spark would ignite this powder keg of trouble.

~~~~~~~~~~~~~~~~~~~~~

City Councilman Matthew Brooks had a full barber shop of customers and the discussions centered squarely on the closing of the White Dog Saloon. "What's to keep some low-down dirty politicians from closing any business they want?" asked one of the angry customers.

Brooks, who had easily mastered the art of clipping hair while talking, replied, "Just isn't right to deprive a working man a couple of beers or whiskeys and a free lunch counter. I mean, what's the harm anyway? I cut hair even better after I enjoy a few shots under my belt."

One of his old-time customers laughingly spoke up, "That ain't sayin' much!" Everyone started laughing at the barber's expense, who clearly did not appreciate being the butt of the man's joke. Brooks continued to cut hair in silence.

A young man of about fourteen spoke up, "My brother works at the Thompson Plant and he says there's gonna be
~~~~~~~~~~~~~~~~~~~~~

trouble over this." Very quietly the Barber returned to the conversation, saying, "I wouldn't be a bit surprised if your brother isn't right."

~~~~~~~~~~~~~~~~~~~~~

As the noon whistle blew, both William Dorsey and Frank Livingston watched with deep concern as the men proceeded outside. A small group of them walked towards the White Dog Saloon, either in defiance or to simply see if the reports of its closure were true. Upon its tiny door was a painted wooden sign saying **Closed Until Further Notice**. Reluctant to return to the plant, many of the men simply stood around the closed saloon and discussed their options.

~~~~~~~~~~~~~~~~~~~~~

Justin had been so busy since he was appointed deputy marshal that he realized he hadn't written his parents and brothers back on the farm in Ohio. Sitting down at the office desk, Justin was surprised at the amount of information he was able to write. He had certainly been busy since his arrival. Justin chose not to mention Miss Samantha, at least not at this point. It was just too early, and the couple had yet to even kiss. He tried to find every excuse he could to be around her as much as possible, but there was a sense that perhaps Samantha was in no hurry in this mild but friendly relationship. He did know one thing for certain: she was the first thing he thought about in the morning and the last at night when he closed his eyes.

Taking his letter in hand, Justin walked down to the white wooden framed post office. Outside was the postmaster's bicycle and a crowd of people had already gathered. His timing was perfect. Moving up to the edge of the assembled men and women, Justin could hear names being called out. "Wallace."

From inside the group, a faint voice was heard, "Here," as the letter was passed from hand to hand to the lady. Many names were called with some not in attendance. Justin had just about given up hope when he heard his name called. "Here," he replied, as a thick letter was handed to him. After mailing his own, Justin walked along reading the news from back home.

~~~~~~~~~~~~~~~~~~~~~~

After lunch time had ended, the tension within the Thompson Bottling Plant was at a fever pitch, with the general feeling that something might happen at any time. With the 10,000-bottle order from a customer out of New York, men were busy producing the aqua-embossed bottles as fast as they could. This was a new customer, The Great
~~~~~~~~~~~~~~~~~~~~~~

Doctor Kilmer's Swamp Root - Kidney, Liver, and Bladder Cure. One would expect it to cure even the common cold with a bold title like that. Truth be told, it was just another quack medicine but business was business. Thompson's would not think of turning a good, solid customer down.

Suddenly, the shouts of "Fire! Fire!" were heard as black smoke erupted from a corner inside the packing warehouse. Rushing to the scene, William Dorsey pulled the chain on their local fire bell, sounding an alarm for all employees to cease production and help fight the fire. Men were rushing to and fro trying to clear away other combustible materials in and around the fire in order to make a fire break. Dorsey grabbed a Babcock fire extinguisher and emptied its contents upon the base of the fire. The fire was discovered early and, with the efforts of many, extinguished quickly with little actual damage, mostly just smoke.

Witnessing the incident, Plant Manager Livingston soon approached his shop foreman, "Any idea how the fire started, Bill?"

"No sir, not yet, but I'd guess someone was smoking around all the packing materials again. If I have told them once, I have told them a thousand times not to smoke around the combustible packing." Patting his good friend upon his shoulder, Livingston thanked him for his quick actions.

"Thanks to you it was extinguished quickly, and we didn't have to involve the local firemen." Privately, both he and Dorsey were wondering the same thing, *Were the men sending a signal to management?*

~~~~~~~~~~~~~~~~~~~~

The rest of the week was uneventful around town, and the hope was that maybe everything might start returning to normal. No other incidents were reported at Thompsons. *Funny thing*, Marshal Brewster had thought, *none of the other factories had had any serious difficulties at all prior to the closing of the White Dog Saloon.* The workers of the other factories in town went about their business, a few drinks and a free lunch at saloons close to them, then back to work. He had never been called to these locations for disturbances in the past, only at Thompsons. They must have a rough crowd working there he finally determined.

His two nighttime deputies reported in at the end of their shifts but pretty much stayed totally out of sight. Brewster had noticed their very cool reception toward his new deputy and figured some jealousy might be underway on their part. Blake didn't seem bothered by their coolness anyway so Brewster guessed it wasn't really important that a friendship developed as long as it didn't become an issue on the job. He wouldn't put up with that.

One day, Justin was sitting in the office reading the night reports when Brewster came in. "Any coffee on?" he asked.
~~~~~~~~~~~~~~~~~~~~

"Yea, Zeke started a pot a while ago, should be ready anytime." As if hearing his name, Zeke appeared and started filling up three coffee cups. The old bearded man had taken a liking to Justin and was always good for an old story or two.

Justin did have a question on his mind for Brewster. "It seems to me that we should have our own building away from this fire barn and the activities of the firemen. Is anything like that in the making?"

Before the marshal could answer, Zeke jumped in, "Been that way since '67, can't see no reason ta change now."

Brewster just shook his head in amazement and replied, "Well, for one thing, it would be wonderful to get away from the fire barn horse smell."

Zeke seemed surprised, "What horse smell you talkin' about, Marshal?"

"Maybe you should take a bath once in a while and you might notice the difference, Zeke."

Both officers laughed but Zeke didn't seem to catch on to the joke. "Yep, been that way since Granny Bradford's cow use ta wander the streets of Jonesboro. No sense in changin' nothin' now."

~~~~~~~~~~~~~~~~~~~~~~

It was a lovely Friday afternoon and Justin hadn't been able to see Samantha all week due to his work schedule. He
~~~~~~~~~~~~~~~~~~~~~~

managed to just happen to be on patrol at the schoolhouse as the children were leaving for the evening, happy for the start of a weekend. Out walked little Martha next to her teacher and both seemed to brighten up on seeing him. He could only hope Samantha brightened more than the child.

"Good afternoon, Miss Stokes, and how was your day in school?" Justin joked. She gave him a phony hard stare then laughed.

"It was a wonderful day. The children were all attentive and I really hope I may be getting through to a few of the others that learning can be fun," she said.

"And how was your day, Mr. Deputy Marshall? Shoot any bad guys?" Without missing a beat, Justin replied in a serious tone, "Only three." As they walked, he apologized for not being able to walk her home more often.

"Maybe I can ask Alvin Jensen to fill in for you some," she said it in a teasing manner.

"Let's leave him out of our plans, shall we? Say, if you are not busy tomorrow, how about joining me for a ride on the *Helen Boyd*? I was able to get the entire day off at work." Samantha smiled at the thought.

"I can bring along a picnic lunch while we rest along the river in a nice shaded spot." Justin told her he could hardly wait and would rent a buggy and pick her up at 11 a.m. Samantha informed him she would prefer to walk since everything was close by anyway, and being cooped up in a schoolroom made her desire to be out walking in the fresh air. As he reached her doorway, she told him, "Don't let it rain tomorrow," and quickly ran inside. He would check in later with weatherman Zeke Miller as to tomorrow's local forecast. Fingers crossed, it would be a beautiful day.

Chapter 9

Saturday morning was indeed a beautiful day as old Zeke had assured Justin it would be. Arriving at Samantha's home precisely on time, she met him at the door with a picnic basket under her arm and a blanket to place on the grass for comfort. Justin was admiring the lovely emerald green touring hat upon her head. "This should do nicely in keeping the sun out of my eyes," she told him.

"It's very pretty," he said, taking the picnic basket from her. Together the couple walked as Samantha placed her arm within his. Anyone seeing the young couple on the street would secretly smile to themselves that these young people were destined to be together.

Walking down the buggy pathway, they approached the docked *Helen Boyd,* named after the owner's daughter. She was a small wooden steam pleasure craft that provided visitors, couples, and anyone else a pleasant two mile sight-seeing adventure up and down the river to each mill dam. All this for the fare of five cents per person. The owner, a man dressed in a captains hat, welcomed the young couple aboard and assisted Samantha to her seat. The couple sat together, placing the picnic basket at their feet, and appeared to be the only visitors for this trip until a distant voice sang out, "Hold, please." Another young man ran up quickly and stepped aboard. It was the reporter Alvin Jensen.

"Hope you don't mind if I tag along," he said to Justin. Whatever Justin was thinking at that point probably could not be repeated in mixed company, so forcing a smile to his face, Justin replied, "Of course not, it's a free country."

Alvin knew full well what he was doing. Upon seeing the young couple in the distance with a picnic basket in arms, he had decided to invade Justin's space a little. A subtle message that he was not the only person interested in the lovely Samantha Stokes. "Good morning, Samantha," he said as he tipped his hat. "My, that's a lovely dress you are wearing."

"Thank you, Mr. Jensen," she replied in a slightly forced pleasant voice. The "Mr. Jensen" was certainly not missed by either Alvin or Justin. Already, Alvin regretted his actions but had to remain pleasant until the boat ride was over.

"So, Deputy Blake, what do you think of our little boat ride?" he asked.

Looking up slightly harshly, he replied, "I am off duty now, Alvin. You may call me Justin. But to answer your question, it seems to be a beautiful river. I am happy it's not as high and swift as it was the day of my arrival. We are looking forward to a day of relaxing under the sun and enjoying each other's company." *That should signal this guy to back off*, Justin thought. Unfortunately, it did not.

"You wouldn't know it now by the looks of things," Alvin said as he attempted to dominate the conversation, "But all of these shore lines once held a thick forest miles deep. My uncle says that saw mills in old Harrisburg shipped enormous quantities of black walnut timber to Germany for the construction of furniture while heavy oak was shipped east for ship building. There was even an old steamboat company in Jonesboro for the construction of river craft and flatboats for shipping produce all the way down to New Orleans. Unfortunately, all of this cutting resulted in an enormous drain upon our woodlands."

The couple said nothing and, without emotion, stared into his face. Alvin was able to read their signals quite clearly and ended his unwanted sight-seeing oral presentation. Even the owner of the boat occasionally glanced over his shoulder as he steered the *Helen Boyd* back upriver. After the completion of the boating excursion and the *Helen Boyd* had safely docked, reporter Jensen tipped his hat, wished the couple a good day, and was gone like a flash. Samantha looked at Justin as they both began to laugh. "I'm glad he's gone!" Justin said as he and the captain assisted her out of the boat.

The captain simply shook his head, "I'm sorry I wasn't able to pull away fast enough to keep him from ruining your boat ride, young man." Reaching into his pocket for a tip, Justin told the captain not to be concerned as he and Samantha still had a wonderful time anyway, and together, the couple started walking in the direction of the perfect place to picnic. "I'm hungry, let's go have some fun," a laughing Justin told her.

Soon, they arrived at a good shaded destination, and Justin spread out the blanket upon the ground. "It smells wonderful," he replied, "And what do we have here, Miss Stokes?"

Handing out plates and silverware, Samantha answered, "Fried chicken, potato salad, and dinner rolls. You better be hungry, Mister Deputy Marshal, as I had to get up early this morning to prepare this feast for you." She made his plate up first by scooping up a large chicken breast and three helpings of potato salad. "Save room for the apple pie, dear."

Dear, she said. This is the life, Justin was thinking. *I am in the company of a beautiful woman who is educated, refined, and a great cook. How can my life get any better than this?*

By early evening, Justin Blake was one sick puppy, having all the symptoms of a bad stomach flu. He couldn't hold anything down and was forced to make frequent trips to the privy. He was pale, dizzy, and feverish with chills. His condition was observed by his kindly landlady, Ma Richards, who took it upon herself to send a runner to fetch Dr. Baxter. Soon upon his arrival, the Doctor found the young deputy flat on his back in bed. After a brief initial examination, Baxter asked him, "What did you have to eat today, young man?" Between a series of dry heaves, Justin managed to say, "Picnic basket, fried chicken, potato salad, apple pie," as he grabbed again for the bucket Ma had placed there for his quick use.

"We got to send him to the Pest House, Doc?" Ma asked him. Dr. Baxter shook his head no, saying, "Potato salad and the heat of the day don't mix. It probably spoiled just enough to give him a case of food poisoning. He will be alright in a day or so. Just keep giving him water to flush it out of his system. I'll check back on him in the morning."

Within twenty-four hours, a weakened but improving Justin Blake left his sick bed and went outside for a few minutes for fresh air. He wrote a short note to Samantha and paid a young boy to deliver it to her house. By early afternoon she arrived at Ma Richards Boarding House and upon knocking, asked if she could visit her sick friend. Ma told her it wouldn't be proper for a young lady to enter the room of a gentleman but that she will inform him of her arrival, and see if he is up to a visit on her front porch. Justin was thrilled to hear that she had come to check on him.

"Oh my poor dear," she told him, "You must think me terrible to have fed you spoiled potato salad! I feel simply terrible and embarrassed to know I have caused you such misery."

Justin smiled and stopped her, "It was just a little something that didn't agree with me. Are you all right? Were you sick?" She shook her head no. "I didn't eat but a couple of small bites of the salad. It's not one of my favorites, but Mother thought it appropriate for a picnic, so I made it. Justin **dear**, please forgive me!"

"There is nothing to forgive, so please don't blame yourself one tiny bit. By the way, I like the way you use the word dear when you speak to me."

It embarrassed Samantha that she had used the word and that HE had caught her using it on his behalf. "I better be on my way home. Evening services will begin shortly," she told him as she walked away.

"Please give your parents my best," Justin said as he waved her goodbye. It was getting harder and harder to say goodbye to that special pretty young lady!

~~~~~~~~~~~~~~~~~~~~~~

Big Jim Malone was quite annoyed. It seemed that after the judge's stern warning to his three paid thugs that two of them had chickened out and snuck out of town. Only
~~~~~~~~~~~~~~~~~~~~~~

the loyal Kruger remained. Oh well, more muscle could be found to replace those two nitwits. With the White Dog Saloon closed, Kruger had no place to go and was always underfoot.

It is time to find something productive for Kruger to do and I have the perfect job in mind, he thought. *Kruger will become my campaign manager. With city elections scheduled for November 7, I will announce to everyone my intention to run against Mayor Huffman for the position of city mayor. Since Huffman is a Republican and running unopposed by anyone on either ticket, I will run as a Democrat and give the people a choice. It will be up to Kruger to persuade the workers of Gas City to choose me. I will run on an open town platform that allows anyone to open more saloons, brothels, pool halls, underground gambling joints, you name it. And of course, I will be entitled to a certain percent of their profits. Not only will I become a political powerhouse within the community, I will, also, stand to become one of its wealthiest too. I must also replace that marshal with one of my own men, maybe Kruger, who will enforce my will within the community. I look forward to this election and may the better man win...and of course that will be me!* With that, Big Jim went down to the city office and filed the paperwork to appear on the ballot as a candidate for Mayor. He then went into the office of the Gas City Journal and gave them their headlines for tomorrow's newspaper.

Unbeknownst to anyone else within Gas City was Big Jim's secret investment plan. It came about, thankfully, by the actions of the state legislature in February. It was then that the state legalized gymnastic exhibitions and athletic contests of science, though prize money and betting were still unlawful. In other words, prize fighting! This act opened the door for much to come. It must be remembered that the main railway stop between the cities of Chicago, Illinois, and Louisville, Kentucky was, in fact, Gas City, Indiana. Many people traveled to the fair city, and not all of them were of the highest caliber. Hoodlums, large and small, all the way up to Chicago crime bosses passed through and were known personally to Big Jim. In return, he was well-known and respected within the crime family, so receiving important visitors from time to time was not a surprise to him. They had arrived here in late February to make him an offer.

In exchange for an investment of $25,000, Big Jim would become one of five silent partners in building and operating the Columbia Athletic Club Arena and Racetrack. The planners had chosen a location very wisely, a small berg of a town called Roby, Indiana, just on the upper western tip next to the Illinois line. A modern prizefighting arena would be constructed in addition to a press box, several private boxes for wealthy customers, reserved, and general seating holding about 18,000 boxing fans. Rail and boat service from Chicago for boxing fans were also to be provided. The public would eagerly line up in droves with the wealthiest men ready to pay as high as five dollars each for a private box seat.

A public stooge would be named as the president, who has a squeaky clean background but would eagerly do as he was told by the owners. Their goal was to complete construction quickly and have the athletic club ready for its first boxing match by early summer. Of course, additional big money would be made from the private wagering that gentlemen will undoubtedly be conducting. Mob members were happy to ensure that bets would be collected, if needed, the hard way. The plan was to hold a few clean boxing exhibitions in order to satisfy the Indiana state boys, then to quietly and slowly start the public betting without it becoming obvious. By then, the state boys would start becoming comfortable with the side gambling or the Mob could pay the holdouts off with cash or rig a sex scandal to end their political careers. "Are you interested, Big Jim?"

"Yes," he told them. He was very interested but required a couple of days to collect that amount of cash, as he would need to put up his local properties as collateral in order to swing the deal. He then made plans for his visit to Chicago by train, and they would complete their business dealings. He thanked his fellow business partners for allowing him to get into this gold mine on the ground floor. Once the popularity of prize fighting began, he was certain that more athletic clubs such as this would start springing up all over the state. He already had a location in mind for the one he would build here in Gas City. Since early March, Big Jim has made weekly two-day trips by rail into Chicago to watch his investment starting to take shape. The fortunes of war were indeed smiling upon him. Once the money started rolling in and he was elected mayor, he could have anything he wanted approved. *Maybe we could change the name of the town again... this time to Gold City!*

~~~~~~~~~~~~~~~~~~~~~

It was past 8:30 a.m. before Marshal Brewster made it into the office. Both Justin and Zeke were a little concerned as Brewster normally was the first man in the office every morning. Brewster came in holding his jaw with pain written all over his face. "Good afternoon Marshal," Zeke said in a playful way, teasing about his lateness.

Brewster refused the cup of coffee he was offered and sat down at his desk. "Blasted toothache...been up all night with it. Just won't stop hurting. Nothin' helps."

Zeke leaned closer to Justin with a grin on his face, "Reminds me of a story. Old colored man north of here named Uncle Eli Hollingsworth got quite a reputation as a tooth extractor. I heard him sayin' many times that the only thing that kept folks from dyin' was that the tooth lets go
~~~~~~~~~~~~~~~~~~~~~

just before death receives um!" Justin burst out laughing as Brewster moaned loudly and ran outside while still holding his jaw.

Zeke stood up and began walking toward the door. Pausing, he looked back and replied, "I'll be back soon as I get me my pair of forceps out in the horse barn and pull the Marshal blasted old tooth fer him." Justin poured himself another cup of coffee and waited to hear the inevitable scream he knew would soon be coming. *I'm so glad I was blessed with good teeth*, he was thinking as a huge scream of anguish filled the air.

Chapter 10

In the cover of darkness, the group of four White Caps met again north of town at their usual rural location. Instructions were given and a plan was clearly laid out for all to understand. This next victim was different from the others in the past, but even so, everyone understood that orders are orders and must be followed through as directed.

Today was the final day of school for the children, and Justin had made arrangements to meet Samantha at the school so he could carry a few of the heavy books she wanted to return to her home. The children were in an excited mood, knowing that they could now enjoy the summer months free from the drudgery of schoolwork. By now, Justin had become an almost constant fixture after school and many that knew him gave him a friendly wave as they raced home to play.

"I'll take all those books for you," Justin said as he removed the stack from her desk. "Now that school is out,

Miss Stokes, maybe I can start seeing a little more of you," he joked.

Samantha's smile disappeared from her face, "I'm afraid I have something I must tell you. Mother and I are going away for four to six weeks to visit her sister in Indianapolis." Justin's grin also vanished upon hearing this bit of unwelcomed news. "Mother says it was my idea to go away but I don't remember ever suggesting it to her. Perhaps she wants me to spend some time away from you for my own benefit. She suspects I am beginning to care a great deal about you. So tomorrow we shall be leaving here on the 8:45 a.m. southbound train."

A saddened Justin then asked, "Do you? Do you really care for me?"

Her tearful eyes said the words before she uttered them, "Yes, yes I do. Much more than perhaps you know." With that, she rushed into his arms as he held her tight and kissed her.

~~~~~~~~~~~~~~~~~~~~

Justin arrived at the depot at 8:30 a.m. hoping to have a few minutes alone to speak with Samantha, but found that both mother and daughter had already taken their seats in the car as they waited for the train to depart. He quickly located their window and lightly tapped upon the glass. Samantha,
~~~~~~~~~~~~~~~~~~~~

upon seeing him, moved to lower the glass window. “Good morning ladies, I hope you have a wonderful time in Indianapolis,” Justin said. Mrs. Stokes smiled but clearly was not pleased that Justin had arrived in time to catch them. “Please write to me,” he asked of Samantha, as the train came to life.

“I will,” she replied. “I will, good-bye Justin, good-bye.” Mrs. Stokes closed the window. He remained standing on the platform long after the train was out of sight. *Mrs. Stokes knows*, he thought to himself, *she knows I am in love with her daughter. Mothers always seem to know these things.*

~~~~~~~~~~~~~~~~~~~~~~

Walking back to his office, Justin passed the Western Union telegraph office. The operator was sweeping his floor outside on the street and seeing Justin, asked that he come in. “Got a telegram last evening for you folks. I couldn’t find your night deputies to give it to. Here you go.”

Taking the envelope he replied, “Thanks, I’ll pass it along to the marshal.” As Justin walked back to the office, he began to think, *She’s gone and for quite some spell, so no use fretting about it, I got work to do.*

Walking inside, Brewster looked up at him, “So you saw the little lady off, did you?” and he smiled. Now that his bad tooth was pulled, he could smile again.
~~~~~~~~~~~~~~~~~~~~~~

“How did you know she was leaving this morning?” a puzzled Justin replied.

“Son, there isn’t much I don’t know about here in town and besides, love is written all over your silly face.” Justin didn’t comment but handed the marshal the twelve-hour old telegraph and walked over to get a cup of coffee, but found the pot empty. “I’ll make a pot; Zeke’s falling behind in his chores.”

After opening the telegram and reading it, Brewster handed it to Justin. It read:

> *Marshal of Gas City, be on the lookout for a Wilbert Vance, age twenty, 5’6”, one hundred thirty pounds, brown hair parted down the center with a waxed mustache. Last seen heading east on horseback, possibly your location. If found, apprehend. Wanted for questioning of the murder of Phoebe Johnson, this city. Signed, A.D. Williamson, Chief of Police, Kokomo.*

“I’ll check all the hotels and saloons today and tomorrow. That fella should be rather easy to spot if he’s coming our way,” Justin replied as he went out on patrol. He had searched about half of the establishments when he entered the Panhandle Hotel and Restaurant down by the depot. Looking casually among its occupants, Justin’s eyes fixed upon a man sitting alone at a small table. Thinking back on the wanted man's description, he couldn't help but feel that this was his man. Approaching from the side so as not to allow the man to notice him, Justin stopped by his side with his hand resting upon his weapon.

"Your name Wilbert Vance?" He spoke with some authority. The man froze in place with his fork halfway up to his mouth. It clearly was him. "Now I want you to move very slowly, Vance, as I have my weapon trained on you. Stand up and lean over the table with your hands wide. Don't try anything, Vance, I'm warning you." What happened next came as a complete surprise to Justin. The wanted man started crying. I mean, bawling his eyes out, begging not to be shot and all. Thinking it might be some kind of sick trick, Justin stood ready to shoot as he quickly frisked the crying man. "Please, sir, I don't even own a gun let alone carry one," he continued to plead. The search produced no gun or knife on his person.

"Put your hands behind your back, Vance. Do it now!" Justin ordered him. The trembling young man did as he was told. "Now, where do you carry your money?" Justin demanded to know.

"You gonna rob me, mister?" he asked as he stood there trembling.

"No, I'm a deputy marshal and you are under arrest, but first, you gotta pay for that meal and a tip would be nice for all the trouble you have caused these nice folks during their mealtime." Finding out which pocket contained his coins, Justin dug into it and paid for the meal plus a generous tip to boot. "This way, start walking." The pair then left the restaurant and proceeded uptown towards the jail.

Marshal Brewster was on his own daily patrol when he noticed the pair approaching the fire barn. *Good work, Justin*, he thought, as he walked across the street to meet up with them. "Here's our boy, Marshal, I'll lock him up for you." Having Vance enter the cell and face the wall, Justin removed the handcuffs and securely locked the cell door.

"Where'd you find him?" Brewster asked.

"Down at the Panhandle feeding his face like he didn't have a care in the world."

"Good work. I'll go over to the Western Union office and let Kokomo know we got their murderer," Brewster said as he left the office.

"Please, you gotta believe me," the man in the cell was bellowing like a lost calf. "I didn't kill anybody. I'm innocent!" Seeing that there was a little coffee left, Justin poured a cup and sat down to finish his written report.

"Mister, this is what happened and you gotta believe me. I am a traveling shoe and boot salesman for the Brown and Desnoyers Shoe Company out of St. Louis. Our plant has 600 workers producing 5,000 pairs of shoes and boots per day." Justin swiveled his chair around so he could look at the man as he drank his coffee. "I had just recently checked into my room at the Flintlock Hotel in Kokomo, and was reviewing the contents of my traveling display cases when I heard a muffled scream. I opened my door and stepped into the open hallway, wondering what I had heard."

"Suddenly, the door across from mine opened and a large black man with, I swear to God, red hair, came busting out of the room and almost knocked me to the floor as he ran to the rear stairs doorway. Confused, I happened to look into the open room and there upon the floor was a lady lying in disarray and bloody. I, at once came to her aid and upon a quick examination, noticed a knife sticking into her bosom. Blood was gushing out from the wound as I tried to stem its flow, using my own personalized handkerchief. The lady was quite pained and dazed by this terrible attack and was, in fact, trying to tell me something of importance when two ladies appeared at the hallway. One of them started screaming, 'Murderer, Murderer!'

"I tried to explain to them about the large black man with red hair but they were terribly frightened and pointing into the room at me, and told another gentleman that I had stabbed this poor woman. At that point, I fear I panicked and, afraid for my life that I was to be accused of doing this terrible deed, I too fled down the rear stairs. I hardly remember finding my horse and riding out of town, as by now everything seemed like a terrible nightmare. I rode all night and arrived in your town just this morning totally famished from hunger, and utterly confused as what I shall do now."

Thinking about his story for just a brief moment, Justin replied, "The worst thing you could have done was run, Vance. That in itself makes you look guilty. Anyway, it's not for me to judge you. That will happen once we return you to Kokomo." With that, the prisoner laid upon his cot and softly cried.

Brewster returned to the office and informed Justin that he had notified Kokomo that the suspect was now in their custody. "I was thinkin' that maybe you might want to transport the prisoner over to Kokomo yourself." He motioned for Justin to follow him over to the large framed area wall map. "Here we are and here is Kokomo straight west, a little less than thirty miles. You can do it in a day and a half easy, but don't push it. Take the two days going and comin'. Maybe a little bit of hard ridin' will help get that pretty little gal out of your system. I told the Kokomo chief of police we would return his prisoner for him. I owed him a favor from long back anyway. Are you willing to do this?" "Sure thing, happy to do it," Justin quickly replied. "I'll get me a horse from the stables and we'll get an early start in the morning."

~~~~~~~~~~~~~~~~~~~~
~~~~~~~~~~~~~~~~~~~~

That afternoon it got very hot and sultry without any wind moving to help break up the heat of the day. This was the first real hot one of the year, and by evening, many families were just sitting outside on their porches rather than face the stifling heat inside their sun-baked homes. Justin had packed everything he and the prisoner would require for the ride to Kokomo, placing both horses inside the fire barn. *What the firemen didn't know wouldn't hurt them.* He would have both horses saddled and ready to start come daybreak. Now back in his room, Justin tried to rest up for the long days ahead, but sleep would not come. Because his room was so hot, he had decided to sleep with his window open, and the moonlight shining into his room also brightened it and kept his mind from drifting off. He tried sleeping on his back, then on his side, then with the pillow over his face. Nothing seemed to work.

So rather than keep beating a dead horse, Justin just laid on his back and stared at the ceiling. In his mind he was rehearsing the next two days. *Can't turn my back on the prisoner... innocent or guilty is not my problem... got to deliver him as promised and on time.* His mind was snapped back to reality by the sound of what sounded like a twig being broken outside his window. Probably a raccoon out prowling around, he thought. Glancing into the direction of his open window, Justin was startled to see what suddenly appeared outside his window. It looked to be a ghost!

Justin forced his mind to study this spooky figure while he tried to rationalize exactly what he was seeing. *That's not a ghost...it's a flour sack over someone's head.* Suddenly, a pistol was also being pointed in his direction. Justin leaped up and rolled off the back side of his bed as his pillow erupted into a mass of flying feathers. The White Caps had taken a shot at him! Justin grabbed his pistol and leaped out the open window but could not see or hear his assailant who had vanished into the darkness of the night. Ma Richard began pounding frantically upon his door as Justin opened it. To her great relief, he had not been murdered but was quite upset to discover that a bullet had been fired into her guest's bed. Justin reassured her that all was well and that he would personally pay for the damages. With the excitement over, Ma and the other guests returned to their own rooms for the night. Justin pulled out his pocket knife and pried the bullet out of the wall behind what was left of his pillow. Satisfied that the assailant would not return, Justin pocketed the knife and the bullet for further study later. Within minutes he was fast asleep.

~~~~~~~~~~~~~~~~~~~~~~

Justin arrived at the jail early the next morning saddled their horses, picked up his prisoner, cuffed his hands together in front of him, and off they rode through the quiet streets
~~~~~~~~~~~~~~~~~~~~~~

crossing over the covered bridge spanning the Mississinewa River and headed due west. The pace was slow but steady. There was just no need to place a physical hardship upon the animals. The only hardship Justin felt was that his prisoner would not stop talking. If he heard, "I'm innocent and I didn't do it," once, he heard it a thousand times. After a while he started wondering if this Wilbert Vance was the greatest play actor of all time, or perhaps the guy really was innocent. Anyway, that was up to a judge and jury to decide.

The men were about two miles out of town when Justin happened to glance back at the road they had traveled and he thought that he'd caught a glimpse of another rider possibly following them. Thinking little of it, they continued on. He occasionally glanced behind but saw nothing of another rider. They continued on. Justin kept his prisoner's horse within ten feet in front of himself in case the man got any fancy ideas about escaping. If so, Justin was ready for him. It happened about noon when both horses had just cleared a line of thick trees.

Out of almost nowhere, a rider rushed in at Justin with a pistol aimed directly at his chest. There was nothing Justin could do.

"It's me, Mr. Deputy Marshal, your old pal, Kevin Martin. Seems like you killed my brother a spell back and locked me up in that jail. I warned you I'd be a lookin' fer you and dat day is here. Say ya prayers, deputy!" The rider's actions caused Justin's horse to spook a bit, slightly turning his body and that quick movement prevented the gunman's bullet from entering his chest. Instead, it buried deep into his left shoulder, dropping Justin to the ground. Seeing the cuffed man on the other horse, Martin told him to get away quick, as he then rode off in triumph.

Wilbert Vance sat upon his still horse in shock over what he had just witnessed. The deputy marshal now laid upon the ground, shot and probably dead. That little voice inside his head started talking to him. Vance's life spread before his eyes in a flash. Here was his only chance. Get the keys to remove these handcuffs, grab the deputy's gun, and scatter into the wind. No matter what, he was sure to be blamed for killing the deputy now and would hang for it despite his innocence.

Then another voice spoke to him, a calmer voice of reason. He had run away once and it had proven to be the wrong thing to do. He would not run away a second time. He would stay and take his chances. Slowly, he lifted his right leg over and came off his horse as he approached the stricken deputy. Checking the man's vitals, he could see that the young deputy was still alive but bleeding badly. Rummaging through the man's pockets, Vance located the key to his handcuffs, removed them and was free to move about easier. He started packing the shoulder wound with cloth. The deputy was turning pale from the loss of blood, so trying to stop or at least slow the bleeding was his first priority. Glancing about, he saw that the deputy's horse had become spooked during the shooting and had run away. He would have to ride double now, as it was imperative that the injured man gets to a medical doctor as quickly as possible. He could easily die in route. It was just a chance Vance now had to take.

With great difficulty, he managed to set the unconscious, but much heavier deputy upon his own horse. Funny how added strength could come during a critical time when it was desperately needed. Catching his breath, Vance saddled up directly behind the deputy, held fast to the man's body, and started retracing their steps back to Gas City. If he died in route, he might be blamed for killing this man but the inner voice told him that this was the correct thing to do. Vance's running days were over.

Chapter 11

It was early Sunday morning as Plant Manager Frank Livingston and his family were preparing to leave for morning church services when there was a knock upon their door. Upon opening it, there stood William Dorsey, breathing somewhat heavily. “Real sorry to bother you on a Sunday morning, Frank, but I hoped I could catch you before you left home.” “What’s the problem, Bill?”

A deep concern quickly spread over Frank’s face. “That half drunk night watchman we have just informed me that someone broke into your office sometime in the night and scattered papers and furniture all over the place.”

“Didn’t he see or hear anything? That’s what we pay the man to provide security for.”

“Claims he didn’t know anything until he made his final rounds this morning before going home. We may need to consider hiring-twenty four-hour security men.”

Frank thought for a moment before replying, “I want you to go home and spend time with your wife. I will go down after lunch and clean it all up. Whoever did it will expect that we'll discover it Monday morning and I don't want to give them that satisfaction. I don't keep money or valuables in the office, so whoever did it must have just wanted to put fear into our heads. I will not back down to thieves and thugs. Go on home now and don't be concerned. I will take care of this. Thanks for letting me know and, please, give our best to your wife. Good-bye, my friend."

The description of things thrown everywhere was certainly no exaggeration, but by evening Frank had the biggest part of it all cleaned up and he would sort the remaining files Monday afternoon. When he had finished no one would ever be able to tell that the office had been ransacked that weekend.

~~~~~~~~~~~~~~~~~~~~

The blood completely drained out of the face of Marshal Brewster when a group of men informed him his new deputy had been shot. *I'll never forgive myself for putting that young man in harm's way*, he thought, as he ran over to where others were removing Justin from the horse. "Get him straight over to Doc Baxter's office and please be gentle with him." A million things were going through the Marshal's mind as his eyes suddenly became fixed upon the other young man standing there with a blood-soaked shirt. "You! You shot my
~~~~~~~~~~~~~~~~~~~~

Deputy!" He accused as he tried but fumbled badly in an attempt to draw out his pistol.

"No, Marshal, it wasn't me. I'm the one who brought him back. A fellow just rode up from nowhere, pulled a gun, and shot your deputy."

"Let's talk inside," Brewster said as he motioned him inside.

"There must have been more to it than you are saying. Out with it, boy!" Walking over to the water bucket, which was always kept full for making coffee, Wilbert Vance poured himself a cup and drank it down quickly without stopping. "Yes. The shooter said, 'it's me Deputy, your old pal Kevin Martin.' Then something about his brother getting killed, then he just shot him." Now everything suddenly made sense to Brewster as he realized the truth. This wasn't Martin's fault as he could have come gunning for Blake anytime, day or night.

"Anything else?" he asked the exhausted and filthy young man.

"Oh, he did look at me and I thought I was going to be shot next, but when he saw the handcuffs he told me I was free and to get going."

Brewster looked at him with curiosity, "Why didn't you run, then? You had my deputy at a full disadvantage. You could have just left him there to die and disappeared."

Vance looked at him with steely eyes, “Running scared is what got me into this mess to begin with. Had I stayed in Kokomo, I’m sure I could have explained it enough to clear myself. That was a mistake, a big mistake on my part and I don’t believe in making the same mistake twice.” With that, Wilbert Vance walked over to the open jail cell and stepped inside. Brewster thought himself a good judge of character, but he had completely misread Wilbert Vance.

“You are a bloody, stinky mess, Vance. I want you to go across the street to the Emporium and have them give you a new shirt. Tell them I said to put it on my bill.” Vance suddenly realized the trust and the favor the marshal was trying to provide him and he was grateful, mighty grateful for the gesture. “I got the money to pay for the shirt, Marshal. Your deputy packed all of my personal belongs in my saddlebag before we left here, but aren’t you a little concerned I might just run away and not come back?” he asked. Brewster, with a solid no-nonsense reply, said, “Nope, not at all. You said it yourself; your running days are over.” As he walked out of the office Vance stopped, “Thanks, Marshal. It’s not every day that a man gets a second chance to grow up.”

~~~~~~~~~~~~~~~~~~~~~

By the time Marshal Brewster arrived, Doc Baxter had already removed the slug from Justin’s shoulder. Brewster
~~~~~~~~~~~~~~~~~~~~~

had dealt with Doc before in these types of situations and knew to have a seat and wait in his office while Doc was operating. Soon, the door opened, and Baxter stood up awaiting word on his young deputy. "He's lost a lot of blood," Doc replied as he took a seat and rubbed his tired eyes, "but I think he'll be fine. Whoever compressed the bleeding probably saved his life."

Brewster, holding his hat in both hands was visibly relieved. "When can I speak with him, Doc?" Shaking his head, Doc replied, "Not for a while. He's still unconscious and when he does wake up you can only talk to him for a moment. Come by later tonight and we will see." "Thanks, Doc. I'll do that but first, I got to pay a visit to the Martin residence."

Kevin Martin now felt free as a bird at his family home. He had gunned the no-good deputy that had killed his brother and avenged his family's honor. It would be quite some time before the body was found and everyone would automatically assume the prisoner he was taking somewhere got the jump on him and killed him. It had all worked out just fine. The prisoner, not himself would get all the blame.

Probably the stress from all of the excitement had caused Martin to feel the call of nature, and he was just sitting out back in the outhouse taking care of business, humming a tune to himself. Before he could react, the door burst open, and bright sunlight temporarily blinded him as someone grabbed him by the shirt and pulled him off the throne, spilling him onto the ground. Finding himself lying in the dirt with his pants around his ankles made him furious with whoever had pulled this dirty prank upon him. Then he heard a voice he instantly recognized, “Pull up your britches, Martin, you are under arrest for shooting Deputy Marshal Blake.”

Within a short period of only eighteen hours, Justin Blake was sitting up in his bed as Ma Richards fed him some of her famous chicken soup. There was a small knock upon his bedroom door. It was Marshal Brewster. “One of your lodgers let me in. How is your patient feeling this afternoon, Ma?” With a smile on her face, she replied, “As long as he minds what I tell him, I think he’ll mend just fine. Come in, Marshal, and sit a spell. I was just about finished, so I’ll be leaving you men folk to talk your manly business.”

Justin replied, “Thanks, Ma, that tasted great.”

“So, how are you feeling, and is your head still fuzzy?”

Justin was happy to see the marshal so he could now discover exactly what had happened. “I vaguely remember speaking with someone last night, or was it a dream? Which is it?”

“Doc told me you probably wouldn’t remember what I said to you, so let’s bring you up to date. I went out and captured Kevin Martin last evening. Got him locked up safe and sound. He was sure surprised to hear that you were alive. Judge McKinsey should be setting his trial date in a couple of weeks."

"But, how did I get into town? Did I ride in? Did my prisoner get away?"

"Actually, it was Wilbert Vance that managed to control your bleeding, and he rode you double back into town."

"Well if that doesn't beat all." Justin chuckled at the thought of the prisoner coming to the aid of the deputy.

"There's more to it than that. Once Doc had removed the bullet from your shoulder, I wired the chief of police in Kokomo and explained how you got ambushed, and there would be a delay in getting the prisoner returned to them. Seems that the woman who got stabbed regained consciousness long enough to tell the police that a large black man with red hair had stabbed her. One of the officers knew of such a man and later found him hiding out with friends. He has confessed to the crime. Kokomo only asks that Mr. Vance return to testify for the prosecution at the man's trial, so he is a free man today."

"That's wonderful. He said he didn't do it. I wish I could shake his hand and thank him for saving my life."

"Funny you should say that, as he's standing outside waiting to say good-bye to you. Can I bring him in?"

Justin broke out in a big smile, "Yes, please bring him in." Within a minute Wilbert Vance entered the bedroom. "Say, you're looking a might better than the last time I saw you, Deputy."

"I understand I have you to thank for saving my life, Mr. Vance. I want to thank you. I am in your debt, sir."

"Nah, think nothing of it, Deputy, you would have done the same for me. Actually, by saving you, I saved myself."

Justin didn't quite understand that statement but added, "Justin, my friends call me Justin, not Deputy."

Smiling, he said he needed to get going. "Thanks to the marshal wiring my employer saying I was needed to testify at two hearings, I think I still have a job. The chief of police in Kokomo has my display cases, and I will be testifying there in a few days. Then I'll be returning to testify against Martin. So I expect to see you up and on your feet by the time I return. Deal?"

"Deal, and Wilbert, the drinks will be on me!"

"Make it Sarsaparilla, and you got a deal!" They shook hands as he departed.

Brewster then asked the question that had been working in his mind, "Now what's all this about someone taking a shot at you last night?"

With Justin out of commission for a while, all of the daytime office work and patrols fell back on the shoulders of Marshal Brewster. That's when an odd thing started to happen. Old Zeke Miller started playacting like his temporary replacement. After checking on the fire horses and feeding them, if one of the firemen got tied up, Zeke started *makin' rounds* as he called it. It was noticed by some of the more observant members of the community, and old Zeke quickly got the nickname Deputy Jr. One of the tasks Deputy Jr. took upon himself was to always be at the post office when a group of people started forming outside, indicating mail had arrived. When its postmaster called out names, anything for the marshal, Justin, or the two nighttime deputies was handed over to him. With three letters in hand, Zeke proceeded over to Ma Richards Boarding House to see Justin. "Got one regular and two good smellin' letters for you, Justin." Justin was pleased to see Zeke and far more pleased to receive three letters. One was from his mother and the two good smelling ones were from Samantha. "I'll read them later, Zeke, but thanks. How are things going?"

Zeke pulled up a wooden chair and sat down. "Ain't been no crime ta speak of lately. I did get in to a bit of a hollern' match within a fireman over the lack of care of their fire horses, Old Betsy and Prince Phillip, got Sunday. Nobody came in ta feed and water them poor horses. Some mix-up he tried ta blame off and such. I'm ah thinkin' their men got too much smoke on their brains. Them poor animal was really glad ta see me cum Monday mornin'. When you comin' back ta work?"

"Dr. Baxter is pleased with the way it's healing and says I can come back and do paperwork in a few days. I'll sure be glad to get out of bed and back to work!" Zeke stood up "Well, I needed ta get a goin' and let ya read them fancy smellin' letters. Get well, Justin."

Checking the oldest postmark Justin opened the first of Samantha's letters. She told him things about her visit, places she had been to, and concerts she had attended but nothing much about missing him or when she might return. He needed to write to her but thought it best not to tell her about his injury, so as not to worry or spoil her trip. His mother's letter did contain some distressing news. His father had sliced his leg wide open while splitting firewood, and he was bed ridden. A local doctor had sewed it up but his old man was determined to get up and resume his chores. His mother would keep him informed in another letter within a few days, but not to worry. *I need to make a trip home this fall for a quick visit,* he thought.

Justin felt deep concern and worry over this news about his father and, perhaps, a little guilt for leaving the farm. His thoughts were interrupted by a light tapping on his door. "May I come in?" asked the Reverend Stokes. Justin sat up taller in bed, pushed the letters to the side and welcomed the Reverend into his room.

"I was deeply saddened to hear of your injury, Justin. I have come by to say a prayer for your complete recovery."

After the prayer, the Reverend seemed a bit at a loss for words, then finally came out with what was really on his mind. "I do have something I feel I need to say, and it's from the heart of a father and not from a minister of God. It's about you and Samantha. I cannot help but wonder where all of this is leading and felt the time most appropriate that we should speak together privately."

"Son, Mrs. Stokes and I both think the world of you as a person, but we are concerned where this may be leading you and our daughter. Look at where you now lie, shot down by a madman's bullet. The life of a peace officer is dangerous, and I cannot help but worry what kind of a life it would offer Samantha. Have you ever considered the harm and stress her constant worry would have on her physically? Every day that you left for work, she would be living in fear until your safe return that evening. Yours is a dangerous profession and it's quite possible the next bullet might, shall we say, be far worse than this one."

Justin realized how hard discussing this subject was for the Reverend Stokes. "Perhaps if I took up another job, say in a factory..."

"All I ask of you, son is to consider what I have said, and please, proceed slowly and cautiously when she returns this summer. I must leave you now, so, I wish you a speedy recovery. Good-bye, Deputy Blake."

Justin considered everything the Reverend Stokes had said, knowing that much of it was true. He enjoyed the life of a peace officer, but it certainly wasn't the life for a married man. Justin was glad that her father let him know they were only concerned for their daughter's welfare. He could either go with what his head was telling him and slow down his involvement with Samantha, or follow his heart and, ultimately he hoped, ask her to marry him. Lying in his bed with a bullet wound in his shoulder, he had the next few days to decide what he should do.

Chapter 12

Big Jim Malone and his four silent partners were well-pleased with the finished results. The construction of the athletic club arena was completed May 27, on time and on budget. Now the massive promoting would begin with newspapers all over the states of Indiana and Illinois, each with full-page advertising promoting legalized contests of scientific boxing to be held at their brand-new facility starting on June 2nd. Easy access would be provided by rail or steamboat. Come to Roby, Indiana and enjoy this new, exciting public exhibition of boxers' skill and daring.

Big Jim sat inside one of his many low-end saloons and read the Gas City Journal newspaper boxing advertisement over and over. Since no one knew of his involvement in the project, he could simply sit back and listen to the many comments he was hearing from his patrons. If their discussions were an indication, it seemed that the Athletic Club would become a tremendous success. While these men were most likely too poor to travel north by train, many other men in and around town, as well as elsewhere, were already planning on attending the first of many public boxing events. And, of course, Big Jim would be on hand each time to enjoy the event and later to split up the take.

The night of the first fight produced only about four thousand attendees. The match was stopped at the completion of round 22, as an exhausted fighter could not or would not answer the bell. The crowd seemed well pleased with the event and would no doubt return again, and maybe bring a friend next time. As promised, the fight was squeaky clean, no side betting of any kind, nothing that would give the local authorities any provocation. As long as the local police and political leaders were happy, then the bi-monthly fights would continue. After a private meeting with his four silent partners, expenses paid out and a game plan established, Big Jim returned to Gas City with his share of the take. While not as much as they had hoped for, each knew that word of mouth would double tonight's attendance at the next event. Things were moving along very nicely.

~~~~~~~~~~~~~~~~~~~~

Justin returned to work doing paperwork and making rounds of the town. He found it painful to mount a horse, but once in the saddle, he could ride short distances with little difficulty. As to Samantha, he realized that her father
~~~~~~~~~~~~~~~~~~~~

was justified in asking him to back off for a while to allow their relationship to cool for the time being. As a result, he chose not to answer her letters, thinking it might be best to follow her father's wishes. Within a few days, he received another letter from her. In it, she said she received a letter from a friend who informed her that he had been shot but was recovering. She also said she now knew that it was the reason why he hadn't written to her.

Ouch. Now it looks like I will have to write, after all, he thought to himself. Forcing himself to do so, Justin explained that his job was dangerous and maybe they should reconsider their affection for each other. All this broke his heart writing it, but maybe her father was right after all and she deserved better than to become a young widow. He mailed the letter and waited, but no further letters arrived from her. Brokenhearted, Justin threw himself into his work.

Kevin Martin's jury trial was set to take place June 11 in Gas City. A few days before, Wilbert Vance walked into the marshal's office and welcomed Justin back on the job. Sarsaparilla flowed freely that evening as promised. "I quit my job with the shoe company," Wilbert told him. "I think after the trial, I will look for something around here. I kinda like this little town."

Justin seemed a little surprised, "The factories pay well, you might try them." Shaking his head, Wilbert replied that he would much prefer a position working in an Emporium or something of that nature. "I'm not exactly the physical type," he joked.

"I don't know, you sure picked me up and carried me back into town, but I am happy to hear you will be staying locally. Here's a toast...to your future success in Gas City."

~~~~~~~~~~~~~~~~~~~~~~~

"Tell us about your involvement with the White Caps, Martin, and maybe the judge will go easier on you," Marshal Brewster continued to question his prisoner. Like he had told them time and time again, "I don't know nothin' about no White Caps." Taking a break from the questioning, Brewster and Blake stepped outside for a little breather. "I'm afraid he's telling the truth and isn't part of that gang. He knows he'll probably hang and informing on them might just save his neck, but it's the same answer every time we ask."

Justin was equally disgusted. "I was sure he was one of them or maybe its leader. Now we are back to square one. Well, let's keep at it for a while longer."

~~~~~~~~~~~~~~~~~~~~~~~

The second boxing match filled the athletic club's arena three-fourths of the way up. The crowd really got into the fighting as both fighters at one time or another seemed to have their opponent on the ropes, but somehow, the injured man managed to continue on. It was getting late, and finally, the promoter made the decision to call the fight a draw at round 57. The crowd seemed happy, as they certainly got their money's worth. This was when the promoter made his huge mistake.

Entering the ring, he announced to the crowd that the match would be considered a draw, and then made the stupid remark concerning the distribution of prize money to each fighter. Since the payment of prize money was illegal, this was the chance that the local sheriff was looking for and quickly arrested the promoter, taking him and a few others he managed to capture to Crown Point, Indiana. All were later bailed out by an attorney working for the partners who quickly paid their fines. The matches then continued on as before.

~~~~~~~~~~~~~~~~~~~~~~

Each and every day brought about improvements in Justin's injury. One afternoon he and Zeke were on their afternoon patrol looking in the shopkeepers' windows, talking and generally watching people as they went about their daily business. That was when both men witnessed it happening. A husband and wife were strolling along very casually about thirty paces ahead when the lady's small
~~~~~~~~~~~~~~~~~~~~~~

black coin purse became dislodged from either a pocket or her purse and fell onto the ground. Not realizing what had happened, the couple continued along. Justin was about to shout out to the couple when a young boy about eight or nine pounced upon the coin bag and shoved it into his pocket, then casually started to walk away. Justin was angered by this and began moving toward the boy when Zeke put out his arm to stop him. “Let me handle this my way, Deputy, and just play act along with what I say.” Justin was more than curious concerning what was about to happen.

Picking up his pace, Zeke walked up to the boy. “I saw what you did boy, a thievin’ of that ladies coin purse and all. You’re under arrest.” The boy’s eyes got wide as fear gripped him.

“I don’t have no ladies’ purse,” he pleaded to Zeke and Justin, who was trying very hard not to smile.

“Oh yea, show me and dis deputy marshal what’s in dat pocket!” Realizing he had been caught, the boy handed the black coin bag to Zeke.

“Its finders-keepers,” the boy tried to explain.

“Think we need ta lock him up in jail, Deputy?” Zeke said speaking in an official manner.

“Well, yes, that’s the standard punishment. Ninety days bread and water while we send his parents to the poor farm. Come along peaceful, son, and no tricks.” By now the boy was starting to cry, saying he was sorry and all. A few people noticed but quickly caught on when Zeke's facial expressions implied they should just ignore this. The three entered the jail office, and immediately the young boy's eyes made contact with the empty cell door standing wide open. "Think he's a bit too small and might just squeeze 'tween them bars, deputy?" Zeke inquired. Justin was catching on. "One way to tell, go stand in that cell and try to squeeze between the bars," he commanded. Slowly with great trepidation, the small boy entered the cell and showed that he could not fit in between the bars. *Of course*, Justin thought, *Old Zeke is putting the fear of God into the boy. I wonder what he has up his sleeve now.*

Ordering the boy to take a seat, the young lad was mighty quick to vacate the open jail cell. Looking the boy in the eyes and speaking softly in a fatherly manner, Zeke told the boy he had a true story to tell him and he had better listen up close. "I remember hearin' dis story back when I was about your age, back when only a few settlers lived in deez parts we now call the town of Marion, just north of here. A stranger had hired Martin Boots and his son, 'bout your age too, ta guide them around all the wilderness that existed back then. All three were on horseback and going up a hill when the boy noticed somethin' droppin' out of the stranger's saddle. The boy stopped and picked it up and handed it to his father who then handed it ta the stranger. It was a land speculators purse containin' $8,000. The stranger was so delighted with the honesty of the boy dat he went and offered the boy a $100 reward. The boy rejected the reward on account of high moral purpose, just doing what was right, knowin' that doing right was reward enough. If not fer the honesty of dat boy, none of deez here towns would be here today."

The boy had listened quietly and seemed to grasp the importance of the story. Justin could no longer sit and watch "So whats the right thing for you to do now, son?"

Without any hesitance, he replied, "I need to give the coin purse back to the lady." That was the answer both men were waiting to hear.

"Do you know who she is, and where she lives?" Justin asked of him.

"Yes, they live close to my house," he replied. Justin then told the boy he expected him to take the coin purse to the couple's home, tell them he had watched it fall out of her pocket, and spent some time learning who the lady was and where she lived. "Then make sure you don't accept any reward. Doing what is right is reward enough."

The boy quickly agreed. *No bread and water today, and no poor house for ma and paw!* As he was ready to leave, Zeke made one additional point, "After you do all of this, tell your pappy you saw it drop and returned it with no reward taken. He'll be mighty proud of you for ah doin' what's right! Now get!" Looking over at Zeke, Justin couldn't help but feel that a life's lesson was shown to him today, one that he should use in the future if warranted. “You know something, Zeke... you would have made a great father.”

~~~~~~~~~~~~~~~~~~~~~~

The trial of Kevin Martin was a big event in Gas City so, to accommodate the large crowd of people, the proceedings had to be moved to the fire barn. Kevin had requested a jury trial thinking he might have a few friends on the jury to keep him from hanging. The trial started on time with the prosecution first calling Deputy Marshal Blake to the stand. He explained to the jury everything that had happened that day before being shot by Kevin Martin. Then Wilbert Vance was called to the stand. He then told the jury what he had witnessed before and during the shooting. “He told me I was free to run, probably so the shooting would be pinned on me,” he told the jury.

The defense admitted that his client did, in fact, shoot the deputy but that it was in self-defense. He also told the jury that since the deputy had murdered his brother in cold blood, he just wasn’t right in the head and shouldn’t be held responsible for his actions. This caused a mild chuckle from a few jury members. In the end, it really didn’t matter as the sentence was passed upon Kevin Martin, guilty of attempted murder and sentenced to hang by the neck until dead on June 14. Case dismissed.
~~~~~~~~~~~~~~~~~~~~~~

~~~~~~~~~~~~~~~~~~~~~

It was an established policy, a gentleman's agreement if you will, that the clergy would be rotated from among the group in town, to any defendant of a capital offense judgment handed down. Today, it was the Reverend Stokes' turn to minister to the condemned man. As he approached the fire barn jail cell to perform his sacred duty, Stokes found it ironic that it would be him again involved with this man. This man who had attempted to dishonor his very own daughter. This man who broke a church window long ago, this same man who he would now have to face just before he was scheduled to die.

As he approached, Martin made it very clear he did not want the Reverend to enter his cell and to just go away. "My son," the Reverend spoke to him in kindness, "let us pray together to save your soul so you shall be welcomed in heaven as you meet your maker." A hateful Martin only replied, "I'll be shaking hands with the Devil soon enough and I'll give him your personal regards." At twelve noon, Kevin Martin went to his end the way most people fully expected him to do.

~~~~~~~~~~~~~~~~~~~~~

Indiana Governor Claude Matthews was running for re-election. A Democrat running on a law and order platform, he had crisscrossed the state by train, stopping in town after town to campaign and shake hands with the voters. It was only natural that at some point he would arrive in Gas City. His private secretary had already contacted the mayor with the governor's schedule and asked that proper arrangements be made for his safety and comfort. Mayor Huffman, a Republican, was more than pleased to welcome the governor to his fair city. The local Democratic Party quickly leased the use of the Lovett Opera House on Main Street for the governor's public address that evening. This large room was said to hold up to 200 people sitting side by side in portable wooden seats, which when removed allowed the local basketball team, the Owls, to play ball games inside.

The governor arrived on a busy Saturday afternoon, June 15, to a huge welcome at the depot. The mayor was on hand to welcome and introduce the governor to his prosperous city. Crowds pushed in order to catch a glimpse of the man, mothers held their small children up over their shoulders, and saloons closed in order for the men to participate in the democratic process and hopefully keep everyone sober. Speaking only briefly at the depot, the governor invited everyone to hear him speak that evening at 8:00 p.m. at the opera house. Completing this, he was escorted by coach down Main Street and into his hotel room at the Mississinewa

Hotel. This was a day to remember that no one present would soon forget.

Marshal Brewster and Deputy Blake were on hand at the hotel to prevent the curious and any pesky office seekers from bothering the governor during his period of rest. He dined promptly at 6:30 p.m. (pork chops, as recommended) with city dignitaries, gave an interview to Alvin Jensen of the Journal, and seemed more than anxious to begin his evening campaigning.

Since it was very much required, Brewster had all three of his deputies on duty with him at strategic points to ensure the Governor was well-protected. Justin was positioned outside the building watching all who entered by way of the stairwell, to ensure there was no mischief, like someone bringing a sack of tomatoes or eggs to throw. Justin saw no problems and was surprised at how Gas City residents had dressed up for the occasion. Men and women sat on hard wooden chairs with poor air ventilation anxiously awaiting the governor's arrival.

A few minutes before 8:00 p.m., the governor and his party then walked across the street to the open stairway that led to the third floor Opera House. Outside, Justin began to wonder what would happen if a fire should break out? With only a wooden center stairway and a cast-iron exterior fire escape, he hoped and prayed nothing would happen tonight. From up at the top of the stairway he could hear someone making an announcement, "Ladies and gentlemen, the governor of the great state of Indiana, the Honorable Claude Matthews." All Justin could hear at this point was thunderous applause. He would have to read the paper tomorrow to see what was said tonight.

After the governor's well-used stump speech, he agreed to take a few questions from the audience. As a seasoned campaigner, he had heard just about every question put to him and had a well-rehearsed answer ready for them. The one question that did catch the governor a little by surprise tonight came from a Catholic priest. He asked the governor about the boxing exhibitions underway up in Roby, and if prize money and betting were now part of his law and order campaign.

This question clearly made the governor uncomfortable, but he quickly stated that the payment of prize money and betting was not allowed under Indiana law, and would not be tolerated. At that point, he ended the session and reminded everyone to become a registered voter and to please vote the Democratic ticket. A thunderous applause erupted as people began to exit the building. One of those who remained was Big Jim Malone. He did not like the governor's answer one bit. He would have to tell his silent partners about this.

Chapter 13

The following day the private secretary to Governor Matthews released the following statement to the Indianapolis Star Sun, which was quickly picked up by other newspapers.

> *"The governor has made up his mind effectually and for all, that prize fighting in any guise cannot take place in Indiana, and all efforts of the Roby managers to deceive the public by calling their noxious fistic carnivals exhibition of skill will be of no avail. If the sheriff finds himself powerless to prevent the occurrence of the fights, the governor will more than likely call out the state militia." - Indianapolis Sun Star*

The prize fighting continued.

In July, the Columbia Athletic Club announced it would hold a heavyweight championship fight with a purse of $45,000 between challenger Charles Mitchell and reigning champion James J. (Gentleman Jim) Corbett in December at their facility. Excitement reached a fever pitch as it soon became the talk of the entire state.

"Do you think the governor is bluffing, or will he do it?" asked Big Jim.

His silent partners did not seem at all worried. "The championship fight is being discussed all over the country," one of them replied. "People will flock to Indiana to witness this great event. The governor is only playing this out for political purposes. He can see the added revenue it will bring to Indiana, as well as Illinois. If it will make you men feel any better, I'll have one of my men contact his office privately for a meeting. Campaign contributions have a way of changing a politician's mind. All we need him to do is just look the other way until he's re-elected. Gentlemen, we stand to make a small fortune on the Mitchell-Corbett fight!"

The prize fighting continued.

~~~~~~~~~~~~~~~~~~~~

It was now early July, and Justin had heard through a casual remark that Samantha and her mother had arrived back in town. The news sent a mild lightning bolt through him and he considered going straight to her house, take her into his arms, and explain it had all been a huge mistake. Then reality struck. *So close, yet so far away*, he thought.
~~~~~~~~~~~~~~~~~~~~

I'm bound to run into her somewhere in town, how will I handle it? Will she even speak to me? No doubt, Samantha feels betrayed and may even hate me now. Why didn't her father just stay out of our business?

Justin had returned to the office from his afternoon patrol of the town. Old Zeke had a feeling something was troubling young Justin so he came inside and took a seat.

"I ever tell ya the story of Paddy Morgan?" he asked. Justin set his pencil down and gave Zeke his full attention. "Well, sir, Old Paddy got a job he invented all by himself deliverin' newspapers to folks' homes every day. Gets ten cents a person come collectin' day too! Well sir, Paddy Morgan rides a mule named Ruben and sometimes da mule would throw him off. Once a bunch of rags was seen ta go over da mules head, and Paddy was in um." The amusing story had no effect on Justin's sour disposition.

"Go see that little gal," he told him. "Beats just a sittin' here ah pinin' away fer her." Justin pounded his fist onto the table.

"You're right, Zeke, I'll do it!" Off Justin went straight to the home of the girl he loved, and father or no father, he intended to tell her.

Reaching the home of the Reverend Stokes, Justin paused momentarily to compose his thoughts, then tapped the door knocker three times and waited. Unfortunately, it was Mrs. Stokes and not Samantha that opened it. "Good day, Mrs.

Stokes, I was wondering if I might have a brief word with Samantha, please."

Instead of inviting him in, she replied coldly, "My daughter does not wish to speak with you, and if you would be so kind, please refrain from any further contact with her. Good day, Deputy," and she closed the door in his face. A confused and dejected Justin then walked back to the fire barn and told Zoko what had transpired.

Sounds like dat little gal threw you over like dat mule did Paddy Morgan.

~~~~~~~~~~~~~~~~~~~~

An interesting editorial appeared in the July 14 issue of the Indianapolis News. In it, the governor was heavily criticized for dumping the enforcement of the state's no gaming law into the hands of the under-equipped local sheriff. In it, they demanded that he enforce the law and obtain warrants to arrest the management of this illegal fighting establishment in Roby, Indiana. The following was from the editorial article:

> *"Are we to fold our arms and let a game of plug-uglies defame our good name and make Indiana synonymous with indecency and shame; leave her, challenged by rascality, powerless to protect herself?*
~~~~~~~~~~~~~~~~~~~~

We demand in the name of an outraged State, in the name of a State that is jeered at and scorned, that this vile, insulting Roby be wiped out. No measures are too large, no cost too great to accomplish this object."- Indianapolis News

The prize fighting continued.

~~~~~~~~~~~~~~~~~~~~

After Justin was back at work, he made a point of asking Zeke to accompany him on his rounds and provide helpful advice on important matters such as which saloons water down their drinks, which men on the street are known to be thieves or troublemakers, and who he could count on in a pinch at help protect his back. Justin had developed a great admiration for old Zeke and would listen closely to anything the old man would tell him. Facts, not meaning much today, might provide useful clues down the road.

"Zeke, I'm still learning more about you all the time, but I'm curious, did you serve in the war?" he asked. Pride quickly filled the face of the old-timer as he answered, "Yep, fought with da 19th Indiana, Company H, under Captain Kelly. Seen enough death to last a feller a lifetime. I ever tell you about the strangest battle I was ever in? Well, sir, it was *the Battle of Jonesboro*."
~~~~~~~~~~~~~~~~~~~~

Justin started laughing, knowing the old man was putting him on. "I knew that Confederate General John Hunt Morgan raided into Southern Indiana and Ohio before getting caught, but I didn't know he came all the way up here!"

"Wasn't Morgan, let me tell you all about it cuz I was there, son. Some of us boys in blue was home on furlough when we got word that a group of Copperheads, that means Northern men agreein' with the South, was gonna pass through Jonesboro. So a bunch of us soldiers was a layin' fer um. Course, whiskey-fueled much of our anger. It was a pure night of terror, women, and children fearful ta stick their heads out the door. One local got himself wounded. Shouts, pushin', fightin,' and egg throwin'. Next day we held the high ground and the Reb lovers skedaddled out of town covered in blood and eggs. Battle of Jonesboro was as real ta folks den as the Battle of Mississinewa was ta the Injuns. I still belong to the G.A.R. Post in Jonesboro."

~~~~~~~~~~~~~~~~~~~~~~

Thompson Bottling Plant Manager Frank Livingston entered the barbershop of Matthew Brooks for his monthly haircut. Brooks seemed happy to see him, "Afternoon Mr. Livingston, please have a chair, only two people ahead of you today." Livingston located a day-old newspaper to look over and waited his turn.
~~~~~~~~~~~~~~~~~~~~~~

"Like I was saying, Matt," the customer in the barber chair was talking, "The White Cappers have been mighty quiet since the law hung Kevin Martin. I'll bet ya $2 he was their ringleader all along." The barbershop always tended to be the focal point of all conversations, whether it was the weather or any recent incident occurring within the town. "I don't know," the barber commented, "seems to me that enough time hasn't passed to make that assumption. What do you think, Mr. Livingston?"

All eyes within the barbershop were now upon the plant manager as he laid his newspaper to the side. "I'm afraid I haven't kept up with that group's supposed activities enough to even venture an opinion at this point. Only time will tell if this gentleman is correct or not." Soon it was Livingston's time for the barber chair.

As Brooks placed the barber's cape around the neck of his new customer, he brought up a subject he knew the plant manager wouldn't like at all. "How are the problems down at the plant going?" Livingston replied that things had been quiet, keeping the incident within his office private from the general public.

"Well, the reason I am asking is that I have been approached by the owner of the White Dog Saloon about allowing them to reopen. It's been almost three months since the city council, to whom you know I belong, voted to close them. If your difficulties have subsided, I am thinking of bringing up another vote this next week when we meet to reconsider returning their liquor license to them."

This was not news to Frank Livingston, as word had reached him earlier that the city council might do just that. He then replied, "If the vote goes against us, we will have to keep our fingers crossed that the men have learned their lesson and have profited by it. Otherwise, if serious troubles return, we may have to relocate the plant back to Ohio." *Perhaps word of this veiled threat will spread to our workers and put an end to all of the troubles once and for all*, Livingston thought.

~~~~~~~~~~~~~~~~~~~~

The next week the Gas City Council voted four to one to allow the White Dog Saloon to reopen the following day. Since its closure three months previously, Kruger saw to it that all whiskeys and kegs of beer had been relocated into other saloons belonging to Big Jim Malone. In only a couple of hours, the White Dog Saloon was restocked and ready to open again that Friday. Big Jim himself authorized a deluxe free lunch spread of fish, ham, sausages, crackers, and bits of cheese to the hungry workers who gladly paid their money for beer and whiskey. The saloon was soon packed with happy Thompson Bottling Company employees, but thankfully, no issues developed later at the factory. Kruger
~~~~~~~~~~~~~~~~~~~~

once again began to feel like the real boss he always pictured himself to be.

Later that night, word reached Frank Livingston that his friend's wife, Mary Dorsey, had taken a turn for the worse and wasn't expected to live much longer. What can you say to a friend who is about to lose the love of his life? What words could be spoken to aid and comfort this poor stricken man? He and his own wife had been friends with the Dorsey's for many years. For such a close bond to exist between upper management and a man who advanced through the ranks as Dorsey had done was quite unusual in these modern times. While neither ever spoke about the actual division between their stations in life, each simply held a deep and understanding friendship that was far more important to Livingston than wielding power over a subordinate.

On Saturday afternoon, Mary Dorsey succumbed to the cancer that had taken her life at the young age of only thirty-six. In respect to his friend, for the first time in history, the Thompson Green and Amber Glass Bottling Company closed on a workday out of respect for William Dorsey. Livingston would see that the men received a full day of wages using the plant's emergency contingency fund. The production work itself would have to be made up at a later date. A memorial service was held that day to honor her memory and was heavily attended by its Thompson Glass workers, who came to show respect for their well-liked grieving foreman. Throughout the ordeal, Frank Livingston stood by his friend's side, as Mary Dorsey was laid to rest.

There would be no further incidents at the Thompson Bottling Company.

~~~~~~~~~~~~~~~~~~~~

One should not be given the wrong impression that the single ladies, wives, and mothers in town were pleased that their husbands and fathers were spending a great deal of their earned wages within the halls of the numerous saloons operating in and around Gas City. But women, still lacking the vote that would take another generation to grant to them, still made their displeasures known. A group of these ladies called themselves The Temperance Crusaders who openly and vigorously demanded the closing of all saloons. Ministers of God often spoke in their defense, knowing full well the effects that alcohol was having on the poor working man's families as wives struggled, trying to save what was left from their husbands' incomes that seemed destined to be turned over to the saloons. As a result, physical abuse was on the rise against women and children.

Many of the older ladies remembered fondly the Francis Murphy movement that had swept the county in the 1870s. Anti-saloon fever swept the community though no actual league officially was established here. Ladies of that time
~~~~~~~~~~~~~~~~~~~~

donned a badge upon their clothing consisting of a little blue-colored bow. Perhaps, some ladies speculated, we should return to using that proper identification method today.

Otis Blackburn was a living example of what these ladies were fighting against. He was employed as a day laborer at the Chicago Edged Tool Company bringing home earnings of almost $9.00 for a seventy hour work week, very good pay by the standards of the day. Unfortunately, his favorite saloon, The Snake Hole, received more than their share of his wages as his wife and two children often went hungry and were reduced to receiving assistance from friends and family. Neighbors would be quick to testify that screams of terror often penetrated their tiny rental property next to the railroad tracks. Stumbling home late at night, he had no problem in knocking his wife around a little when she pleaded with him. "The rent must be paid...the children are hungry..." but he sees nothing wrong with unwinding with his friends after a hard day at work. This scene is repeated over and over in many of the factory workers homes as lives are destroyed while Big Jim Malone rakes in the daily proceeds.

East of town at a long abandoned log cabin, plans are being made this evening to send a strong message to all offenders. Outside, a pot of a certain substance was cooking under a small fire and waiting for its owner to arrive. It will not have to wait long.

Late at night under a moonless sky, Otis Blackburn staggered toward his home. He had left The Snake Hole a little later than normal as he had managed to hide away some of his paychecks from the old lady. *What she don't know ain't gonna hurt her none*, he thought as he tried to walk as straight as possible without bumping into obstacles within his path. The motto of the saloon was "Just give a rabbit two drinks of whiskey and it will spit in a wildcat's eye." That's how he felt tonight, able to tangle with any wildcat that came his way. Otis Blackburn didn't have long to wait to meet his own wildcat.

Chapter 14

Otis Blackburn proved to be an easy target as he seldom varied from his late night schedule. Four hooded members of the White Caps lay in wait, hidden by the darkness. As he approached, the largest hooded figure stepped out from behind his concealment and struck the man on the back of the head. In seconds, Blackburn was unconscious and lying upon the ground. Without a single word being said, the hooded group using hand signals, brought up a small horse drawn wagon and quickly laid their victim in it under a tarp. The driver removed the flour sack over his head and stuffed it into his shirt. As he slowly rode out of town his compatriots quickly vanished into the night. All would meet up at the pre-determined location. Justice would once again be served this night.

With the wagon's arrival, the group went about their pre-determined plans. A groggy Blackburn's mouth was heavily gagged as his hands were tied behind his back. A large thick wooden post had been buried into the ground and

Blackburn was then tied to it standing up. One of the hooded figures produced a long knife and began cutting away all the clothing off of the man leaving him quite naked. His clothing was then burned in the open fire underneath the pot. Setting inside the fire, resting upon the glowing ambers laid a branding iron.

A bucket of cold water was thrown into the face of the captive. He quickly was able to sober up enough to know that he was in fact in a terrible predicament, one that he seemed powerless to escape. A voice sounded out from the darkness.

"Otis Blackburn, you have been found guilty of being a wife beater, and a drunkard who is not fit to live. It is the judgment of the White Caps that you be branded WB for a wife beater, tarred and feathered, then left to die in this miserable location."

The speaker then picked up the cherry red branding iron and slowly approached the victim. Blackburn kicked and bucked as much as he could but found himself unable to prevent that which he fully understood was coming. The speaker advanced to within inches of the man's chest then paused, savoring the moment of pure anguish on the victim's face. Then the branding iron found its mark as the man howled in agonizing pain. Pulling the iron back within a few seconds, the mark WB was now clearly branded upon his body. The iron was then placed back into the fire, awaiting further use. Soon his entire body was branded with the initials.

Within thirty minutes, unconscious and nearly dead, Blackburn was again subjected to another bucket of cold water. He was barely conscious when the boiling pot of hot tar was poured over his body. Old feather pillows were then sliced open and their contents dumped upon the blacked oil. A message had now been sent to all wife beaters and worthless drunkards that their conduct will no longer be tolerated. The White Caps had spoken.

Many days had passed before a squirrel hunter, seeking shelter from a heavy downpour, discovered the grizzly remains and notified Marshal Brewster.

Doctor Baxter commented this was certainly the work of deranged lunatics. Several who witnessed the body later said the image would haunt them the rest of their lives. “Same type of knot,” replied Brewster. The darkened brand marks stood out on the body as several speculated what WB stood for. The decision was made to just send for the funeral director and let him bag the remains up. Clearly, this man was tortured to death. Several days earlier, the wife had reported him missing but Brewster felt she needed to be spared the shock of seeing this. He wished he had also been spared. Any trace of footprints was long ago washed away. Parts of the man’s clothing still remained in the cool ashes of the fire. A bucket with tar remains was all that was left behind. Catching this killer or killers was now paramount. If actions didn't produce results soon, Brewster knew he might find himself out of a job.

~~~~~~~~~~~~~~~~~~~~~~

"Marshal Brewster," came the voice of Zeke Miller as he tracked him down on the street. "Afternoon Zeke, what's up?" He replied. "Well, sir, Doc just flagged me down. Seems one of their ex-soldiers out at the Old Soldiers Home came into town and got himself kicked by a horse. Plum broke his leg, too. Doc set it but wants me ta take the man back to the home in his own wagon. I was wonderin' if I can take young Justin along fer the ride and show him the place?"

"Sure, show the boy around but don't keep him gone too long, alright?"

Catching site of the Deputy, Zeke told him what the marshal said and with the injured man lying flat on the back, Justin climbed up onto the wagon and off they went. "So what is this place anyhow?" Justin asked. "Well sir," Zeke replied, "it opened up about three years ago on what used to be the Elliot farm. Real nice place set up like an army post, sort of. Got their own barracks', mess hall, chapel, hospital, parade field, bandstand and such. Old soldiers go there when they need a place ta live. County gives um free natural gas too. About 586 old soldiers when it opened, probably more
~~~~~~~~~~~~~~~~~~~~~~

now. Some folks like ta go on Sunday afternoons just ta picnic and listen to the band playin' music."

After delivering the patient and answering a bunch of foolish questions, the men headed back to Gas City. "Bin meanin' ta ask if you made up yet with that pretty little gal? Zeke inquired.

"No, and I'm afraid it's all over between us. After speaking with her mother and not receiving a note or anything, I guess she doesn't want to see me anymore. I think her parents probably sat her down and convinced her she could do a lot better than a deputy marshal."

The men traveled on in silence for quite some spell before Justin spoke up. "Did you see yesterday's newspaper?" Zeke then reminded him that he never actually got around to learnin' ta read. "Why?" Justin started smiling, then proceeded with the conversation. "Then you probably don't know about the Professor Victor show at the opera house tomorrow evening? If you are free, why not come along with me? It'll be a great night of entertainment!"

"What's it cost ta get in and what's the show about?" Zeke asked.

"My treat for filling in for me during my down time. As to the show, it's a Hypnotism presentation." Zeke had a strange puzzled look on his old face. "Hypno...?"

"Kinda like a magic show making folks say and do stuff. I was told it will be very funny as Professor Victor is performing in Marion tonight." After a bit of grumbling, Zeke agreed to meet Justin at the open stairwell of the opera house tomorrow evening. Justin asked that Zeke meet him early, say 6:30 p.m., so they could sit up close to see and hear better. It should be a fun evening!

True to his word, Zeke was waiting outside the building the next evening for the show and together they climbed the stairs to the third floor open room. A mass of wooden folding chairs had been set up to accommodate the huge crowd expected. They found two empty chairs in the second row up front and sat down. The show was scheduled to begin at 7 p.m. so they were lucky to get this close, as a large crowd of people was beginning to enter. The Professor had brought with him a simple portable wooden stage capable of holding six or more people and being elevated. It provided easier viewing for the late arrivals in the rear.

Justin was glancing around the room, casually searching for familiar faces when he became frozen in his seat. Entering the room was Samantha on the arm of reporter Alvin Jensen. In an instant, their eyes locked for what seemed to Justin like an eternity. Then she broke off her glance. Samantha must have whispered something to Jensen, as he quickly looked in Justin's direction with a look of complete satisfaction on his face. Justin was tempted to walk over and slap that look right off his face, but thought otherwise and returned looking to the front. Apparently, Zeke had not noticed the couple's entrance, as nothing was said about it.

The seating soon began to fill up as Justin's pocket watch showed only ten minutes to go before the show started. The gas lighting in the room burned brightly and provided great visibility for everyone as they began to converse with their neighbors.

The show began with the introduction of Professor Victor, who entered through the back of the room wearing a black suit with a black cape. He received moderate applause. Justin felt he would need to show this hard-to-sell crowd something before getting the applause Victor, no doubt, felt he deserved.

"Ladies and gentlemen, tonight you will witness feats of hypnotism that will amaze you, events that will astound you, and actions that will thrill you. Little is known of the human mind, as science today attempts to unravel its inner mysteries. Tonight I, with your assistance, will attempt to add to that scientific knowledge. I ask that everyone remain seated unless called upon to come forward. I thank you." By now the crowd was sitting on the edge of their chairs, wondering what was to come next.

Looking into the audience, the Professor smiled and asked two young college age girls to accompany him onto the stage. Six chairs were then placed side by side by the stage crew. "I would, also, like to ask you four gentlemen to accompany us." By now all six individuals were on the stage. "Please be seated, thank you. Just get comfortable and relax." Addressing the six he had chosen, he began the evening's entertainment. "Ladies and gentlemen, before you are several gas lights within this room. I would like you to pick one out and concentrate on it. Look into its flame... look deep within the flame...allow yourself to drift into its flickering light. Concentrate on my voice and the flame... concentrate...concentrate. Your eyes are getting heavy... concentrate on my voice and let yourself drift away. When I snap my fingers you will fall into a deep sleep and will respond only to my voice." SNAP!

The audience seemed a little perplexed as to what had just happened. Professor Victor walked over to one gentleman, who failed to go into a trance and thanked him for his time, and asked that he return to his seat in the audience. Now five people sat in silence under his hypnotic spell.

Turning back to the audience, the Professor explained that the volunteers were in no danger but were under his hypnotic control. There was total silence within the room, with all eyes watching and wondering what was to come. "When I count to three, you will awaken to find yourself surrounded by a huge swarm of bees. One, two,... three!" Suddenly all five people on the small stage leaped to their feet and with flailing arms tried to ward off the imaginary swarm of bees. The audience erupted in great laughter and some applauded as both men and women jumped all around the stage trying to drive off the imaginary insects. "When I snap my fingers, the bees will be gone and I want you to return to your seats." Snap! The five people stopped fighting insects and returned quietly to their seats on the stage. The audience roared their approval as the Professor took a small bow.

Approaching one of the young ladies, he told her, "When I snap my fingers, the person whose shoulder I am touching will fall madly in love with the older bald gentleman on the end of the row. Do you understand? If so, please nod yes." She nodded. The audience could hardly hold their excitement. Going to the bald man, the Professor said, "You will find the girl on the end utterly revolting and want nothing at all to do with her. Nod if you understand." The bald man nodded. "For only these two people whom I have given instructions, when I count to three you will do as I have commanded. When I snap my fingers you will then return to your chairs. One two, three!" The cute young college girl leaped onto her feet and clung to the old bald man, spraying his head with kisses. The bald man found her simply repulsive, attempting to push her away and begged her to leave him alone. The audience roared with laughter and applause. Finally, the Professor snapped his fingers and each returned to their seats. More applause and a small bow.

Now approaching the last girl, he instructed her that she was now eight years old and for her to play with her doll. The girl became an eight-year-old child as she played with her imaginary doll, combing its hair and hugging it. The Professor then instructed the other two men to stand. He then produced a long hat pin, showing it to the audience then instructed one of the men to take it. He instructed the man with the pin that when he counted to three, he was to stick it deep into the hand of the other man. Did he understand? Yes, he did. The professor then told the other man that he would feel absolutely no pain and would not bleed when the hat pin was placed into his hand. Did he understand? Yes. "Here we go, one, two...three!"

The hat pin was stuck into the man's hand with absolutely no reaction. The audience was totally amazed. Instructions were given to remove the pin and that no pain or discomfort from the pin would be felt. When he snapped his fingers each man was then to return to their seats. Snap! Turning to the five on the stage, the Professor asked for a round of applause for them. They sure got one, too. "When I count to three, I will snap my fingers and each of you shall awaken feeling completely refreshed and pain-free with no memories of what has happened. Do each of you understand?" All nodded. One, two...three Snap! Each woke up and was told to return to their original seats as a thunderous round of applause erupted. Again, there was a small bow.

The audience was completely into the Professor's performance and couldn't wait for more to happen. "At this time I need to select a gentleman from the audience..." A chant of "deputy junior...deputy junior" began. It grew so loud that the Professor finally asked, "Who is deputy junior? Is he here with us tonight?"

Poor Zeke, upon hearing that awful nick name slumped down into his seat. "There he is, Professor," someone shouted. "He's in the second row," another laughingly informed the Professor. "Well, deputy junior, your fans would like you to participate. Will you please join me on the stage?" With that, many cat calls and hoots were given by men who knew and liked old Zeke Miller. Instead, Zeke replied, "Naw, just a bunch of fakin' anyway." Smiling with absolute delight at the prospect of fixing this old goat's wagon, the Professor replied, "Then, in that case, you have nothing to fear, do you? Everyone, please give him a round of applause." The place erupted in shouts and more cat calls. Zeke slowly made his way up onto the stage, pulling at his collar and looking mighty uncomfortable in front of all these people.

"What is your name, sir?"

"Zeke Miller."

"Well, Mr. Miller, I would like you to go sit on that single chair for me." Reluctantly he took a seat and stared back at the audience, giving some dirty looks, especially to those that were doing the cat calling. "Just get comfortable and relax," spoke the Professor. "Mr. Miller, before you are several gas lights within this room. I would like you to pick one out and concentrate on it. Look into its flame...look deep within the flame...allow yourself to drift into its flickering light. Concentrate on my voice and the flame...concentrate... concentrate. Your eyes are getting heavy...concentrate upon my voice and let yourself drift away. When I snap my fingers you will fall into deep sleep and will respond only to my voice." SNAP!

Everyone waited eagerly to see if it had worked on old Zeke. It had. "I want you to travel back into your youth, back beyond your teenage years, back to when you were just five years old. Are you there?" Zeke's head nodded yes. "What is your full name, little boy?" In a squeaky, childish voice, he answered, "Zachariah Belvidere Miller." The audience howled at that. The chant of "Belvidere, Belvidere" continued until the Professor signaled for it to end. "Are you a happy little boy, Zachariah?" His head shook no. "Why are you unhappy, Zachariah?" "Cause I wet me britches." The place exploded with laughter, lasting upwards to five minutes. Even the Professor had to walk away for a moment to regain his composure. "Listen to my voice now Zachariah, you are now twenty-five years old. When I count to three you will wake up but everyone you see within this room will appear naked to you. No one but you will have on any clothing. Do you understand?" Zeke nodded yes.

"On the count of three. One two...three!" Zeke opened his eyes and began looking around. *Oh my God,* he thought, *all those people are naked!* Zeke could hardly believe his own eyes! Fat men naked, pretty women naked. Oh my! Oh my! The audience howled at the expression of shock on his face. "Is something wrong?" asked the Professor. Laughing loudly and pointing to the audience, Zeke replied. "Yea, all dem folks is naked!" Again, a couple of minutes of laughter erupted. "Alright, Mr. Miller...on the count of three you need to go back to sleep. One two three!" Off to sleep he went again.

"Now Mr. Miller, on the count of three, you will be changed into a human chicken. One, two, three!" Zeke leaped to his feet, arms fluttering as he clucked and clucked to the audience's absolute delight. The more he fluttered about, the louder the laughter erupted. "Chicken-man, chicken-man," came the taunts from the audience. Finally it was time to bring the show to an end. "You are no longer a chicken, please take your seat." He did. "When I snap my fingers you shall awaken feeling totally refreshed and remembering nothing that has transpired here tonight. On your way to your seat though, I want you to stop and shake hands with every person sitting in the front row. Do you understand?" Zeke's head nodded. SNAP!

Zeke awakened as directed, looked around at the audience, then replied, "Nothin' but a bunch of fakin' anyway," as the audience again burst out laughing. Not understanding why folks were laughing, Zeke stopped and shook hands with everyone on the front row on his way to his seat.

After enough people had told Zeke what he had done up on that stage, he chose to make himself scarce from public view for the next few days.

Chapter 15

It was time to meet again and plan the evening's important and productive work for the night ahead. This person was worthy of the wrath that would quickly come his way. This was a clear message to be sent out once again that the work of the White Caps simply balanced the scales of justice. All transgressors were hereby given notice that the Angel of Death would soon pass their way.

Jethro Lutz was a day laborer who raised dogs on his rural property. Lutz enjoyed conducting an occasional private dog fighting event attended by locals, who used word of mouth to inform only those they knew enjoyed this sick type of *sport*. Money's were heavily waged and Lutz could always be counted upon to provide his homemade brew at a slightly higher than average price to the thirsty attendees. Dogs were forced to fight to the death while financial wagers were made as to whose dog would prevail and whose dog would die. The serious injury and death of a few dogs meant nothing to Lutz. There were always more animals where they came from.

It was well after 1:00 a.m. when the loud barking of a chained up watch dog awoke him from his drunken slumber. Lutz assumed a furry raccoon had entered the property and set the dog off barking, as he was used to the barking of dogs anyway. Lutz just rolled over onto his side and tried to go back to sleep. The evening had been good and profit had been made.

Suddenly his cabin door burst open and four figures wearing flour sacks over their heads entered. Even without visible weapons, their presence at this hour was enough to scare and confuse any man just awakened from an evening of heavy drinking. “Who are you?” Lutz demanded. “And what gives you the right...”

“Jethro Lutz,” their leader shouted. “You have been judged guilty of the crime of dog fighting with a sentence of death to be carried out immediately. Take him away!” Lutz was quickly hustled away to his doom.

August 1st had been a beautiful day, so far. Many of the Hoosier forests along the tracks of the Pennsylvania railroad were at the early stages of changing colors, and this view provided its traveling customers a spectacular view of the changing of the seasons. The first southbound train of the day pulled into Gas City’s Depot for a twenty-minute layover with some of its passengers departing, while others were only beginning their travels. Stepping from the cab of his mighty engine, the engineer Alto Stevens proceeded into the depot to speak with its stationmaster. “You better let your local lawmen know we saw a man hanging from a tree about one mile north of town,” he told him. “Not a pretty sight.”

The stationmaster then asked if the passengers had seen it too. “Some probably did, can’t help it the way he’s just hanging there and all.” Then the stationmaster asked if the tree was close enough to the right of way to be on railroad property. That would require a railroad detective to investigate. “Nope, it’s a way’s back but clear as a bell. Gives your town a bad first impression for folks a traveling through.”

Motioning one of the young boys over who routinely sold food at each stop, he said, “Hey, Billy, I need you to go find the Marshal quick and tell him I need to see him now.” The young boy ran off. Always a helpful lad, young Billy had one dream when he grew up and that was to be an engineer on the Pennsylvania Railroad.

“Marshal,” the out of breath young boy called out. “The stationmaster wants you to come a running.” With that intriguing bit of early morning news, Brewster and Justin headed to the depot. “Let’s take my wagon, my back’s been a killing me all day,” Brewster offered. Pulling up outside the depot, both men were met by the agitated stationmaster. “Morning, Marshal, sorry to drag you down here first thing but we got us a real problem. Southbound engineer reports there's a man hanging from a tree about one mile north of here, close to our tracks. Says it isn't on railroad property so I figured you would wanna know about it. Not a good thing to advertise for folks arriving in our town either."

"Here we go again," Brewster muttered quietly to himself. "Thanks, we'll handle it from here." Turning to his deputy, Brewster motioned for him to drive as the Marshal gingerly pulled himself up on to the seat. The wagon proceeded North running parallel to the tracks. "Backs a killing me so go easy won't you? And try not to hit every hole and rut with the wheels."

It didn't take long to locate the body. It was hanging by a rope from a sturdy branch of an oak tree. No attempt to hide this bit of work. The killer(s) had wanted everyone on the next passing train to see it. It was clearly not a suicide, as the man's hands were tied behind him with that all too familiar knot. The victim's neck was broken and his face had already started to darken in color. Justin asked, "Any idea who he is?" "Yep," the Marshal replied. "Names Jethro Lutz. Worked as a day laborer. I've had a couple of run-ins with him over the years, making illegal shine." Using the Marshal's knife, the rope was cut about five feet from the noose and the body was placed in the back of the wagon by Justin, so as not to add more pain to the Marshal's already aching lower back. The wagon made its way back into town, to the office of Doctor Baxter.

Word of the lynching had already spread and newspaper reporter Alvin Jensen was waiting at Doc Baxter's to find out the identity of the victim. As soon as the wagon came to a halt, the men standing around quickly identified the dead man as Lutz. Alvin Jensen made it a point not to even look at Justin as he asked Marshal Brewster several questions, most of which he just couldn't answer. Word of another presumed White Cap killing spread like wild fire throughout the town. Doc instructed some of the men to carry the dead man into his office for a closer examination, then told the rest to please vacate and allow him to make his examination in peace. Reluctantly, the men moved on. "I'll be down shortly with my report," he told Brewster. "Let me come to you, Doc it's my back again. It's killing me." It wasn't even 8:00 a.m. and Brewster's head already ached now as badly as his back. It was going to be one of those days again.

~~~~~~~~~~~~~~~~~~~~

The fights continued. It seemed that the crowds were getting larger with every scheduled boxing match which took place in Roby. Big Jim Malone and his silent partners again met to divvy up the proceeds and to discuss future events. "We are getting a tremendous response in our
~~~~~~~~~~~~~~~~~~~~

advertising of the Mitchell-Corbett Championship fight for December," one of the silent partners said. "We must continue to build up the excitement with quality fights to ensure the Athletic Club remains packed." Another Chicago-based partner mentioned the side betting taking place, "I have had to get a few of my boys involved in *persuading* some of our more wealthy clients to pay up on their side bets." A few chuckles sounded as each member received a tray of refreshed drinks from the bar.

Big Jim finally asked the question that had to be on the minds of all the partners, "Where do we stand with the Governor?" One partner who had remained quiet spoke up, "That task was my responsibility. I sent a couple of our lawyers to Indianapolis to try to reason with the man, and the cash we offered was no cheap bribe I can tell you that! The man wouldn't even hear our boys out, said he didn't want *that kind of money* then told them to get out. I am concerned his attitude goes far beyond just preaching law and order as Politicians do just to get re-elected, but is serious in his threats to shut us down." These words haunted each member as they said their good-byes and bothered Big Jim plenty on the train trip back to Gas City. *I stand to lose everything if he follows up on his threats*, he thought to himself. There was indeed plenty to worry about.

~~~~~~~~~~~~~~~~~~~~~~
~~~~~~~~~~~~~~~~~~~~~~

While Justin continued on his afternoon patrol around town, he found himself standing in front of Rothinghouse Brothers Drug Store. A sudden craving for a penny piece of hard candy led him inside to complete his purchase. As he was about to depart, the tiny bell mounted upon the top of the shops interior door began to ring. Another customer entered the drug store. It was Samantha, alone. Justin came to a halt, wanting to speak but afraid she would simply ignore him. Within an awkward few seconds, it was Samantha who finally broke the ice.

"Hello Justin, I hope you are well. I wanted desperately to come to you but father told me what you had said, so I stayed away." Justin had a strange look on his face so she responded, "About you not wanting to see me again. I understand." Justin, with a look of pure astonishment, replied, "Samantha, I never said any such thing! It was your father that told me I should leave you alone, that you deserved better than to become a young widow. I was crushed but felt I had no choice but to agree to his wishes. Even your mother told me you did not wish to ever speak with me again."

A look of complete puzzlement spread across her face, "Justin, they told me it was YOU that wanted to break up with me! I cried for days about it." Aware that others in the drug store were clearly listening to their private conversation, Justin suggested they go for a walk and talk it out. Soon they came to the realization that Rev. & Mrs. Stokes had not been honest in their dealings with each of them and was working to prevent them from becoming a couple. Justin suggested for the time being that she say nothing to her parents and they would meet as often as possible to talk. “School will begin again shortly and life shall become quite busy for me,” she reminded him. As they parted, each felt great relief that neither person had turned against the other.

~~~~~~~~~~~~~~~~~~~~

Christmas came four months early for the citizens of Gas City. Or perhaps with clarification, it came early for it’s volunteer firemen. The Fire Commissioner (Chief) had been asking for the replacement of it’s outdated 1873 Truckson LaFrance hand-powered fire pump, which required firemen to pump its handles up and down rapidly. This action caused men to frequently be replaced, due to exhaustion. Exhausted firemen were of little use in a fire situation. With the huge growth in factories and additional housing, a modern steam-powered fire pump was greatly needed. After all, a rapidly spreading fire could easily endanger the entire town. Updated fire protection was an integral part of the town.

The major problem the fire chief had in selling the idea was the steam pumper’s cost- $5,353. That’s when the idea of approaching each industrial factory and business to ask for a donation came to him. Not only would modern
~~~~~~~~~~~~~~~~~~~~

firefighting equipment provide a safer environment but also help decrease fire insurance policy rates. The city council agreed to match whatever amount the firemen were able to raise from businesses and the general public. The ladies of the town sponsored cake and cookie sales, and donation jars were placed in public areas. This made the public feel they had an vested interest in the project and, by summertime, enough money was raised to place the order for the equipment.

The new horse-drawn steam fire pumper was to be purchased from American Fire Engine Company in Cincinnati and transported to Gas City by railcar in early August. On Thursday, August 5th, a telegram arrived stating the steamer had been shipped and was expected to arrive on Saturday, August 7th. Word of its pending arrival created an almost carnival atmosphere in the town as the local band was on hand to play for the crowd while it was carefully unloaded. Children and their parents clustered around the depot to catch a glimpse of the new metal monster, something never seen before by the majority of its town. The brass trim made it shine like the sun rising on a newborn day. It had huge red spoke wheels and a large boiler that, when heated, produced steam to a pump engine that powered pressurized water into the fire hoses.

Old Betsy and Prince Albert, the two fire horses, watched with curiosity as they were harnessed to this strange vehicle. When it was ready, the firemen piled upon this strange modern vehicle for the slow ride back to the fire barn. Everyone cheered as each fireman took his own turn ringing its loud fire bell. The band continued to play lively tunes and a few clever people worked the crowds selling food and drinks. Slowly the new vehicle proceeded up Main Street and turned south onto 3rd Street, arriving outside the fire barn. As the doors were swung open, all eyes fell upon their old hand fire pump that had served them so faithfully. Though some probably would not admit it, there was a small feeling of sadness from replacing an old and faithful friend with a new one. The old hand pump would still be kept back for an emergency backup. Now the work would begin to put this new beauty into operational service and train every man on each aspect of its mechanical use.

Once the steam fire pumper had arrived at the fire barn, the crowds dissipated and went home to leave the firemen to do their business. Since Justin was now friendly with the firemen, having watched their actual emergency responses and training, he felt comfortable asking questions about how the thing actually worked. One of the firemen explained that a small fire was either kept hot or started quickly in the tall water boiler and that steam would then pump the engine that forced water through the fire hoses. The three hard suction hoses carried on its sides would be useful in sucking water directly from the Mississinewa River.

Justin had watched before as the fire horses were placed directly under their overhead hanging collars, which were then quickly lowered in place and clasped before attaching the reins. He was impressed how rapidly the firemen at the fire barn could actually accomplish all of this and be on their way to a fire with bells ringing loudly.

Justin asked him one more question, “This may sound like a stupid question, but I read once over in Europe some fool made a vehicle, like a train, that runs on the dirt roads. With all this steam power, can’t that thing be made to pull itself?”

The fireman laughed, “Not a stupid question at all. To stop any such foolishness here, we got us a law called the Locomotion Act that restricts any such contraption from going over 4 miles per hour in a populated area. And then, a man has to walk in front of the darn thing carrying a red flag just to warn folks to stay away. No, deputy, the good old horse-drawn steam engine is the thing of the future, and it will be just the same in your grandchildren’s day.” Justin totally agreed then left the firemen to their business. *It takes a very special brave man to do what these fellers do*, Justin thought to himself.

Chapter 16

Word had reached Marshal Brewster that members of the city council were unhappy with the way the investigations into these murders were being conducted by his office. Thinking it best that he should take the initiative rather than simply wait to be called on the carpet, Brewster reached out to the Mayor asking for an off-the-record joint meeting. It was quickly agreed to and the meeting was set to take place at 6 p.m. that evening in the office at the bank building. Brewster then asked Justin if he would like to attend, but reminded him he was off duty and under no obligation to do so. Justin quickly agreed to go anyway.

The men met around a large conference table on the first floor. Each council member took his turn asking questions of Brewster, and the extent of his investigation. Most appeared to be displeased with his replies. "What if we offered, say, a $100.00 reward for information leading to the arrest and conviction of the White Caps?" the Mayor proposed. Brewster urged caution, "While this may sound like a good idea, and maybe we will eventually have to go that route, the huge sum of $100 will cause friends to spy on friends or question the whereabouts or movements of their neighbor. My office will be inundated with false leads requiring constant follow up."

"Let's say farmer Jones, for example, goes out late at night to check on a newborn calf and someone sees the lantern and reports him as a White Capper conducting a meeting? I suggest we agree to hold off on that idea for just a while longer and give me more time to crack this case. Even the Grant County Sheriff is perplexed."

After a bit of discussion, it was agreed to hold off on the reward offer for a while. The Marshal was instructed to pursue the investigation to the limits or serious consequences could follow. Brewster did not need that statement to be explained to him at all.

The following morning both officers sat in their office discussing the previous evening's events. Justin had something he wanted to discuss. "You said something last night that stuck in my head. I couldn't quite figure it out and I couldn't sleep, so I just laid there thinking hard about it. An idea came to me. For whatever it's worth, here it is. Maybe we are going about this White Cap business all wrong."

"When you mentioned the Jones' barn scenario with the farmer and the lantern, that got me thinking. Instead of trying to catch them in the act, maybe we need to locate where they are first meeting. Bear with me as I think out loud, alright? It seems logical that there is more than one person behind all of this. One man could not subdue, transport and inflict punishment to this degree by himself. It would also seem to me that the group would have to be small, say five or six, as a larger group runs the risk of one of it's members talking too freely in a saloon or to a woman. So, if this is the case, then we need to concentrate on where and when they meet."

Brewster was giving his deputy his full attention.

"We know they operate strictly in the dead of night so I'm thinking that would be when they would meet. If they did meet in the daytime to plan the night's attack, then how would last minute needed changes to plans get passed on? Also, a group meeting in the daytime runs a greater risk of being observed by someone else. So, unless they meet in a member's home or business, which I'm thinking is unlikely, they must meet up somewhere just before they act. The question, of course, is where? Are you with me so far, Marshal?"

"Yes, go on. So far I'm agreeing with your way of thinking."

"Alright, so do they meet in town, or out of town in the countyside? The risks of exposure would be much greater in town but to meet up somewhere else, say an abandoned farm, cabin, or another location would make more sense." Walking over to the wall map, Justin pointed out the locations where all their victims lived, with all located less than a mile from town, with some living in the town itself. "So in your head, make a circle one mile outside of town. It doesn't seem practical for the members to travel farther than a mile to meet, and then double back into town to conduct their raid. There is only so much time to meet and conduct your raid before daylight. Of course, if all the members live in town and meet here, then this idea goes right out the window."

Brewster moved closer to the map and studied it intensely. "I think you are onto something, Justin. Maybe we should split the town into North, South, East, and West and begin searching any location that shows recent activity or where a body of men might meet. We, also, might come across a clue."

Justin felt he was on a roll. "Moving the two night deputies onto day shift, we can search each assigned area pretty thoroughly. Maybe we'll get lucky."

Brewster started shaking his head no, "I don't want to involve them at all. I've been hearing reports that they are drinking at the White Dog Saloon during the middle of their shift. Men talk too much when they drink. I plan on catching them at it and firing them on the spot if the reports are true. No, if we are to cover all of this ground, it had better be just the two of us doing the searching."

"Three if us, you mean. We can rely on Zeke to keep his mouth shut. Of course, if you actually made him a temporary deputy, I'm guessing he would jump at the chance," Justin grinned.

"More like a secret deputy without a badge. Justin, I think you might be onto something here and I am happy you spoke up. Let's ask Zeke to come in and see if he's interested." Within twenty minutes, Gas City had a secret deputy assigned to the Marshal's Office.

"Will folks comment on the fact that you're packing that forty-five now, Zeke?" Justin casually asked.

"Nope, packed a gun on and off fer years."

Marshal Brewster motioned everyone over to the wall map. "Here are your daytime assignments for tomorrow morning. I want Zeke to do the northern route, check every location occupied or not. I suggest you begin on the western edge of your area and zig zag moving eastward so you can cover the maximum distance. Don't go beyond one mile at this point. If we don't turn up anything, we will start there and extend our outward search another mile later."

"Ask everyone you see if they have noticed any strange activity, especially any lights. I just can't see the group meeting in total darkness to discuss something as important as their next raid. Keep in mind their last victim was cooked with hot tar and a branding iron, so they do have a history of using fire. Justin, use the same type of pattern I just described and take the southern section. I will do the East and West areas myself. Be thorough; try to think like these men do. They might very well meet out in the open, also. Report back tomorrow when finished. Here is our chance to get these guys and put an end to their reign of terror once and for all. A lot of people are counting on us. Any questions?"

~~~~~~~~~~~~~~~~~~~~~~

Justin had finally saved up enough money to purchase a horse and saddle, but had struggled with finding the horse a proper fitting name. It was Zeke who replied that the horse certainly was spunky, and Justin kind of thought that sounded like it fit his disposition, so Spunky he became. This long search would be a test to see if horse and owner could reach a mutual understanding. Justin ate a hardy breakfast before striking out on the search. His gut feeling, which was usually correct, told him that south was a dead end. His bet was westward or maybe northwest, as that was the area the body had been dumped into the river the day he arrived in town. So much had happened since his arrival in April, which gave him much to think about during this long search.

Marshal Brewster had decided to start searching the eastern section first. Not as many farms or old structures and such, but more wooded area to check. Stopping at another farm, Brewster identified himself and asked the same questions. "See anything suspicious late at night? Heard any men on horseback or seen any odd lights or activity?" Every
~~~~~~~~~~~~~~~~~~~~~~

time he received the same general answers. No, nothing. Most folks were asleep between the hours of midnight and 3 a.m. since farm life began early. Brewster covered everything that he felt was a possibility before heading back. Tomorrow he would try the western side, unless one of the men discovered something useful today.

Secret Deputy Zeke Miller started out in the upper northwestern area then started working himself more northward. He had already inquired at five small farms when he approached another. Zeke could see the old farmer was outside pumping water into the water bucket as he rode up. He knew the old farmer from seeing him in town a few times, but couldn't recollect putting a name on him. "Sorry ta bother you but the Marshal of Gas City sent me out ta ask some questions. You ain't in any trouble or nothin' like dat." When he finished filling his bucket, the old man said, "Sit yourself down and have a cup of cold water, then ask your questions, Sonny." *Sonny?* Zeke thought, figuring the man was just joking with him. Zeke stepped down and dipped a cup of water with the tin cup offered him into the bucket. "Thanks, that tasted mighty good."

"Say what you got to say, mister. I got chores to do," the farmer replied.

"Well sir, have you seen anybody ridin' around here tween midnight and say, 3 a.m. or seen any strange lights or gatherin's?" The old farmer seemed a bit startled by the question, "Funny you should ask about lights and all. I tend to my private business in the outhouse in the middle of the night sometimes, and a few times this year I been noticin' some lights over yonder in that old barn across from my field. That's the old Teakwood spread that burned down many years back. Even the missus noticed them. Said them was spooks. Shucks, they aren't spooks. I say it's nothing but late night sparking 'tween folks married to somebody else, if you understand my drift!"

Zeke looked into the distance to where the farmer had indicated that he saw lights during the time frame they were looking at. Perhaps this might be it. "Thanks fer the cold drink and the information'. I'll just be a moseyin' over for a look see." Within a few minutes, Zeke had arrived at the old barn and dismounted for a better look. More of an old dilapidated shed than a barn, it had seen better days. The opening had a swinging door with several pieces of lumber missing. Going inside, Zeke noticed quite a few footprints on the dirt floor.

Looking around, he noticed there were no windows or any other openings. In the back corner of the shed was a stack of hay and hanging up on a wooden peg was a barn lantern. Looking it over, Zeke could see that it had been used recently. Maybe this place was only used by nighttime lovers as the old farmer says...or maybe...? Zeke backed out of the shed leaving everything just as he found it, then resumed his search. He would have much to discuss with the Marshal and Justin later this evening.

FOR CHRIST
CHURCH

Chapter 17

Everyone agreed that Secret Detective Miller might have located the group's possible meeting location. It could, also, be the lover's get away shed the old farmer had hinted at. Brewster stated, "I want to go out there early tomorrow morning and have a look. Let's call it a day. I'm going to be up late checking on my nighttime deputies to see if what's been reported is true. Judging from the groups past activity schedule, I think we have time before they meet and strike again. Maybe by then I will have a plan worked out in my head as to how to catch them in the act." Justin took Spunky to the stables for the night. He was very pleased with the stamina of the animal and the two seemed to have bonded well together. Maybe tomorrow he would be in town early enough to meet up with Samantha. It was time now to go get something to eat and turn in.

~~~~~~~~~~~~~~~~~~~~~~
~~~~~~~~~~~~~~~~~~~~~~

We must strike when our enemies least expect it. We must strike when their guard is down and they rest quietly and peacefully within their soft warm beds. We must strike to maintain fear and trepidation in their miserable lives. We must strike tonight!

~~~~~~~~~~~~~~~~~~~~

It was after one a.m. when Marshal Brewster walked into the White Dog Saloon to find both his nighttime deputies passed out at a table with two near empty whiskey bottles in front of them. *I have seen enough*, he thought to himself as he grabbed each sleeping man by the back of their collars and frog marched them out of the saloon under the hoots and cheers of the other barroom patrons. Brewster did not release them but marched them directly to the empty jail cell awaiting them, after first removing their deputy badges. They could sleep it off. He would fire them tomorrow when they were sober enough to realize what happened. Tossing the door keys onto his desk, Marshal Brewster now only wanted to reach his bed for a few precious hours of sleep. Unfortunately, that would not happen tonight.

He had just stepped outside his office when the sound of a huge explosion shook the very ground he was standing on. Quickly looking up, he witnessed the Reverend Stokes' church completely disintegrate before his eyes in a huge
~~~~~~~~~~~~~~~~~~~~

fireball only two blocks away, as it rained down pieces everywhere. There would be no sleeping anywhere in the city tonight.

By morning, the city had managed to shut the ruptured natural gas line off, and the fire had been contained. The majority of the wooden church had exploded outward and up in a complete circle. Parts of the building were as far as 500 feet away. Now that it was daylight, it seemed the majority of the town's population were trying to see what was left of the church, and wondering what had happened. Marshal Brewster requested the owner of a hardware store to open up and bring him all the rope he had on hand. The area needed to be roped off, to keep everyone from walking through it and picking up souvenirs. It might simply be a terrible accident, or it could be a crime scene. He would have to make that determination based on the report from the Fire Chief.

Standing outside of the rope line stood the shocked Reverend Stokes, with his wife and daughter. People naturally gravitated over to the Reverend to ask him questions and speculate what had happened. They wondered what he would do now. The Fire Chief suggested that all of the lumber and debris be picked up and examined. Afterward, it would be taken out of the roped area and disposed of. Whatever else was left on the ground should be closely examined. To Brewster, it sounded like a lot of work, but he didn't have a better idea so they went to work. The chief also brought in some of his firemen to assist.

Turning to Zeke, Brewster told him about finding the drunken deputies last night. He asked Zeke to go over to the jail and set them free. "Also, while you are at it, casually mention to them that they have been fired." Zeke walked over to the fire barn and entered. Both men were standing up in the cell and peppered him with questions. "Why are we locked up? And what the heck happened last night?" Zeke told them exactly what Brewster had said and opened the jail cell. "Now what are we gonna do?" one ex-deputy said to the other. "I told you we would end up getting caught doing that every night." The other man replied, "Let's get something to eat at the Panhandle, then catch the southbound train out of here." Gas City would now have two fewer residents. No loss at all.

Returning to help out, Zeke informed the Marshal that the men were leaving town, which pleased Brewster to hear. By noon, the majority of the shredded timbers had been removed, and every eye was scanning what remained upon the ground. "Since we don't know exactly what we are looking for, how we gonna know what it is, if we find it?" Justin casually remarked. Brewster told him he figured there were three possibilities: there was an accidental natural gas leak in the church, someone purposely opened the gas keys to allow the church to build up with natural gas or dynamite or kegs of gun powder were used to blow it up. "The Fire Chief said that if an explosive was used, we might find powder blast burns or the remains of a powder barrel. All this may be a waste of time, but we are at least giving it our best effort."

An hour later, Justin noticed that two firemen had taken a couple of objects over for the Fire Chief to examine. Then they were taken to the Marshal. "I think we know what happened, Marshall," one fireman said, as he held out two brass gas piping objects. "These are two different wall mounted natural gas switches from the church. To turn on the gas lighting, the good Reverend would insert a gas key, turn the valve to the flow position, light the overhead gas lights and you have public lighting. When services are over, just reinsert the key, turn the flow valve to the closed position, and the lighting goes out as the gas flow stops. One of the men found a charred gas key earlier, so I tried it on each fitting. As you can see, both valves are turned to the full open flow position. Since the church was empty at that time of night, and the Reverend says he hasn't been in it for several days, someone must have deliberately opened each valve, filled the church with natural gas until the mixture of gas and oxygen was just right, then introduced a source of ignition. It was a pretty sick but effective way to destroy the church."

Brewster shook hands with each of the assisting firemen and thanked them for their work. He, then requested that the ropes be returned to the hardware store, since they were only tied together to create a barrier and were not soiled. Turning to Justin and Zeke, he asked them to mount up so they could visit the location Zeke had found the day before. They made a point of not riding directly to the shed, as there was always the possibility they were being watched. They rode straight west before cutting back north. As they neared the shed, Brewster suggested they tie off their mounts and walk into the area, so hoof prints could be observed. Only one set of prints were seen, and Zeke speculated they were probably his.

Cautiously, they approached the broken door and opened it, finding the shed empty. Zeke pointed out the hay, and the lantern hanging on a wooden peg. "Just like you described it to us," the Marshal stated. "Not quite," Zeke replied. "Da lantern's been turned around and des here matches wasn't here before." Taking one last look around, Brewster ensured everything looked like it had when they arrived. Stepping outside and looking south Brewster's eyes fixed upon a single structure, as he said, "Mount up, let's get back to the office. I gotta plan formulating in my head."

~~~~~~~~~~~~~~~~~~~~~~

Every minister in town made it a point of offering to share the use of their church with Reverend Stokes' congregation. The Reverend was truly touched by their
~~~~~~~~~~~~~~~~~~~~~~

offers, and he blessed each man for their gift of kindness. He was uncertain at this point just how to proceed. Stokes kept having to remind himself not to allow the rage creeping inside of him to take over. It was not his place, but God's, to judge the transgressors who had committed this horrible act. With the strength of his church family and his own, they would survive this terribly tragic ordeal.

As the deputies arrived outside the fire barn, Brewster requested the men to wait for him inside as he had two people he needed to meet with before he coud sit down and explain his plan. Zeke told them he'd put a pot of coffee on as they waited, which sounded pretty darn good to the parched Marshal. First for the Marshal would be the Emporium. Entering the store, he noticed Wilbert Vance dusting off shelves while the owner appeared to be going over his ledger. "Hello Marshal," Vance said, "what can I do for you?" "Plenty," replied the Marshal. "You're under arrest, Vance." The smile on Wilbert Vance's face faded along with the color in his complexion. "Come along peaceably, so I don't have to shoot you." As the words began to seep into his subconscious, Wilbert asked what he had done wrong. Ignoring the question, Brewster turned to the owner saying, "You might get him back in a few weeks if you still want him." Brewster and Vance walked out of the shop.

A look of puzzlement appeared on the faces of Zeke and Justin when Marshal Brewster brought his new prisoner into the office. "Take a seat, Vance, and listen up. I'm only gonna say this once. Here's the deal, I'm asking you to sign on as another Deputy Marshal. We have a special operation starting tonight, and it requires four men to pull it off. I just told your employer you were under arrest in order to get you away from there. If you decide to turn me down, I will walk back with you and tell your boss it was all a misunderstanding. If you accept, you can go back to work and tell him I was just fooling with you."

Wilbert Vance seemed greatly relieved to hear that he was not in trouble. "Go ahead, Marshal, I'm listening." "Vance, this involves long hours at night, working outside in all types of weather, and most likely some personal danger. If you accept you will be sworn in as a deputy marshal and draw full pay like these two do. What do you say?"

Wilbert Vance smiled, "I'm pleased to accept your offer. I feel I owe it to all of you anyway. Sign me up." Wilbert Vance was then sworn in as a deputy.

"Now, I got one more place to visit before I can share my plan with all of you. Justin, go ahead and bring Deputy Vance up to date on what we have learned, and I hope to be back shortly. Zeke, I need you to go down to the train depot and see the station master. Tell him we need to borrow one of those red globe railroad lanterns for a few weeks with no questions asked. Make sure it's operational and full. Bring it here along with a pack of matches."

Walking into the First National Bank building, Marshal Brewster requested five minutes with the bank president. "Hello, Marshal, come in...come in. Have a seat, sir. How may I help you today?" It took five minutes to explain what he needed from the bank president and owner of the opera house and another five minutes to overcome the man's natural reluctance to hand over the key, but Marshal Brewster prevailed. *Now it's time to speak with the men*, he thought.

Sitting down with a small pillow behind his aching back and a cup of coffee in front of him, the Marshal began, "I'm dividing us into two groups, *A shift* and *B shift*. *A shift* will be Vance and me, while you two will make up *B shift*. So as to make this as clear as I can, I will present what my shift will do and your shift will do exactly the same thing the next day. When we leave here momentarily, I want each of you to go home and put together a bed roll, rain gear, change of clothing and anything else to hold you over for a few days. Say nothing about this to anyone. Zeke, bring that pair of field glasses you got in the war. Then I want all of you to go up the stairwell to the third floor of the opera house and wait for me there on the landing. Go up one at a time, so as not to be noticed. I'll meet you there in thirty minutes."

Walking down to Ma Richards Boarding House, Justin packed up a bed roll and some extra clothing. Ma would wonder why he was not sleeping in his bed but there was nothing he could do about it. Within thirty minutes, each man was waiting for the Marshal at the top of the stairway. When the Marshal arrived, he produced a key for the door and opened it. They walked into the now empty opera house. "Just pick a spot and set your stuff down. This building is one of the tallest structures in town, right? From the flat roof above our heads, a person can see for miles on a clear day. Now follow me up to the roof."

The group walked up the narrow stairs leading to the roof and opened the creaking access door. "From here you can see the shed building where we suspect the White Caps have been meeting. So here's the plan, tonight as soon as it's dark, I will take the red railroad lantern, the box of matches, and the office's 10 gauge Winchester lever action shotgun and start walking towards the shed. I will hide on the edge of those trees and out of sight. If the White Caps show up tonight and enter the shed, I will light the red globed railroad lantern. It will stand out from any other normal white lights in the area. Let's call that position the signalman. Vance will be working here, where we are standing, as the watcher. Vance will use these field glasses to watch for my red signal. We should all be in place no later than 10 p.m., and we shall remain on duty until just before daybreak. Now let me cover the duties of *B shift*. You boys will hook up my wagon and team, then park them down below here before it gets dark. Then, I want both of you upstairs in the empty opera house. Sleep, play cards, whatever you want but you must keep quiet as there are offices on the second floor who may start talking if they hear or see us, and that may tip off the White Caps. So if the signalman sees the red lantern, he is to immediately roust the off duty team and, together they'll hightail it to the shed using my wagon. Drive the horses as hard as necessary, as the lone signalman will be trying to prevent the White Caps from leaving the shed. Then, tomorrow *B shift* takes over and does exactly what we did the night before. Then the following day, Vance will be the signalman and I'll be on the roof, and so forth. Any questions?"

"No questions," Vance replied "but I do have a suggestion. In order not to be heard going up the stairwell to the third floor by the occupants below, why don't we use the fire escape on the side of the building? We can tie off a ladder from the top of the third-floor fire escape, tall enough to climb straight up onto the roof."

"Good idea, Zeke. That's your job as soon as we are finished here," Brewster replied. "Oh, one other thing, this round the clock surveillance will leave the Marshal's Office empty at night. Should a need arise, one of the off-duty men will have to cover it. If that happens, beat it back here quickly as your firepower will be needed in capturing these murderers. Guys, we have some long days and nights ahead of us. In a week or so we'll be pretty darn tired, so please don't let your guard down for even one moment. These killers have proven they can strike anytime." Wilbert Vance made his way back to the shop but had no idea exactly what he would tell the owner. Working days, then on special assignment at nights, would become very tiring but, Vance suspected, also very rewarding...if they are able to catch the White Caps.

Chapter 18

Day after day, each man worked his own normal day assignment jobs then was in place after dark for the evening/nighttime schedule. Each learned the art of catnapping when an opportunity graciously presented itself. Night after night turned into week after week as each new shift brought on the possibility that this might be the night the White Caps would return. By now Marshal Brewster was beginning to have some doubt about his plan, and wondered if the others were thinking this was only a wild goose chase. A few times the off-duty shift officers had to respond to nighttime bar fights and such, but overall, the town had been pretty quiet. The worst part of the duty was sitting out in the rain all night. Twice that had happened to the men and it was miserable.

Once again, on an almost moonless night, Justin found himself serving as the signalman at the edge of the woods while stationed behind a large tree, within easy viewing of the shed. He had been on duty for about three hours but, due to the darkness, was unable to read his pocket watch so he could only guess it to be around midnight. In a few more hours, daylight would begin to appear and his shift would thankfully come to an end. Then it would be back to working the day shift for his normal workday. The additional duty was starting to take it's toll. His bed roll would become a welcome relief again tonight. It didn't take too many evenings of the additional duty to halt the evening card playing and bring about much desired periods of rest and sleep.

During these long and lonely nights as the signalman, Justin's mind wandered to Samantha Stokes. He had not seen her in almost three weeks, since that day in the drug store. She was no doubt quite busy getting ready for school to start in early September. *Wow,* he thought, *Summer is almost over. Where did time go? Still, she's no doubt wondering where I am. Boy, do I miss not seeing her. Maybe I should just come on out and ask her to marry me?* Just thinking about holding her made his heart ache with love. Her students were very lucky to have a dedicated and, yes, beautiful young teacher like Samantha. Justin thought back to his teacher, a woman the kids in his class said had to be one hundred years old. She was never seen without the wooden ruler in her hand; always ready to swat any student she felt was out of line. He and that old ruler had become quite familiar by his last days in school.

Justin had heard that the Reverend Stokes' congregation had accepted the invitation to share the Baptist & Methodist church building on West Main Street. Justin had often wondered how both churches met at the same time, since the building itself was not overly large. It had a full partition down the center of it dividing it into two smaller rooms, each having it's own outside front entry door. Stories floated around town that both church groups tried to outsing and out preach the other. Stokes' group agreed to meet on one side mid-afternoon so as not to interfere with the other services. It was very kind of them to do this for them. Justin had not heard if they planned on rebuilding their church or not, but presumed they eventually would.

Justin sat there in silence behind a large tree, contemplating his life, when he heard a noise coming up from behind him. *Probably another raccoon. This place is full of them*, he thought. As the sound grew louder, he watched what appeared to be a hooded figure walking directly towards him. Justin very quietly moved to hide on the other side of the tree as the figure continued to approach and, eventually, came within twenty feet of his position. *Wow, that was close*! *Thank goodness for the darkness*, he thought to himself. Justin watched the figure enter the shed, and within a minute, the light from a lantern glow emulated from the shed. He could see the outline of three other men as they approached from other directions. *Smart to come in from different ways*, he thought. Tonight was the night...the White Caps had arrived!

As soon as the last of the men had entered the shed and closed the old rickety door behind them, Justin lit a match and set the red glow of the railroad lantern ablaze. Now he could only hope and pray that Zeke had spotted the light and was, at this very moment, rounding up the other shift from their sleep and would quickly respond to assist him. Four against one was less than the odds he had expected but, still, he would be hard pressed keeping them trapped inside the shed all by himself with only one shotgun and his own pistol. Now he could only sit tight and wait for help to arrive in time.

~~~~~~~~~~~~~~~~~~~~

It had been a most active and trying night in Gas City. Twice Zeke has had to rouse a heavily sleeping Marshal Brewster out of his bedroll to send him after trouble makers acting up in one of the local saloons. Alcohol could turn a mouse of a man into a roaring lion, and Brewster was forced to club one drunken lion who was threatening to shoot up the place. By morning the lion would once again become a mouse, but that time, with a sore head. Friends had agreed to take the man home rather than let him spend the night in jail.
~~~~~~~~~~~~~~~~~~~~

Zeke had once again resumed his position upon the flat roof and was actively watching the nighttime sky. Shooting stars were everywhere, and Zeke was making wishes upon each and every one of them. He had tried to use his pair of field glasses to obtain a better view but they were just too far away to make out any detail. A little dejected, Zeke glanced over in the general direction of the shed when he noticed a new light. It wasn't another shooting star come to Earth...it was a red light. It was the signal they had all been waiting for. The White Caps have finally arrived!

Now he was deeply concerned. How long had the light burned before he had finally noticed it? Justin needed help now! Zeke quickly climbed down the vertical ladder and onto the fire escape as he jerked open the third-floor exit door shouting, "We got us a red light! Red light! Get a movin', Justin needs our help!" Within a few moments, a heavily armed group of three men were en route to Justin's location, as fast as the wagon horses could take them. Each could only pray to himself that they would arrive in time.

Tonight's mission will be against a cheating husband who is also a drunk and a gambler. Since the laws of this town fail to punish the wicked, it is again up to us, the avengers of justice, to intervene and set an example for other transgressors to learn from. After we capture the man, he is to be quietly gagged and tied, then brought to this location for his punishment of fire and death. We shall

meet next time in another location that is better suited for our needs. That location will be disclosed to you after our night's work has been accomplished. Let us go now and begin our sacred duties of smiting the enemies of a civilized people.

Justin kept an eye peeled for his friend's approach as he watched the entrance of the shed, hoping they would remain inside until help arrived. He could detect movement of shadows from under the door. Suddenly, the lantern was extinguished and the door opened. One man, the tallest of the four hooded figures, took the lead and was three or four paces in front of the others. Realizing he had no other choice at that point, Justin shouted out loudly, "Stay where you are and don't move! You are all surrounded and are under arrest." The three, who were just exiting the barn, quickly dashed back inside and closed the door, leaving the tallest hooded man outside and alone. Realizing he was now exposed in the open, the figure reached for his weapon and began firing wildly, not knowing where the warning voice had originated from. Knowing he had to do something before the figure outside dashed away, Justin leveled the Winchester shot gun at the lower legs of the man and pulled the trigger. The man crumpled to the ground in pain as his pistol was knocked from his hand and into the darkness of the night.

"I hear gunshots," Brewster shouted as the team of horses rushed into the darkness, almost pitching its occupants out of the wagon as it seemed to hit every rock and pothole along the way. Everyone hung on for dear life, with all eyes locked upon the darkened shed in the distance.

Inside the barn, two of the men became frantic with fear as they traded shots through a crack in the door with the unknown peace officer. "They shot Bobby," one stated. "We're trapped in here. What are we gonna do?" "Remain calm," the leader firmly replied. "It appears there's only one of them, or we would hear more shooting. Save your ammunition. When I give the signal, we will burst out and run in different directions. Make sure you find this officer and kill him, while I silence the wounded one to prevent him from talking."

"Ya can't kill Bobby! He's a friend of ours!" The signal was then given by the leader, "Go!" With that, each hooded figure burst outside of the door running in different directions, yelling as they ran. Justin was uncertain who to follow until the group's leader made that decision for him. The person had stopped outside the barn, pulled a long knife and despite the pleading of the wounded man, plunged the knife deep into the wounded man's side. *What kind of a monster would kill his own man?* Justin thought to himself, as he found himself running as fast as he could towards the crazed killer. Seeing Justin approach, the figure tried to swing the knife to stab him. The knife missed it's mark as Justin slammed hard into the killer's body. Though shorter than Justin, his opponent was strong as an ox and came at him with everything, even the old knee to the groin movement, which was thankfully blocked. Using all of his strength, Justin swung the butt of the shotgun and it connected to the face underneath the flour sack, laying the hooded figure out cold upon the ground.

Hearing an approaching wagon, Justin could see that Vance and Brewster had managed to leap from the slowing wagon and commenced to chase down and apprehend the other two killers. Soon all of the White Caps were brought up to Justin's location. Zeke was applying a wad of clothing to the stab wound in an attempt to control the bleeding. Suddenly the feeling of exhaustion each man had earlier felt was completely gone, now replaced with a feeling of euphoria. They had captured the dreaded White Caps.

The hoods of the two captured prisoners, as well as the wounded man upon the ground, were removed and they were unknown to anyone present. Justin reached down to the leader and pulled off the flour sack. Complete shock registered with each man as they recognized the face of the actual leader of the White Caps.

Chapter 19

"Oh my God! It's Samantha Stokes," someone murmured quietly. Justin was completely taken back by this unnerving turn of events. How could his sweet, wonderful Samantha be tied into such a monstrous group? Marshal Brewster having seen enough other strange situations in his many years working in law enforcement, quickly shook off the shock that the local school teacher, and Reverend's daughter, was a cold-blooded killer. He handcuffed each prisoner together, while Zeke cuffed the wounded man's hands together. "Justin, cuff her to yourself," he directed. Justin just stood there looking down at the face of the woman he loved, and had hoped to spend the rest of his life with. "Deputy Blake," he said again, but this time with authority, "Cuff the prisoner to yourself...now!"

Someone had thought to pack a canteen of water in the wagon, so Zeke used the cool liquid to help revive Justin's prisoner. That's when it happened. Strength that no one thought possible from a small woman emerged, almost jerking Justin's arm out of it's socket. The woman jumped to her feet with arms flailing and feet kicking, scratching and spitting. She managed to drive her fingernails deep into Justin's face as she tried to get away. Her eyes were coal black in color, black as the dead of night. She hissed and cussed a string of words that Justin found impossible to contemplate as coming from the mouth of a Reverend's daughter. The biggest shock to him was her voice. It was sweet voice of Samantha Stokes but a deeper, strange voice of another creature. Creature. That clearly described the animal now cuffed to his arm. Life had turned upside down for Justin Blake.

"Zeke," Brewster called out to his secret deputy, "that man's not going anywhere. I want you to collect our red railroad lantern and any other field gear along with the lantern the White Caps used tonight and put it all in the wagon. You men, pick up your injured friend and lay him in the wagon." Struggling, the cuffed men did as they were told. Brewster felt he understood what was going through his young deputy's mind at the moment, so he returned to a gentler voice, "Justin, we need to get all the prisoners loaded up and get back into town, alright?" Finally taking his tearful eyes off of the woman he loved, he gave a simple nod and loaded her into the wagon. During the journey, he tried to speak with her, but she acted like he meant nothing to her. In fact, she maliciously tried to kill him earlier. Realizing she would offer no explanations, the rest of the ride was in total silence as the wagon moved slowly along its pathway back into Gas City.

Zeke, who was driving, stopped the wagon outside Doctor Baxter's office. The two prisoners were directed to bring the injured man inside as Marshal Brewster pounded upon the door of the sleeping doctor. Within moments, the patient was placed upon the examination table as Baxter hovered over the injured man. "You all need to get out of here," he told them, "I'll come over later as soon as I know something." Zeke was told he wasn't needed and helped bring the three prisoners into the fire barn's office. "What we gonna do with the little lady, Marshal, put her in with the rest of them varmints?"

At that point, both men began begging, almost to the point of pleading that she not be placed in the same cell with them. "She'll kill us, sure as shootin', just like she did that time to Old Red," one of the men shouted. In a deep guttural voice, the woman known as Samantha Stokes screamed, "Shut up you filthy dogs or with these puny hands your throats will be ripped out from you."

"See what ah mean, Marshal? You keep her away from us and we'll tell you everything you want to know." That only made the creature howl and cuss even more. "Put them two in the cell, and handcuff Miss Stokes to a bar outside the cell." That seemed to satisfy both men and they began to relax somewhat. By now Justin realized that this was not the woman he loved but a crazed killer who would stop at nothing to escape. He securely placed a cuff on one of her tiny wrists then the other end onto a jail bar low enough for her to sit down. Someone brought her a chair to sit on and she immediately tried to use it as a weapon with her free arm. It was quickly removed.

Everyone glanced over upon hearing someone entering the office. It was Doc Baxter. "Never stood a chance," he replied. "Stab wound caused massive bleeding." Everyone in the room now knew that an additional murder charge would be added to this woman at her trial. Brewster replied, "Thanks Doc, we know you did the best you could. Zeke, put on a pot of coffee, we're gonna need it tonight. Vance, I want you to go over to the Stokes residence and wake them up. Tell them I need both of them down here immediately, but don't say why. That grim task will fall upon me." Sitting down in his office chair and placing a small pillow behind his back, Brewster then told the prisoners to start at the beginning and tell them what he wanted to know. "Doc, I would like you to stay and witness what you're a hearin' too. Someone get Doc a chair."

Both prisoners looked at each other and one said, "Go ahead. You start, Fred." The man glanced over at the handcuffed woman, perhaps to make sure she was in fact tied up, and then he began. "Well sir, my friend here and I moved over from Marion in early January. We got us a job working as boys at the Thompson Bottlin' Glass Factory. One of the few friends we met there was Old Red. He'd moved up here from Southern Indiana last fall, and he kinda took us under his wing. Well, sir, one night, over a bottle, Old Red started talkin' about the White Caps that were active in them parts where he used ta live. Red said it might be fun to start us a group here in town, you know, just to push around some darkies and have a little fun. You know what I mean."

Now the other man started speaking, "We found this old shed and the three of us got some old flour sacks, and cut some eyes holes out and decided to cane an old darkie we saw around town. We didn't kill him or nothing like that, just caned him real good. Then we told him to keep his mouth shut or we were going to come after his family. It was great fun ...but probably not for the darkie. We heard later he skipped town for good. The next evening we were sitting down at the White Dog Saloon sharing a bottle, maybe two bottles, when a painted up whore came up to our table. Guess with all the whisky we bragged, and said too much, as she heard about when we planned to meet again and where. We all hoped to get lucky with her but she said maybe later and left. You take it from here," he told his friend. "Makes me sick just thinking about it."

"On the night we planned to meet up in the barn, we were talking and making plans for who we were to grab and cane when the door opened up and she came strutting in. We were shocked to see a woman we all knew to be the local preacher's daughter and schoolmarm. She walked in saying she was gonna be the new leader of the White Caps."

Justin could not contain himself any longer and asked, "What happened next?"

"Well sir, we all busted out a laughin', which made her angry. Old Red said something like *come here, little lady, and I will show you a good time,* or something like that. Ya should have seen the look of pure hatred that woman had. Her eyes were black, like the Devil's eyes. It was about then that Old Red recognized her features as the painted up whore in the saloon. Well, sir, she suddenly produced an axe handle she was hiding under her skirt and began to hit Old Red over the head. She kept hitting and hitting him until the top of his head looked like a busted watermelon. Killed him plum dead."

"We were standing there in shock as she started laughing at what she did to Old Red. She enjoyed killing him fer sure! That voice was plum fearful. She removed the blood splattered flour sack from Old Red's pocket, then tied him up to his saddle with his head a draggin' the ground, and slapped the horse's rump sending it racing towards town. Then she turned to us, put on Old Reds sack over her head, and said we were next to die unless we agreed to her being the boss and all. We had no choice, as we weren't armed that evening. She then made us swear allegiance to the Devil. I tell you Marshal, she is the Devil!"

"Red must have been the man we found earlier this year. His face was completely unrecognizable and the top of his head was gone," Doc Baxter replied. The other prisoner added, "We saw her once on the street and we tried to speak with her, but she acted like she didn't know us and was scared of us too. We thought it was very odd."

"So, how did you all communicate to set up your meetings then?" the Marshal asked.

"She was kinda smart about figuring that out. She said we were to watch her bedroom window every night at 10:30. If it was dark, no meeting would occur that night. If there was an oil lamp sitting on the table by the window lit, we were to meet at the shed at Midnight. If she was seen moving the oil lamp side to side, then meet at 1 a.m. If she made a circle with it, that meant 2 a.m."

Everyone was chilled at what the creature then injected into the conversation, "This stupid girl was made to fry up your picnic chicken breast after first soaking it in rat poison. But the hot grease must have dulled its effect. We cannot allow this silly girl to fall in love. We wanted you dead...we STILL want you dead! Ha, ha, ha!"

"So it was you who ordered one of these thugs to shoot at me as I laid in bed?"

"We did...too bad we didn't blow off your stinking head, Deputy! Killed by orders from the love of your life. If only SHE knew what WE made her do!"

Justin knew that what he was hearing from this creature in a woman's body was true, but felt himself getting sick just thinking about it. He looked over at her face to see what type of reaction this conversation was having upon her. Despite the large lump forming along her jaw line from making contact with the butt end of the shotgun, the woman's face was actually glowing with pride.

Marshal Brewster then asked, "Were you behind all of the problems at Thompsons?" Nodding yes, one of the cellmates said, "She wanted us to stir things up a bit, just for the excitement. Maybe the factory would pack up and leave town."

A stillness hung in the air as each man struggled to fathom the meaning of all they have been told. Coffee was passed out as they waited for the arrival of the Reverend and Mrs. Stokes.

Within twenty minutes, Deputy Vance had returned with the girl's parents. As they entered the small room, their eyes naturally came upon their only daughter, chained like an animal to the cell bars. Mrs. Stokes immediately rushed to her daughter's side. It was then that the young girl spit directly into her mother's face. The deep evil laugh that originated from what appeared to be their daughter made her parents take pause. Doc Baxter escorted Mrs. Stokes to her seat and offered his hankie to clean the spittle from her face. Dreading exactly what he had to say, Marshal Brewster was preparing to inform the couple of the seriousness of the situation when Justin spoke up. “I am afraid your daughter and these men have been operating as a group known as the White Caps, killing and mutilating people late at night. We all watched as she stabbed another member to death tonight. She even tried to kill me with a knife.”

Mrs. Stokes openly wept as her husband tried his best to comfort her. Mr. Stokes slowly made his way over to where his daughter stood. Seeing the crazed look in her eyes and facial expression, he tried to speak comfort to her. “Get this fraud away before we strike him down by the powers of Satan, as we did his church,” she cried out. Any lingering doubts Reverend Stokes might have had were gone. He would publicly acknowledge that which he and his wife had long feared, but kept locked away at home.

“Doctor Baxter, I am glad you are here to hear the story I am about to share with these gentlemen of the law. Perhaps you can make some sense out of it, as both my wife and I are completely baffled. It all started about a year ago. Our family normally retires for the evening around 10 p.m. My wife and I have an upstairs bedroom while Samantha continues to use her old bedroom on the ground floor, in the back of our home. Late one night, my wife awakened me to say she feared a prowler was in our home, as she could hear strange noises downstairs. I immediately proceeded to discover the cause of the strange sounds. They were originating from behind our daughters bedroom door.

I gently tapped upon it, to announce my presence, when I came upon the creature you see before us. Yes, gentlemen, I said creature, as the woman who then stood before me was as you see here tonight. She attacked me with flailing arms and used the most hideous profanities I have ever known. I managed to light her table lamp and was shocked to see the face of a wild beast before me. I will never forget the look on her face. Her once lovely blue eyes were now a darkened black, and the voice emitting from inside of her sounded like the raging Hounds of Hell. I stayed with her for over two hours and would not open the door for my wife, knowing that to see our child behaving like this would surely break her heart."

"By 3 a.m., whatever had possessed my daughter had disappeared and her sweet wonderful features returned. She appeared quite confused and asked me what had happened, and why I was in her bedroom. May God forgive me, but I told her a lie, saying that she had undergone a terrible nightmare and that I was only there to comfort her. That seemed to satisfy her curiosity and soon she drifted off in my arms. That night was not the end, gentlemen, but only the beginning."

"I was naturally forced to inform my wife of what had transpired. When she questioned our daughter the following morning, she discovered Samantha had absolutely no memory of any of the events that had transpired. I was forced to keep a secret ledger of the dates and times that Samantha changed into what we privately referred to as *the evil one*. It seemed that she would rest easily for about three weeks before another episode occurred. These events always occurred very late at night and never in daytime hours. For that, we were most grateful to God. She could continue to teach school and, I am almost ashamed to say, we could keep all of this quiet and private."

"It was very early this year when we again heard the terrible sounds emitting from our daughter's bedroom. Upon investigating, I discovered her bedroom door open, her closet ransacked, and to my horror, a can of facial powder and lipstick paste, all of which are never used within our family. Not knowing what to do I sat upon the edge of my daughter's bed until early morning. Much to my horror, she returned looking like a painted woman of the night. Samantha was completely confused as to why she found herself walking around outside at night and, naturally, returned home. She began to scream and cry when she saw her reflection in her looking glass."

"Gentlemen, our daughter is a Christian and would never stoop to being anything but the lady she is. Thank God, it appears that none of our neighbors has seen her dressed that way, and I'm am ashamed to say, I feared to lose my church over it. Again I told a lie, this time saying she had become a sleep walker and to prevent further humiliation to her, we would securely lock her within her bedroom at night. Eventually she came to believe this to be our only solution. Gentlemen, I assure you we had no idea that she started slipping out her bedroom window at night to join in these horrid and ghastly proceedings."

Doctor Baxter then spoke up, "Reverend, why didn't you come and speak to me about all of this?"

Hanging his head as his wife softly wept, he replied, "Fear...fear of ridicule...fear of losing my church...fear of our sweet daughter becoming the talk of the town. I know now it was wrong for us to continue to hide our shame. Look at what my stupidity has now caused. People are dead because of my personal vanity and pride."

"No Reverend, you and your wife are not responsible for this," Doc assured him with a gentle touch on the shoulder. "Your daughter has developed mental problems far beyond anything either of you could control."

"Justin, this is why my wife and I tried to break up your involvement with our daughter. We hoped to spare both of you the pain of final discovery."

Stokes spoke, "I took Samantha to a specialist in Indianapolis, not my sister's home, as you were told.

We informed Samantha that they were going to treat her sleepwalking sickness, which my husband and I knew did not exist. Strange, but while we were away, her evil side never appeared, so the doctors had no choice but to discharge her."

From across the room, a guttural deep laughter erupted from the creature chained to the cell door. "We knew the tricks you were playing upon us, and we were determined not to show our self to anyone. This foolish girl knows nothing about us but we know all there is to know about her. We lay in wait for the proper opportunity to venture forth to conduct our fun. We enjoy killing. We may even kill all of you tonight!"

Doctor Baxter was very curious about what he had just heard. He approached the girl, "You refer to yourself in the past tense. What is your name? I demand you tell us your name!"

With a look of pure evil, the creature replied, "We are Lucinda, Daughter of Darkness, Angel of Death." One could have easily heard a pin drop, due to the stillness of the room. A deep chill ran down Justin's back. He realized that he has lost the woman he loves forever.

Marshal Brewster finally broke the silence, "We are not set up to house a female prisoner, so I suggest that two of our officers escort the woman back to her home and handcuff her to her bedpost securely. Is this idea acceptable to you and Mrs. Stokes?" Each looked into the eyes of the other as Mrs.

Stokes replied, "Yes, and I wish to remain in her bedroom for the remainder of the night. I feel I need to be there when our daughter's mind returns before daylight." Brewster thought it was a good idea. He looked at Justin, "Would you mind staying there to guard the prisoner? If it's too painful, I can ask one of the others to do it."

Without pausing, Justin agreed to do it. He knew deep down that he was the only one to accomplish this awful task. It would be a long night of waiting for everyone.

Chapter 20

After an exchange of telegrams, the Grant County Sheriff's office agreed to arrive in Gas City around noon to transport the White Caps over to the Marion jail, where accommodations for a female prisoner could be arranged. Justin had made no attempt to communicate with Samantha when she returned to her normal self early in the morning. It was a blessing for him that both of her parents were in her room when her mind returned to normal. They would then explained the entire terrible situation to her. Justin could hear a great deal of crying outside of the bedroom door, but tried to keep his mind focused on the grim task before him today. Even though it personally killed him to do so, he would have to escort the love of his life in handcuffs to an awaiting train of police officers.

By 11:30 a.m., the bedroom door opened and Justin was told she was ready. It was difficult for her mother to properly dress her daughter while still handcuffed to a bed post. It was time for the family to accompany the deputy and their daughter to the train depot. Justin had obtained a small carriage for everyone to ride in, but the prisoner had requested that she be allowed one final walk through her town. With a lump in his throat, Justin agreed and everyone began the final journey together.

Justin couldn't help but feel terrible as he saw the huge bruise on Samantha's face from the impact of the gun stock. She had not spoken to him directly, and for that, Justin was entirely grateful since he felt sick inside. Together, they continued their walk. He had to hand it to her for she was holding up from this terrible ordeal very well. While she had absolutely no knowledge of the terrible things she was told she had done, Samantha seemed to realize that she had no choice but to pay a stiff price for what something deep and sinister inside her mind was totally responsible for. Sometimes life just wasn't fair.

"Mother, what will become of my schoolchildren?" Mrs. Stokes was unable to answer. Justin fought hard from breaking down at that question, as the party arrived outside the depot. Looking at his pocket watch, Justin saw that he had only ten more minutes before the train from Marion would arrive. Glancing about, Justin noticed Alvin Jensen standing back all alone watching the situation. Was he there today as a newspaper reporter or for personal reasons? The tears rolling down his face answered that question.

As if on cue, both of her parents announced they would wait on the platform with the Marshal's group and allowed the couple a final few minutes to be alone together.

It was Samantha who broke the silence. "Well Justin, I guess this really is good-bye. Mother told me that whatever possesses me scratched up your face and tried to kill you last night. I'm deeply ashamed, but you've got to believe me. I have no memory of any of those terrible events and I would never, ever hurt you, or anyone else for that matter."

Justin turned and looked deep into her beautiful green eyes. "I know that, and I don't blame you personally for any of this. Samantha, darling, I was going to propose marriage to you the very next time I saw you." Tears swelled up instantly in her eyes as she responded, "And I would have accepted." The sound of the arriving train drowned out any further conversation. Together, they walked up to the Marshal and his two male prisoners. As soon as the train had come to a stop, a group of Grant County sheriff deputies approached the group. "Your prisoners, sir", Brewster replied, as his cuffs were removed and the county's cuffs applied. Both sheriff deputies were a little uncomfortable with a woman being in custody, but accepted it as necessary. In a show of mutual respect, both the Reverend and his wife were allowed to hug their daughter one last time, as the group waited for a northbound train's arrival to complete the journey.

Unable to watch it's departure, Justin walked directly back to the office. Sensing his young deputy needed his space at the moment, Brewster suggested that everyone take the next two days off. He looked at Wilbert Vance and told him, "You have handled yourself quite well and if you desire it, the job of a nighttime deputy is yours." Vance, with a grin on his face, replied, "Somebody's got to teach me how to shoot a gun, though." Shaking his head, Brewster laughed and told him there was plenty of time to learn that part of the job.

As Justin walked alone, he had made up his mind just what he would do next. Entering the office, Justin sat down at the desk and pulled out a sheet of paper and a pencil and wrote *I do hereby resign the position of Deputy Marshal* then signed it. He removed the silver badge he had been so proud to wear, holding it in his fingers gently before laying it upon the paper, and left the office. *Well, he thought to himself, that's that.* Justin walked over to his room at Ma Richards and began packing up his travel bag. He didn't know where he was going, only that his horse Spunky would not sleep in the stables here in town ever again. Any place but here was preferable. Too many memories here now. Just too much pain. Taking a final moment, he looked around his room to ensure he had packed everything before closing up his travel bag. He had been quite happy here. He would miss Gas City.

There was a tiny rapping upon his open door as he turned to see who it was. There stood the Reverend Stokes. "I was hoping I could catch you before you left," he replied. "I had a feeling today you might do this, so I hurried my wife home and came straight to your office. I read your letter on the desk and saw your badge, so I came straight over here."

Justin began to explain but the Reverend held up his hand, "Hear me out first, son. I realize why you feel you need to get away. Mrs. Stokes and I also feel like running. We have lost our only daughter, and you lost the woman you loved. Oh yes, we knew. We have known all along and that is why given what we knew, we tried to keep you from getting hurt. The next few weeks will be most difficult for us. Some of our congregation will want nothing more to do with us, as if we are responsible for our daughter's sickness. I understand that and will accept it. We are not running. We will stay here and fight."

"I will preach a sermon every Sunday, only if my wife is there to hear it. In time, others will overcome their own concerns and return. I cannot judge them for their actions. Your friend, Wilbert Vance, learned that one cannot run away from his problems in life. Only by staying put and fighting back can one begin to overcome them. The same now applies to you. Stay and fight your demons, and in time, they too shall pass away. This town needs you, Marshal Brewster needs you and Ruth and I need you."

"How can you even look me in the face? I am the one that placed your daughter under arrest and into the hands of the authorities," Justin said.

"Listen to what I'm about to say to you, Justin. I spoke with Doctor Baxter about what was wrong with Samantha, and he told me there is much we simply do not understand yet about the human mind. Doc said there are cases similar, where a person's mind can create an alter ego of themselves. We both know that Samantha is a good and loving person who would never hurt a fly. Somehow an inner subconscious sickness has developed that becomes the stronger side of her at times. An evil side that only comes out at night when she sleeps, when she is at her weakest. Doc then told me that unlike the two men who will probably be hanged, she most likely will be declared mentally incompetent, and sent to Richmond State Hospital for treatment here in Indiana so my wife and I may visit her. They have doctors there that better understand her form of mental illness. Doc plans to testify as to what he witnessed, as does the Marshal. We greatly appreciate their kindness"

"I pray they won't hang her. I loved her...I wanted to marry her," Justin replied.

"I know, son, but you've got to let go of all of this bottled up pain and guilt. She needs mental help now, and that's all any of us can do for her. Our lives must go on. She would be the first to tell us that. The choice is yours, but many of us hope you will stay." With that, Reverend Stokes left the room.

Justin sat down on the edge of the bed and considered all of his options. A half hour later, Justin walked out of his room and back into the office. Nobody else apparently had been there after the Reverend's visit. Justin picked up the badge and pinned it back upon his chest. He crumpled up the written note. Justin Blake's running days were also over.

~~~~~~~~~~~~~~~~~~~~~~

On September 4th, 1893, Indiana Governor Claude Matthews followed up on his given word by dispatching 700 soldiers to surround the Roby arena, and pointed a Gatling gun at it's front door. In response, the athletic club's president, Dominic O'Malley, agreed to the military threat by postponing the scheduled December heavyweight championship bout. By November, with no other fights allowed to occur, the Roby Athletic Club closed it's doors for good.

Big Jim Malone was now a financially ruined man who had gambled, and lost it all, in his bid to become a major player within the area's crime syndicate. Of course, the people within Gas City had no idea that he was now broke and were no doubt surprised when his body was found early one morning hanging under the wooden bridge over the
~~~~~~~~~~~~~~~~~~~~~~

Mississinewa River. Some thought another group of White Caps were still active within the area. With his passing, life continued on as before, as if Big Jim had never existed.

As for the Corbett-Mitchell bout, it was rescheduled to occur at the Duval Athletic Club in Jacksonville, Florida, and "Gentleman Jim" Corbett won.

Mayhem... in a Small Town

Historical Fiction

Part Two

The Assassin

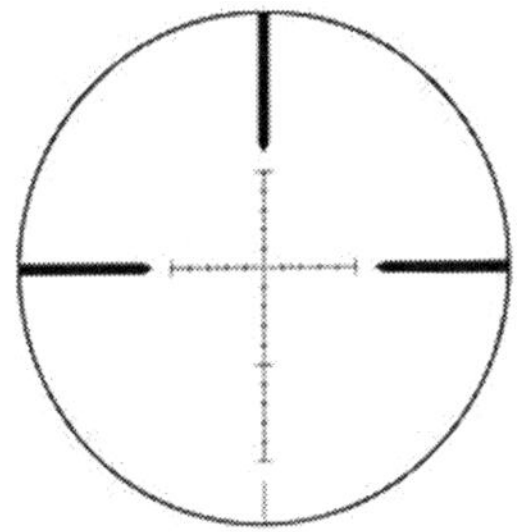

Alan E. Losure

Prologue

Mayhem... in a Small Town is again set in the actual small town of Gas City, Indiana, situated between Fort Wayne and Indianapolis, during the Natural Gas Boom that existed during the late 19th century. This story begins in the Spring of the following year- April 1894.

From time to time I have inserted actual historical events that did, in fact, take place in or around this small town but the majority of what you read and the characters portrayed will be fiction. If you are interested in learning more of Gas City's history, please visit their web site www.gascityindiana.com.

Alan E Losure

Returning Cast of Characters

Justin Blake	Main Character Deputy Marshall
Kenneth Brewster	Gas City Marshal
Wilbert Vance	Nighttime Deputy Marshal
Zeke Miller	Older Man and Friend
Alvin Jensen	Reporter, Gas City Journal Newspaper
Doc Baxter	Town Doctor
Matthew Brooks	Barber/ City Council Member
Mayor Huffman	Town Mayor/Head of City Council
Kruger	Local Crime Boss/Hoodlum
Clarence Stokes	Reverend
Ruth Stokes	Wife
Samantha Stokes	Lost Love of Justin Blake
Harris	Postmaster
Spunky	Justin Blake's Horse
White Dog Saloon	Local Drinking Establishment of Low Caliber

New Cast of Major Characters

Timothy Merrell	New Gas City Marshal
Cecil Merrell	Chief Deputy Marshal, Brother
'Squire Hiram Jones	Local Legal Justice of the Peace
Smiley Lewis	Head of Local Break-In Gangs
Charles Weir	Brother of Mrs. Edith Stokes
Marsha Weir	Daughter
Happy Hollow	Local Saloon of Low Caliber
Dooriya	Gypsy Girl
Jal	Father
Beval	Gypsy Girl's Boyfriend
Tommy Two-Fingers	Carrier Pigeon
Councilman Davidson	City Council Member

Chapter 21

April 1, 1894

Gas City, Indiana Marshal Kenneth Brewster found himself in a terrible situation. Being in his late 50's and quite honestly overweight and past his prime, he had suffered lower back problems for over a year which had caused him much pain and concern. Being an active lawman required much in the way of physical activity; walking, riding, sitting, and other necessities that develop from time to time. His back pillow became a familiar sight to anyone entering his small jail office located inside, of all places, the fire-barn. But it was mounting, riding, and dismounting that had caused his greatest physical issues up until recently.

Thankfully, winter was mercifully coming to an end. It had been the worst winter since '77, with deep blowing snow accumulating everywhere. The old veterans at the Marion National Soldiers Home were completely closed off from the world for a time, due to the high drifting snow on the streetcar tracks. Just leaving their barracks in order to go to the mess hall proved a great challenge for these old ex-warriors. The local ice men had a field day cutting river ice, as thick as six inches, to sell to homes and businesses. "Lay in your summer supply of ice now," was their selling point, and customers were happy to buy it. Finally, the end of March had produced a warmer melting temperature, turning the winter's accumulation of ice and snow into a slushy mess.

Brewster has been so very careful all winter long while walking, but today he stepped on a hidden patch of ice and fell hard on his back. There he laid, in the middle of the street, for what seemed to him like hours but was actually only a few minutes, before onlookers and friends came rushing to his aid. Even with their assistance, Brewster was unable to stand on his own feet since the new pain in his lower back was excruciating. As a result, he was carried over to Doctor Baxter's office. Brewster sent word through a friend to contact his daytime deputy, young Justin Blake, and inform him of the situation. While the shooting pains down his legs and lower back were terrible, Brewster worried more about the image he was leaving in the minds of the town folks of a town marshal unable to stand on his own two feet. A million things were now going through Brewster's mind, and none of them were any good.

It seemed only natural that the four men who carried Marshal Brewster into Doc Baxter's examination room would try to remain and learn more of his medical condition, but the kindly old Doc would have none of that and quickly shooed them all outside. “I fell on a slick patch of ice and the pain is killing me,” Brewster said. Doc Baxter pulled up the Marshal’s shirt tail and began feeling around on his lower back as Brewster whimpered in pain. “Tell me what you are feeling,” Baxter inquired. “It’s bad, Doc, much worse than before. I feel pain shooting down my legs and some numbness. Can you give me something for the pain?”

Doctor Baxter had known this man for quite a long time and wished he had better news to tell him. “Yes,” he replied, as he sat down in his wooden chair, took off his glasses, and started rubbing his eyes. “Laudanum or Cannabis will help ease your pain. But you have some spinal trauma in your lower back that medicines will not cure. If I could somehow look inside of you, without cutting you open, I would know exactly what we are dealing with.”

Marshal Brewster was not surprised by what he was hearing, having suspected that his days as the Gas City Marshal might now be over. “Are you suggesting I have an operation, Doc?” Baxter took a few moments before he answered. “It’s not something I would try myself, but I do know of a good surgeon in Indianapolis that has some experience with these matters. I can send him a telegram if you’d like, to see if he would examine you there and give you his best medical opinion.” The very thought of having his lower back split open like a watermelon did not sound very encouraging to Marshal Baxter, but neither did the idea of spending the rest of his days sitting in a wheelchair. After a few more questions, Baxter agreed for Doc to send the telegram and wait for a response.

Deputy Marshal Justin Blake was kicked back and enjoying a cup of coffee inside the Panhandle Hotel and Restaurant down by the railroad tracks. Marshal Brewster had taught his young deputy the advantages of observing who enters and leaves town by rail. As it was, nobody of any interest had gotten off the morning southbound train, and a cup of coffee on a cool morning sounded mighty fine to Justin. It was hard to believe he had lived in Gas City for the past year while working as a deputy marshal. It was a job Justin had grown to like, and he enjoyed the good people in the town. Marshal Brewster was like a father figure to him and had certainly provided solid police training and friendship to him. He also enjoyed the friendship of the other young deputy, Wilbert Vance who worked the night shift and was asleep at that time of day. Brewster was a top notch lawman in their eyes, despite his age. He had even agreed to update their police work by installing one of the newfangled telephones in their office.

Together the three officers had managed to keep the gas and oil booming little city quiet and peaceful, once that awful White Cap business was finally brought under control. That night was the last time Justin had been forced to draw and fire his Remington 44-40 revolver. The terrible night that changed his world forever. Justin could not allow himself to keep dwelling on the past so he forced himself to live each day now as it came. Hopefully, the personal loss he felt would become lighter to bare. At least, it's what he'd been told by many people.

A man approached his table and broke his concentration, "Justin, Marshal Baxter fell on the ice and hurt his back real bad. He's a callin' for you ta come quick." It was his friend, old Zeke Miller, the man who took care of the fire horses in the fire barn and helped around the office occasionally. Old Zeke was known for spinning tall tales and making bad coffee. He had filled in when needed as a secret deputy, and was considered a great friend to everyone in the Marshal's office. The look of deep concern appearing on the old man's wrinkled face told Justin that this could be serious.

Walking together, they approached Doc Baxter's office in time to see the marshal being wheeled outside while in Doc's old wicker wheelchair that he kept around for emergencies. Brewster saw his deputy and Zeke approaching. "My men are here, they will take me from here. Thanks again for your help Doc." Brewster waved the man away while managing a painful smile.

Approaching Brewster, both men could not fathom seeing Marshal Brewster sitting in a wheelchair. "Quit your gawking, and push me to my house. I don't want folks to see me like this," Brewster told them in a cross voice. "We'll talk once we're inside." They soon reached Brewster's home.

The marshal owned a small four room house one block south of the main street. It was big enough for him since he lived alone. He never felt the need to marry. Brewster had chosen instead to marry his job as a law enforcement officer. Life had been good for him until today. Both men had to lift his wheelchair into the air in order to clear the threshold steps.

"We need to build some kinda ramp or somethin'," Zeke mentioned. "I'll get some lumber boards and work on it today," he assured the marshal. Once everyone was inside the house, Brewster filled them in on what had happened to him, and that doc was going to telegraph another doctor in Indianapolis about his condition. He hoped to learn something within a few days.

"Marshal," old Zeke said, "I'll be happy ta go with you ta Indianapolis and help out. You're gonna need a feller like me ta get you on the train and push you around the big city, and keep all of the pretty ladies away from you." Brewster was clearly moved by Zeke's act of personal charity, and thanked him for his assistance. "Now, let's discuss the present situation," Marshal Brewster said. "Clearly my days as the town marshal are over."

Looking up at his lead deputy, the marshal continued, "Justin, I will be submitting my letter of resignation to the mayor today, and I'll be recommending you to take my place." Justin thought to himself for a few seconds before replying, "Maybe that's a bit premature, Marshal. The doctor in Indianapolis might be able to fix your back."

"I'm not gonna let anyone split my back open like a watermelon. It probably would kill me, or put me in bed for the rest of my life. Doc Baxter didn't think too much of my chances for a full recovery anyway. He can give me medicine to control the pain, so I can at least sit up. I'll just wait and see what the Indianapolis doctor says, if he agrees to see me." Both Justin and Zeke knew that what Marshal Brewster just said was probably true. Still, it was a hard pill to swallow, seeing their friend in this bad situation.

"Don't concern yourself about me. I'll be fine. I've lived a frugal life, and own this little house free and clear. I'll get by. Now, acting Marshal Blake, don't you have work to do?"

Realizing it was time to leave, Justin reached out and shook his friend's hand. "Call upon any of us anytime you need something, Marshal." Brewster shook his head, "My name is Kenneth or Kenny, if you prefer, not marshal. Now go, but leave Zeke here to carry my written resignation to the mayor."

Stepping back outside, Justin felt the weight of the world on his shoulders. He would do his very best to make Marshal

Brewster proud of him. It was time to make his patrol of the town. No doubt, many people would have heard about the marshal's accident by now and would be asking him many questions.

~~~~~~~~~~~~~~~~~~~~

Mayor Huffman read the letter of resignation twice before thanking Zeke Miller, and sending him on his way. Gas City required a full time marshal, so a special public town council meeting would need to be scheduled as soon as possible. Brewster was a good man, and would be hard to replace. Huffman only wondered if young Blake was up to the task.

~~~~~~~~~~~~~~~~~~~~

The man known only as Kruger, smiled broadly upon hearing the news of the town marshal's resignation. Since the departure of his boss, Big Jim Malone, Kruger made it his goal to take over the local crime syndicate in the town, and its local communities. Kruger's first act was to obtain ownership of the White Dog Saloon for himself. Since it, and other properties belonging to Malone were mortgaged, Kruger made it a point to inform the new owner that "accidents" could easily happen to one's family unless people were reasonable in dealing with him. Within a short time, Kruger's measly financial offer was accepted and, overnight, Kruger became its owner. The odd name of the saloon resulted from a stray white dog that found it's way inside over a year ago. His newest purchase was a lively little watering hole called Happy Hollow, where all types of seedy activities transpired with Kruger always receiving his share of the cut.

Owning saloons wasn't nearly enough for Kruger. He wanted as much money and power as he could accumulate in as short as time as possible. Unlike his ex-boss Malone, Kruger saw the profit in purchasing and installing automatic games of chance machines on countertops in retail stores, tobacco shops, and bars around town. A player simply inserted a coin and activated the device, depending on which machine the player was using. A winning player might win a cheap cigar, free drink token, or some other prize awarded by that shop or bar. Men, and yes women, were seen at all hours of the day and night inserting their coins and taking a chance on winning. The profits he raked in were huge, and Kruger placed more and more of those little beauties everywhere. *If only a way could be made to make those machines larger and pay off the players in nickels rather than cigars*, he thought, *I would make a killing.* Another moneymaker of his was the selling of Louisiana lottery tickets. At a steep price of $1.00 per ticket, Kruger always suggested that men join together, and then split their winnings. Of course, nobody ever won since the tickets he sold were all fakes. A sucker truly was born every minute.

Kruger also had a mob of local thugs who conducted break-ins of local businesses and homes at night. Of course, he always received his percent of the take from these after-hour activities, and occasionally accompanied his men, just so they could see that he was willing to take a risk, as well. One might be surprised how a few threats to a store owner about his families "health" could result in a cash windfall, and an unreported crime. Marshal Brewster was a threat to Kruger and his mob, but now that he was out of the picture for good, that only left the two young deputies to deal with. Things were indeed looking up.

~~~~~~~~~~~~~~~~~~~~

By the end of the day, Doctor Baxter had received his reply from the Indianapolis surgeon concerning Brewster's back condition. The man agreed to examine Brewster, providing he could travel to Indianapolis soon. Zeke Miller quickly agreed to accompany Brewster on the journey, and purchased with Brewster's money, two tickets to Indianapolis for the following morning. The station master, who was an old friend, suggested the marshal be wheeled into the mail car for his journey south, rather than require him to sit on
~~~~~~~~~~~~~~~~~~~~

the hard wooden passenger seats. Since ramps existed for loading cargo and such, this option was quickly agreed upon. Brewster knew it would be a very difficult experience, but he felt he needed to try it for his own piece of mind. He knew he would have to live with the results either way.

The next morning, Justin Blake and Wilbert Vance were at the train station to see their friends off, and to wish them a safe and productive journey. Zeke was a good man and would be a great help to their injured friend. "Let us know what you find out," Justin told Zeke, as the wheelchair was rolled into the mail car. "Looks like we're ridin' shotgun on the mail car again, Marshal," Zeke laughed, as the door was slid shut. Soon the train was out of sight, and Justin could only hope that something could be done for his friend's condition.

~~~~~~~~~~~~~~~~~~~~~~

Justin and Wilbert attended the special public town council meeting the next evening. If Justin was to be given the marshal's job, he planned on bringing Wilbert onto day shift with him, and then hire another man for night duty. Wilbert Vance had proven to be a very good deputy and a close friend. Mayor Huffman struck the gavel a few times, "Everyone please take a seat and remain quiet. This meeting is called to order." Huffman read out loud Brewster's letter
~~~~~~~~~~~~~~~~~~~~~~

of resignation, and explained that he was now in Indianapolis getting another doctor's medical opinion. "On behalf of the city, we wish Marshal Brewster the best of luck, and we hope that something can be done medically to aid his pain and suffering." At that point a motion was made to award Marshal Brewster, should he not return to duty, one hundred dollars severance pay from a grateful city. That motion was quickly seconded and passed unanimously.

Council member Davidson then asked for the floor. "We now come to the part of selecting Marshal Brewster's replacement. I realize it was Brewster's wish that young Deputy Blake is selected for that position. I know I speak for everyone present in acknowledging his efforts in bringing the White Caps reign of terror to a halt last year. But I do find myself wondering if one short year on the police force is enough experience to assume the difficult position of Gas City Marshal. I sincerely mean no disrespect in saying this, but I cannot help but wonder if working under a more experienced law officer might be beneficial. As it so happens, I have a cousin assigned to the Fort Wayne police force that has many years of experience and has expressed a strong interest in the Marshal's position. I now put in motion that our council consider hiring a more seasoned lawman, and offer the position of Gas City Marshal to Police Officer Timothy Merrell."

After a great deal of questions, and some back and forth, the council voted three to two to offer the position first to Officer Merrell, and keep Justin Blake as a backup.

Councilman Davidson suggested that he represent the city council in making the job offer to his cousin. This, too, was agreed upon. The meeting was then adjourned. Justin didn't quite know what to think since the idea of obtaining the marshal's position seemed a foregone conclusion to him. Justin noticed many eyes on him as he left the meeting room. He would not allow his disappointment to show publically. Outside, Justin and Wilbert discussed what had just happened, and began to make plans for a transfer of power to the new marshal, if and when he arrived in town.

The following afternoon a telegram arrived and was taken to the marshal's office. It stated, "Position of Marshal accepted. Stop. Will arrive with Deputy tomorrow by rail. Stop. Timothy Merrell." Justin stared at the telegram wondering about the "with deputy" portion of the message. *Oh well, the more help the better*, he thought to himself. Going outside to the hitching post, Justin mounted up on his horse, Spunky, and rode west to the railway station to discover the time the new marshal and his deputy would arrive. With Zeke gone, Justin also needed to do a little office cleaning for the new marshal. It was inside a fire barn after all, and sometimes the odor reminded everyone of it. A quiet little voice inside of Justin was saying to him that this might not work out as he had hoped. Justin forced himself to shake it off and began to make things ready for the new men's arrival.

Chapter 22

Deputy Marshals Justin Blake and Wilbert Vance were on hand to welcome the new marshal and his deputy to Gas City. It was a particularly slow travel day for the Pennsylvania Railroad, with very few passengers exiting the car, so both men were quite easy to spot. One was following close on the heels of the other, as they stepped down off of the platform. Justin extended his hand, "Welcome to Gas City, gentlemen. My name is..." At that point, Justin was cut off by the leader of the men, who shoved the handle of his traveling bag into Justin's outstretched hand. "Here," the man said in an annoyed voice, "Take our bags to the Mississinewa Hotel and register us. I'll talk with you later." With that rude dismissal, both deputies stood in total silence. "I'll take their bags, go home and get some sleep," Justin told his friend. "We'll talk later." With that, Justin rode off in Brewster's wagon toward the hotel with all the baggage. Whatever he was thinking, it was probably best not to say it out loud anyway.

Both of the Merrell brothers walked over to be greeted by Councilman Davidson, who was standing next to the Gas City Journal reporter, Alvin Jenson. After being introduced to the brothers, Jensen requested an interview for his newspaper. It was then agreed that the reporter should join the group for dinner that night at 7:30 p.m. at the Mississinewa Hotel. Councilman Davidson then escorted the brothers to his awaiting carriage for a short ride through town.

"Let me give you two a quick tour of our fair city before we meet up with the Mayor," stated Councilman Davidson. "As I mentioned earlier, Gas City and it's surrounding community are experiencing an industrial boom with the discovery of endless supplies of natural gas and oil. Factory after factory has opened up providing high paying jobs for the newly arriving workers. This dirt street we are now on is Main Street. Within a few short weeks, contractors will start paving it with bricks, fifty feet wide and extended from the railroad yard all the way past the Mississinewa Hotel, around 1/2 mile long. It's costing our city $65,000 and is estimated to be completed within three months. Progress has arrived, gentlemen, and there's money to be made here by everyone."

Timothy Merrell spoke next, "So tell me about this Mayor Huffman. How do I get on his good side?" The Councilman replied, "He's a strong party man who is very much respected within the community. He is honest, fair, and very ambitious. I fully expect him to run for higher office soon, and I intend to replace him as Mayor when he does. But to answer your question, Mayor Huffman is deeply interested in the financial aspects of the city. We have many ordinances on the books that impose fines on those who neglect to obtain the necessary permits required to do legal business within the city. Marshal Brewster was friends with almost everyone in town, and often overlooked that aspect of his job. If you concentrate on enforcing these ordinances by adding more revenue to the city coffers, Mayor Huffman will no doubt be very pleased. Well, gentlemen, we have arrived. Let's go inside and get you both introduced, and sworn into your new official positions."

"Mayor Huffman, I would like to introduce you to our new marshal, Mr. Timothy Merrell and his brother, Deputy Cecil Merrell," Councilman Davidson said with a deep smile. "Welcome to our fair city, gentlemen," the mayor said, as he shook their hands. "Do you have any questions or concerns before I swear you both in?"

"Yes, I do, as a matter of fact," replied Timothy Merrell. "I was offered thirty-five dollars a month as marshal. However, I won't stay for less than forty for me and thirty-five for my brother, Cecil. He will be working days with me as my chief deputy." There was an awkward tension in the room, as nobody spoke for a few seconds. "Well," the mayor finally replied, "I will need to bring a motion at the next city council meeting to do this, but I think we can accommodate both of you." With that both officers of the law were sworn in.

~~~~~~~~~~~~~~~~~~~~

Deputy Marshal Justin Blake remained inside the marshal's office and completed a little clean up, as he waited for the arrival of the Merrell brothers. There were activities that commanded his attention, but Blake felt it only polite to be in the office when his new boss arrived, along with the other deputy. First impressions could sometimes be wrong, he reminded himself over and over again. Justin was willing to give them a chance to disprove the old saying. Hours passed without their arrival, so at the end of his day shift, and feeling some hunger pangs, Justin left to get something to eat and return to his room at Ma Richards Boarding House. He would meet them officially tomorrow morning.

~~~~~~~~~~~~~~~~~~~~

Gas City Journal reporter Alvin Jensen entered the lobby of the luxurious Mississinewa Hotel to find both Merrell brothers and Councilman Davidson waiting in the lobby. Together the four men were ushered into the dining room and seated at their reserved table. A snappy waiter approached the men and handed each their menus. "I highly recommend the pork chops," Jensen said to the new officers. After each man's order was placed, the reporter began his interview. "Gentlemen, I appreciate being invited to accompany you here tonight. My readers will want to know more about you, and what your impressions are of our little town." Marshal Merrell, puffing up somewhat, replied, "I can see great potential for this community, and I along with my brother, look forward to meeting it's leading citizens. Cecil here will be my Chief Deputy and assigned to days working by my side. We both have many years of police experience working in the much larger city of Fort Wayne, so I expect no trouble in adapting to this little town."

Jensen, seeing an opportunity to take a dig at Deputy Blake, replied, "What about Deputy Marshal Blake? He is currently working the day shift." Without blinking an eye, Marshal Merrell responded, "Not anymore, he's going on the night shift with the other deputy, until I can decide which man I will let go." The interview ended as the food arrived, and only polite small talk took place for the remainder of the meal.

~~~~~~~~~~~~~~~~~~~~

Justin was inside his room reading an interesting Western novel when there was a loud knock on his door. Opening
~~~~~~~~~~~~~~~~~~~~

it, he saw Deputy Marshal Wilbert Vance standing there. Justin had fully expected his friend to drop by this evening to discuss this new working situation. "Sorry to bother you Justin, but Marshal Merrell wants to meet with us in his office now." Off duty, Justin Blake was used to being called out for important matters of law enforcement, but this order struck him as being very odd. "Give me a moment to change back into my uniform and I'll be right with you, Wilbert." Together the men walked briskly over to the fire barn.

They say a man can tell a lot from another man's handshake. A crushing handshake indicates superiority over the other; a firm shake indicates respect and a genuine interest in meeting the other. The handshake Justin received from both men was light and cold. "My name is Marshal Merrell and this is Chief Deputy Merrell. You will address us, as such when you address us both publicly and privately. You will take your orders from my brother when I am not around. Pointing to Justin he continued on, "As of tomorrow, you will begin the night shift with Deputy Vance. I will, then, make a determination soon as to which man will remain employed. If you don't like this decision, you are free to quit here and now." Justin did not allow anything to show on his face and remained rigid while facing his new employer.

Marshal Merrell continued, "Fine, now that it's settled, let's move on. I expect everything to be accomplished by-the-book. I will not tolerate incomplete paperwork or sloppy police work. Do I make myself clear on this point? Tomorrow evening you will both report to this office first and there will be a bulletin board hanging on that wall. You will check it daily for written instructions from me. There will, also, be a list of city ordinances that were not enforced by my predecessor, but from this day forward, will be rigidly enforced. Now that I have made myself clear, I want you, Deputy Vance, to remain in the office tonight and scrub it down completely with a bucket of soapy water and a hard scrub brush. Just because our office is inside a fire barn doesn't mean it has to smell like one."

Without thinking about it, Wilbert Vance cast his eyes on Justin to see his friend's reaction. "Don't look at him for advice," Merrell ordered. "He's not your boss... I am. I'll be inspecting your work in the morning. Do I make myself clear?" Wilbert, with a cold stare, replied, "Yes." Showing his anger, Marshal Merrell stated harshly, "That's yes, sir." Without saying a word, Wilbert left the office to obtain the necessary cleaning materials from the horse barn. Looking over at Justin with a satisfied look on his face, he said, "You are dismissed." Justin was very tempted to slam a few doors on his way out but held his temper in place as he headed for home. *This is not the time*, he thought to himself.

~~~~~~~~~~~~~~~~~~~~
~~~~~~~~~~~~~~~~~~~~

The following day, the noon train from Indianapolis arrived at the depot and Kenneth Brewster, wheelchair and all, was unloaded from the mail car by Zeke Miller. Brewster had informed Zeke earlier that he didn't want to speak with anyone, and to push him home as quickly as possible. Several folks noticed their arrival but, with a negative shake of Zeke's head, remained at a distance. Word quickly spread around town that they were back and the news wasn't good. Arriving at the Brewster home, Zeke pushed the ex-marshal up the newly constructed ramp and into his house. "I want to thank you again for all you have done, my friend. Now I would just like to be left alone," he softly said to the old man. Zeke replied, "I'll be back ta check on you sometime tonight. Rest easy Marshal." "Zeke, how many times do I have to remind you the name is Kenny now? I'll see you later, go get some rest." With that old Zeke headed over to the fire barn to inform Justin that the doctor didn't have any solutions without surgery and even with that, there was no guarantee it would help.

Arriving at the fire barn, Zeke entered to find a stranger sitting at the desk. Looking up and clearly evaluating Zeke's somewhat rough appearance, the man said, "Something I can do for you?" Zeke took an instant dislike to the fellow but politely informed him that he was the guy who took care of the fire horses and helped out around the office. Before he could ask about Justin's whereabouts, the stranger said,

"Then I suggest you return to the barn and take care of the horses." Zeke stood there and turned beat red from being spoken to like that before walking out and returning to his own lodgings, seething with anger. He asked the first fellow he met on the street who that man was and what's going on. Zeke was not pleased with the answers he received.

~~~~~~~~~~~~~~~~~~~~~~~

Barber Matthew Brooks had three people waiting for a haircut when a stranger walked into his shop. "I'll be with you after I'm finished with these customers," he said. The stranger stated, "I'm not here for a shave or haircut, but to introduce myself. My name is Cecil Merrell and I am the new Chief Deputy Marshal. I understand you are, also, on the city council so I just wanted to drop by and say hello. My brother, Tim, is the new marshal." After shaking hands and nodding to the customers, the new deputy told them he had better get going as he had many new folks to meet, and then he left the barbershop.

The customer sitting in the barber chair spoke up, "Sure gonna seem odd not having Marshal Brewster in charge. That new guy seems nice enough, has anyone here met the new marshal yet?" No one had. "How's come Justin didn't get the job, Matt?" Barber Brooks then replied that the council had voted to hire a more experienced man for
~~~~~~~~~~~~~~~~~~~~~~~

the job, but that it wasn't a negative reflection on Deputy Blake. With that, the topic quickly turned to the warmer weather. Another visitor soon entered, a woman holding the hand of a young boy ready for his first real haircut. Any man would tell you that the mood of a barbershop totally changes when a woman enters the halls of it's manly domain. Barber Matthew Brooks continued to cut his next customer's hair in total silence as the little kid squalled, and each customer wished he was somewhere else.

'Squire Hiram Jones was a very busy man these days. His elected position as the town Justice of the Peace required much more from him than just marrying folks. He had limited powers to try criminal and civil court cases. He had been called by many names such as magistrate, 'squire, and simply judge. For some reason, the local paper continued to refer to him as 'squire, an old English term from the twelfth century. 'Squire Jones presided over many cases, such as: drunkeness; adultery; imposing fines; issuing arrest warrants; ordering the removal of disorderly people; criminal misdemeanors; infractions; and to jail those persons who needed it for short periods of time. His position was very useful in handling these types of minor offenses locally rather than to tie up the criminal legal system at the county seat. A person could only imagine that with 25 saloons, scores of loose women and factory men galore, business would be good and it certainly had been hectic.

Hearing that the new marshal was now on the job, 'Squire Jones decided to pay him a visit and introduce himself. Normally he would have sworn in the new man himself but his wife was suffering from the flu, and he was needed more at home. From what he had heard, Mayor Huffman performed the task just fine, and now they had two new men on the job. The men and women in town were a polite bunch when meeting 'Squire Jones on the street. A tip of the hat or a friendly good morning was always greatly appreciated by the fifty-eight year old man. Jones had moved here from Ohio years ago, when Gas City was then known as Harrisburg.

Entering the fire barn, Jones spotted the new man sitting at his desk. The first thing 'Squire Jones noticed was the fancy new uniform the man was wearing, full of large shiny brass buttons. Jones quickly thought that his coat reminded him of a circus ringmaster. Holding that thought in check, 'Squire Jones introduced himself. Upon realizing that his visitor was a man of importance, Marshal Merrell stood up and he shook the older man's hand. "Please pull up a seat, Your Honor. I was planning on looking you up today so you saved me a trip. I have obtained copies of our city ordinances and will be instructing my men to enforce them as required. Things will be run by the book around here from now on."

"I see," replied the 'Squire. "Sounds like my work will be picking up around here. Anyway, I wanted to meet you and to offer my services anytime they are needed. My house is only four streets away from your office, and I look forward to working with you and your brother. Good day, sir." As he started his walk home, he couldn't help but chuckle out loud, "*Brass Buttons*." With the departure of the 'Squire, Marshal Merrell felt it was time that he began his daily walk about town to allow the people to see him and to know that, indeed, there was a new marshal in town.

~~~~~~~~~~~~~~~~

The man known only as Kruger sat in his small private office inside the White Dog Saloon, counting the profit from the previous night's take. Kruger visited each of his saloons during the day, doing the same thing, and clearly business was good. Though he owned other establishments, the White Dog is his sentimental favorite. This time last year Kruger was only the manager of the White Dog, and the ex-boss' muscle when needed. Today his empire was expanding, with hopes of achieving what "Big Jim" Malone had in the next few years. He was deep in thought as he heard a knock on his door. Opening it, one of his thugs stuck his head inside. "Boss, there's a new Deputy Marshal outside asking to speak with you." Kruger sat back within his chair while scooping the cash on his desk into a drawer. He reached for a ledger book, picked up a pencil then replied, "Show the man in."
~~~~~~~~~~~~~~~~

Chief Deputy Marshal Cecil Merrell entered the room, introduced himself and shook hands with Kruger. “Please be seated, deputy,” Kruger said, “How can I help you?” Deputy Merrell got right to the point, “I’ve been told that you are an important man around town, and a good person to know.” Kruger pretended to close up the ledger book and put it to the side. “I don’t know about that, deputy. I’m just an honest businessman trying to make a living the best way I can.” That brought a smile to the visitor’s face, that bothered Kruger somewhat, but he didn’t allow it to show. “I wanted you to know that my brother is the new marshal now, and I thought, perhaps I should explain a few bits of information that might help you. Kruger leaned forward and, with a jovial smile on his face said, “I am always ready to assist the law in any way I can.”

“Mr. Kruger, I know my brother very well. I know how he operates and I can see in advance what his next move will be. I just thought it might be in your own financial interest to know about it so you can make sure you have all of your bases covered, as they say in baseball.” Kruger was interested. “Go ahead, Deputy.” “Well, sir, my brother is a stickler for paperwork. He is a by-the-book type of man who only sees things either black or white, right or wrong. Now me, I see a lot of grays. I’m a live and let live kind of fellow, if you know what I mean. So, here’s a piece of free advice on the house. Within a day or so, my brother will instruct the two night deputies to visit your places of business and search for all required permits, or other, shall we say, female vices that might trigger further police involvement in your honest places of business."

Kruger could not contain the genuine smile that crept up on his ugly face. "That's mighty nice of you, Deputy Merrell, to let me know this in advance. It will give me time to post my liquor license and any other permits in public view, and we can, as you say, ensure any loose ladies who might be present without my knowledge be given the opportunity to depart the premises. Mighty nice of you sir, to take the time from your busy schedule to meet with me today."

"Think nothing of it, Mr. Kruger. I am but a poor public servant making thirty-five dollars a month, and trying to do his civic duty. From time to time, there may be other bits of 'nice to know' information that I may casually mention, all in the spirit of community service, of course."

"That's a pitifully small sum to pay a man of your fine civic distinction, Deputy. Perhaps something might be done to ease your burden."

With that, Deputy Merrell stood, shook hands again with Kruger, and started for the door. "Oh, by the way, I like that idea very much. Good day, Mr. Kruger," he said as he started to leave the saloon.

"Allow me to see you to the door, Deputy," Kruger said. Upon entering the open saloon, Merrell started for the door but his eyes fell on the free lunch spread. He walked over to it, picked up a piece of Rye bread and some smoked meat and dabbed some mustard on it. Then casually walked out the door eating the sandwich. Kruger couldn't help but admire this man's grit, as any man who failed to purchase a drink while eating at the free lunch counter could expect a club to the head by the bartender. Merrell knew this unwritten rule as well as the next guy. Kruger stood there wondering if he had read the deputy correctly, or if it was some sort of slick police trap.

Turning to one of his men, he informed him to bring the manager of the Happy Hallow Saloon to him immediately. Going back into his office, Kruger opened the drawer holding last night's cash and counted out one hundred and fifty dollars in bills. The saloon manager arrived quickly. "Take this money to the clerk's office and obtain the proper liquor permit for the Happy Hallow. Also, post a NO DISCHARGING OF FIREARMS ALLOWED sign above your bar. Keep a couple of bouncers on hand for the next couple of nights. You need to, chase off any whores or wild drunks. I want that place to appear to be a quiet little bar, if and when the law pays you a visit. Now go!" Sitting back in his chair, Kruger considered his options. Having a reliable source within the marshal's office might prove to be a gold mine, if it were true. "Now bring me my other saloon managers," he told his men.

Chapter 23

Not working the day shift was a new experience for Justin Blake. His body was totally used to sleeping at night, so the change in routine would take some getting used to. Justin was feeling restless so he felt it was time to speak directly with ex-Marshal Brewster, to see what he found out from the Indianapolis doctor. He had heard rumors but desired to know the facts. Approaching Brewster's home, he saw the ex-marshal and Zeke Miller sitting outside on the front porch enjoying the mild April weather. "Morning," Justin said. Seeing an empty wooden chair, he pulled it closer and sat down next to the men. A moment of awkward silence hung in the air before Brewster spoke up. "Not much can be done about my back without splitting me open," he said. Justin had suspected as much, but held out hope that something other than drugs would help his friend's pain.

"I don't care fer that new marshal one darn bit," Zeke said in changing the subject. "He talked ta me like I was a dog.

If he says ta make him some coffee, I might get some water from one of the fire horses!" With that everyone chuckled.

"I got put on nights with Wilbert, so he can decide which of us to let go. I am tempted to just quit now and save everyone the trouble," griped Justin. Brewster sat up straight in his wheelchair, looked Justin square in the eyes, and replied, "Don't do that, son. I have seen his kind come and go during my long years in law enforcement. His kind never lasts, as he doesn't have anyone's back, nor will they have his in a pinch. You and Wilbert need to just stick it out. I know it will be very difficult to do but think of the town. You can't let these good people down. 'Every dog has his day' and 'what goes around comes around', so he'll get his just rewards soon." Justin considered the marshal's words. "I guess you're right. I'll try to stick with it, but I will only put up with his nonsense to a point. He has a bunch of written rules he wants to be enforced that we are to read over tonight. I guess time will tell if this works out or not. I guess I'll be moving on now. See ya fellows."

"Den I'll be a visitin' with you fellers come evenings from now on," Zeke said as he waved to his friend.

~~~~~~~~~~~~~~~~~~~~~~

Reverend Clarence Stokes was proud of the work that had been accomplished. His church rebuilding project had
~~~~~~~~~~~~~~~~~~~~~~

taken quite a while to begin since so many in his congregation seemed to have blamed him and his wife, Edith for the prior fire. Many had deserted him during his hours of greatest need, but fortunately the other churches in town came to his aid. He had since used the church on West Main Street in order to preach. Slowly, many of his old congregation began to return, and the feeling of anger started to fade away. Now a new frame was being erected over the charred remains of the old one. Like the book of Isaiah says, 'the Lord's favor will bestow on them a crown of beauty instead of ashes.' Both the Reverend and his wife were at the job site almost every day, except Sunday, to do all that they could to assist. Justin had heard that the church was being rebuilt, but had avoided making contact with the couple. Seeing them from a distance, Justin thought it was time to face his own personal demons and approached them.

Tipping his hat to Mrs. Stokes, Justin said, "Good afternoon Mrs. Stokes, Reverend Stokes." The Reverend broke out in a large grin, as he offered his hand while Mrs. Stokes gave him a motherly hug. "It's great to see you, Justin. It has been a long time. Too long, in fact. How have you been?" the Reverend asked.

"Still plugging along, I guess. I see you're making good progress on the new church."

With a bit of pride showing on the Reverend's face, he replied, "Yes, it's going up very nicely now. We hope to have it completed by late summer or early fall, but that will depend on the continuing generosity of many fine people. You know you're always welcome here, son." The word struck home for a few seconds. There was a pause in speaking as everyone looked at the structure but knowing the question Justin would soon be asking. Seeing an opportunity to step away momentarily, the Reverend Stokes excused himself. Another short period of awkward silence passed, finally Justin found the nerve to ask, "So, how is she?"

The look on the sweet face of Mrs. Stokes changed at the very mention of the question. "Her mind is now completely gone. She doesn't even know who we are." As she spoke, tears began to run down her cheeks. "Her once beautiful brown hair has turned to snow white." Mrs. Stokes fought to hold herself from breaking down. "Justin, it's an awful place where they have her. There are constant shrieks and screams coming from the patients. If there is a hell on earth, it has to be the Richmond Mental Institution." Justin hated himself for even asking about Samantha, and putting her poor mother through this agony. He reached out and held her as they both grieved together in silence.

~~~~~~~~~~~~~~~~~~~~

Justin and Wilbert arrived in the marshal's office, at 7 p.m. to begin their night shift. They found Councilman
~~~~~~~~~~~~~~~~~~~~

Davidson leaving the office and Chief Deputy Cecil Merrell sitting at the desk. "Evening men," he said. "Marshall Merrell asked me to hang around long enough to brief you on a few things." Justin and Wilbert pulled up a chair and sat in front of the desk to await the briefing. "Let me start off by saying I am not my brother. I know he's a bit of a stickler for rules and regulations, while I see things from a more practical side. I will be happy to serve as a go-between for your benefit until my brother finally adjusts to his new position. Do you have any questions or problems?" There was total silence from the deputies.

Seeing that his friendly approach didn't seem to pay off, Merrell switched to a more authoritarian style. "Here is the new pass-on book. We want everything, and I mean everything, that happens to any of us documented inside as a permanent record of all police activities. Marshal Merrell will review what you write every day, so make it clear and precise. Over on the bulletin board, you'll find a list of rules of conduct and city ordinances that must be followed to the letter. Tonight you are to visit all city drinking establishments for an inspection of license documentation and to enforce all ordinances. Jail those who do not comply as a message to everyone that this little town has a new marshal who will enforce the law, and not show favoritism to his friends. The marshal wants everything properly documented. Am I understood? Pass on your normal city patrols tonight, and concentrate on saloon inspections. Don't stop until everything has been accomplished." With that, the new chief deputy departed.

"I don't trust that guy as far as I can throw him," Wilbert told Justin. Together they walked over to read the written rules and do a quick review of city ordinances. "We are already familiar with the city ordinances anyway, nothing new here," Justin said. They read the rules:

Rules of Conduct-

The following police guidelines will be enforced at all times.

(1) A board of police will now exist made up of the marshal, his chief deputy, and all other deputy marshals, with the approval of the Gas City Council. Any and all merchant police hired by saloons, hotels, or factories within this city must follow all rules of the police board. The payment of any merchant police will not be paid from city funds.

(2) All city law enforcement officers must be able to read, write, speak the English language clearly, and buy their own uniforms. No exceptions.

(3) No officer may enter a house of prostitution, gambling establishment or, dance hall, or associate with said persons on or off duty. You may only enter said premises while on official duty. No officer may accept favors, gifts, or money from said premises, or it will be viewed as a bribe with termination upon discovery.

(4) Any officer who willingly knows of a fellow officer's immoral conduct but fails to report it, will be considered a co-conspirator and subject to termination and/or prosecution.

Signed,
Marshal Timothy Merrell

Neither officer had much of a problem with these new rules of conduct, so little was actually said. The rule concerning reading English was clearly aimed at keeping Zeke Miller out of any official working position. Both men prepared for the evening's work ahead, and after a quick discussion agreed to divide the list of known drinking establishments in half for inspection purposes. "Before we do this," Wilbert said to Justin, "Something occurred late last night that I fear may come back to haunt me." Chuckling, he continued, "Haunt is a word I could use in describing it." He then went on to tell

Justin the full story, before separating for the night's work. Each agreed to meet up at the railroad depot when finished.

~~~~~~~~~~~~~~~~~~~~~~

One of the petty criminals working for Kruger stuck his head into the boss's office, "It looks like the information the new deputy marshal gave us might be true. The boys just reported back that both night marshals are going to each saloon with clipboards in hand." Kruger could not believe the good fortune that was just handed to him.

"Tell Smiley Lewis I want to see him immediately," Kruger ordered. Smiley was the leader of all breaking and entering gangs that existed in Gas City. No burglaries occurred within city limits without the expressed planning of Smiley Lewis. Any individuals who felt they could operate by committing robberies on their own without Smiley's control were quickly taken care of. The man certainly knew his business; how to pre-plan, what to take, and especially plan for a safe getaway. To date, none of his gang members had ever been caught. "Come on in, Smiley, and close the door," a welcoming Kruger stated. "It looks like the town is wide open tonight since both deputy marshals are going to saloons looking at paperwork. How many gangs do you have at your disposal?" Both men made plans for an exciting and prosperous night.
~~~~~~~~~~~~~~~~~~~~~~

~~~~~~~~~~~~~~~~~~~~~~

By the time that Justin had finished his third saloon, he sensed that word of his inspections had already spread to the other saloons. All of Kruger's saloon keepers already had their paid up liquor license laid out for him to inspect. The normal influx of highly intoxicated men, and a few loose women, were not present tonight. No gunfire, a common occurrence when heavy drinking and arguments mixed, had been heard all night. The saloon and red light districts were quiet as a church mouse. Justin and Wilbert had found very few violations to report. Finally they met down at the railroad depot to compare notes during the early morning hours. "I don't think the marshal will be very pleased with our reports tonight," Wilbert said.

"Yea, it's like they knew we were coming. We might as well head back to the office. I could use a cup of coffee," Justin replied. The men walked the few blocks together but, as they approached the horse barn, they could see in the darkness a few people outside waiting on them. The telephone could be heard ringing inside the office.

"It's about time you two returned," one man shouted. "I was robbed tonight." Another exclaimed, "Our home was broken into, and my money is gone." Another shouted, "My wife is terrified about our home intrusion." Justin was stunned by the number of break-ins that occurred while he
~~~~~~~~~~~~~~~~~~~~~~

and Wilbert were inspecting the saloons. "Everyone, please come inside and we'll take your reports," Justin assured the victims. This would be a long difficult night. Both men were finalizing their reports in the morning when the Merrell brothers entered the office.

"What the heck is going on around here?" the marshal exclaimed loudly, "I'm being bombarded by angry citizens about mass breaks-ins last night. Were you two asleep or just drunk?" Justin almost exploded with anger over the false accusations being hurled their way. He gritted his teeth while replying. "We were out inspecting twenty-five saloons, as we were told to do. It's like the criminals knew we were not patrolling, and took advantage of it."

Marshal Merrell shook his head, "I just can't buy that. We're going to be working on these break-in reports all day now." Changing the subject, the marshal then demanded to see their inspection reports. "Is this all you found?" He tossed them down on his desk, with some of the loose papers finding their way to the floor. "I expect...no, I **demand** better police work than this out of you two. Shape up quick or both of you can start looking for another job."

Wilbert had heard about all that he was going to take and took a step toward the marshal. Justin held out his arm to restrain his friend. "Come on," Justin commented. "Our shift is over and we both could use some fresh air." Both deputies left the office in total disgust. As they departed from the horse barn, another group of robbery victims approached. Justin informed them that the marshal was inside and would be happy to take their complaints.After walking a few paces, both deputies looked at each other and burst out laughing. "I hope the Merrell brothers enjoy their quiet day," Wilbert remarked.

Seeing the group of angry citizens approaching, Marshal Merrell directed his deputy brother to make out their robbery reports. He scooped up last night's break-in reports and went outside to find a peaceful shady spot to read them. *This is not how I expected this job to be*, he thought. One man's report stated that the thieves had entered his bedroom while he lay sleeping, and that he always hung his trousers on the bed post, but by morning they were gone. He found the trousers laying on the kitchen floor with the pockets turned inside out and his coin purse, containing $16.40, was gone. Another said that two masked men entered their home, having crawled through a window, and held his family at gunpoint until all jewelry and money were surrendered. The bandits then tied up the family and escaped. The complaints went on and on. Marshal Merrell, quit reading and began to wonder about all of this. What had that night, deputy said, he wondered? *It's like criminals knew we were not patrolling and took advantage of it.* Scooping up the reports, Marshal Merrell went back into the office to face the difficult tasks that lay before him and his brother today.

~~~~~~~~~~~~~~~~~~~~~

The man known only as Kruger smiled deeply as he was briefed by Smiley Lewis on last evening's take. His break-in gangs had done very well, and all with the knowledge that the night, deputies would be elsewhere and could not interfere. The tip that the new deputy, Cecil Merrell, had provided, proved invaluable. Some sort of "thank you" now seemed appropriate. Not only were homes entered last night, but several local businesses were broken into and valuable weapons, tools, and money stolen. Kruger knew well enough not to try to pawn any of the stolen materials around town. No, everything was hidden away in a safe place, and would be eventually taken to another town for resale.

~~~~~~~~~~~~~~~~~~~~~

'Squire Jones had heard of a large number of break-ins last night, and was very surprised he had none of the usual drunks, loose women, or petty theft crimes to preside over that day. Going outside to his rear storage shed, he grabbed up his fishing pole, dug some earth worms and headed to the river for a nice relaxing day of fishing. Upon arriving at a good fishing location, 'Squire Jones noticed lots of dead fish floating on the river bank. When he cast his baited line into the river, he noticed a thin scum laying on the top of the water. He mentioned the substance to another fisherman across the river and was told the stuff was being discharged into the river by the Tin Plate factory.

~~~~~~~~~~~~~~~~~~~~~

With all of the town's commotion, most of it's people had not noticed the new marshal's spiffy new deluxe uniform with large brass buttons. One man who did stated that he thought the uniform looked more like that of a Civil War general than a marshal of a small town. Soon the nickname "Brass Buttons" was used in mentioning the new marshal. If Marshal Merrell thought the worst part of his day was behind him, he was sadly mistaken, as a group of laughing townsmen brought in the afternoon Gas City Journal paper for him to read. The headlines read:

> **A Ghost on Wheels-** *This morning, Deputy Marshal Wilbert Vance had a wonderful story to share with a few friends. The night before, between the hours of midnight and 1 a.m., he was startled to see a white figure on a bicycle gliding along Main Street. The figure appeared so unearthly that Deputy Vance's heart almost ceased to beat for a time. When directly opposite the officer, the figure waved it's long arms and chuckled a fiendish laugh, and then, turning*
~~~~~~~~~~~~~~~~~~~~~

quickly, guided around the corner to Grant Street. The wheels of the bicycle seemed to emit sparks of fire from the stone pavement. The officer does not deny that he was startled by the spectrum, and he soon gave chase to the moving phantom. This time he saw it's face, and he swears that it looked like the face of the dead. He attempted to block it's flight, but with a "hellish" laugh, it passed him like a streak.

The officer had not chased a ghost before, but had decided to arrest it if he could. He gave chase and saw the ghost and it's bicycle disappear in the lumber yard south of town. A young man here in town is the owner of a bicycle and a sheet, and what the deputy doesn't realize about the ghost is not worth mentioning here. Boo! - Editor

An angry Marshal Timothy Merrell wadded up the newspaper and threw it into the trash while the assembled men laughed at the new marshal's obvious discomfort.

~~~~~~~~~~~~~~~~~~~~

"Here comes Brass Buttons' now, get ready," a voice shouted next to the window inside the barbershop. The newspaper story of the night deputy chasing the ghost riding
~~~~~~~~~~~~~~~~~~~~

a bicycle through town had become the talk of, or more like, the laughing stock of the town. One of the patrons had obtained an extra barber's cloth from the barber, placed it over his head and stepped outside making ghostly howls. Marshal Merrell was not amused and made a quick detour, much to the wild laughter he heard emitting from the barbershop. *Maybe I should have just stayed in Fort Wayne*, he thought.

Chapter 24

Chief Deputy Marshal Cecil Merrell returned to his room in the Mississinewa Hotel when he noticed an envelope had been slid under his door. Stooping down, he picked it up he opened it and found a ten dollar bill inside. There was no name or address on the envelope. He didn't need a name to know where the money had come from. Pleased with the reward for his services, Merrell placed the bill inside his near empty wallet. What Councilman Davidson had told them on the day they arrived was certainly true. There was money to be made in this town.

~~~~~~~~~~~~~~~~~~~~~

The following morning Justin Blake decided to walk over to the tiny post office on Main Street once he noticed the bicycle of Postmaster Harris was leaning against the building, signaling he was open for business. Already a small crowd of people were beginning to line up to see if
~~~~~~~~~~~~~~~~~~~~~

they had any mail. Quite soon Justin's name was called and an envelope was handed to him. He recognized his mother's handwriting and was walking along fully engrossed in news from back home, when a voice spoke to him, "Deputy Marshal Justin Blake, I would like to introduce my brother Reverend Charles Weir." Justin quickly recognized the voice as coming from Mrs. Stokes and, composing his thoughts, shook hands with the stranger. "Charlie is starting a sabbatical after working tirelessly the last year in helping to relocate Taylor University from Fort Wayne to Upland. Why don't you come over for lunch Sunday after church so you two can get to know each other?"

The older brother spoke up, "I would like that, deputy. I'm still trying to meet all of Edith's and Clarence's friends."

Looking over into the face of a nodding Mrs. Stokes, Justin agreed to drop over after church services. "You know you're always welcome in our home anytime, son."

~~~~~~~~~~~~~~~~~~~~

While out on his daily walk around town, Chief Deputy Cecil Merrell was stopped by a young man. "Officer, I want to surrender to you." This was a new experience for Merrell, a criminal who walks up and offers to surrender.

"What's this all about?" he asked the stranger.
~~~~~~~~~~~~~~~~~~~~

"Well, sir, I am guilty of a robbery last fall and I want to make amends for my crime. I robbed a Hebrew peddler in Kokomo. I heard him bragging about how good business was, and made plans to rob him. The peddler had a man employed to take him to Peru, so I made up a dummy and stood it near the road where they would be traveling. I ,also, placed a fake gun in the hand of the dummy. As they approached, I jumped out and robbed both men. All I got was this five dollar gold piece and a cheap watch. Here they are sir," the man said as he handed both items over to Merrell. "I thought that his name might be on the watch so I could return it myself, but I can't read the Hebrew writing engraved on the lid."

"Who have you told about this?" the chief deputy asked.

"Nobody knows. I am deeply ashamed of my behavior, and I am ready to pay for my transgressions."

"I'll see that these are returned to the Kokomo police. Maybe they can find the peddler or will have written knowledge of who he was, or find someone who can read Hebrew. As for you, leave this town at once. You have learned your lesson that crime doesn't pay. Go and say nothing of this to anyone." The young man was very happy not to find himself locked up for his crime, and thanked the deputy over and over for his generosity. After the young man was gone, Chief Deputy Cecil Merrell shook his head in amazement, and pocketed the easy money and gold watch for himself.

Wilbert Vance was embarrassed beyond words by the newspaper story. He had only mentioned what had happened with the bicycle to a couple of friends, but had no idea that somehow the story would be picked up and printed. That reporter Alvin Jensen clearly had something out for him, or must have something out for the marshal's office. As a result, Wilbert spent most of the day holed up inside his room which he had recently changed to Ma Richards Boarding House, the same as Justin. The worst part of this terrible day would be facing the new marshal and his brother. He might even get fired over the embarrassment he had brought on himself and his occupation. Tapping on Justin's door, Wilbert found that his friend had already left. *Guess I don't blame him for not wanting to be seen with me*, he thought as he walked to work.

When Wilbert entered the fire barn office he saw that Justin and Zeke were already there, and no Merrell brothers were present to report to. That was good, no actually that was very good since Wilbert might come to regret anything he might say tonight in anger. Justin was the first to speak, "The message on the bulletin board says we are to resume our normal patrols. I had a little talk with our reporter friend, Jensen. Since the community enjoyed the early Halloween story they ran, he's planning on another ghost story that doesn't involve us, thank goodness." Zeke, who could not read but only heard others speak of the story involving

Wilbert, spoke up, "Say, did he say what ghost story he was runnin' soon?" Thinking back on the conversation, Justin replied, "Yes, something about a real haunted house two miles out of town, or something like that. Going to run it day after tomorrow. Why do you ask?"

Slapping himself on his own leg and laughing, Zeke replied, "I know of that ghost story myself. Heard friends of mine tellin' it long ago. Seems four of dem when they were younguns' heard the old folks a tellin' bout it. One night they took a wagon out ta the Timpson House, northeast of town ta visit it after dark. That was once a fine little farmhouse but wasn't lived in for some spell. They planned to rush any ghost they saw and capture it for folks ta see."

"They hitched the wagon ta a tree on the corner of the road by the path a leading ta the house. They then hid in the tall weeds a growin' all around the old empty house. After waitin' near an hour, they was fixin' ta give up when they heard an unearthly scream and groanin' ah comin' from inside. Then they heard a woman weepin' and chains rattlin' and they skedaddled it right back ta town. Folks say the people who lived there had a worthless son, Adam by name. He decided ta get the money his momma possessed and hid away, as she had no trust in banks. He put her in the cellar and chained her ta the wall ta make her tell where it was hid. She finally broke down and told where it was hidden, but he left her chained and ran off with the money. Neighbors found her dead long after, and farmers say her ghost still screams and weeps ta this day at about midnight."

Justin and Wilbert just couldn't help but to laugh at Zeke's story. He sure knew a mess of them to tell. "We better start making our patrols. We'll see you, Zeke. Say hello to Marshal Brewster for us." Stepping outside, a young man came running up to them.

"Sir, I'm the one who spoke with the other deputy earlier. I just wanted to say thanks again and that I'll be leaving town in the morning, as he told me to."

Justin explained that they had just come on duty and didn't know anything about it, so the young man told them the entire story and that the deputy would send the five dollars in gold and the Hebrew watch to Kokomo. After the youth had left, both deputies stepped back inside to read more about what transpired inside the pass-on book, but discovered that nothing at all was documented by the Chief Deputy. Very strange.

~~~~~~~~~~~~~~~~~~~~~~

Larson's Hardware store was a popular business along Main Street. While not the only hardware in town, Jeb had a solid reputation among the townsfolk as an honest hardworking businessman who was known for going the extra mile in providing customer satisfaction. His store
~~~~~~~~~~~~~~~~~~~~~~

carried the latest home gadgets; kitchen utensils, clothing, weapons, knives, and ammunition. If it existed, Jeb either had it or could get it for you. He had also been planning a big birthday surprise for his soon-to-be sixteen year old son, Jeremiah. Jerry, as he is better known, worked without payment after school to help his father in the store, and seems to have an actual attachment to it's operation. Next week will be his birthday, and on that special occasion Larson's Hardware will officially become Larson and Son Hardware. The new sign was being painted today and will be installed at the business on his birthday. Jeb could only imagine the joy and happiness it will bring for years to come. "Jerry, run on home now and tell your mother I'll be closing up and will be home in fifteen minutes. Business is slow, and I'm hungry." With that information, the young boy raced out of the doorway towards home. Turning off the gas lighting fixtures, Jeb walked up to the front door to flip over the window's "we are open" sign to the "sorry, we are closed" sign just as the bullet shattered the glass and penetrated his heart, exiting his back. Jeb Larson was dead before his body hit the floor.

The night deputies had a busy night, already arresting two drunks who started a bar fight and a man who seemed very happy to keep firing his revolver into the ceiling of the Happy Hollow Saloon, claiming he was shooting flies. All prisoners had been made to walk the distance to the awaiting jail cell, thinking the walk may sober them up. Just as Wilbert had secured the cell, word of the shooting reached them. Why would anyone shoot and kill Jeb Larson?

A large crowd of people were assembled outside of the hardware store, attempting to have a look at the body. "Move along now, go home," Justin told them as he and Wilbert arrived at the crime scene. Doctor Baxter arrived but he quickly realized that Larson was beyond hope. The body had been covered by a shop apron that the Doc found hanging on a wall hook by the counter. "Shot straight through the heart, deputy. Never knew what hit him." Justin could see that the bullet exited through his back, so his eyes scanned the rear wall until he found what he was looking for. Removing his pocketknife, Justin removed the bullet buried deep into the wall, looked at it then placed it inside his coat pocket. He then walked over to the counter cash register and pushed the no sale button. The money drawer opened to reveal a drawer full of cash and coins. He found a paper bag and placed the drawer's contents inside. "Some of you men, come inside and find some boards and nails to cover the shattered glass door." There seemed to be a slight hesitance before two men took it upon themselves to enter the crime scene to fix the door. Reaching into the dead man's pocket, Justin removed the door key so the store could be locked up when the final examination was made. "Wilbert, I think you should fetch the marshal," Justin said. Wilbert quickly agreed and left for the Mississinewa Hotel.

"Has someone gone to fetch Mrs. Larson?" he asked the outside crowd. Doc Baxter stood up and informed the deputies the body needed to be carried over to his office for a closer examination. Hearing that, four men volunteered to do it. "Let's get it moved before his wife arrives. We wouldn't want her to see this," one of the men spoke. "Jeb was a fine fellow. I hope they hang the dirty..., well, you know what I'm saying." Stepping outside to speak with the crowd, Justin asked if anybody saw or heard anything. Some thought they may have heard a muffled shot coming from the north. "Anybody see any strangers in town or anyone running away?" The answer was "no", as the group began to dissipate. Soon the entire town was buzzing with news of the murder.

Marshal Merrell and his brother quickly arrived, and informed Justin that he and Deputy Vance were relieved and that the case was now in their hands. Justin handed the key for the shop to the marshal and walked out still holding the bag of money. He would deliver it into the hands of the family. He assumed correctly that they would assemble in the waiting room at Doctor Baxter's. "Come on Wilbert, let's go bust a few more drunks for the marshal."

The next day was a busy one for 'Squire Jones and his civil court. Three intoxicated men fined five dollars each, and two days in jail. One charge was for discharging a weapon within city limits was fined five dollars with time served. Another was charged for allowing his mule to wander unattended around town, fined two dollars. A youth was fined one dollar for being out with older friends after curfew, and he was turned over to a waiting father and his hickory switch. After the completion of court, 'Squire Jones asked for an update on the killing. Marshal Merrell had little to offer and seemed stumped for a cause. The victim had no known enemies, had not been in any altercations recently, and certainly did not gamble or owe money. He was a much respected family man, and now a great loss to his friends and family.

~~~~~~~~~~~~~~~~~~~~

Upon finishing their night shift and logging everything in the pass-on book, Justin and Wilbert decided to eat a little breakfast at the Pan Handle Restaurant before turning in. Between bites of food, both discussed the tragic events that had occurred. It was then that Justin remembered the bullet he pulled out of the wall and placed inside his pocket. "Maybe I will visit Marshal Brewster first before I turn in. This bullet may mean something to him. I'll see you this evening." With that, Justin started off toward Brewster's house, where he noticed Zeke and the marshal sitting outside on the front
~~~~~~~~~~~~~~~~~~~~

porch. "You should be in bed rather than checking up on an old useless cripple," Brewster said to him. "Actually I am in need of your professional assistance," Justin stated, as he produced the bullet from his pocket.

"Zeke told me what happened. Terrible. Everyone liked Jeb Larson. What a terrible thing to happen. Has your new marshal solved the case yet?" Brewster said, with a smirk to his tone.

"Take a look at this, and tell me if you know what it is? I pulled it out of the wall after it passed through Mr. Larson."

Holding it in his hand, the ex-marshal studied it, "It's a .50 caliber hexagon bullet fired from an old .451 hexagon barrel Whitworth rifle. I haven't seen one of these in a long, long time. English made weapon and ran through the blockade during the war, to be used by Confederate sharpshooters. The Whitworth is a heavy beast but can knock a man out of the saddle at a thousand yards. Maybe even further. See here, the ends still show the hexagon shape of the bullet."

"So this is a powder rifle?" Justin asked.

"Yes, takes about 100 grains of black powder. A very lethal weapon and not at all common. If your killer uses this, he can pick off any law enforcement officer long before he could return fire," Brewster replied as he handed it back to Justin. "What does your new marshal have to say about it?" Justin smiled as he informed them that he had *forgotten* to give it to him when he was removed from the case last night.

Turning to Zeke, Brewster asked him, “You have any dealings with this rifle during the war?”

Zeke only shook his head no, “Can’t say I have, but heard of them though. Say, maybe the killer is one of the veterans out at the Old Soldiers Home, still fightin’ the war in his mind?”

Brewster spoke next, “I really doubt it’s one of those boys. The Home won’t allow them to keep firearms there, but I guess one could be stashed away somewhere else for use. I’m guessing it could belong to almost anyone. These were made to either be supported on a tree limb, or mounted upon some sort of stand rather than to hold and fire. From what we all know now, even a woman is capable of doing this.” As soon as he said it, Brewster cringed and wished he could take that back. Justin made like he didn’t hear it, knowing that it was not said to hurt him.

“Well, I guess I better take this back to the office before I turn in. Thanks again for all of your help.”

Brewster seemed in a much better mood by now, “Anytime I can help, feel free to drop by.”

Walking into the office, Justin tossed the bullet onto the desk of Marshal Merrell and left without saying a word to either man. Let them figure it out.

The funeral of Jeb Larson took place that Friday afternoon. Almost everyone who knew him or did business with him was in attendance. Justin had heard that the hardware store would open for business the following Monday morning, and that Mrs. Larson would be assisting her son in it's daily operation. It took real guts to do that, and Justin was positive the Larson Hardware would have a solid clientele from now on. Even the killer of Jeb Larson planned to continue to do business there.

Friday and Saturday evenings proved busy, with many of the same types of arrests. Justin found himself looking forward to having lunch tomorrow at the Stokes' home as a welcome relief. He had not stepped inside their home since Samantha lived there. Justin found himself thinking about Mrs. Stokes' older brother, Charles Weir. With him being a reverend, it seemed a natural fit for the Stokes family. Anyway, it would be good to get away from all of the hustle and bustle, and enjoy a great home-cooked meal for a change, and maybe a story or two.

~~~~~~~~~~~~~~~~~~~~~
~~~~~~~~~~~~~~~~~~~~~

Chapter 25

Since he was invited to have lunch with the Stokes family, Justin felt he probably should attend their church services at the temporarily shared building on Main Street. Arriving late, he took a seat on the rear pew and heard the Reverend Stokes introduce his brother-in-law, the Reverend Charles Weir to the congregation. Stepping up to the small podium, Reverend Weir said, "I want to thank all of you for allowing me a few minutes this morning to brief you on our important work at Taylor University in Upland, only 7 miles from your fair city. As many of you already know, our institution was originally established in Fort Wayne, Indiana in 1846 as Fort Wayne Female College. By 1850 men were admitted and it's name was then changed to Fort Wayne College. Then only four years ago we acquired the former facilities of a nearby medical college and voted to change our name once again to Taylor University to honor Bishop William Taylor."

"It was through what some would say a chance encounter, while I believe it was God's will, that the President of the

College, Mr. Thaddeus Reade, met with civic-minded people in Upland. They laid the groundwork for our permanent relocation to Upland. We settled upon the property then owned by the Upland Land Company. Since then, we have provided only the best in Christian education to our youth. One day we hope to be recognized as one of the leading Evangelical colleges in the nation. I played only a small role in this affair, but I could not have done so without the full love and support of my family. I would now like to take this opportunity to introduce you to my lovely wife, Lois, and our daughter, Marsha. Please stand ladies." A warm round of applause emitted from the congregation, but Justin didn't actually hear it. His eyes were fixed upon the lovely Miss Marsha Weir.

She was gentle in appearance, standing with poise and dignity. She had sparkling blue eyes and long blond hair, which was tucked inside a simple green bonnet. Justin could not help but recognize a family resemblance between the girl he loved and lost, and her young cousin, Marsha. He took her to be around 25 years of age, and hoped that his staring went unnoticed by Reverend and Mrs. Stokes. Hesitation began to formulate in Justin's mind that perhaps he should make excuses and not attend the family dinner after all. Memories of Samantha swept over him like a tidal wave... memories he had tried so hard to put behind him. He had tried to move on with his life. No, he thought, it would hurt the feelings of the

Stokes not to attend after being invited by them. By the time Justin had gotten all of this sorted out, the church service was over. As members were in the process of leaving, the voice of Mrs. Stokes called out to him, "Justin, a moment, please. I would like to introduce my sister-in-law, Lois Weir, and my niece, Marsha."

Justin felt rather awkward, but managed to pull himself together. "Good morning, ladies. A pleasure to meet you both." When Marsha's eyes met his, Justin felt like a lightning bolt had passed through his body. "Justin is our town's deputy marshal and a friend of our family," Mrs. Stokes mentioned. "Will you ride with us in our carriage, deputy?" Mrs. Weir asked of him. "Thank you," he replied, "But I have my horse tied up on the side and will follow you home." As everyone left the church, Justin and his horse, Spunky, rode a short distance behind the carriage, and once he thought he saw the lovely Miss Marsha glance his way. Or was to simply his imagination?

Arriving at the house, the men entered the library while the ladies went to work in the preparation of the meal. "So how do you like police work, Deputy Blake?" asked the Reverend Weir.

"Please call me Justin, sir. I find I like it very much but would prefer working days rather than night shift. The job does allow me to meet all kinds of people, most of whom are good."

Chuckling, the Reverend said, “In a way, both Clarence and myself are policemen for the Lord. You fight the Devil’s work on the street, while we fight the Devil himself.” After a little more small talk, Mrs. Weir appeared before them to say that everything was ready. The meal, as usual, was wonderful and reminded Justin of his own mother’s cooking. Little table talk occurred, with most of it directed as casual questions to Justin. Miss Marsha said nothing, and made no eye contact with him as she ate in silence. To liven things up a bit, Mrs. Stokes informed Justin that she and her husband had attended a very interesting lecture last month at Taylor University, thanks to her brother’s suggestion. “I think you may remember me telling you of our family’s involvement in the Abolitionist movement?” Justin nodded at the memory as she continued.

“The speaker was a seventy year old Negro man by the name of Daniel Irish. He had been searching for his family since 1862, and had only recently found his children living in Franklin, Indiana, which is south of here. He had been a member of the Society of Friends in Richmond, which was an underground Abolitionist organization. Daniel had learned that several free Negros in Ohio had been captured and sent south into slavery. He was determined to find them and return them to freedom, so he bid his wife and children goodbye in 1857 and set out on his dangerous rescue mission.

He almost succeeded, but was betrayed by a false friend and imprisoned for aiding slaves to escape."

"There he laid in prison, until he was freed in 1862 by Union soldiers. He then returned to Richmond in search of his own family but discovered they were gone. In time, Daniel joined the Union army and served as a private until the end of the war. Daniel continued his search but was unable to obtain any leads on their whereabouts."

"In 1860, not having heard from her husband in three years, she had to consider him dead and remarried, moving to Franklin, Indiana. Within a few years, she died but her grown children were determined to find out what had happened to their father so they hired an attorney to look into the matter. After contacting Daniel's family members, the lawyer was soon able to locate the missing man. Learning of the whereabouts of his grown children, Daniel Irish moved to Franklin to be near them. After a separation of thirty-six years, they were finally reunited and will spend the rest of his life telling his life's story. I cried as he told it to the audience. Poor fellow"

Justin was moved by the story. "One cannot help but feel sorry for that poor man and his entire family. At least he is with his children again, but at his advanced age probably not for long." Justin thanked all of the ladies for the invitation to dine with them, and was preparing to excuse himself and return home to the boarding house, when Mrs. Stokes spoke again, “Marsha, why don’t you and Justin take a little walk and get to know each other, we can clean up here without any assistance.” Glancing into the face of Miss Marsha, Justin noticed a slight blushing of her cheeks and wondered if she would prefer to remain behind with the family. He was ready to say something, to give the young lady a polite way of declining, when she said she would be happy to do so, and rose from her seat. “Have a nice walk,” her father cheerfully said, as the couple walked towards the door.

They had walked to the edge of the property when Marsha said, “Do I remind you of her?” The question startled Justin somewhat, but after only a bit of an awkward pause, replied, “Yes, in a way you do.” Coming to a complete stop, she looked straight into his eyes.

“I am not my cousin, Samantha. I am a completely different person with different likes and dislikes than she had. I heard mother speaking privately with my aunt about you and your personal involvement with my cousin. While you may take this as bold advice coming from a young lady you have only just met today, I feel I should encourage you to drive away whatever guilt you feel deep inside and move on with your life.”

Her words seemed to resonate deep within his soul as he pondered her advice. “My cousin was a wonderful young woman until the Devil obtained his control over her mind. That was not your fault, and in a way, it was also not her fault.

There is evil in this world, but we cannot allow ourselves to give in to it. I have a friend who owns a bicycle. He says that when someone falls off of the bicycle, it's best to get back on and overcome their natural fear of trying again. I hope you will not think I am too bold in saying these words to you, but my aunt and uncle feel nothing but the deepest affection for you. They pray that you will learn to forgive yourself." *Forgive me? Maybe that's what I needed to hear to release the pain inside,* he pondered.

"I appreciate your advice," he told her, as they began to walk again. "I know it is time for me to move on. Thank you for your kind and sincere advice, Miss Weir."

"My name is Marsha, Justin. Please consider me a friend, but not her replacement. I am a completely different young lady." With that, Justin felt that the huge rock he carried on his shoulders had slipped away and was finally gone. It was, indeed, time to move on. Changing the subject, she then asked him if Gas City was his original home.

"No, I moved here from Cleveland, Ohio a little over a year ago. I was a dockworker, loading and unloading cargo onto the Great Lake cargo ships. And what about you, are you originally from Fort Wayne?"

"Yes," she replied. "It's a nice town with much to do, but I am enjoying Upland now and consider it my home. I work as the college librarian and, also, help new students register for their classes. Does a working girl shock you, Mr. Deputy Marshal?"

Justin laughed, "The world is changing every day. It sounds like you work in a safe and professional environment, being around books and education every day." With a coy smile on her face, she also informed him that she considered herself a suffragette.

"I feel women should have the right to vote the same as any man, maybe even run for President one day." She seemed to wait for his argument but none came her way.

Justin grinned, "Yes, the world is changing every day." With that the couple returned to the house and Justin said his goodbyes to the family. It had proven to be a wonderful day after all.

~~~~~~~~~~~~~~~~~~~~~~

Marshal "Brass Buttons" Merrell was no closer to solving the murder of Jeb Larson than the day it happened, despite the wild claims he made to reporter Alvin Jensen and Councilman Davidson that an arrest was imminent. He and his chief deputy brother had taken the bullet fragment, that Deputy Blake had recovered, all over town to show it to many of the shop owners. Nobody had seen one like it before, but they were positive that it was fired from a black powder rifle of unknown type. "What if you showed it to
~~~~~~~~~~~~~~~~~~~~~~

the retired marshal here in town. Maybe he might help us?" Brother Cecil suggested.

Marshall Merrell adamantly refused. "I saw Mayor Huffman this morning, and he was complaining about all the loose horses and mules wandering around town unattended at night. I'll write up instructions for our boys tonight to concentrate on rounding these animals up so their owners will be fined. City ordinances must be enforced." Standing up from his desk, Marshal Merrell told his brother he was going down to Matthew Brooks barbershop for a haircut and would be back soon.

The gears began to turn within the mind of Chief Deputy Cecil Merrell. Maybe another opportunity had presented itself. Cecil felt it was time to leave the office and walk around town to consider the matter. Across the street, a movement caught his eye. It was old Tommy Two-Fingers and he was drunk again. Every town had at least one man who qualified as the town drunk, and old Tommy was Gas City's entry. He developed the nickname Two-Fingers for obvious reasons, as his left hand only contained the large middle finger and part of a thumb. Nobody was quite sure if this was a war wound or a birth defect, as Tommy showed up one day in town and remained intoxicated almost all of the time. Most folks gave Tommy a few handouts or allowed him to work a little now and then and, with a few coins in his possession, he went straight to any saloon that would have him. Simply by buying a beer, Tommy would be allowed to eat at the free lunch counter. That was pretty much Tommy's life, other than all the nights he slept his stupor off in jail. 'Squire Jones had long ago given up on sentencing Tommy, as the poor old man got the shakes very badly when he was deprived of his beer.

An idea quickly entered the mind of the chief deputy. "Tommy, come over here, now!" he told the old drunk. Tommy slowly staggered over to the other side of the street.

"You gonna arrest me Mr. Policeman?" the old man asked.

"Tommy, how would you like to make an easy ten cents today?" Tommy's blurred eyes lit up in excitement. Ten cents would buy two beers and some free lunch. "Yea, what do you need, mister?" was his reply.

Looking about to see that the few people on the street were not watching them, the deputy told Tommy to step inside the office quietly. Cecil Merrell then sat down at the desk and wrote out a short note and sealed it in an envelope. He wrote a name on the front and handed it to Tommy. "Here, take this and give it to the bartender at the White Dog Saloon." Tommy took the envelope but could not quite make out the name since he was still seeing double. He shoved it into his pocket.

"Say, what about my ten cents you promised?" Reaching into his pocket, he handed a dime to the old drunk. Tommy put the dime in his pocket and staggered out of the office. No one would think anything about seeing Tommy leaving the marshal's office and staggering towards a bar. Folks had pretty much come to expect that of Tommy.

It took a bit of time before Tommy arrived at the White Dog Saloon, as walking in a straight line was normally beyond his ability. Entering the early morning saloon, Tommy shouted out, "Give me a beer!" Shaking his head no, the bartender demanded to see his nickel first. Tommy slowly searched all of his pockets until he located the dime and laid it and the envelope on the bar. "What's this?" the bartender asked as he picked it up and read the name written on the outside of the envelope.

"Feller gave me a dime to bring it to you," Tommy said as he snatched the beer from the counter and drank the entire contents down. "Give me my second one," he shouted. Without saying a word, the bartender walked with envelope in hand and knocked on the office door of Kruger. "Message for you, sir," he stated and remained in the boss's office awaiting any response. Reading the short note brought a rare smile to the face of Kruger.

"How did you get this?" he asked the bartender.

"Old Tommy Two-Fingers brought it in." *Of course, Kruger thought. The perfect carrier pigeon.* "Give him two bits worth of free beer and send him away before our noon crowd arrives. Nobody wants to eat at the free lunch spread after him anyhow. Filthy drunken pig." Returning to his desk, Kruger started making his evening plans. "Go get Smiley Lewis," he instructed one of his men.

~~~~~~~~~~~~~~~~~~~~~~

Marshal Merrell was happy to be finished with his haircut and out of that place. All people did was ask him nosy questions. "Did he know who killed the hardware store owner?" "What leads did he have?" More and more questions. He finally had to tell them, "Look, you'll know something when I am ready to tell you something." With that, all conversation stopped and the barber then cut his hair in total silence. Stepping outside, Marshal Merrell's arm was suddenly grabbed by an excited young man, "Fight, Marshal, you gotta break up the fight." Looking out into the street, he could see two men fistfighting and rolling around on the dirt street, punching away at each other in front of a wagon full of bricks. The marshal succeeded in separating the two brawling men. "What's going on here?" he demanded to know.

"He's cutting our wages," the angry driver of the brick wagon yelled. The job boss, who represented the two actual contractors, was sporting two black eyes. He responded, "Business is business. We can find cheaper help out of town to complete the street brick laying project."
~~~~~~~~~~~~~~~~~~~~~~

"Like the blazes you will! Our boys will go on strike and shut you down for good." That evening the bricklayers and teamsters agreed to walk off the job and demanded a fifteen cent per day increase. All work on the street bricking project came to a halt. Management made plans to bring in cheaper labor to finish the project.

~~~~~~~~~~~~~~~~~~~~~~

A few of the more interesting legal cases that were brought before 'Squire Jones that day that would appear in tomorrow's edition of the Journal were the following:

(1) The traveling Wagner Opera Company who have been conducting performances at the Lovett Opera House in town, attempted to leave without paying their $103 bill at the Mississinewa Hotel. Once 'Squire Jones threatened to sell the company's assets, the money for the hotel's bill was produced.

(2) Schmidt's Saloon on South H Street was fined twenty-five dollars for selling intoxicating liquor on a Sunday.

(3) Sammy Roll, married twice and never divorced, was preparing to marry again- fined $50 with sixty
~~~~~~~~~~~~~~~~~~~~~~

days in county jail. The second wife was given an annulment and she quietly left town this morning.

Inside the marshal's office, Deputy's Blake and Vance found their written instructions for the night shift. They were directed to round up all loose horses, mules, and whatever animals were found roaming the streets at night unattended. All such animals were to be placed in the stray pen and owners of said animals would be brought before 'Squire Jones for fines. This action was to be their priority tonight. "You've got to be kidding," Wilbert Vance said while shaking his head.

Justin totally agreed, "I hope there isn't another major crime wave tonight, as we chase loose animals around the city." Said in jest, the men had no idea that these words might prove very true.

By five a.m. they had located and penned ten stray horses, mules, and even some cattle found roaming around. Wilbert had learned the hard way that a mule will only go in the direction it wants to go, and he spent a great deal of the night trying to encourage the beast to see things his way. "I'm tired, let's put on a pot of coffee and finish up our entries in the pass-on book," Justin suggested. As they approached the fire-barn, a crowd of angry citizens awaited their arrival. "Oh no, not again!" exclaimed Wilbert. They were still taking break-in reports when the Merrell brothers arrived at seven to relieve them. The talk around town wasn't good, that the marshal had his men rounding up stray animals all night as the city experienced an epidemic of break-ins. The complaints of a few animal owners were nothing compared to the fury unleashed upon the Merrell brothers by the citizens of the town who demanded action in halting this reign of terror.

Returning to his room in the Mississinewa Hotel, an exhausted Chief Deputy Cecil Merrell was pleased to find an envelope underneath his doorway. Again there was no signature or letter, only a crisp new ten dollar bill which Merrell added to his billfold before lying down to help ease his pounding headache. The money was just the remedy the doctor had ordered.

Chapter 26

It seemed that everyone liked to hear about a juicy sex scandal, as long as it didn't involve them or their own family members. Boy, or boy, was there a juicy one. Originally whispered about in bars and back rooms, the subject was now the talk of the town. Since it involved prominent members of the local community, well, all the better gossip many would say. The man and woman involved had broadcast their guilt to everyone within hearing distance. The scandal involved Mrs. Virginia Howell and her husband, James. Mr. Howell was a well-known and respected loan officer at the First National Bank here in town, with a beautifully decorated home on East Main Street. Until recently, Mrs. Howell had been a solid member of society and active in many local civic and church affairs. The couple had been married twelve years, and their union had produced a nine year old daughter and a seven year old son. In the eyes of the community, the Howells were the example of the perfect couple. All that changed when Virginia Howell met Franklin Ernest.

From what Mrs. Howell had told those still speaking to her, she had been very lonely in her marriage and, at age forty-two, felt that her youth and good looks were quickly passing by. How the lovers met is not known, but affairs of the heart, or more likely affairs of the flesh, quickly escalated from minor flirtation to an adulterous relationship. It was whispered that Mr. Howell was tipped off by a neighbor that something was amiss, and arrived home early before the children returned from school. It was said that Mr. Howell entered his bedroom during the act, and seething with anger and rage, threatened to shoot his wife's lover then and there, before sanity returned and good judgment prevailed. At that point, Mrs. Howell was told to pack her bags and depart his home at once. She then moved in with her new boyfriend, openly, in a ramshackle house near the railroad tracks. It was said that Mr. Howell sat on the edge of the bed with a pistol in hand contemplating taking his own life due to the disgrace inflicted upon him. His sister, who lived nearby, prevailed in reminding him that he must live for the sake of his children. She packed the clothing of his children, and when they returned home from school, informed them that they would be spending a few weeks living with her. Fortunately, the small children did not fully understand the situation, and happily departed with their aunt. They were still curious about the whereabouts of their mother.

Most of this information would not have become public knowledge except that Franklin Ernest, a day worker at Thompsons Green and Amber Bottling Company, liked to talk over a few beers down at the White Dog Saloon. Such was the tragic situation that had torn a family apart, and set many busybody tongues a wagging. Somehow, Mr. Howell had managed to pull himself together, at least outwardly, and returned to work at the First National Bank. He had already contacted a lawyer for a legal separation, and, ultimately, a divorce on grounds of adultery. He hoped and prayed that his children might be spared the image of their mother with that terrible man. If only they had the decency to move out of town.

Across town next to the railroad tracks, a tired and unhappy Virginia Howell scrubbed the Monday wash outside in the heat of the day. Washing, cleaning, and cooking were tasks she had not personally performed in many years as her home on Main Street. She had servants to do these physical tasks. Taking a much needed break, Virginia looked about and evaluated her new surroundings. Living in poverty was terrible, and she missed her children. The wild, exciting physical relationship she had discovered with Frank was beginning to wear thin. He was drinking almost every evening, and she was thinking now that she had made a terrible mistake in trading a good loving man, home, family, and her reputation for this. Maybe she had failed to realize that her husband was absorbed in his work and that she had not given him an opportunity to change. Maybe if they had communicated better... She had heard that he almost shot himself that night, due to the pain and disgrace she had brought upon him. Well, her choice was made and she had to live with it. *Will Frank grow tired of her and put her out on her own? He seems to have already changed. Maybe having her is not as strong as wanting her? Maybe to Frank, she was simply the forbidden fruit that has now been sampled, and ready to be discarded?* Her thoughts enveloped her.

Looking down on the tub of wet clothing, Virginia picked up a pair of Franks work pants, rung out the water by hand, and pitched them over the clothes line. As she was placing the second clothes pin in place, a bullet sliced through the center of the pants and exited through her head. Virginia Howell was dead before she hit the ground.

~~~~~~~~~~~~~~~~~~~~~

Deputy Marshal Justin Blake was already dressed for work when he was startled by a loud pounding on his door. Opening it, he saw the visitor was Zeke Miller. "Been another shootin' down by the river someplace. That's all I know fer sure," he told him.

"Thanks, Zeke, please let Wilbert know about it. I'm going there now." Since Ma Richards Boarding House wasn't
~~~~~~~~~~~~~~~~~~~~~

all that far away, Justin hurried along on foot looking about for the location, until he saw a crowd of people standing on the property. It was hard to tell just what was going on since the crowd seemed determined to get as close as possible to see what they could. Catching a glimpse of Justin, Marshal Merrell shouted for Justin to get the people to back off. "Please, folks, step back and give us some room to conduct our investigation," he encouraged. Sensing they were being told politely, rather than the harsh demands of the marshal, the crowd did back away twenty feet or so. Pulling out his pocket notebook and a pencil Justin attempted to interview any witnesses to the shooting. None had seen a shooter and only a couple actually heard a shot. "I thought it was a firecracker myself," one witness reported.

A newcomer to the group asked, "Who was shot?"

"It's that harlot, Virginia Howell. You know, the one who left her husband and kids to move in with her boyfriend," one of the women assembled offered.

Someone else replied, "Serves her right, she got what she deserves."

By now, Justin was able to clearly see the body of the dead woman underneath the clothesline. She was surrounded by both of the Merrell brothers and Doctor Baxter, who was examining the terrible wound in the center of her forehead. From the back of the crowd, Justin heard someone state that they saw the dead woman's estranged husband approaching.

The poor man had to push his way into the crime scene, and as soon as James Howell saw the remains of his wife's beautiful head, he rushed to the side and vomited. Who could blame the poor man? As soon as he composed himself and cleaned his face with his hankie, the shaken and ash white man asked the doctor, "Is she...."

"Yes, I'm afraid so, Mr. Howell. If it's any consolation to you, she never knew what hit her," the kindly doctor told him. James Howell fell to his knees, clenched fists pounding the ground, as he shouted "No! No!" He then began to cry uncontrollably and had to be removed to the sidelines by Doctor Baxter.

Marshal Merrell turned to his brother and suggested he escort the man home. "Shouldn't we lock him up first?" Cecil Merrell enquired loud enough for all to hear. "Nine times out of ten it's the husband who's behind it and, from what I hear, he sure has the motive. Let me lock him up for twenty-four hours and I'll get a confession out of him!"

Justin was appalled by the total lack of sensitivity of publicly accusing Mr. Howell accused of murdering his wife, without any proof whatsoever. Hearing himself being accused of the crime, Howell pulled himself together enough to proclaim his total innocence. "I didn't kill my wife," he pleaded. "Until two weeks ago we were a happily married couple. You got to believe me, I had nothing at all to do with it!"

"Yea, sure you didn't," shouted the sarcastic chief deputy marshal. "Tell us who you've hired to do this, and maybe the judge will go easy on you. Tell me or I'll beat the truth out of you!"

Justin by now had heard enough, "Shut up Cecil. This is not the time to go into all of that."

The Chief Deputy jumped quickly into the face of Justin Blake, "Nobody talks to me like that, you little pipsqueak. I'll pound you straight into the ground!"

Marshall Merrell leaped between the officers, telling them to stop it. "Blake, escort the prisoner... ah, I mean, husband, home. He is not to leave town. Is that understood?" Giving a weak nod in acknowledging the instructions, Justin led the weeping man away.

Looking directly at both of the Merrell brothers, Doctor Baxter told them, "You, too, should be ashamed of yourselves. That was very unprofessional conduct and you said it in front of all those people." The body was then transported to the doctor's examination room. Afterwards it was turned over to the local undertaker, who noted that business was picking up, for sure.

Instead of escorting James Howell directly home as ordered, Justin detoured to the private residence of 'Squire Jones. "Come in my friends, come in," the 'Squire offered.

"Sir, sorry to bother you but there's been another shooting, and I thought you might recommend legal counsel for this man."

"James! You? You shot someone? What the devil is going on here?" Between sobs, the entire story was told, as well as other information filled in by Justin before the 'Squire held up his hand.

"Gentlemen, I probably should not hear anymore since this case might very well end up in my court, although I probably would recuse myself, having known James and Virginia for a long time. As for legal counsel, if I were ever in need of an attorney, I would pick Hugh Williamson. He's made quite a reputation for himself as a dependable and competent lawyer. Deputy, is my friend here under arrest?"

Justin then filled the 'Squire in on what the Merrell brothers had said in front of everyone present. "Preposterous!" the 'Squire said in a loud voice. "If my friend is brought to trial, the marshal's public accusations may well have poisoned the local jury pool. Things like that spread quickly in a small town. If you are arrested James, I will push for a change of venue to Marion. Please take my friend home now, deputy, and I'll see that Mr. Williamson is notified to contact you. Good day." As it turned out, no arrest was ever made, and within days the grieving husband returned to work at the bank.

~~~~~~~~~~~~~~~~~~~~~~

The brick layers street worker's strike was in it's second day. Management remained firm in their demands that the daily payment of $1.25 for the laborers be reduced, to help cut unexpected costs. The workers, instead of feeling empowered, demanded a fifteen cent per day pay increase. Wagonloads of bricks lined the streets, abandoned just where the striking teamsters had parked them. Management then advertised in the surrounding cities that work was available at $1.15 per day for brick layers and teamsters. Several new men arrived eager to work for that pay only to find that the strike was not over, as they had been told, and all refused the work. By the end of the day, the onsite supervisor, black eyes and all, met with the two contractors of the brick laying street project at the Mississinewa Hotel to consider their options. They had clearly underestimated the will of the working men. In the end, management agreed to increase the worker's pay twelve and a half cents per day, and so the strikers returned to work. The brick laying street project, though delayed, was now expected to be completed by September.

~~~~~~~~~~~~~~~~~~~~~~

Mayor Huffman felt it was time to discuss a few legal problems with 'Squire Jones. Entering the rear of the courtroom where the 'Squire remained, when not on the bench, he approached, "A word with you, Hiram, if you can spare the time?" Setting aside the legal brief he was studying, 'Squire Jones seemed happy for the interruption. "Certainly, Mr. Mayor, anytime. What's on your mind?"

Pulling up a chair to the table, the Mayor began. "I'm having some serious doubts about the Merrell brothers being the right men for the job. So far, no arrests have been made in regards to the break-ins that have plagued our town. These two murders are very troubling. I heard that the deputy marshal all but accused poor old James Howell of killing his wife right in front of a large group of people. The entire town is talking about it. We both have known Jim for a long time, and I cannot see how he would be responsible. Anyway, I wondered what you thought about all of this."

Leaning back in his stuffed chair, 'Squire Hiram Jones assumed his judicial posture before responding, "Yes, so far it appears the Merrell's are in over their heads. The break-ins puzzle me, as they appear to be a coordinated effort. As to the murders, well... I think we may have an assassin on our hands."

Looking a little surprised, the mayor asked if he thought the two killings were connected. "Yes, probably so. Somehow, those two people may have had something in common." The mayor then informed him that a petition was being circulated around town to fire the four law enforcement officials, and he expected the topic to be brought up at tonight's city council meeting. "I'll be there to watch all the fireworks," the 'Squire jokingly told him as the mayor departed.

The headlines of the Gas City Journal said it all: **No Arrests in City Murders or Break-Ins. Marshal's Office Baffled.**

Coming in to work Justin and Wilbert saw that the newspaper was placed for them to read upon the desk top. There were also written instructions on the bulletin board to continue interviewing the neighbors of the break-in victims, to see if they knew or heard anything that might help. So far, nothing had turned up. Both deputies were pleased to see their friend, Zeke Miller, enter the office. "Been a while since I set foot in here," he told them. "Got no love fer them Merrell brothers." Even though Zeke never got around to learning reading and writing, he was well aware of the newspaper story, having heard folks talking about it all over town. "Anything good in that newspaper?" he asked. Justin picked up the folded paper and skimmed it quickly before finding something to read out loud.

"Here is something you might like, Zeke. *To the Editor of the Gas City Journal: That man who is around my house on the corner of C street knocking on the windows, had better take warning as he will be entertained with cold lead next time."* Laughing and slapping his leg, Zeke enjoyed that one. "Here is another one: *Tom Venter and a colored man named Preston Thomas, employed as a boot shine, had a one hundred yard footrace for a small purse. Pres Thomas was the easy winner."*

"Yep, I know Thomas. Fast as greased lightnin'," Zeke said.

Or this one: *"Ely Shoe Store is offering a free street car ride to Marion and back with the purchase of a pair of shoes."* Shaking his head Zeke announced he didn't need any shoes.

"Then what about this one? *The marriage of a 60-year-old widow worth twenty thousand dollars, to a 19-year-old farm hand.*

"Sounds like true love ta me," joked Zeke. Everyone got a chuckle out of that one. "Well, if you'll excuse us, we better get to work," Justin told Zeke. "Tell Marshal Brewster I'll try to drop over soon to check up on him. Good-bye."

"I also have an idea about the Hebrew watch. One of us should just ask Cecil what time it is, then take hold of the watch to see if it's the one described by the peddler." Wilbert said he would do it, and let Justin know what he discovers.

~~~~~~~~~~~~~~~~~~~~

Mayor Huffman was surprised at the large public turnout at the city council meeting. He had asked Marshal Merrell to give the council an informal briefing on the break-in situation around town, knowing that any criminal investigation into
~~~~~~~~~~~~~~~~~~~~

the two murders could not be discussed in a public meeting. Striking his gavel, he called the meeting to order and the clerk called roll and made notes of the meeting. "Thank you all for attending tonight. I do have one piece of business I wish to discuss, and it involves these gaming or token machines all over town. Some, I have been told, are now starting to pay off in coins. Gambling is illegal within the state of Indiana, pure and simple. It's time we put an end to this corruption once and for all. I now make a motion to outlaw these mechanical gaming devices, effective June 1st. That will allow the owners a month in order to be legally notified and remove these machines from within city limits."

The motion was seconded and opened for discussion. There were no strong objections, and the motion was passed unanimously. "I see the Journal's reporter present here tonight, so I'm sure he will see that the banning of these devices will appear in the newspaper. Marshal Merrell, I instruct you to see that the written notices that we will have printed up, are taken to each place of business that has these devices and posted. After June 1st, any such machine found operating within city limits is to be confiscated, with it's owner arrested and facing prosecution."

Sitting in the crowd of visitors was Kruger. The city council's actions were only a minor inconvenience, as these machines had already paid for themselves ten times over and more. Besides, he could easily sell them to store owners out of town and start raking in high profits there.

A resolution was offered by a citizen to eliminate the positions of city marshal and deputies. He had obtained the signatures of one hundred-sixteen local citizens, calling for their termination. He stressed the city could not continue to afford the expense of police officers, and that they were not effective in crime prevention or the solving of local killings. He felt that the Grant County Sheriff could handle all local police matters. Marshal Merrell sat there quietly as his red face clearly showed his anger at being called out for termination. The resolution failed to be seconded and died on the spot. Still, a fire had now been lit under the marshal's office to solve these crimes pronto.

And now it was 'Squire Jones' turn to speak. He told the council that he had gone fishing down by the river recently, and discovered a great deal of dead fish floating along the bank and a thin whitish film covering the water. Jones then expressed his view that whatever was killing the fish was being dumped there by wastewater from the local tin plate factory. With that, the river pilot of the *Helen Boyd* steam launch stood and stated he was witnessing the same thing during his river cruises. Councilman Davidson then asked "Even if so, won't it just wash itself down the river?" He then stated that these factories were the lifeblood of the community, and if they were told to stop dumping their waste water into the river, that they may simply close up and move elsewhere. Mayor Huffman then turned to the city attorney and asked if any laws were being violated. Caught off guard, the attorney didn't think there were, but would have to check on it and report back at the next scheduled council meeting.

Chapter 27

A small knock on his door brought Kruger out of his deep thoughts. "Got a minute, boss?" he was asked. "Sure, what's on your mind Smiley?" Kruger replied.

"You probably noticed that band of gypsies camped down by the river this morning. Well, sir, I recognized one of the men, a fella I've done business with a few times before. I was wondering if you might be interested in unloading some of the jewelry and silver sets the boys acquired for us. Gypsies love jewelry and know how to sell it on the sly. When you see one band, you can expect another is close by."

Kruger pondered the idea for a few seconds. "Maybe we can unload some of that fake stuff on um, too?" Shaking his head no, Smiley replied, "Boss, gypsies are experts on telling the difference. Get one mad at you and they all cum looking for you." Realizing that Smiley knew those people a lot better than he did, Kruger agreed for Smiley to make the offer and see what they had to say.

One of the reasons Justin frequented Matthew Brook's barbershop for either a shave or a haircut, was just to listen to the topics being discussed among the waiting customers. It was also a good source of information, although often he found the stories embellished a little bit. Entering the barbershop, he saw three men ahead of him and one in the chair. Picking up the back half of the Journal newspaper, Justin began reading, but always with an ear open. "Yep, a bunch of gypsies is camped down by the river. The missus already made plans on us going there tonight to get her fortune read," the man in the chair said.

Barber Brooks asked, "You don't actually believe in all that stuff, do you?" Sensing everyone was looking at him for his response, the customer quickly replied, "Not me, no sirree, but the wife thinks there's something to it, and she's only spending two-bits of the household money. I hear tell they got a little gal that's a real cutie, doing the fortune-telling. Pretty enough to stop a young man's clock." One of the waiting customers butted in, "Tim, your clock stopped ticking a long time ago." With that, everyone laughed and the conversation ended.

Having a few hours before he was to report to work, Justin thought he might just mosey on down to the river and check out the gypsies' encampment. Thinking back, he remembered as a youngster being taken to a county fair outside of Cleveland by his parents. The gypsies stood out in his memory due to their colorful clothing, and that his own mother had her fortune read. He remembered asking her what the gypsy woman said, but his mother only laughed and said it was a bunch of foolishness. As he walked west down the sidewalk, he bumped into Zeke Miller talking to a drummer, who had a small sales stand of men's dress ties along the street. Justin stopped and listened in on the conversation.

"You going to start wearing a tie around town, Zeke?" Looking a bit startled at the very thought, he replied, "Nah! I was tellin' this gent the marshal is a real stickler for peddlin' permits around here." Nodding yes, Justin informed the peddler that he was an off-duty deputy marshal, and suggested the man obtain the required city permit before the chief deputy runs him in.

"How much do they cost?" the tie peddler asked. Pulling the information from memory, Justin replied, "One day is $1.50, two days $4, one week $6, two weeks $10 and one month $20." With this information in hand, the peddler folded up his display case and announced he was going elsewhere to sell his ties. Looking over at Zeke, Justin kidded him by saying, "You would have looked great in that tie, Zeke."

Continuing his walk down to the river, Justin entered the encampment of the gypsies. Colorful wagons and tents were set up for the expected customers, and there were signs advertising fortune-telling and spiritualism sessions. As he looked around at the wondrous sights, he heard a girl speak to him, "Would you like your fortune told? Past, present, and future events will be revealed to you." Justin turned to look at the girl and was shocked by her great beauty. The man in the barbershop was right, she was a real looker. She had shiny long black hair with a braid holding it in place. Her eyes sparkled like diamonds and her lips pink and full, the type of lips just asking to be kissed. Justin shook off the cobwebs in his head and asked her how much she would charge him. Finding it to be only two-bits, Justin followed the girl as she led him to an open tent. He was surprised to see only a few townspeople were milling about, but the word of the gypsies arrival would no doubt bring people out tonight.

Holding out her small delicate hand, Justin realized she wanted to be paid FIRST before his life and future were told. *Why not*, he thought, *this might be fun.* She then directed him to sit down at a small table that contained some sort of glass globe. The lovely girl proceeded into a type of trance, as she moved her fingers seductively over the glass globe. Justin was surprised to see the globe begin to light up and wondered how she did it.

"My name is Dooriya, and I am the vessel through which the spirit world shall speak to you today. The information they provide could be good or bad news to you, so do not blame me for I am their messenger. I see that you are not originally from this town," she said. "You arrived from east of here. You have an important job within the community.

You like to help people. You are a good man and much respected. I see that you have loved deeply and lost that love, and you are unsure if you will ever love again. I can tell you that you will, in fact, find happiness in the arms of another." By now Justin was intrigued by what the lovely Dooriya was saying, and he could not take his eyes off of her face as she continued, "I see advancement in your position. I see danger... grave danger....I see... I see the death of a dear friend." The smile faded from Justin's face but he quickly changed back to his smile. "You are now allowed to ask the spirit world one question," she informed him.

Without missing a beat, Justin asked, "Would you ask the spirit's vessel if she will take a short steamboat ride with me?" This clearly brought Dooriya out of her practiced fortune-teller pose, but she quickly composed herself. "The spirits are asking if you are paying?" With that, the session ended and the light within the globe darkened. Justin was pleased, Dooriya seemed somewhat pleased, and no doubt the spirit world was pleased. After all, they could see the future, right?

"Mother, I shall be gone for a brief period of time with this gentleman, please cover for me," she informed her mother, who produced an almost sinister glare towards Justin. "I don't think your mother likes me," he told her.

"I am bequeathed to my father's friend, Beval, but he left camp bright and early this morning, so what he doesn't know won't hurt him. So, tell me about this steamboat ride. I noticed it earlier tied up at a pier."

"The *Helen Boyd* is a small steam launch belonging to the Gas City Land Company, who is the major land owner in town. The boat ride takes about thirty minutes and visits both dams, up and down the river," he told her. As Justin assisted Dooriya with stepping into the *Helen Boyd*, the boat pilot realized the lady to be a gypsy and made an unconscious move to check the security of his coin purse before the small boat left the docks. "It's a beautiful day for a ride on the river, and the spirits and I wish to thank you. What should I call you, marshal, sheriff, deputy or just plain officer?" Her question completely caught Justin off guard, which only made Dooriya laugh, knowing that she caught him totally by surprise. "Justin Blake, Miss Dooriya. Deputy Justin Blake. But how did you...?"

"It's very simple, deputy. We always know to expect a law enforcement officer within the first day or so. They don't wait for the crowds to form, and always arrive early. Sometimes they arrive in uniform and, sometimes, dressed like you. I could explain more but it would violate trade secrets." Laughing, Justin could see how this identification system would work.

"At least I got to meet you and get my fortune told! Where are you from, Miss Dooriya?" Taking her eyes off of the still and calming water, she replied, "I was born in the caravan. My parents arrived from Europe, and a group of them simply formed up in wagons and traveled the country. My father, Jal, is our leader. At least I get to see a lot of new places along the way. I'll let you in on another trade secret, probably one you didn't notice. As we got in, the boatman reached for his purse to ensure it was safe. We see a lot of this from people who think we are all thieves."

Justin replied that he didn't catch the movement, but in his position as a deputy, catching little things like that might save his life one day. He will have to pay more attention in the future. With that, the couple sat back and enjoyed the boat ride.

~~~~~~~~~~~~~~~~~~~~

Justin and Wilbert checked the bulletin board for instructions, but didn't find any, a first for the Merrell brothers. Peeking his head inside the office, Zeke Miller did a quick glance before coming in. "Wanted ta make sure Brass Buttons wasn't around," he joked. Both deputies had heard other people calling the marshal by that nickname, but hearing it from Zeke made them chuckle. "Gonna have a big wind, heavy rain and lots of lightnin' bout eight tonight. Better get things tightened down good," he told them. Wilbert looked out the window and commented that the weather was
~~~~~~~~~~~~~~~~~~~~

perfect, but Justin had learned to take Zeke's word on the weather. He was always right in his predictions. Always.

"Thanks for the advanced warning, we'll see that the word gets out to everyone." Both men split up and began walking the town, warning everyone they saw. Once people heard that Zeke had said bad weather's coming, they took it as gospel and set about tying down everything that needed it.

Justin thought about the gypsies and Dooriya's tent, and he headed down to the river. A large group of townspeople were present, with quite a few standing in line to have their fortune told by her. "Bad storm is coming tonight about eight o'clock," he shouted out to the gypsies. "Better get your tents and animals tied down before it hits."

One of the gypsy men heard this and rushed up to Justin. "Officer, are you using scare tactics to shut us down? We are not breaking any laws and have the right to be here." Pointing up at the sky, he said, "Not a cloud in the sky, the weather tonight will be wonderful." Justin knew that an explanation of Zeke Miller's uncanny ability to predict bad weather would not be believed, and tried to reason with him.

"I'm not trying to shut you down. I'm telling you that bad weather will hit at eight tonight, and you better get your people ready for it. Many of the town's people heard this and asked if Zeke said it was coming. Upon confirmation, the majority headed for home.

Seeing their evening's income leaving, the angry young man ran up to Justin, "You'll pay for this." Ignoring the threat, Justin pleaded with Dooriya to find shelter. She seemed both confused and a bit angry at him.

"That man was Beval and will soon be my husband, so he speaks for me. You better leave here, deputy," she told him. Justin felt he had done all he could do to warn the gypsies, and returned to town to help people prepare for the worst. At eight p.m., the sky turned dark with high winds, heavy pelting rain and lightning.

Within an hour the storm had passed. Justin and Wilbert went out to survey the damage and tend to any injured. The city firemen responded to two house fires caused by lightning strikes, and brought them under control. Lightning had, also, struck the chimney on a house on North D Street, destroying the chimney and cracking the plastered ceiling. Fortunately, everyone in the home escaped injury. Recently one of the fire barn horses, Old Betsey, was retired and a new fire horse named Roscoe was trained to take it's place. Roscoe performed very well, making each of the firemen very proud. Once an opportunity presented itself, Justin went down to the gypsy encampment and found it in complete shambles. All of the tents were ripped in pieces, their wagons blown over, and the animals scattered everywhere. Justin found only women present, since every able-bodied man was out searching for their livestock. Looking about, he found Dooriya who was wrapping a bandage around her mother's injured leg. Seeing him, she continued working, as she said, "We should have listened to you. Now everything is damaged or missing."

Seeing that she appeared safe and sound, he replied, "Do you have many injured? We have a doctor in town. I can get a wagon and take the injured to his office." Stopping her work, she looked him straight in the eye and said, "We'll be fine, but thank you for your concern. We are not used to kindness from strangers." Justin paused a few seconds, then said, "I don't want to be a stranger to you, Dooriya." He smiled at her, turned away and headed toward town.

By the next morning, most people had agreed it could have been worse, if not for the early warning by Zeke Miller. Someone even suggested to Zeke that they erect a statue in his honor, but Zeke said he didn't want birds a poopin' on his likeness for eternity. Justin was exhausted and didn't even bother to eat before turning in. Let the Merrell brothers help with the final cleanup.

At noon Justin was eating lunch at the Panhandle Hotel and Restaurant when an idea hit him. By two o'clock, he had enough volunteers and materials to begin. They were going to assist in rebuilding everything that was lost by the gypsies. At first, an elderly man, that Justin soon learned was Dooriya's father, Jal, told the assembled volunteers that gypsies didn't need the help of strangers in their rebuilding. Justin informed him that the town folk were no longer strangers, but neighbors here to help, and with a little more coaxing, overcame his objections and soon the repairs were underway.

Broken wagon wheels were soon replaced, missing livestock rounded up, replacement canvas found to make tents and much more. It was not as pretty as what existed before, but functional. The work was completed by early evening. "I don't know how we can ever repay you for your kindness. We are not used to it," replied Jal. "Dooriya informs me that you tried to warn my people of the coming of the storm. As a show of our gratitude, tomorrow evening will be a celebration in our camp, and all of your townspeople are welcome. We will entertain with music, dancing, fortune-telling and spiritualism, all free of course." Everyone agreed that it sounded like fun, and the ladies of the town made their plans to supply the food.

The following day Kruger called Smiley Lewis into his office. "How did it go?"

Smiley, who never actually smiled, nodded, "The man sold the stuff to another band of Gypsies camped close to Greentown. Here is the cash." He handed it to his boss.

"Expect any trouble from your gypsy contact? He doesn't know anything, right?"

Smiley replied, "He only recognizes my face and I always use an alias when dealing with his kind. There will be no problems from him."

There was a general feeling of excitement throughout the town, as most of its population was planning on attending the festivities at the gypsy encampment. Though on duty, Justin and Wilbert planned on being around quite a bit. Long tables were set up with ample food being dished out to any and all comers. Once the eating was over, the singing, dancing and musical festivities began. The town's people loved it, clapping along to the beat of the music. It seemed the gypsies really went out of their way to make things pleasant for everyone.

Inside one of the new tents was a unique speaker for the evening. He spoke on a topic that many knew nothing about, but it proved to be entertaining and a bit spooky and unnerving to several. He began by telling the crowd that he was "a Sopister- a special type of teacher of the hidden arts that ruled the universe and the great beyond." It certainly got their attention. "With a show of hands, how many of you have ever had a vague remembrance of a place you've never visited before, or that strangers seemed familiar to you?" Quite a few hands slowly went up. "You know positively that as far as the present existence is concerned, it was impossible for you to have seen the person before, or to have been to that now familiar location. I have often met people with whom I have become intimate with at first sight because it seems I have known them all my life. The Hindu religion calls this oddity reincarnation." There was a bit of mumbling in the crowd as a few of the people active in their churches felt uncomfortable hearing the discussion on such a topic, but everyone remained subdued. This was, after all, entertainment.

"I will now tell you a true story of a person that has experienced this rare phenomenon. She was the daughter of Isaac Fulton from Effingham County, Illinois. Twelve years ago he buried this daughter named Maria, who was taken away just as she was reaching young womanhood. A year later, Isaac Fulton moved to the Dakotas, where he still lives to this day. About three years after his daughter's death, the family was blessed with the birth of another daughter they named Nellie. Once the little girl grew old enough to speak, she insisted upon being called Maria. She became quite angry when told her name was Nellie. She told her parents the name belonging to her was Maria, as that was the name they used to call her. You can imagine the confusion this had caused her parents."

"As she grew older, a matter of business required Mr. Fulton to travel back to Effingham County, and the decision was made to take Nellie along. The father was very surprised at the knowledge this little girl had of the place, a place she has never been to. She not only recognized the family's old home but many people the first daughter had been acquainted with, calling them by their name. About a mile from their old home was a schoolhouse where Maria had gone to school. Little Nellie had never seen the place, yet she gave an accurate description of it to her father, and expressed a strong desire to visit it. Accordingly, Mr. Fulton took her there, where she promptly marched straight up to the desk her sister had occupied. "This is mine," she told her father. Mr. Fulton felt that his first daughter had indeed returned from the grave, but the child's mother would have none of it. She said if that were true, she had but one child and yet God had given her two. So ends my story tonight, and I hope you have enjoyed it." There was mild applause from the audience. "Now anyone who wishes to have their fortunes read, please line up in one of our two lines. Thank you."

For obvious reasons, the line for Dooriya's fortune-telling session was much longer than her mother's. With each reading taking about two minutes to complete, both lines were slowly making progress. Mr. and Mrs. Prescott of Gas City was standing near the head of Dooriya's line when Mrs. Prescott noticed something that changed the entire evening's festivities for everyone. "That girl is wearing my mother's stolen brooch!" she shouted. It got very quiet when everyone heard that. Justin and Wilbert approached Mrs. Prescott, "What is the problem, ma'am?"

Pointing at Dooriya, Mrs. Prescott said, "That's my mother's brooch that was stolen from our home last month. I would recognize it anywhere." Sensing that things could get ugly very quickly, Justin said, "Lots of jewelry can look the same, perhaps you are mistaken." Mrs. Prescott was adamant, "On the back of the brooch is engraved *To Lidia With Love.* Now it was Dooriya who got upset, "I did not steal this brooch. It was given to me." Knowing he needed to examine the brooch closer to determine if it was the lady's stolen piece or not, Justin asked Dooriya if he could see it. Pausing briefly, she removed the brooch from her white blouse and shoved it toward him on the table. Turning it over, Justin found it did indeed have exactly what Mrs. Prescott had stated it had. "I'm going to have to hold onto this for a while," he said to Mrs. Prescott "but you will get it back soon. That's a promise"

Dooriya sat still with arms crossed, glaring up at Justin. "Dooriya, where did you get this brooch?" The young girl said nothing, but the fury from her dark eyes said much. "You said someone gave it to you. Who was it?" Dooriya continued to be still.

From behind, a male voice spoke, "I gave it to her, so what's it to you?" Turning around Justin could see that it was her future intended, Beval. Looking hard at Beval, Justin said, "I am asking you officially in my capacity as s deputy marshal, where did you get the brooch, Beval?" Shaking his head and looking into the faces of the gypsy men for the support, he replied, "I'm not telling."

Justin had no other option, "I am now forced to place you under arrest for possession of stolen merchandise," he stated as Wilbert placed handcuffs on him. The festivities had come to an end. The party was clearly over.

~~~~~~~~~~~~~~~~~~~~~

The following morning Smiley met with his boss Kruger, "So tell me exactly what happened last evening?" Smiley had obtained his information from one of his best men who was at the gypsy camp. "I naturally stayed away so as not to be identified, but I did have a dependable man present." Smiley was clearly agitated. "My contact in the gypsy camp apparently pocketed one of our bits of stolen merchandise and the fool gave it to a gypsy woman who wore it in the camp, and it was noticed by the ex-owner. The deputy marshal then arrested him and locked him up in the jail."

Kruger slammed his fist in anger upon the desk. "Can he hurt us? Can he identify our operation? Smiley replied, "Well, if he breaks, he can certainly describe me. I'm not that hard to identify." The wheels inside Kruger's head began to turn, "Here's what we're gonna do"......
~~~~~~~~~~~~~~~~~~~~~

Chapter 28

The Merrell brothers worked on Beval all day trying different approaches to get him to confess his crime, but far more importantly, to give names in this fencing operation. So far, they were not having any luck. Neither threats or special pleas seemed to have any effect on him. Presently, he would only face 'Squire Jones with a charge of selling stolen merchandise, though one could say he didn't sell the brooch but gave it to his lovely girlfriend. The question was, how did he obtain it and where was the rest of the stolen jewelry? Clearly, he knew but refused to speak. Perhaps the 'Squire's courtroom would get his attention. Marshall Merrell told his brother to keep an eye on the prisoner while he took a break and visited with 'Squire Jones about tomorrow's courtroom proceedings. As soon as his brother was out of the office, Chief Deputy Cecil Merrell attempted to play a little hardball with the prisoner. "You might as well tell me what I want to know, or I'll pull you out of that cell and beat you to a pulp."

Still, nothing worked so Merrell picked up the newspaper and began reading. A loud ruckus outside got his attention, so he stepped out of the fire barn to investigate. Five grown men were fighting each other, directly across the street next to the home where sick people were quarantined. His shouting of, "You men break that fighting up," seemed to have no effect, so the chief deputy proceeded over to the fight and attempted to pull the men off of each other. It seemed that as soon as he separated two men, a third or fourth jumped in and the ruckus started again. On and on it went until suddenly a faint whistle was heard and all the men seemed to stop fighting at once and ran off in the same general direction. The chief deputy was sure he had made his point and impressed upon these hooligans that fighting in the streets would not be tolerated.

Merrell dusted his clothing off, and retucked his shirt tail back in before going back inside to resume his newspaper. The sight before him prevented any further reading. The prisoner in his charge now lay prone upon the floor in a puddle of his own blood.

Somehow the Journal reporter, Alvin Jensen, learned of the murder and had arrived on the scene before Doctor Baxter. Jensen was asking a multitude of questions to discover what had happened and who did it, but was not learning anything from the Merrell brothers. Marshal Merrell was more than angry at his brother for being drawn outside for a fake fight.

Clearly, it was a ruse to gain private access to the prisoner by someone who was concerned he might talk. Someone was willing to kill in order to protect a secret. The more his brother made excuses, the angrier Marshal Merrell became, and all of this was witnessed by the newspaper reporter.

"I want everyone out of here now!" he shouted. "Just let the Doc in when he arrives." Losing a prisoner would be another perceived blot upon his professional image as marshal. *If only this had happened at night with those two deputies on duty,* he thought.

"Make a way, please, thank you." Doctor Baxter had arrived. "Marshal, will you light that desk lamp and bring it over here, so I can examine this man?" At a glance, Baxter knew the man was dead by the huge volume of blood, and the fact that it was no longer being pumped out of the open wound. "Someone stuck a knife in the left side of his neck and sliced a jugular vein, from what I can tell." Looking around and under the body, the marshal was unable to locate the murder weapon anywhere. "Not even bloody footprints leaving the scene," Doc mentioned. "Anyone see anything?" Shaking his head, Marshal Merrell stepped outside for some fresh air. "Please have someone take the body over to my office. I should be able to give you a little more information as to the size and possible type of weapon used. Oh, you might want to send someone to tell those gypsy's that their man has been murdered." Merrell's mind hadn't processed that far yet, but he knew just who to send. "Cecil, I have a task for you," he said.

As would be fully expected, the gypsy camp was in total shock when learning about the murder of Beval. Dooriya's father, Jal, who served as the leader of the group, knew it fell upon him to obtain the body that evening after the investigation was completed, for burial. Who could have done such a horrible thing to Beval, and why? Dooriya remained inside her wagon, alone and not willing to speak with anyone. Jal called the camp together and made a vow that Beval's death would be avenged, with or without the approval of the people of the town.

Justin Blake had one goal in mind tonight and that was to start interviewing the gypsies for any possible motive for the killing. Seeing a list of items on the bulletin board, Wilbert told him to go ahead and that he would take care of what was written down. As Justin approached the camp, the feeling of warmth and happiness experienced last evening was gone now - replaced with a suspiciously cold stare and a closed door. If he was to make any progress in this case, he would need Jal's help. If the old man would cooperate, the others might come around. It took a bit of coaxing before Jal would even open the door on his traveling wagon. "Haven't you caused us enough harm, deputy? Poor Beval would not be dead if it were not for your people. Please go and leave us in peace."

At this point, Justin was more determined than ever "Sir, help me find Beval's killer so we can bring peace to his tortured soul. Somebody must know something that might help. Dooriya told me that Beval had left camp early one morning. Where did he go? There must be a connection on what he did with any possible stolen merchandise, and those trying to silence him. Can't you see, by not helping me you are helping his killer remain free."

Justin stood outside the doorway hoping he might have gotten through to the old man. The wooden door opened and Jal stepped outside. "Perhaps you are right. I simply do not wish to tarnish the memory of a man who was to be my son-in-law with wild speculation." Justin reached out and touched the shoulder of the man, "I only want the facts so that justice will prevail." Shaking his head and quietly laughing, Jal spoke, "Justice. You speak of justice. But there is no justice for gypsies. Town after town tells us to move on. We are called thieves and bandits wherever we travel. Why should I add to that image?"

"Sir," Justin replied. "It was this town that came to your aid when you most needed it. It was this town that sang and danced with your people just a day ago. No, sir, this town is not your enemy. Your enemy is the monster who killed Beval. By helping me you are helping everyone."

The old man sat down on a small stool and motioned for Justin to do the same. "Alright," he finally said. "Beval borrowed a freight wagon from someone in town to go to another one of our people's campsites over by Greentown. He had some merchandise he was going to try to sell to our people over there. I did not pry, as we all look for ways to make a dollar."

Justin nodded, "Did he mention any names or other information?"

Thinking back Jal replied, "Ringo, he mentioned the name Ringo, and that he knew him from before."

Pondering the name, Justin said, "That name doesn't ring a bell with me. It may be an alias. Do you think Dooriya would speak with me? He may have said more to her." Shaking his head, the old man asked that she be left alone. "My daughter was not happy when I promised her to Beval, but I think she came to respect him as a man. Our ways are different from yours, deputy. My wife was promised to me in marriage, as well as my grandmother to my grandfather. That is our way." Sensing that he had received about all the information he could get at this time, Justin offered his hand in friendship and promised to be in touch with whatever he discovered.

It was Jal who replied, "No, it is I who will be in touch with you." Returning to the office, Justin pondered those words and their meaning.

~~~~~~~~~~~~~~~~~~~~
~~~~~~~~~~~~~~~~~~~~

"They're gone," replied the chief deputy to his brother, as the marshal entered his office the following morning. "Must have pulled out during the early morning hours - lock, stock, and barrel. Nothing left down there but the memory." Marshal Merrell produced a happy face and told his brother, "Good riddance." He then went about his normal duties. Wilbert had taken it upon himself to scrub the jail cell floor as clean as he could. His landlady, Ma Richards, had suggested to him that he use ammonia, soda, and borax on the stains, and this mixture worked pretty well. At least he had exchanged one strong odor for another.

Marshall Merrell was indeed unhappy when he saw the morning Journal newspaper headlines: **Gypsy Suspect Murdered in Police Custody By Unknown Assailant.** Reporter Alvin Jensen had written an editorial on the crime and murders taking place without any arrests, as well. His editorial summary stated: *"Our once fair and peaceful community has now become a battleground for robberies, murders, and general mayhem that goes unresolved by our new marshal. This latest outrage of allowing a prisoner in his custody to be murdered, while the killer easily escapes, is the final straw. We call upon Marshal Merrell to put an end to this madness once and for all, or we might soon put an end to the career of Marshal Merrell."*

As expected, the article and editorial became a hot topic around town. A man in the barbershop jokingly stated that

Marshal Merrell spent all his time polishing his brass buttons. That jest spread all over town, finally reaching the ears of the marshal himself. Being the butt of jokes made Merrell even more determined to put an end to these break-ins and murders, but without solid leads he just didn't know where to start. Walking over to a clothing store on Main Street, Marshall Merrell peeled off his dress coat and handed it to the seamstress on duty, "Remove all these brass buttons and replace them with black ones. I'll be by later today to pick it up." Going back to his office, he thought, *that should put an end to all those brass button jokes for good.*

Justin Blake thought it was time to visit again with his friend, ex-Marshal Brewster, and see if he had any ideas that could help him to solve the murder. Approaching the house, he saw that Brewster and Zeke Miller were sitting on the front porch enjoying the early morning mild temperatures and drinking some of Zeke's bad coffee. "Why aren't you in bed?" Brewster joked, upon seeing the now off-duty Justin walking up his sidewalk. "Plenty of time for that after we visit. Any of that bad coffee left?" Justin replied. Zeke pretended to be offended but, knowing Justin was only joking, proceeded inside and poured a cup for the deputy. Pulling up a chair, Justin evaluated his friend's condition. Brewster didn't look good as the reality of sitting in a wheelchair, maybe for life, has gotten to him.

"How are you feeling?" Justin asked.

"Well, as good as can be expected, I guess. My legs are pretty numb and I must keep a shawl covering them, since I'm always cold. When an old horse gets sick or injured, the humane thing to do is to put it down." Justin didn't want to hear that kind of talk. "Stop that, you still have much to offer, and that is exactly why I wanted to stop by and pick your brain this morning." He then brought Brewster up-to-date with everything that had happened.

"Your new marshal won't be happy with you for speaking with me about the investigations, Justin." Lowering his head in disgust, Justin replied, "I don't care what that man or his brother thinks. Neither are professionals nor instill public trust like you did." With a smile, Brewster thanked him for that. "So what are your thoughts, marshal?"

Brewster sat up straight in his chair and said, "Give me a minute to think about it." By now Zeke had returned with the deputy's coffee and began to speak, "Justin, I was tellin' the marshal here that I got an idea about his back and all. I shot a deer the other day and field dressed it in the woods when I noticed something. I had the deer hangin' upside down by the rear legs as I was a lettin' the meat to cool for strippin' it's hide, when I saw its spine bone separatin' a little bit. If we were to hang the marshal here upside down by his legs, it might take some of the pressure off his back."

"Which one of you are going to field dress me?" Brewster laughed. "I appreciate the offer *Doctor Zeke* but I think I'll stay just where I am for the time being. On a more serious note, you said the old gypsy mentioned the victim borrowing a wagon in town and leaving early. I suggest you ask anyone you think might have been up that early if they saw him. They might recognize whose wagon it was."

Justin smiled. "Thanks, Marshal, that's an idea. I'll see who I can find. Zeke, don't lynch the marshal by the legs while I'm gone." The word "lynch" got the marshal to thinking.

"Justin, do you know the history of that word?" Shaking his head, Justin sat back down to hear the story. "Well," Brewster continued, "after the Revolutionary War ended, North Carolina was plagued by a band of misfits, Tories and common criminals who inflicted much pain and suffering upon the local population. There was no established law enforcement to handle the situation, so a Colonel Charles Lynch developed a plan of action. He contacted men of quality and distinction and presented his plan to them. Together they would hunt down these criminals and capture them. One would think today that they were instantly hung, but that was not the case. His men served as a jury with Col. Lynch as the judge. The accused criminal was allowed to present his own case. For lighter offenses, guilty men were often flogged and told to leave the country. Those judged with a harsher sentence were hanged. Somehow the name just stuck."

"Kind of like that medical doctor, Gatling, the inventor of the Gatling Gun." Zeke then spoke up, "Maybe I'll be a remembered one day fer Zeke's Leg Lynchin' Cure."

~~~~~~~~~~~~~~~~~~~~~~

A tragedy occurred in the nearby town of Marion that quickly became a hot topic in Gas City. Pan Handle train No. 20, east bound at speeds of up to forty mph, struck a carriage at the unguarded railroad crossing at Western Avenue the previous day, killing the two occupants. Gas City was no stranger to its own close calls. During the Spring, a local young couple was thrown from their buggy as a Pan Handle train clipped their real wheel, sending the occupants tumbling onto the road. God was clearly with the young couple that day since their only injuries were cuts and bruises, but their buggy was destroyed. There had been other close calls involving the Pennsylvania, Cincinnati, Chicago and St. Louis railroad tracks, and so the people of Gas City watched to see what might come from this tragedy. Something had to be done to alert the public about the approach of the fast moving trains.

In a show of unity, all Grant County mayors who had active railroad tracks intersecting their town's public roads, attended a joint meeting to determine a united course of action. At the conclusion of the meeting, each mayor would
~~~~~~~~~~~~~~~~~~~~~~

introduce to their own city council an ordinance requiring the placing of watchmen/flagmen at each dangerous crossing, with the cost of such an employee being paid by the railroad in question. It was asked that all trains announce their approach to any crossing by way of the train's whistle. All such ordinances were to be submitted to the city attorney for proper evaluation prior to being introduced for a vote. Should the ordinance be approved, a copy of said ordinance had to be submitted to the railroad in question.

A suggestion was made about a daily fine, up to fifty dollars, to be imposed if failure to comply was not carried out and would take effect within thirty days from written notification. Gas City's ordinance went on to state that flagmen must use proper and continuous signals to warn all of the oncoming locomotives, and to keep pedestrians and carriages off of the tracks. The flagmen were to be stationed from March 15 through October 15 from 6:30 a.m. to 7:30 p.m. daily, and from October 15 through March 15 from 7 a.m. to 7 p.m. daily. A special city council meeting was called where the ordinance was introduced and passed unanimously.

'Squire Jones and two area farmers also appeared, to discuss the polluting by factories on the Mississinewa River. One farmer stated that there was a sickening smell that was becoming unbearable, with a black scum one inch thick on its surface. He then stated that his cow entered the waters and the legs of the poor beast began to swell. 'Squire Jones pointed out that no animal life was being noticed along the river's banks anymore. He went on to add that he took it upon himself to scoop up some of this scum in fruit jars and mailed them off for proper scientific evaluation to the Indiana University Chemistry Department. 'Squire Jones then reported that their detailed report stated a heavy concentration of lime, muriatic acid and other harmful chemicals present in the river water sample. With this report in hand, he said he approached the manager of the Strawboard Company, who only laughed at the report. "We make a hundred dollars a day and don't care," the manager actually said, 'Squire Jones then went on to recommend that the city attorney file a lawsuit on behalf of the city against the Strawboard Company. The city attorney then asked for time to prepare such a document, and it was agreed to discuss it further at the next council meeting. Councilman Davidson urged caution, and to consider the reactions that harsh decisions could have on all of the present factories.

The Pan Handle Railroad, as well as the "Penny", chose to simply ignore the written ordinance provided to them. They felt that flagmen at every intersection would cost the company too much money. Their lawyers stated it was the responsibility of pedestrians and wheeled vehicles to watch for oncoming trains.

With everything seeming to happen all at once, the marshal's office became a very hectic place to work, especially for Chief Deputy Cecil Merrell. His brother's attitude was unbearable, demanding results now to problems two months old. *He seems to forget I'm his brother and not the two knuckleheads who work nights*, he thought. *I deserve to be treated better than this. Maybe it is time to conduct a little more after hour's business but on a much larger scale.*

The June first deadline for the removal of all gaming devices within city limits was fast approaching. Kruger had instructed Smiley Lewis to ensure all machines were picked up by the end of May, as he didn't want any police involvement looking into any of his business adventures. "That gypsy returned the freight wagon with a broken axle," Smiley said. "And that was the wagon I was planning on hauling all the machines in to distribute to other towns. Want me to have it fixed or borrow another?" Smiley asked. Shaking his head, Kruger said that he saw the Gas City Hardware got in a few new wagons this morning. "Go look at them, and if they are solid, buy all he has." Kruger then opened his cash drawer and pulled out a wad of money. "You know where to store them. Just get the guys to use one for now and start picking up them machines tomorrow morning."

Smiley could see the unloaded freight wagons sitting outside of the hardware store. *They seem strong enough*, he thought as he entered to speak with the owner. "Tell me about those freight wagons you got parked outside," he asked the owner.

"They arrived this morning. Made by the Smith Wagon Company out of Perkins, Illinois. Solid as a rock," the owner said with pride. "I wanna buy them." Smiley told him. Not quite sure just what he heard, the hardware store owner asked, "You want to purchase one, sir?" Smiley replied, "No! I wanna buy all four, complete with full hitching equipment."

Chapter 29

Justin knew that to act on the advice Brewster had given him would require some off-duty investigation work. After sleeping until noon, he proceeded to stop by every shop along Main Street to see if anyone remembered seeing the gypsy man driving a wagon through town early that morning. He also questioned people he met on the street, anyone who might have been up early that morning, but so far he wasn't having any luck. As he entered the Gas City Hardware building, he couldn't help but notice three brand new freight wagons sitting outside. He wondered if one of those could be converted into a patrol wagon. It would be useful for piling all the nighttime drunks and trouble-makers in, rather than the long walk back to the fire barn. It sure would be nice. Entering the hardware store, he waited until a lady customer was taken care of before asking his questions.

"Come to think of it, I do remember a man on a wagon going by as I was opening up because the rear wheel was squeaking. I didn't pay any attention to who was driving it."

That was the closest thing to a lead Justin had obtained so far, and it might not have been the gypsy's wagon after all.

"I was admiring those three new wagons out front. We could sure use a patrol wagon that we could mount a cage or something in for prisoners. Just out of curiosity, what would one of those cost?"

"Sorry deputy, those three are already sold. Actually, one man came in today and bought four." A puzzled look came over Justin's face. "Four? Why would one man buy four new freight wagons?" Chuckling the owner said "I wondered the same thing, especially once I remembered who he was. It's that sour looking man who works or manages one of the low-end saloons down by the river. You know, the one that never smiles and looks mad all the time, so people call him Smiley. He pulled a huge wad of bills out of his pocket, and never batted an eye at the cost. He has already picked up one of the wagons and he said other men will come by and get the others this afternoon. Now I wish I had asked for more money."

Bells began to go off in Justin Blake's head. Why would a small saloon keeper require four brand new freight wagons? Certainly not to haul beer and liquor, as these were delivered by the supplier. Maybe this required a little looking into, but he would have to act fast before the men showed up with teams to haul them away. "Do me a favor. Try to stall the men for as long as you can, because I want to return and do a little investigating for myself." With an agreement to try his best, Justin left and headed straight to Ma Richard's Boarding House. Hopefully, he would find Wilbert there.

"Put your uniform on, we've got a bit of detective work to accomplish before our shift starts," Justin told him, as he filled Wilbert in on the plan. "We might need a third man to make this work. Should we go get our Chief Deputy to give us a hand?" Wilbert told him "Not hardly, let's go find Zeke to help us." "Oh by the way," Wilbert said, "I found the pocket watch laying on their desk. It has engraved writing that looks Hebrew to me."

~~~~~~~~~~~~~~~~~~~~~~

The small entry bell on the door rang to announce customers, as three rough looking men entered the hardware store. Sensing these may be the men he was to stall, the owner made some excuse to visit the back storage room. "We just came to pick up the wagons," one shouted. "I'll be with you in a moment gentlemen, there's a little paperwork to complete first," the shop owner replied. *Now, how am I going to stall with non-existent paperwork?* he thought. The men looked at each other, then began to browse around the store. After a few minutes the men became annoyed with the long delay, so the leader motioned with his head to follow him. Together they left to go outside to hitch up their horses
~~~~~~~~~~~~~~~~~~~~~~

with the new hitching equipment already inside each wagon. Hearing them step outside, the owner left the storage room knowing that was the best he could do to delay their pickup and hoped they wouldn't re-enter his store. Now it was totally up to that young deputy to do whatever he planned.

Unable to locate Zeke, the men walked at a quick pace on their way to the hardware store. "There's Zeke now, talking to a fellow outside the post office," Wilbert said. As the men approached, they could hear that Zeke was in the middle of one of his long-winded stories. "... And so I said to General Grant, let's take the left bank and sneak up and surprise the Rebs..." Justin grabbed Zeke by the arm, "Come on, Zeke, we need your help. You can finish your war story later." A somewhat startled Zeke then asked, "What's up fellers? I was a tellin' how I single handedly won the Civil War." The deputies filled him in as they hurried along.

Arriving within a block of their target, Justin had the group stop. "We got here just in time it appears." Two of the wagon drivers were already waiting for a third to complete his hitching. "Now if all three wagons go to the same location, we won't need you, Zeke, Wilbert and I can follow them on our own. But if they go three separate ways, pick one and follow from a distance to discover where it's being taken. By traveling on foot, we're less likely to get spotted. If time permits and you feel safe in doing so, inspect any barn or shed they park them inside. Report back after our shift starts, to tell us where they are being stored. Like I said, this may be a wild goose chase, but at least it's a possible lead. Wilbert and I appreciate your assistance in this, Zeke."

The deputies didn't have long to wait as the first wagon pulled out into the street, quickly followed by the other two. The first one turned around and proceeded to travel west, the second turned east, and the last proceeded north. Without saying a word, Justin assigned each wagon with a nod to his friends. Now the chase began.

Doctor Baxter entered the marshal's office to inform him of a potential medical situation. "Marshal," he said. "I thought I should inform you that the city of Muncie has experienced some cases of Smallpox, and all the local towns are being asked to take precautions in halting it's spread." Walking over to a large map of the state, both Merrell brothers located Muncie, south and a little east of Gas City. Doc went on, "We haven't had any cases reported yet here in Grant County, but we're doing all we can to help get the word out and prevent it's arrival. I just spoke with the stationmaster down at the depot, and the railroad has already implemented a procedure that no pickup of passengers takes place in Muncie, unless the passengers present a health certificate saying they are free of the disease or have been vaccinated."

Marshal Merrell sat back in his chair pondering the information before asking, "Doc, what procedures would we implement if a case occurs here in town?"

“I will quarantine that person or the entire family.”

“Thanks for the warning,” Merrell said, as Doc stated he had more people to brief and left the office. “Smallpox is a bad situation. I hope they get a handle on it quickly,” he worriedly said to his brother.

~~~~~~~~~~~~~~~~~~~~~

As each man followed behind his assigned target on foot, all were happy the wagon drivers seemed not to be in any hurry to arrive at their final destination. This made Justin wonder if, in fact, he had gotten everyone involved in a wild goose chase. It was early June and quite hot for a long hike on foot. As it turned out, Justin had drawn the out-of-town wagon to follow. After the man drove his rig west, down the almost completely finished bricked main street, he then turned by the park towards the streetcar bridge over the Mississinewa River going into Jonesboro. There he turned left up a long winding pathway surrounded by thick trees to where an old house and shed sat. The man unhitched the wagon, opened the door to the shed, put away his horse, then pushed the wagon inside, closed the door then went into the old house. Justin felt that now was his best chance and took a peek inside the shed and, in doing so, found nothing of interest. Feeling somewhat relieved, he then began returning to the office. If something illegal had been found, Justin
~~~~~~~~~~~~~~~~~~~~~

knew it would have to be handled by the Jonesboro town marshal anyway.

Wilbert had drawn the easiest wagon to follow, traveling east a short distance before turning south at the Gas City Land Company property. A lone rundown barn sat back out of the way surrounded by woods. The small pathway leading to it was grown up in tall grass, indicating people seldom ventured to this location. Wilbert remained hidden as he watched the wagon being pushed inside the old barn. The driver then mounted his horse and returned the way he had come at a slow gallop. Creeping closer to the barn, Wilbert looked around for any signs of activity. Seeing it was clear, he opened the barn door and looked around. Only a large pile of hay in the corner with an empty horse stall, nothing to indicate anything at all of foul play. Pulling out his pocket watch, Wilbert saw that he still had some free time to enjoy before going to the office at 7 p.m.

Where is this feller a goin'? Zeke wondered. After turning north, the wagon began cutting eastward out of town and heading towards a large wooded area. As the driver approached his final destination, Zeke was taken aback by the reality of its location. *There? Is he goin' there?* He thought. After the wagon was backed into the small shed and the man rode away on his horse, Zeke crept up and opened the now familiar shed door. To the right of the wagon were many wooden boxes piled up in the corner. Approaching,

Zeke could see that the lid was off of the top box, and right there in plain sight were three large ladies jewelry boxes. Opening the lids of each, Zeke was a little surprised by the sight of necklaces, bracelets, rings, earrings and other ladies whatnots. Closing the lids, he backed out of the shed and closed the door. Somebody was clearly hiding away these items, and he quickly guessed they were the stolen jewelry items. He then hurried back to brief Justin and Wilbert about his discovery.

Zeke was the last to arrive, but brought news both deputies were very happy to hear, "I found where they are storin' the stolen jewelry." He then proceeded to describe all the wooden boxes and the jewelry.

"Where is it located?" Justin asked. Zeke made a sideways glance over to Wilbert before he answered. "It's the shed where we had the shootout with dem White Cappers."

Justin felt some of the blood drain from his face but quickly recovered to add, "Actually it's the perfect location to store stolen merchandise. Nobody expects lightning to strike the same location twice. I suggest we all go over to see if we can find Marshal Merrell and tell him of our discovery." Zeke had a quick shake of his head, "Not me, got no love fer da Merrell brothers." Both deputies thanked Zeke again for his hard work in helping solve this case.

"Zeke, you make a fine secret deputy," Justin told him as he left the office. Turning to Wilbert, Justin asked if he could provide a description of the driver but like his own, he didn't get much of a close look at the man. "Anyway, we can have the city clerk check to see who owns the properties, and when we arrest them the hardware store owner may be able to identify them." Both men set off to the Mississinewa Hotel in search of the Merrell brothers.

"Let's check the dining room before we go upstairs," Justin suggested. The Merrell brothers were quickly spotted having supper together. Approaching their table, Marshal Merrell looked up with annoyance on his face. "Yes, what is it?" he asked.

Without being asked to sit down, both deputies did so anyway. "We have found where the thieves are storing the missing jewelry." They then proceeded to fill them in on the entire situation.

Chief Deputy Merrell showed his anger in saying, "You should not have used that old coot, but came and got me. I am after all the chief deputy." Both men sat and said nothing waiting to see if the marshal would also be chewing them out for solving these break-ins. Instead, the marshal continued to eat his meal in silence.

Justin then added, "While we cannot give you the names of the three men, I suggest the city clerk look up the property owners. And if they match our general descriptions, we can arrest them. Perhaps later, the hardware store owner can identify them."

Picking up his white napkin to dab his lips, Marshal Merrell then finally spoke, "So that's what you suggest, do you? I don't remember us asking your opinion, deputy." Both Justin and Wilbert were now mad enough to flip the table over and storm out, but before they could act on their rage, Merrell continued. "Here's what we are going to do. You boys go over to the delivery stable and rent a strong rig that we'll use to haul all the stolen materials back to the office. My brother and I will meet you at the livery stable at daybreak. With the theft reports we have on hand, I should be able to match up the recovered jewelry and return them to their owners. Until then, you are dismissed."

Both Justin and Wilbert were furious at the treatment they had just received by the Merrell brothers. "You would think a *good work men* wouldn't have been too much to ask for," Wilbert fumed. "A couple of glory hounds ready to take credit for Zeke's hard work." The thought of laying his badge on the marshal's desk and resigning passed again through Justin's mind before remembering that ex-Marshal Brewster had urged both men to stick it out.

"Let's forget it and go get that rig ready for a daybreak pickup." It proved to be a long night for both deputies, who each dreaded dawn's arrival.

After hearing his older brother brag all evening about the credit he would receive from the community for personally solving these cases, Cecil Merrell had had enough. Returning to his own room, he began to make plans that would involve a much richer payoff than the measly ten dollar bills he had gotten for his past services. It was clearly time to up the ante. Sitting down at his writing table, Cecil Merrell pulled out a sheet of paper and an envelope. Picking up his pen, he wrote the following:

> *Jewelry discovered in shed northeast of town by deputies. Marshal plans early morning seizure. Suggest immediate removal. Signed, a friend. p.s. I fully expect better compensation than before.*

The note was unsigned, of course. He folded the paper into thirds and sealed it inside the envelope. Now he needed to find his carrier pigeon to deliver it to the bartender as before. Placing the envelope inside his breast pocket, Chief Deputy Merrell began his search of the back alleys and low areas in search of Tommy Two-Fingers.

It took only about twelve minutes to find the old drunk sleeping off an afternoon binge as he lay next to an empty bottle in a darkened alleyway. "Wake up Tommy," the chief deputy said, as he prodded him with his boot. Slowly, the old drunk opened his eyes and began to focus on the man speaking to him. "Am I under arrest Mr. Policeman?" he babbled in slurred speech. "No Tommy, do you want to make another ten cents?" Soon his carrier pigeon was flying to it's nest down at the White Dog Saloon."

~~~~~~~~~~~~~~~~~~~~~~~

There was an early morning fog as daybreak began and the Merrell brothers arrived outside of the livery stables. Justin had rented a strong wagon with a pair of durable horses to haul the loot back. Without saying a word or a "good morning", the Merrell's climbed up onto the seat and gestured for Justin and Wilbert to ride in the back to point out the way. Soon the marshal's party arrived at the quiet shed. As soon as the wagon stopped, Marshal Merrell jumped down and ran up to the shed, throwing open the door. There he froze in place as the other officers assembled beside him. The shed was completely empty. The marshal then exploded in anger, "That old fool made all of this up. I have half a notion to place him under arrest!"

Justin calmly walked inside for a quick look around, as his boss fumed and pitched a fit outside. Pointing to where he was told the boxes were stored, Justin spoke, "There are the marks on the ground where the boxes were stored. The place is full of boot prints, and look at the deep ruts left in the dirt from the wagon wheels. Men removed the boxes last night by hauling them out in a wagon. How did they know we were coming?"
~~~~~~~~~~~~~~~~~~~~~~~

Chief Deputy Merrell quickly answered, "I can tell you exactly why, that old fool was seen entering this shed and the gang then removed the evidence." He then tore into both deputies for failing to use proper police procedures, and forbid the use of an old, broken down, dumb civilian ever again. "I got half a notion to ask for both of your badges," he threatened.

Both men were in the act of reaching to remove their own badges when the marshal interjected, "Stop it. If I want anyone's badge it will be by my request and not by anyone else's. Let's go back to town now."

Justin and Wilbert declined the ride in the wagon, and chose instead to walk off their anger when Justin suggested, "Let's go over to the Pan Handle and get some breakfast and coffee. I'm starved." As they walked, they discussed everything that had happened. "I don't think Zeke was seen, do you? He knows to be mighty careful," Wilbert spoke. Justin didn't immediately say anything. Something about the chief deputy had never seemed quite right. "I keep thinking back about that fellow who told us about the Hebrew watch and the five dollar gold piece." By the time they arrived at the Pan Handle, the subject was pretty well talked through and each enjoyed his own breakfast in near silence. Sleep was now exactly what each man wanted the most.

Marshall Merrell contacted the city clerk's office once it opened to discover who owned the properties involved.

It was found that one man owned all three properties, and that man was Theodore Kruger, an owner of saloons near the river. Returning to his office, he informed his brother of who owned the three properties and announced he was going to go find this man Kruger, and threaten him with arrest unless he produced the missing jewelry and the men involved. “Let me handle this. I am after all your chief deputy. I need to show those two nitwits I can handle the situation and you, big brother, need to show your confidence in me,” Cecil interjected. The marshal then suggested that they both go, but again, Cecil Merrell stood his ground and announced he could handle this. With reluctance, Marshall Merrell agreed to allow him to do it alone.

Proceeding down to the White Dog Saloon, Cecil Merrell entered the near empty establishment. The bartender was nowhere in sight, so Merrell just went up and knocked on Kruger’s door. “Come in,” announced a voice from the other side. Kruger was quite surprised to see the chief deputy stroll casually into his office. “Well now, Mr. Merrell, of what do I owe the pleasure of your visit?” Smiling, Merrell helped himself to a seat without being invited to do so.

“You have a problem, Mr. Kruger.” Suspecting a shake down for more money, Kruger sat back and acted innocent. “I haven’t any idea of what you’re referring to Chief Deputy.” Seeing a cigar box setting upon Kruger’s desk, Merrell reached over, again uninvited, and opened it, taking one and placed another in his coat pocket. Kruger tried his utmost not to allow this blatant contempt of power to show on his face. "Yes, please have a cigar. May I offer you a light?" A cocky Cecil Merrell then announced, "Thanks but I'll smoke them later." Tired of the games this man was playing, Kruger went right to the point, "Then say what you got to say, I got work to do."

"Now that's no way to speak to a friend who saved your bacon this morning, Mr. Kruger. I was sent here by the marshal to ask you some questions about stolen jewelry and three men who apparently are in your employment who may be connected with these thefts." Merrell then told Kruger the entire story about how the three men were followed and that the marshal now knew Kruger owned the three properties. Sitting in silence for upwards of a minute, Kruger finally spoke, "Yes, I see this is a problem. You need a man you can claim was responsible for the jewelry theft, someone, shall we say...to take the fall? I'm guessing if some of the jewelry was also returned, perhaps the case might be closed, figuring the rest had been sold?" Merrell simply smiled back at him. "Of course, you realize I personally know nothing about any of this. It seems that a man under my employment has taken it upon himself to run afoul of the law, and to use one of my honestly acquired properties to store his illegal merchandise, of which I am shocked to learn has happened."

“Yes, that pretty much sums up your problem, Mr. Kruger. Now, what shall I tell my brother?”

“Tell him that you have discovered by interviewing yours truly, a humble and honest businessman, the name of the culprit who it appears is the lone break-in bandit. That he was found to be a dishonest fellow, and upon a discovery that he was wanted for questioning, his name and address was gladly provided to you by myself.” Opening up his pocket watch, Kruger saw that it was 10:15 a.m. “If you will arrive at the rooming house whose address I will provide, say at 1 p.m, perhaps this guilty man may be discovered along with a box of jewelry. Should this poor individual put up a fight and you were forced to defend yourself and shoot him, well, that might just wrap everything up clean and proper. Kruger then scribbled an address on a piece of paper and handed it to Merrell. “He’s a dang foreigner named Tony D’Agostino, by the way. You should come out of all this as some kind of town hero, Chief Deputy. Does this solve my problem?”

Rising from the stuffed chair, Chief Deputy Cecil Merrell began walking towards the door. “Yes, that solves your problem very nicely, but it doesn’t solve mine. I expect a much thicker envelope under my doorway when I return to my room tonight. Good day, citizen Theodore Kruger.” Merrell mentioning that awful first name really made Kruger quite angry. *This man is becoming a problem*, he thought in anger. Going into the saloon, he told one of his men to run next door and tell Tony he was wanted by the boss. Soon Tony arrived. "You want to see me boss?" he said in his Italian brogue. Kruger, in an unconcerned manner, replied, "Tony, I need you to get a couple boxes of the jewelry and take them to your room. Stay there with them as one of the out-of-town boys will be coming by later to pick them up as payment for a favor." Tony gave Kruger a smile, missing several of his front teeth, and quickly left the office to accomplish the task. Kruger did not feel any remorse, or even the least bit uncomfortable in offering up one of his lesser men's life. He only hoped the new chief deputy was a good shot.

~~~~~~~~~~~~~~~~~~~~

Arriving back at his office, Chief Deputy Merrell briefed his brother. "Mr. Kruger was very cooperative and understanding. As to the properties, he has acquired some holdings strictly for investment purposes. He plans on purchasing O. Gordon's furniture store on Second and Main soon, and will need delivery wagons. He has asked us not to publically mention that, as the business offer is still at the early stages of negotiations. It seems that one of his employees, a Mr. Tony D'Agostino, a recent immigrant from Italy, may be our break-in bandit. Mr. Kruger was most upset to learn that stolen merchandise had been kept at one of his properties by this man, so he provided the individual's
~~~~~~~~~~~~~~~~~~~~

address on South B Street and stated he will terminate his employment effective immediately if found to be guilty. I came by Mr. D'Agostino's one room lodging, but he was not there. I will continue to do so later so I may ask him some questions, and of course, place him under arrest." The marshal was quite happy with this news and urged his brother to keep at it. "I'll give him time to eat lunch then mosey on over. He should be in our custody by mid-afternoon."

After eating his own lunch, the chief deputy pulled out the Hebrew pocket watch to check the time. Seeing that it was nearing the appointed 1 p.m. hour, he found a secluded location to inspect his weapon, a Colt .45, to ensure everything was ready. Killing this man would bring him headlines while solving the problem those night deputies caused with their meddling. He would see that they get their ears pinned back, and never again take the initiative in a criminal investigation. Knowing there would be the possibility of an inquest, Cecil made a point in playing it straight for the benefit of any witnesses. "Hello, I'm Chief Deputy Cecil Merrell. I'm looking for a Mr. Tony D'Agostino," he asked an individual as he entered the boarding house. "Down there, last door on the end," came the reply. "Thank you, sir," came his cheerful reply, as he gently tapped upon the door which opened quickly for his entry. Thinking no more about it, the man in the hallway walked away until he heard a loud shout, "Don't go for that gun!" as two shots rang out.

Quickly stepping back outside, Cecil Merrell told the startled man to go fetch the marshal pronto as he stepped back inside, and told anyone else who tried to enter to remain outside. It had been so easy. With D'Agostino fully expecting a visitor, the man had allowed him in quickly and didn't notice the uniform until it was too late. Cecil had hoped that the man would make a grab for a gun so killing him would be easy, but instead, the man simply stood there motionless. Knowing that he now required a bit of acting, Cecil Merrell shouted "Don't go for that gun," before pumping two bullets into the unarmed man. Knowing that this might be a possibility, Cecil had brought a small, single action Derringer along. Slipping it into the dead man's hand, he now felt he had all the proof he needed to prove self-defense.

Chapter 30

Off duty, Justin Blake was only a block away when he heard the two gunshots. Reaching the home he entered to find a group of people outside the doorway. "Deputy Marshal," he told them, "Please stand aside." He entered the room. Chief Deputy Merrell, upon seeing Justin, went into the entire pre-rehearsed presentation. Justin walked over to see two wooden boxes of jewelry setting upon the bed. "Funny the victim would have kept them on his bed, of all places. It's like he was expecting someone to show them to," Justin said out loud to nobody in particular.

"There's the gun in his hand that he aimed at me. I had no choice but to shoot." Looking at the sprawled body on the floor, Justin noticed the two bullet wounds in the man's chest. "Why did you shoot him twice?" Clearly upset by the question, Merrell ordered him to go ensure the marshal was, in fact, on his way. Justin again cleared a path through the crowd to the outside but heard a voice call out to him. Turning around he saw a man approaching.

"Officer," the man said to him, "Something about this isn't right." Justin asked him what he meant by that. "Did you notice the small derringer in his hand?" Justin nodded, "Yes. Why?" Looking back over his shoulder to see that nobody else was listening, he went on. "I was the first one to see the body after the shooting. The derringer was resting inside of his right hand but I know for a fact that Tony was a southpaw, you know, left-handed. The way your weapon is carried says you are right-handed, so would you draw yours with your left hand?" Justin thought back on the crime scene and clearly remembered the weapon in the man's right hand. Pulling out his notebook, Justin took down this man's name. "I may be in touch with you later on," he told him.

Once Doctor Baxter examined the body, Marshal Merrell could hardly wait to remove the boxes of jewelry and take them back to the office, where the two officers could begin to match up the pieces from the theft reports. A few lucky women received word that their missing jewelry was found and would soon be returned after 'Squire Jones' required inquest in the shooting was completed.

The morning newspaper headlines read: **Break-In Bandit Killed, Jewelry Recovered by Chief Deputy**. Cecil Merrell enjoyed the attention and the congratulations he was getting from the people of the town. Even his brother seemed to show pride in him that he rarely displayed to anyone. That morning his brother had been notified by 'Squire Jones that the required inquiry would take place later that afternoon. That was standard procedure anytime a law enforcement officer was involved in a shooting. It was mostly a routine matter that from start to finish would be completed easily in less than thirty minutes. Chief Deputy Merrell would give testimony, along with any witnesses to the shooting. Only with negligence or any indication of criminal activity or perjury, would the case then be heard by a higher court. This was an inquiry that both Justin and Wilbert fully planned on attending. Since it was a public affair, anyone seeing them would automatically presume that they were present in a show of support for their brother officer. In reality, that was not the case at all. After telling Wilbert what the shooting witness had told him, Wilbert urged Justin to inform 'Squire Jones of what was said. Maybe even the witness should give testimony at the inquest. Normally Justin would not jump the chain of command, but Marshal Merrell was not someone you could take doubts of his own brother to. No, Wilbert was right and Justin planned on speaking with the 'Squire privately, after resting and eating, so that Jones could make that final determination.

It was well after 1 p.m. before Justin arrived outside the office of 'Squire Jones, who was busy preparing himself for the inquest. "May I have a moment of your time, Your Honor?" Glancing up at the wall clock, 'Squire Jones replied, "Yes, come in deputy. Have a seat. I'll be right with you." Within a few moments, Justin explained the entire conversation with the witness concerning the placement of the gun in the hand of the victim. "Have you discussed this information with Marshal Merrell?" Jones asked. "No sir, he is not the type to listen to anything negative about his own brother." Nodding, 'Squire Jones admitted that would put Justin in a difficult situation with the marshal. Reaching into his desk, the 'Squire pulled out a paper and scribbled something on it. "Here, have this paper served to the witness that he is to appear at our 3 p.m. court inquest. I want to hear his testimony. Thank you for bringing this to my attention, deputy."

Learning that the witness, a Mr. Allen Buckley, was a night shift worker at one of the factories, made finding him in his room very easy. Justin handed the form to him with instructions that he must appear as a witness or face possible charges himself. With great reluctance, Buckley agreed to appear. *This inquiry should be most interesting*, Justin thought.

Arriving fifteen minutes early, Justin and Wilbert were a little surprised at the large crowd already seated, so they chose to stand against the rear wall. Gas City had yet to build its own city building, so they conducted city business in either room number five of the First National Bank building, or the clerk's office located in the Mississinewa Hotel. Today the inquiry was being held inside the bank. 'Squire Jones began the inquiry by stressing that this was not a trial but only a hearing into the shooting that occurred involving Chief Deputy Merrell and the deceased, Mr. Anthony D'Agostino, which took place inside the deceased's living quarters. The Chief Deputy was placed under oath, then questioned by 'Squire Jones.

"So, please tell us everything that led up to the shooting," he was asked. By now he had his story down pat having recited it many times, and naturally made no mention of meeting with Kruger... "So upon our office receiving a tip involving a robbery suspect, I knocked on his door and the deceased let me in. I then noticed the boxes of jewelry setting upon his bed, and at the same time he apparently realized I was not who he expected, but a deputy. Suddenly I saw him reaching for a small derringer setting on the table, so I shouted a warning not to reach for the gun. He continued to do so and I was forced to defend myself." 'Squire Jones leaned forward in his chair, "So the derringer was lying flat on a table when he reached for it?" Nodding his head, "Yes, that's exactly what happened. It was either him or me, so I drew and fired." "What type of a weapon do you carry deputy?" "A Colt .45 caliber, sir." "May I ask why you pulled the trigger twice?" That was a question Cecil Merrell had not planned on, but quickly replied, "It was only a reflex, I guess." "One last question, since you and the deceased were standing so close together, why didn't you just tackle the man and subdue him? I mean, you certainly had the height and weight advantage?" For this, he had no solid answer.

Thanking the deputy, 'Squire Jones then called the witness Allen Buckley, who was sworn in. Cecil Merrell was very surprised to see him, but felt he would only collaborate the plan he had made on entering the home anyway. "Mr. Buckley, please tell us in your own words what you witnessed that led up to the shooting." Allen Buckley was a simple man, not at all used to being in the spotlight. As he began to speak, 'Squire Jones instructed him to begin again but to speak louder. "I said, I was in the rooming house when this deputy approached and asked me if I knew where he could find Mr. D'Agostino. I told him where to find his room then thought nothing more of it until I heard him shout "Don't go for that gun" or something like it. Then I heard two quick shots. I ran and opened the door to find the deputy was stooped over and Mr. D'Agostino was lying dead on the floor in a puddle of blood." 'Squire Jones began to ask him questions, "Did you notice anything else?" Nodding, he continued, "I saw two bullet holes in the center of the chest area and I noticed a small derringer in his right hand. That's what troubles me as I know for a fact that Mr. D'Agostino was left-handed." What the witness just said hit Cecil Murrell like a freight train.

"How do you know that the deceased was left-handed?" the 'Squire asked. "I knew Tony quite well and have helped him with paperwork. Being from Italy, English is...ah, was his second language. I recently helped him fill out some government paperwork and watched him sign it. He did everything with his left hand." 'Squire Jones then asked him why he felt this information was important. "Well, sir, I'm right-handed and, if I was forced to reach for a weapon, I would only use my right hand. Even if you startled me, by reflex I would only use my right and never my left. I figure Tony was the same way."

Doctor Baxter was then questioned. "Doctor, how many times was the deceased shot?" "Twice from about four feet I have judged, Your Honor."

"Did it require two shots to produce death?"

"No, sir, either bullet would have killed the man."

'Squire Jones then proceeded to ask about being left-handed, "Doctor, can you cast some light on this subject about being left-handed, and the question of using a gun with his right hand?" Shrugging his shoulders, Doctor Baxter then explained that some people are simply ambidextrous and have the ability to use both hands equally. That pretty much resolved that question. Finding no reason to think otherwise, 'Squire Jones cleared Chief Deputy Cecil Merrell of any wrongdoing in the fatal shooting. The inquiry was finished. Marshal Merrell shook his brother's hand and walked out of the room happy as could be that the issue had been laid to rest. Justin Blake was not so sure about that matter.

~~~~~~~~~~~~~~~~~~~~~

It seemed that almost every neighborhood had a family who owned a barking dog. The Beck family had such a dog. It was a cute looking Beagle, but that dog sure could bark, bay and howl at all hours of the day and night. The Beck family must have been completely deaf not to know that "Bluto" was completely driving all of their neighbors batty. Neighbor's complaints were going nowhere, and more than one person considered throwing a poisoned chunk of meat over the fence to the dog. It was early evening and Bluto was baying away for hours upon hours only stopping, apparently, to occasionally catch his breath. It was during another baying session when the bullet impacted his skull, essentially blowing the dog's head from it's body. A deep stillness in the air quickly followed. Bluto would bay no more. The assassin had seen to that.

~~~~~~~~~~~~~~~~~~~~~

Kruger set a plan in motion using the four heavy-duty freight wagons he recently purchased. He was invited to become part of a select group of criminal bosses awaiting their own shipment of special items. They would add to his already growing fortune, counterfeit quarters and dollar coins all dated 1892. He was shown examples of the products recently while he was away on "business" in Kokomo and they were good replicas. In fact, they were very good and the only way a person could probably tell the difference between a real coin and his fakes was by the ringing of the metal when dropped or struck. How many people did that anyway? Several members of his local gang had questioned why he purchased the four new freight wagons from the local hardware store. All Kruger would say was "for business purposes." Kruger had ordered twenty wooden barrels full of these fake coins; some that would be passed as change at all of his saloons and businesses, while others were to be passed off to his creditors in Marion and Muncie. The coins were packed tightly in beer barrels so anyone who bothered to look at them would not consider it unusual at all. That is, unless someone attempted to lift one. It took two grown men to carry each one.

Kruger asked Smiley to enter his office for a very private meeting. "Smiley," he told the man, "I am very pleased with your work. You have rapidly advanced through the ranks, and are a trustworthy and loyal man. My enterprises are growing by the day and I need someone I can depend on to help carry the load. Therefore, I'm promoting you to be my lieutenant who will take over managing all of my saloons, their books, and keep the men in line." Smiley Lewis with his typical harsh blank look, responded, "Thanks, boss, I'll do my best to make things run smooth."

"I need you to make one last run though, before you move up, because there isn't anyone else I can trust to do it right," Kruger told him.

"Sure thing, boss, but there's something I need to discuss with you. The boys are upset that deputy snuffed out Tony and are saying we need to avenge him." Kruger sat back in his chair and thought before answering. "The boys are probably right, but this is not the time. Tell them it will come soon, when the deputy's usefulness is no longer required."

Kruger then dispatched Smiley Lewis and another man to Kokomo with two of the freight wagons to make the final payment and return with the barrels of fake coins. Two barrels of quarters would be stored behind the real extra beer barrels inside the supply room of each saloon. The dollar coins would be passed throughout town to the merchants and to cover payrolls. By the time the Feds discover they are fake, it will be too late to determine where they came from, and Kruger will be richer... much richer and more powerful than ever.

~~~~~~~~~~~~~~~~~~~~

Labor troubles were brewing down at the local Tin Plate factory. About thirty young boys who were employed to work the night shift voted to go out on strike for higher wages. Their complaint was that they only make eighty-four cents
~~~~~~~~~~~~~~~~~~~~

for working the entire night shift, while girls who worked the daytime shift earned nearly the same at seventy-five cents. The boys demanded their pay be increased to one dollar and twenty cents for working nights. Management flatly refused and fired the instigators of the strike. Management then stated they would purchase a new machine that would replace the boy workers. After heated discussions, the remaining boys returned to work and the strike was called off. This was hardly the first such incident of the summer in and around Gas City. While its main street brick laying project had been resolved, a similar project in the town of Jonesboro did not go as well. Seeing the need for paving its own main street with bricks, the contractor for that project tried the same trick and announced a reduction in workers' pay, cutting each man by twenty-five cents a day. The bricklayers already at work immediately called for a strike, but in the end a compromise was made that still reduced workers' wages. There were several fights and brawls within local saloons between the union and non-union men, resulting in fines being imposed by 'Squire Jones.

Workers at the U.S. Glass Works who were on strike, began boycotting any local business or merchant who sold supplies, either to the company or it's executives. In retaliation, non-union scab workers were hired from out of town, and the factory supplied special police to escort them from the railroad station to the factory through angry strikers. More than one fight broke out keeping the 'Squire's afternoons quite busy. One of the scab workers at the Tin Plate factory had the tip of his second finger sliced off and received local first aid.

One of the worst of these incidences involved a warehouse fire at the Thompsons Glass Factory. Despite the quick application of Stemple Fire Extinguishers, the warehouse was a total loss. Thompson made plans to rebuild it. Then an engineer working at the Tin Plate factory was charged with assault and battery after spitting his coffee into the face of a female plant worker. This caused a wild brawl resulting in plant property damages. After refusing to pay his fine for damages, 'Squire Jones had no choice but to give him thirty days in the county jail. In an attempt to improve labor relations, many of the factories began to form baseball teams from their own members who would then take their rivalry out against other sporting teams and not against management, while instilling pride in one's own factory team. Clearly, management did not become management by being stupid, only cheap.

A story quickly spread all over town that a prize fight was to take place at 8:15 p.m. that evening down near the Thompson Bottling Works, between a white man from Gas City and a colored man from Jonesboro. About one hundred men gathered to watch the fight, but after waiting one hour, nobody appeared. So much for listening to rumors.

The Gas City Council met again with the following items scheduled on the agenda:

(1) Doctor Baxter reassured the public concerning the outbreak of Smallpox in other local towns.

(2) The council approved the purchase of two thousand feet of fire hose at sixty-five cents a foot.

(3) The city engineer will give a briefing on the deteriorating condition of the streetcar bridge, badly crippled from constant use with a cracked support timber and it's stone base support settling. The bridge needs replaced, but funds are not at present available.

(4) Explanation on the lawsuit proposed by Gas City against the Strawboard Manufacturing Company for its pollution of the Mississinewa River.

(5) Status of warning flagmen to be posted at all railroad/ street crossings. So far no action has been taken by any of the railroads to comply with these ordinances.

(6) City Council member will introduce a plan to build a new schoolhouse on the southeast part of town. The building will have eight rooms and cost eighteen thousand to build.

Justification: We currently have six hundred students, but the current school holds only two hundred, with overflow meeting in various locations including the Mississinewa Hotel.

(7) Mr. Joseph Townsend, a saloon owner on Main Street, asked the council that saloons not be required to pay their annual one hundred and fifty dollar liquor license fee up front, but in payments. After discussions, it was voted to allow a seventy-five dollar down payment with the balance within four months.

While all of these public activities were going on, the assassin made final plans for another killing. The 4th of July was soon approaching, and a different type of fireworks would add to the festivities of this little town. Yes, this would stir things up quite nicely.

Chapter 31

Off duty, Justin Blake was approaching the small white wooden frame post office building on Main Street, when he noticed a man out front handing out flyers. It was the Reverend Stokes. "Justin," he called out, upon seeing the deputy approaching. "Here you go. We are conducting our first service in our new church this Sunday. I hope you will attend." Justin took one of the flyers, then commented, "I didn't know it was completed yet." The Reverend continued to pass out flyers to passersby as he continued, "Only the exterior is completed. We'll use folding chairs for the service, then continue interior construction the other days of the week. Please come to dinner afterward. My brother-in-law and family will also attend our dedication. I think you remember my niece, Marsha?" With her name mentioned, Justin broke into a wide grin. "I sure do." With a coy smile on his face, the Reverend replied, "I'll even ask my wife not to bore you with anymore of her long-winded stories. Please come." Justin replied that he enjoyed her stories and thanked him for the invitation.

Seeing that he had no mail, Justin felt it was time to confront the marshal and his brother on the lack of progress being made in solving these killings. He entered the fire barn only to find the marshal by himself. Looking up at the off-duty deputy, Marshal Merrell said nothing and waited for Justin to speak first. "Marshal, I feel it is time we should talk."

Merrell replied, "So go ahead and talk." Pulling up a chair, Justin took a seat and tried to show no emotion. "Marshal, I think we could accomplish better results around here if things were not so hostile. From the very first day, you have ridden Wilbert and me pretty hard. This job should be a team effort. Believe it or not, Wilbert and I want you to succeed, but this isn't a very pleasant place to work. We both have the threat of being fired hanging over our heads daily. It seems to me that if we worked together closely, rather than as individuals, we might crack these murder cases wide open."

Justin's attempt to reach out to his boss clearly showed failure upon the marshal's face, even before he replied. "Blake," he said sternly, "If I want your advice I will ask for it. Do you understand me? If you want hugs and kisses you won't get that from me, and maybe you should just quit and save us both the hassle. Solving these murders, and, yes, I believe it's only one person doing all of this, is my responsibility. I will solve it when I'm good and ready. Just do as you are told and quit bothering me with your suggestions. Now if you are finished, I have work to do." Justin slammed the door very loudly on his way out.

Justin needed to vent his anger and frustrations to someone and he knew just the person who would be willing to hear him out, his old friend ex-Marshal Brewster. As he approached the man's house, he saw him again sitting outside on his porch, but this time Zeke was not present. "From the look on your face, I'm judging you just tangled with somebody," the very observant man stated. "Pull up a chair and chew the fat with me. Gets mighty lonesome just sitting around here these days." Justin filled him in what had just happened. "I agree with you about the murders. Two different people altogether, completely separate issues. One uses a sniper's rifle to execute people, and the gypsy was killed to prevent him from squealing about who he got the stolen items that he was selling from."

Justin was pleased that he had sought out Brewster for support. "That Marshal Merrell and his worthless brother are a huge mistake, and I'm not saying that because I was passed over for the position. His attitude is hostile with almost everybody." Nodding his head, Brewster reminded Justin of what he had said before, that Merrell's type doesn't last long in this type of work. "Stick with it. I know it's very hard but stay the course." Thanking his friend, Justin felt better and decided it was time to move on and drop the subject. He then shared the story about the gun being in the wrong hand of the thief that the Chief Deputy shot and killed. 'Squire Jones ruled it a justified shooting and ended the inquest but Marshal, I'm not so sure. Something just doesn't add up to me." Pausing before replying, Brewster reminded him that there were some dishonest police officers, luckily very few. Justin then told him about the man with the gold coin and the Hebrew watch. Hearing that story the ex-Marshal Brewster offered a simple solution, which Justin put in the back of his mind for future use.

Justin enjoyed entering the various merchant stores along Main Street during his afternoon slack time. It gave him an opportunity to see and speak with a nicer clientele of people, as he was becoming frustrated in dealing with nighttime drunks, fights and other petty arguments. Stopping in front of the Larson Hardware, Justin thought it might be time to allow the wife and son, who were now operating the business together, to ask questions about the murderer of Jeb Larson. Justin only wished he had the answers. "Afternoon, deputy," Mrs. Larson said. "Anything I can show you?" Shaking his head, Justin said he just wanted to look around some. "I'm afraid I haven't any updates on apprehending your husband's killer, Mrs. Larson," he told her. She clearly heard him but had no comment and began to busy herself behind the counter. Looking into the large glass display case of pistols and knives, Justin became so absorbed in looking at them that he almost didn't hear what Mrs. Larson had just said to him.

"We got a nice selection of small derringers. Your other deputy bought one a few weeks ago, and I will give you the same deal I gave him, if you are interested." Justin shook out the cobwebs in his head and asked her to repeat what she had just told him. Reaching into the case she removed the weapon and laid it on the top glass. "I can see where an officer of the law might find a tiny weapon very useful when hidden away in a pocket for emergencies." Picking up the weapon and turning it over in his fingers, Justin asked her which deputy had recently purchased one.

"The other one, the brother of the new Marshal. He said it might save his life one day. I sure hope he doesn't need to use it, as their accuracy isn't all that good unless you are up close." Justin handed the weapon back to Mrs. Larson with the promise he would be in touch soon. So the Chief Deputy recently purchased a small derringer, just like the one found in the wrong hand of the victim. Justin could hardly wait to speak with Wilbert about this.

That evening while they were out on patrol, Justin told Wilbert about Cecil Merrell purchasing a small derringer three weeks before the shooting. Both men were thinking the same thing, but how could they prove it? "We need to tell somebody, but who?"

Wilbert spoke. "I don't think we should drag Marshal Brewster into all of this, do you?"

Justin gave a nod of his head, "Probably not. I'm guessing he would say to go see 'Squire Jones for a legal opinion. One thing's for certain, if we make any accusations and they don't stick, Merrell will fire both of us on the spot."

Wilbert replied, "Let him, as I'm about ready to quit anyway. Let's go see the man and see what he says."

'Squire Jones was in his study half asleep when the men knocked on his door. "Hello deputies, what have you got for me tonight?"

Justin replied, "No, sir, it's not anything like that, but may we have a few minutes of your time?" After explaining the story of the man with the gold coin and Hebrew watch along with the purchased derringer, the 'Squire began to ask questions.

"Have you spoken with Marshal Merrell about any of this?"

"No, sir."

"Have you confronted the Chief Deputy about your concerns?"

"No, sir." "Have you identified the inscription inside the deputy's watch as Hebrew?"

"No, sir."

"Well, deputies, your case against the Chief Deputy is only circumstantial, unless Mrs. Larson can positively identify the derringer found in the hands of the man as the exact one she sold your deputy earlier. As for the watch, your witness isn't here to identify his property any longer, correct?"

Justin replied, "Anyway, that's the situation. We just wanted to let you know of our suspicions." As he walked the deputies to the door, the 'Squire stated, "Obtain solid evidence and take it directly to your Marshal. Brother or no brother, he's appointed to enforce the law."

Upon returning to the fire barn, both men were surprised to see a gypsy wagon and team sitting across the street. Stepping down from the seat was Jal. Justin walked over and offered his hand. "I told you that I would see you again, Deputy Blake. Have you discovered the killer of Beval?"

Justin had to tell him no. "I suspect the killer was from the lower sections of town, but so far nothing has turned up. I give you my word that as long as I am employed here, I will not give up." Nodding but saying nothing, Jal motioned for the men to come with him to the back of the wagon. Jal opened pulled back a tarp to reveal three boxes of jewelry, rings, silver and other stolen items.

"I traveled to the other gypsy encampment to see if Beval had been there and discovered he had. I explained that the jewelry Beval had sold them was stolen, but they said nothing. I then told them about the wind storm that wrecked our encampment and that you tried to warn us of it's approach, and that afterward your own townspeople came to our aid. I told them I did not have the money to purchase the stolen items back from them, but asked that they honor my request and voluntarily return all as a gesture to your people that there is honor among our people as well. I have no idea if everything was returned, but I would say most of it was."

Justin and Wilbert were almost speechless. Jal and his people had proven beyond any doubt that they were men and women of the highest caliber. He continued, "Perhaps this small effort on my part will work to erase decades of rumors and mistrust between my people and yours."

Shaking the man's hand, Justin replied, "Today your people and my people are one and the same." Together they carried the items into the Marshal's office. "I bet the Merrell brothers will take total credit for the return of all of this, but Wilbert and I will see that the truth is spread." Once they were finished, Justin and Wilbert followed Jal back out to his wagon. "Please tell Dooriya hello from me," Justin said with a wave.

"Jump up here and tell her yourself, she's down by the river where we camped before. We'll be heading out at daybreak for parts unknown." With a smile and a wave, Wilbert assured him that everything was under control and he'd see him later.

The following morning both deputies remained in the office just so they could see the look of astonishment on the faces of the Merrell brothers when they took a gander at all of the returned merchandise. To ensure that the truth would get out properly, reporter Alvin Jensen was told the story the previous evening. The town needed to know the truth about the gypsies. The Merrell brothers spent the entire day matching up the merchandise from the theft reports while Justin and Wilbert each slept in a restful peace.

~~~~~~~~~~~~~~~~~~~~~~

It was Saturday afternoon and Justin was having lunch at a small diner close to the tracks when he heard two people discussing a railroad accident. It seemed the Pennsylvania Railroad Special No. 20, which passed through here daily at 3:30 p.m., had its sleeper car jump the tracks near Columbus, Ohio last evening. Luckily no one was hurt. This turned the conversation into the railroad's unwillingness to provide warning flagmen locally. "It's just a matter of time before one of our folks are hit and killed by these flying bullets." His dining friend, Councilman Davidson, agreed, "The Council passed a city ordinance requiring them to provide warning flagmen, but so far they have not. The railroads are just too big and powerful. Somebody ought to break up their powerful monopoly..."

~~~~~~~~~~~~~~~~~~~~~~

Smiley Lewis and his workers returned to town that morning very quietly without fanfare. Anyone who bothered to glance upon the freight wagon would only see kegs of beer. Everything had worked out just as Kruger said it would. Entering the White Dog Saloon, Smiley made eye contact with the bartender and nodded towards the door. He received a gentle nod back that the boss was indeed in. After a short tap on the door, he was welcomed in by Kruger. "How did everything go? Any problems picking up the stuff?" He was assured there had been no difficulties as another gentle tap on the door resulted in two barrels each of the counterfeit coins being brought into the office and sat down by his thugs. Going over to one of the barrels, Kruger flipped open a long knife and pried one of the top boards off of the nearest keg. It contained the dollar coins. "Great, you did very well. Like I promised, you are now officially my lieutenant with all the benefits that goes with it. I have an idea I would like to discuss with you. Please pull up a chair... Mr. Lewis." If Smiley could smile, I am sure that might have done the trick, but instead, the sober stern look on his face did not waver.

"What if we have all of the gang come by individually today, and you hand each man twenty of the counterfeit silver dollars? You can tell them the money is a bonus for their loyal support and, at the same time, that each and every one is required to address you as Mr. Lewis. We might as well start getting the coins into circulation. Let's run through the dollars before we circulate the quarters, which will work best in the saloons. I want you to pull out a hundred dollars for yourself. There's your new desk. Go try it out, Mr. Lewis."

Smiley sat down and seemed most content but, of course, nothing showed on his face. "I like the plan. I'll stack the coins up so the men will see them as they enter," Smiley said. Kruger nodded, "Then I'll leave you to your business, Mr. Lewis. I'll tell the barkeep to contact the boys. Enjoy the moment," And he left his new lieutenant to enjoy being a boss.

Off duty, Justin Blake observed the raising of a fireworks tent down near the park at the river. *Somebody was pretty smart to think of ordering a large quantity of fireworks to sell,* he thought. *I bet it will be very difficult for me to sleep after work once they start selling them.* In only two days it would be the 4th of July. Mayor Huffman was head of the parade committee, and much work had gone into preparing for the popular event. Zeke Miller, with his uncanny ability to predict the weather, promised no rain all day Monday, so great excitement was beginning to be felt by all.

The Journal newspaper had stated that the city's band would lead off the parade. Mayor Huffman's twelve-year-old daughter, Zelda was picked as "Miss 4th of July Festival Queen," and she would ride on a hay wagon covered with small American flags. Huffman himself would ride directly in front of his daughter's float, on the seat of the one-year-old fire department's steam engine. He would sit next to the driver, the man folks call Smokey, due to his love of running into smoke-filled homes to rescue anyone trapped inside. Smokey was getting up there in age but nobody had the heart to suggest that maybe it was time for him to step aside. All would be joined by a marching band and the local Grand Army of the Republic Post in Jonesboro. Justin had also been told that Marshal Merrell, on horseback, would lead the parade. It was scheduled to begin down by the river and travel slowly up the new brick street until finally reaching Fourth Street. Justin planned on rising early Monday morning so as to not miss anything.

~~~~~~~~~~~~~~~~~~~~~

The envelopes of cash had stopped appearing underneath Chief Deputy Cecil Merrell's hotel room door, as he had nothing to pass on to Kruger. Merrell needed money for gambling debts as he continued to live beyond his means as a deputy marshal. The night before he had written another message to be delivered by his messenger pigeon, once he could be located. It contained an idea for an even bigger take if Kruger had the guts to pull it off. Merrell then stated he expected a larger reward for his services and naturally left the letter unsigned. Telling his brother he was going out on patrol, he scoured the town looking for Tommy Two-Fingers.
~~~~~~~~~~~~~~~~~~~~~

Where is that old drunk hiding? He thought as he checked all of the normal locations before finally finding him passed out in the alley behind the pool hall. Using the toe of his boot so as not to have to actually touch the filthy man, Cecil Merrell finally succeeded in awakening Tommy enough to stand, receive the letter, and of course, receive his dime. Tommy then staggered towards the White Dog Saloon. Now all Merrell could do was sit back and wait for another payday envelope.

The Saturday night shift had been quite busy as a larger amount of drinking seemed to result in more fist fights, cat fights between loose women, gun discharges, and drunks. Justin was always amazed at how easily Wilbert had taken to rounding up these people without having to knock too many heads together. From salesman to deputy marshal, he had done remarkably well, and Justin was proud of his friend's accomplishments. Probably the biggest change in the nighttime routine had been the new fireworks tent. Once that sales tent opened, groups of men, women, and especially young boys lined up to make their purchases. With the extent of fireworks going off already, Justin wondered if anybody would save any back for the Fourth. There would be little sleeping after this shift, but he didn't care as Sunday morning meant church and a meal at the table with Marsha Weir.

A groggy Justin Blake finally forced himself out of bed and prepared himself for the 10:30 a.m. service, arriving just in time to find a seat near the front. *Why do people always take the rear seats first?* He wondered. Looking at the brand new building, Justin could see why the Reverend Stokes was proud of his new church. Justin also made eye contact with Marsha, who gave him a gentle wave of her hand. *Was she watching for me?* He wondered. After the service, Justin approached the Stokes and Weir family before singling upon Marsha Weir. “Good morning, Deputy Justin Blake,” she said in an almost teasing manner. "Shoot anybody recently?" Justin laughed, “Miss Marsha, a pleasure to see you again and no, I haven’t shot anyone recently.” Reaching her arm toward his, she asked that he escort her to their awaiting carriage. “Maybe you will take me for a walk after lunch down at the park?” she asked in a teasing manner. “I would be delighted,” he replied. Once she was properly seated, Justin mounted his horse, Spunky, and rode behind the carriage to the home of the Stokes family.

As the ladies busied themselves completing the meal, the men remained inside the library and out of the way. The Reverend Charles Weir then said, “My sister tells me you were able to retrieve many of the stolen items back from the gypsies. I guess I haven’t had much experience with them, and, unfortunately, succumbed to the idea that they were of a lower class of people.”

Justin saw an opportunity to correct this misconception, “I have found them to be a noble group of loyal and friendly people who feel persecuted for just being different from the rest of us. Without their leader, Jal, none of the missing jewelry would have been recovered. I had very little to do with any of this I'm afraid."

Interjecting himself into the conversation, the Reverend Stokes replied, "That's not the way I heard it." Before Justin could answer, a voice from the kitchen announced that the meal was ready, and the men adjourned to the dining room for a feast of fried chicken, fried potatoes, fresh corn on the cob, and homemade bread, all with which Justin filled himself to the brim.

As everyone was finished and enjoying a cup of coffee and a slab of apple pie, a happy Mrs. Stokes spoke, "My husband has instructed me that I am not to bore our company with any more stories of mine, so it will be up to him to begin any table talk." All eyes fell on the Reverend Stokes who, looking around to see that everyone was looking at him, dabbed his lips with his napkin and cleared his throat. "Well... I guess I am pleased to see that the popular prejudice against the trolley is finally dying out. At first, you'll remember there was a great outcry against the system for fear of electricity, but that seems to be subsiding. I think the present system is much nicer and definitely cleaner than the old horse cart, and soon its use, a familiarity to all of us, will become lost to the younger generation. I guess that's progress."

“My own concern, though, is with the railroads. I am in fear that it’s only a matter of time before someone is hurt or killed by a high speeding train as their carriage or wagon crosses it’s tracks. I pray that I am wrong, but stationing a flagman would cost the railroads very little in money and might save a life.” This conversation continued on and on until Marsha interrupted, “I’m ready for that walk in the park you promised me, Deputy Blake.” Thanking his host again for the invitation to dinner, the couple left the room and ventured outside.

“I couldn’t take another moment of that topic,” she told him. Together they started walking towards the park. As they walked in silence she finally spoke up, “I cannot help but feel you are a different person that when we first met. I mean that in a positive way, Deputy Blake. You no longer appear to be carrying around the baggage you seemed to have before.” This observation by this very cute young lady pleased Justin very much.

“It’s Justin, Miss Weir, and yes, all of that is now behind me. I credit you for finally helping me to release my pain, and I have indeed moved on.” Smiling up at him, Marsha replied, “I’m very happy to hear you say that, Justin.” She reached out and held onto his arm. It proved to be a wonderful day to be young and alive.

Chapter 32

The 4th of July arrived beautifully, just as Zeke Miller had predicted. People expected the temperatures to continue to rise to the low nineties, with a strong and gusting wind that might help cool down the town people who were expected to line both sides of the newly brick paved main street. The gusts of strong wind were playing havoc with some of the float decorations and mounted flags.

Justin had risen earlier than normal, thanks to exploding fireworks and the general excitement of the festivities. Eating a hardy mid-morning breakfast, he began to walk around and take in the sights. Mayor Huffman was already on the scene directing people, and resolving the parade order of vehicles and marchers. The firemen had clearly spent a great deal of time polishing up their new steam fire engine and had already arrived. Due to the high temperatures and the fact that the parade would not begin until 11:00 a.m., the firemen had relocated their two fire horses under a nearby shade tree with several buckets of river water at their disposal to rest the animals as comfortably as possible. Today would be a scorcher for sure.

By 10:30, Mayor Huffman was beginning to have everyone start the process of lining up their vehicles and marchers for the parade. People were already beginning to gather along Main Street, and Justin caught site of ex-Marshal Brewster in his wheelchair and Zeke, who was wearing his old Civil War uniform, positioned at the edge of the street. They had staked out good positions across the street from O. Gordon's Furniture store near the end of the parade route, which allowed easy viewing both directions. Justin could see that both of his friends had become quite a pair these days, and he was very happy to see the smile on their faces. "Morning guys, mind if I join you here?" Ex-Marshal Brewster replied he was happy to see him. "Justin, I had better be ah gettin' down ta the parade so as I can march with my G.A.R. Post. Will you watch over the Marshal for me till I can get back?" Justin said he was happy to do so as Zeke left to join his comrades. "I don't require a babysitter, Deputy Blake," Brewster said in mock anger. "You're stuck with me either way, Marshal, so just sit back, relax and enjoy the parade."

Marshal Merrell had arrived down at the starting point, sitting atop a borrowed mount. He would lead the parade, followed by the fire engine driven by Smokey with Mayor Huffman, then the hay wagon with "Miss 4th of July Festival

Queen." Then the marching band, the old soldiers carrying flags, followed by other floats - many of which were local merchants with advertising signage. All these were decked out in red, white, and blue ribbons to mark the celebration of the event.

While the mayor tried his best to organize everybody and to tend to last-minute questions, two young boys who went unnoticed, crept up to the hay wagon where the young Zelda Huffman sat. "Go ahead, I dare you," the older of the two told his friend. Looking around to see that he was not being observed, the youngster removed a pack of matches from his pocket, lit one and touched it to the thick straw hanging off the back of the wagon. Seeing that it was successfully lit, both boys slowly walked into the back of the crowd. Suddenly with the help of a gust of wind, the rear of the wagon erupted into flames. "Fire! Fire!" someone shouted, as it quickly started advancing forward. Upon seeing his daughter in danger, Huffman rushed to her aid and lifted her to safety. Firemen standing next to their fire horses grabbed the buckets of river water setting about and doused the majority of the flames, as they pulled the rest of the straw off the wagon and onto the ground where it was left to burn itself out. "Who did that?" shouted the mayor and several others, as anyone even close by became an instant suspect. Nobody moved, nobody had actually witnessed anyone setting the fire. With no suspects to be found, the remaining unburned hay was quickly spread around to cover the bare spots, and Zelda remounted the stack on the wagon where she had previously sat. She then found herself looking back from time to time, to ensure everything was safe. Looking eastward, any one could see that now both sides of the streets were packed with people five or six deep, all anticipating the start, all watching westward for the command to begin.

The ruckus caused a small delay, but everyone eventually reformed and were now ready to begin once Huffman gave the signal. As many of you know...'boys will be boys' and those two were not finished with their pranks. "Your turn," the younger boy told his friend. Slowly the older boy pulled out a large full brick of firecrackers from a paper bag, lit the fuse, and tossed them directly under Marshal Merrell's standing horse. People still to this day laugh about what they saw. Once the firecrackers began to detonate in mass application, both horse and rider jumped high into the air. Merrell held on tightly as his terrified mound leaped and kicked like a wild bronco. All eyes in the crowd watched as the horse jumped and took off through the grass where Marshal Merrell was sent flying into the air, finally rolling to a stop. At first nobody said a thing, then suddenly wild laugher circulated all along the lines on both sides of the street. Chants of "Brass Buttons" could be heard among the crowd. It took only a matter of moments before the laughter had filtered all the way to the end of the parade route, as each neighbor told the other neighbor what had happened. A bruised, but deeply humiliated Marshal Merrell raced to chase down his terrified horse, who still seemed spooked by the wild laughter. Finally able to calm the horse enough to remount, Merrell focused his eyes straight ahead as he slowly rode back down Main Street to the jeers, hoots, and finger pointing of the crowd. Merrell tied up the horse outside the horse barn and stormed inside his office. His parade was now over.

~~~~~~~~~~~~~~~~~~~~~~

Watching all of this from a safe distance was the assassin who, while amused by these childish antics, was ready for the parade to begin. It was hot up here and the longer he remained in place, the greater his chances of discovery. His .451 hexagon barreled Whitworth rifle with scope was loaded and ready for the kill, his victim picked out, and a clear message to be sent today in front of almost the entire town.

~~~~~~~~~~~~~~~~~~~~~~

"Looks like your Marshal won't be riding in the parade after all," Brewster mentioned to Justin. "Are you going to take his place? If so, don't worry about me. I'll be just fine here until Zeke returns." Justin reassured Brewster he wasn't going anywhere, and he guessed the Chief Deputy would now fill in for his brother. All eyes began to look west as the band began to play renderings of patriotic music. The parade was finally beginning.

Mayor Huffman was glad this was finally underway. Trying to get everyone lined up and ready was quite an endeavor, but gladly that was all behind us now. Everything would be fine, unless one of the marchers passed out from all the heat. It's a real possibility, and one that he forgot to plan for. "Beautiful day for a parade, Mr. Mayor," Smokey said as he expertly handled the team of fire horses, holding them to a slow pace for the benefit of the marchers. The sun was scorching hot beating down upon his head as the mayor used his hat to wave to the crowd. Thank goodness for the wind gusts that were helping to cool things off a bit. Huffman finally decided to leave his hat on his head and just wave to the crowd saying, "Larger turn out than last year, don't you think, Smokey?"

Block after block the parade limped along, and finally, the steam fire engine was approaching the main section of town. Both Justin and Brewster began waving to the mayor when a large gust of wind caught the brim of the mayor's hat and flipped it off the front of his head. Instantly Huffman jerked his head back, trying to catch it as the bullet whizzed past where his head had been only a second before and struck Smokey straight on the left side of his face. The poor fireman's face exploded into a pinkish cloud of goo, as the bullet passed cleanly through him and ricocheted off the brick surface. As if in slow motion, Smokey's lifeless body began dropping off the seat and onto the bricks below.

It took several seconds for the waving people along both lines to realize what had happened before the screams and stampede of pure terror began. Fathers grabbed for their children, and ladies shrieked in fear as the realization of the horror began to set in. The body of Smokey now lay along the edge of the bricks in it's own puddle of blood, as some of the braver men in the crowd moved forward to catch a glimpse of the scene. Justin leaped into action. "Get that fire vehicle out of here, now," as someone guided the fire horses off of the street. Rushing up to the scene, Justin shouted for someone to find Doc Baxter as he held the crowd back. Ex-Marshal Brewster had managed to roll his wheelchair up to the body, and his many years of police training kicked into gear, giving directions and doing what he could. "Any idea where that shot came from?" he asked everyone. "Somewhere behind us" came the reply from a group of men. "Justin, I'll take charge here, go see if you can spot the shooter. He can't have gotten far," Brewster shouted. "Be careful!"

Justin took off running north, looking high and low for any movement of anyone running away from the parade. Glancing back he saw a few other men running after him, no doubt also looking for the shooter. Justin had managed to look over two city blocks of homes when he heard someone calling for him. Responding, Justin followed the shouting until arriving at the new church of Reverend Stokes. The church's tall wooden construction ladder was leaning up on the back side of the church, and what appeared to be a common horse blanket laid down on its roof for the shooter to lay on to protect him from the heat. The perfect high location for a clear shot into the parade only one block away. Unfortunately, the shooter had simply vanished. This would be a 4th of July that nobody would soon forget.

~~~~~~~~~~~~~~~~~~~~

Marshal Merrell sat in silence as each member of the city council, as well as the mayor, shouted at him at the same time. "That shot was clearly meant for me, and if that gust of wind hadn't blown off my hat, it would be me laying at the undertakers now instead of poor old Smokey," Huffman yelled. Justin returned from the crime scene to see Zeke pushing the ex-Marshal home. By now Wilbert had met up with him and was filled in on the situation up to that point. Now they needed to brief the Marshal on the discovery of the shooter's nest, but hearing all the shouting coming from inside the fire barn caused them to pause. *No sense in getting mixed up in all of that mess,* each man thought. Finally,
~~~~~~~~~~~~~~~~~~~~

the mayor and city council came out still bickering among themselves, walking past without even acknowledging them. It was now time for the deputies to brief the Marshal on their discovery.

Entering the office, both men noticed the Marshal sitting at the desk with his head laying in his hands. The sight made both men feel a little uncomfortable, as if they were intruding upon a private personal moment. Making a little noise so as to announce their presence, Marshal Merrell looked up at them with a deeply troubled face. He then motioned for the deputies to pull up a seat as he straightened himself. "Alright Blake, I'm asking now. What do you suggest I do?" Merrell's change in attitude caught both men a little off guard, but Justin felt he had finally been given permission to offer advice.

"First, I suggest you look at this as two separate murder cases. The gypsy was killed by someone to keep him from providing names of the gang. The Italian was also killed to prevent him from talking. These other killings are by an assassin, someone with a grudge or agenda. He is probably the same man who shot Mr. Larson and Mrs. Howell. This insanity must be stopped before he kills again. I suggest you assign your deputies to specific cases."

"Second, I suggest you develop a working relationship with ex-Marshal Brewster. He has thirty years plus experience in criminal investigations, and knowing this man the way Wilbert and I do, I feel he would be more than happy to assist in any way possible. It was Brewster who identified the remains of a .50 caliber hexagon bullet that killed Jeb Larson. It was Brewster that identified the murder weapon as a .451 hexagon barrel Whitworth English rifle, a very rare rifle used by a few lucky Southern snipers during the war. Today Marshal Brewster took charge at the crime scene and directed me where to search for the killer. We came very close to catching him, too. Upon returning, I discovered two small children were hit by ricocheting brick particles from the bullet's downward impact. Doc Baker says the children will thankfully recover just fine."

"Third, I suggest we run an advertisement in the Journal asking our people if they know of anyone here who owns such a weapon. Fourth, we should speak with every store owner in town that sells ammunition to find out if anyone stocks or purchased this type of very rare bullets. If nothing is discovered, we add our search to Jonesboro and Marion. Of course, the assassin may have a stockpile already on hand but it's a shot in the dark, no pun intended." The last bit of a joke was only said to try to lighten the conversation a bit. Justin then sat back and awaited the Marshal's response.

"The other day my brother and I spent all day matching up stolen jewelry to it's owners and making quite a few people happy. They thanked us for getting their belongings back, but none of this would have happened had it not been for you. You took the time to develop a relationship with the man called Jal, while I never bothered to even speak with him."

"Today some kids with firecrackers turned me into a figure of public ridicule. I heard them all laughing and calling me 'Brass Buttons'. I was even hiding here in my office when a killing took place, and a man in a wheelchair had to take charge of the murder scene. The mayor is right, I no longer am in control of anything. They are considering asking for my resignation. I guess, under the circumstances, I can't blame them. All I ever wanted from these people was their respect."

Wilbert chimed in, "Respect has to be earned, sir, and comes later. First, you must build friendship, trust, and confidence, then the rest will happen. The one thing you did do right, Marshal, is that you rode your horse down Main Street afterward."

"That took guts, and secretly everyone knows that you stood up to the ridicule with pride." Still lost in thought, Merrell then answered, "Alright, I'm assigning both of you to work on this assassin's cases. I'll have Cecil stay on the gypsy and the Italian murders." Justin was only waiting to respond when he asked, "Where is your brother anyway?" "He asked for the day off in order to take care of some personal business. I fully expected today to be a quiet and peaceful day anyway. Anything else you gentlemen have to offer?"

Justin considered telling him of the other two incidences involving his brother, but reconsidered. Even the suggestion that his brother was not one hundred percent honest would completely undo any good already accomplished here today.

~~~~~~~~~~~~~~~~~~~~

"So how did the men like their twenty dollar bonus?" Kruger asked his new lieutenant. Smiley replied they were very happy to get the silver dollars and that the entire counterfeit operation was proceeding according to plan. Very pleased with that bit of news, Kruger then opened the envelope containing the note Chief Deputy Merrell had sent earlier by way of his favorite carrier pigeon, Tommy Two-Fingers. Shaking his head Kruger then passed it over to Smiley Lewis.

It read: *The perfect time for your operation is today while almost everyone is at the parade. Easy pickings. p.s. I expect a thicker envelope for this valuable information.*

"I don't like it one bit," Smiley said. "Why take chances in broad daylight when our boys can use the cover of darkness to their advantage?" Handing the note back, Kruger wadded it up and pitched it into the trash saying, "Now the guy is telling us our business and then has the nerve to demand money in return. I'm getting mighty uneasy about this guy."
~~~~~~~~~~~~~~~~~~~~

Smiley nodded in agreement, "Just say the word and he'll be taken care of."

"Start making the arrangements," Kruger told him, "His usefulness has expired. Do what you think is best when you think it's time, but make it clean and untraceable."

Chapter 33

Smokey's funeral was well attended by the good people of Gas City. The victim's wife was in total shambles as the sealed wooden coffin was lowered into the small cemetery east of the river. One of those in attendance was the assassin who was slightly upset with himself for hitting the wrong man. Missing his intended victim was not his norm at all, but due to the high gusting winds, these things could occasionally happen. He had watched and laughed from a safe location as the men swarmed around the church where he had fired from only minutes before. It was just like the local police to be a day late and a dollar short.

~~~~~~~~~~~~~~~~~~~~~~

Alvin Jensen wrote a full spread in the Journal on this senseless public murder, and asked everyone to report anything out of the ordinary they might have witnessed. There was also the suggested request for information on
~~~~~~~~~~~~~~~~~~~~~~

anyone owning a .451 hexagon barrel Whitworth rifle to inform the Gas City Marshal's Office. Hopefully someone from the reading public would bring forth information that would lead to a quick arrest. Justin and Wilbert approached every store in town that handled any type of guns or ammunition, to see if they have sold .50 caliber hexagon bullets, but came up short. Marshal Merrell then sent a request for area town marshals to do the same. Now the wait began. Marshall Merrell then asked his brother for an update on the killing of the gypsy and the Italian but got nothing he didn't already know. "Maybe I'll have to get involved in these cases myself," he told his brother, in hopes of building a fire under him. From the look upon the Chief Deputy's face, it may have worked.

Cecil needed time to think, so he began to walk down by the Pan Handle Depot to observe passengers arriving into town. As he stood by waiting for the passengers to step off the arriving train, a commotion and scuffle caught his attention. It was that old Irish drunk from the Old Soldiers Home again, acting up and causing more trouble. The Chief Deputy has had several dealings with the man they call Toby before. He loved to drink, and when he did he was ready to take on the world and the Southern army. On several occasions he has had to spend some local jail time over these incidences, and it looks like he will be doing so today. 'Squire Jones only sends him back to the Old Soldiers Home so they can deal with him, and asks that he not be allowed to return. When his first opportunity arrived, Toby jumped onto the trolley, came to town, and it all began again. "Come along peaceful now, Toby. I don't want any trouble from you," the Chief Deputy calmly stated, as he reached for the man's arm. Suddenly Toby's eyes flashed with a wild hatred that caught Cecil Merrell completely off guard as the man swung a hidden knife, burying it deep into the side of the Chief Deputy. The attacker then bolted away as a startled group of railroad passengers and townspeople watched helplessly and ladies screamed in sudden terror.

Deputy Marshal Wilbert Vance had just sat down at the lunch table in the Pan Handle Restaurant, and was contemplating his meal choices, when word reached him of the attack upon his fellow officer. Reaching the scene, he saw the Chief Deputy lying upon his side writhing in agony, as the depot station master was compressing a towel over the wound to try to control the bleeding. Someone who had a buggy close by arrived, and several of the men lifted the injured man into it. "Get him to Doctor Baxter quickly," was heard as the injured man was transported away. "Who saw this happen?" Wilbert shouted.

"I did," a local man said. "It was that man called Toby from the Marion Old Soldiers Home. He was drunk again, and the officer here was removing him when Toby flashed a knife and stabbed him." Wilbert was very familiar with the suspect.

"Anyone see where he went?"

A woman answered, "I think he ran towards that terrible Happy Hollow Saloon. I pray that someone should burn that awful den of iniquity to the ground."

Knowing that Merrell's injury was being attended to, Wilbert Vance set off to apprehend Toby. Searching several out buildings, he found nothing so he entered the notorious Happy Hollow Saloon. From the hard looks he received from it's clientele, Wilbert suspected the man he was looking for was indeed hiding away inside. Now to find him, which he did, hiding behind the bar. "Come on out, Toby," he firmly instructed," and lay the knife on the bar." Instead of complying with the order, Toby came up yelling, "I'll kill everybody," as he lunged towards Wilbert. Pulling his own service revolver, Wilbert sidestepped the lunge and clubbed Toby on the side of his head. He went out like a light. Wilbert placed cuffs upon the man's wrists and picked up the still bloody knife. He noticed, then, that some of the men along the bar began moving his way in a threatening manner. Clearly, they did not like what they had just witnessed. "This man just stabbed a deputy marshal in cold blood, then threatened to kill all of you. Is he worth your protection?" With that information, the men took a step back and returned to their prior conversations as Wilbert marched the dazed man out of the saloon and towards the jail.

As Wilbert escorted his prisoner to the jail, it became very apparent the man was cold sober and only pretended to be intoxicated in order to lure the Chief Deputy in. During this time, someone had thought to go fetch the Marshal and inform him of his brother's attack, as the office was empty when Wilbert locked the prisoner up. He then proceeded over to Doctor Baxter's residence to see about Cecil's condition. The pale look on the Marshal's face said it all. "He's still alive but has lost a lot of blood," Merrell informed him. "I got the man who stabbed him and locked him up. He's from the Marion Old Soldiers Home and has caused a lot of problems here in the past." This information clearly passed over the Marshal as all his attention was now focused on his brother. Both men remained silent in the waiting room as the minutes ticked away and they awaited word from the doctor.

Looking up from his desk, Smiley Lewis informed Kruger, "It's been handled." He then told of hiring a known troublemaker from the Old Soldiers Home, with a few mental issues, as the perfect patsy. The badly injured deputy was hauled off to the Doc's office with a deep stab wound. Live or die, he wouldn't be a bother any longer. Kruger was pleased with the way it was handled.

"Now that the Marshal's Office is one man short, maybe it's time to set out teams to work tomorrow night?" With that, Smiley set to work in organizing tomorrow's robberies.

~~~~~~~~~~~~~~~~~~~~~~

Once Justin Blake learned of the attack on Cecil Merrell, he immediately donned his uniform and reported to work. Finding his colleagues awaiting word, Justin reported to the office to see if he could obtain a confession from the prisoner, as well as a motive. Wilbert had told him that in the heat of the moment he had forgotten to search the prisoner, so Justin made a point of patting the man down, and was surprised to discover twenty silver dollars inside the man's pocket. "Where did you get the money, Toby?" The prisoner became very agitated at the mention of the money. "That's mine! I earned it, give it back to me!" he shouted. "We'll keep it for you out here. How did you earn it?" With a grin on his face, Toby replied, "By stabbing that Johnny Reb spy! That man told me that the Reb was a saying all Yankee soldiers were cowards and horse thieves. He told me the fella was saying I was crazy, and I was glad to do him in for money." Justin made written notes of each question he asked and the answers the prisoner provided. Clearly, this was a paid assassination attempt upon Cecil Merrell but the questions remained, why and by whom?
~~~~~~~~~~~~~~~~~~~~~~

"Who was the man who paid you to stab the Rebel spy? What is his name?" Shaking his head, he replied, "Don't know his name, just what he looks like. A mean looking feller too." Justin was unable to obtain any further information from the prisoner, so he picked up his notes and walked over to the courtroom located inside the First National Bank. 'Squire Jones was ruling on a civil case, so Justin remained outside until the proceedings were over. "You wish to speak with me, Deputy?" the 'Squire asked. Justin then filled him in on the attack on Cecil Merrell and showed him the statement the prisoner had made. "It's unsigned, you'll need him to sign it," the 'Squire told him. "Since he is an occupant of the Old Soldiers' Home he would fall under Federal jurisdiction for final punishment for something this serious, but I can still hold a local inquest to determine the motive and possible accomplices." Looking for his ledger book, the 'Squire continued, "Tomorrow afternoon is open. I suggest you send a telegram to the Soldiers' Home and tell them about all of this, and request they provide an officer to take the prisoner into custody after the inquest tomorrow." Justin agreed to do just that. "By tomorrow we will probably know if this will be an assault or a murder case. It will also give the Marshal a little time to pull himself together. I expect a large public attendance, so we may need to use the horse barn. You might have Zeke clean it out, just in case we have to relocate there."

Justin walked over to the Western Union office and had the telegram sent. “Please have someone deliver any reply to the Marshal’s office,” he informed them and no, he had heard no more updates on Deputy Merrell’s condition. Feeling he must maintain a presence inside the office, Justin put on a pot of coffee and awaited further word. “I’d like a cup of that when it’s ready,” Toby said. “Sure thing,” Justin replied. “Once you sign this confession.” Without any hesitation, he took the offered pencil in hand and signed the paper. “Please date it also. Today is July 9.” Handing it back, Toby seemed very pleased with himself. “You should have seen me in action today. I took care of that Reb real good. Isn’t gonna spy on me no more, that’s for sure!” Justin, in a somber tone, finally had heard enough bragging. “That was a deputy town marshal you stabbed. The Civil War ended over thirty years ago.” Those words had no effect on the old soldier, who woke up every day thinking it was 1862.

About an hour later, Wilbert entered the office. “I thought you might need a break. Is there any of that coffee left?” Pouring what was left into a cup, Justin filled him in on tomorrow’s inquest and showed him the written confession. “I’m almost afraid to ask how he is.”

“Still hasn’t awakened. Doc said he’s done all he can and now it’s in God’s hands.”

With a deep sigh, Justin then asked how the Marshal was handling it.

"He's not talking at all. He just sits at Cecil's bedside holding his hand. Doc wanders in from time to time to check his vitals, but mostly he just remains outside. I needed to get away myself."

Inside the jail cell, the old confused soldier was singing a little jingle, "*Got me a Johnny Reb today... I got me a Johnny Reb today...*" Justin looked up at Wilber and, with a point of his thumb at the prisoner, said, "It's not been a picnic in here either. Well, with you here I'll mosey over to the Doc's and see if I can brief the Marshal on tomorrow's..." Just then the door opened as a crestfallen Marshal Merrell entered the office. Wilbert got up from the desk to allow the Marshal to sit down. Both men searched Merrell's saddened face for the answer. "He's gone," he told them. With that, both deputies left the office to allow the Marshal some privacy, as the jailed prisoner continued to ssing, "I got me a Johnny Reb today…"

Chief Deputy Cecil Merrell was buried at 11 a.m. the following day, with a solid turn out of town support. Two police officers from the Marion Old Soldiers Home were on hand to pay their respects before the scheduled 1 p.m. inquiry. As expected, the large public turnout for the hearing forced the use of the larger fire barn. Zeke Miller had worked well into the night to clean and refresh it. The firemen also relocated their steam engine and fire horses to another location close by. The inquiry began on time as a few witnesses were brought up and placed under oath to tell of what they had seen. Marshal Merrell was physically present, but clearly, his mind was elsewhere and not on the inquiry itself.

Wilbert was then called up to testify and placed under oath. He told how he was ready to eat lunch when informed of the assault upon a fellow officer. How he saw others attempting to save the deputy's life and how he was directed to where the perpetrator was hiding out and, finally, how he was subdued and arrested. Then Justin was called and spoke of questioning the prisoner and writing down his questions, along with verbatim what the man had said. The signed confession was then given to the court. The prisoner who had been sitting quietly between two soldier's home policemen, began singing, "I got me a Johnny Reb today…"

A man stood up from the courtroom, "Your Honor, if I may have a brief moment. My name is Doctor Steadman, and I am this man's physician at the Soldiers Home. I can attest to you that Toby suffers from severe emotional trauma from fighting the Civil War. At times he believes he is still fighting it as a soldier, and he is not mentally competent to stand trial, so I ask that he be returned to us for further medical evaluation and treatment."

After a brief pause, 'Squire Jones stated he would recommend that the county provide a second expert to evaluate the accused man's mental condition, and leave it up to the county sheriff to defer charges if he was found mentally competent. That ended the inquiry. With that, Marshall Merrell stormed out of the courtroom. After all, who could blame him for his anger since his brother's killer may have just walked away scot-free.

A subdued Marshal Merrell entered the office and immediately told both deputies, "Let's talk." Justin began first, "I think I have made a discovery that probably involves this case. While I was questioning the prisoner, I began to fiddle with the prisoner's silver dollar coins and, without thinking, started tapping one on the desk. It took me a little while to determine what was wrong. The coin rang dull, not like the sound of silver being tapped. I picked up each coin and tried the same experiment, and all had a dull sound. I then reached into my pocket and pulled out one of my own, and tapped it on the desk. It sounded totally different. Marshal, Toby was given counterfeit dollar coins as payment. I made a point of showing the two soldier home policemen the difference and told them I was holding these coins over as evidence. They are here in the corner of the desk. Try them for yourself."

After tapping them for himself, a slight smile and a bit of color returned to the Marshal's face. "Good catch, Deputy Blake." He then examined each coin. "Every one of these are dated last year, 1892, and all look uncirculated. I think we have the beginning of a major counterfeiting ring here, and it may very well play into what I am about to share with you now."

"Cecil woke up and spoke before he passed away. He asked that Doctor Baxter come in to witness what he wanted to tell me. He informed us of some things I am greatly depressed about, that he had been working with a man he called Kruger, who is behind the recent break-ins. Cecil said he provided information from our office by using an old drunk called Tommy Two-Fingers to pass along notes to Kruger, who would then slip a pay envelope underneath his hotel room door. He feels Kruger set up this attempt upon his life to get him out of the way. He went on to say there were other things he would share after he began to recover, but then he began drifting off and never awakened. My own brother was working against us."

Justin felt this was the right time to inform the Marshal about the man with the watch and the issue of the derringer. While these bits of additional damning information were probably cruel, they needed to be aired. Nobody spoke for a few minutes until Justin shared an idea that just popped into his head. If this Kruger was behind the break-ins and fencing operation, he was no doubt behind the killing of the gypsy and the Italian. I'm guessing he's somehow connected with the counterfeiting operation, too, or Toby would not have twenty fake coins in his possession."

Marshal Merrell perked up at this information and began to formulate a plan. “Here is the witness statement Doctor Baxter wrote out after Cecil died. I asked him not to mention anything for the present and he promised to do just that, and I feel I can count upon his discretion. Here is my plan...”

‘Squire Jones listened intently as Marshal Merrell laid out his plan, after first allowing him to test the counterfeit silver dollars for himself and to read the doctor’s statement of Cecil’s confession. “I’m sure all of this is very painful for you Marshal but you’re doing the right thing with your plan. I have no problem issuing the search warrants, but I cannot take part in the search myself as I may be asked to judge this man later on. Wilbert had been successful in rounding up Mayor Huffman and all of the members of the town council, and each was arriving at the marshal’s office as directed. Of course, a few were annoyed at being kept in the dark but were told all their questions would soon be answered. Wilbert had also been directed by the Marshal to round up Tommy Two-Fingers after tonight’s work was completed, and place him under protective custody as a material witness. With paperwork in hand, Marshal Merrell arrived back at his office. Seeing that Zeke Miller and reporter Alvin Jensen were also invited to participate by his deputies, Merrell realized they needed all the help they could muster. Their additional help would be very welcomed.

"Gentlemen, I must apologize to each of you tonight for rounding all of you up from your supper tables, but you are desperately needed tonight for a very important mission. The information I am about to share with you cannot leave this room." He then began to show each man the counterfeit silver dollars and how to tell real ones from fakes. "If we do not act quickly, every business in town will suffer great financial loss from accepting these coins in trade. This is where all of you come in. 'Squire Jones has issued search warrants for every saloon owned by a Mr. Theodore Kruger. We think somewhere inside each saloon there is a stash of these fake silver dollars. Each of you will search your assigned property thoroughly. Leave no stone unturned. We must find these coins and put a halt to their being spread. I cannot tell you how they will be stored, but it only makes sense that all will be kept the same way. Once we discover the first one, that information will be quickly spread to each of you. We will travel together by wagon down to the saloon district, and each of you needs to wait in place until I have Kruger apprehended before you make your move to your assigned saloon. Now if each of you will raise your right hand, I will swear you in as temporary deputy marshals..."

Zeke drove the wagon to a central location already agreed upon, and each man stepped out and waited for their signal. The Marshal then said, "Blake and I will enter the White Dog Saloon first and place Kruger under arrest. As soon as you see I have him in custody, jump into action before they can spread the word." Merrell knew that Kruger was inside as he had a man verify it earlier by peeking through the window of his office. Both men quickly entered the saloon that contained many hard-drinking men, and proceeded unannounced to enter Kruger's office. "Hey," the bartender shouted, "You can't go in there." He reached for a club kept hidden behind his bar. Justin pointed his Remington 44-40 into the man's face. "Police business, I suggest you stop right where you are. We have a warrant for Kruger's arrest. So unless you want to join him..." The bartender's mood changed and he returned to filling drink orders. Marshal Merrell shoved the door to Kruger's office wide open and pointed his weapon at the crime boss. "Theodore Kruger, you are under arrest. Make no move towards a weapon, or I'll shoot you down like the murdering dog you are." An agitated Kruger demanded to know what this was all about.

"You are under arrest for ordering the killings of the gypsy, Beval, the Italian worker, and of course, for my brother Cecil. I also have a warrant signed by 'Squire Jones for the search of this and all of your properties for stolen property and counterfeit coins."

Seeing that he had no other option but to cooperate, Kruger stood and placed his wrists together as Justin cuffed them. Merrell was then led out of his office, but began to shout instructions to his bartender. Taking the prisoner outside, Merrell then cuffed him to the wagon wheel to prevent his escape. By that time, all of the temporary deputies began entering their own assigned saloon by announcing, "I am a temporary deputy marshal and I have a written search order to inspect this place. Do not interfere or you will be arrested." With that, the majority of the men in each saloon realized they had other pending appointments and quickly left. One bartender demanded to know what was going on. "Health inspection, we got word there are flies on your free lunch counter." The bartender, not realizing the joke, replied, "But I swat the little buggers as soon as they land on the food!" Hearing that, Councilman Davidson privately swore off eating at any more saloons. The Marshal's office now had all eight saloons covered. If only something positive would turn up or there would be heck to pay.

Justin began his search of the White Dog starting in Kruger's office and turned up nothing. He then inspected the main saloon, even looking for loose floor boards. Nothing. Now he began looking into the store room. Boxes of whiskey were stacked neatly one on top of the other, and unopened kegs of beer lined four deep along the rear wall. Justin moved every box of whiskey and found nothing. Looking down at the wooden beer kegs, he gave each a light push but was startled to discover the beer kegs would not move. It took great effort to finally pull one out, and using some tools lying about, pried the lid of one open. It was full of twenty-five cent coins. Picking up a handful, he found that all were dated 1892. *So this is how they brought them into town*, he thought to himself. *Pretty clever*. He then pried off the top of another and discovered the silver dollars. Justin stepped to the front door and called for Marshal Merrell, who was then led into the storeroom. Merrell broke out into a huge grin and bolted to the door to inform his deputies where to look. It required a great deal of manpower for all of the barrels of coins to be removed from the saloons and placed inside the wagon for the trip back to the jail. Kruger's smug attitude completely changed once he realized his prize catch of coins had been discovered. Prior to leaving the White Dog, Marshal Merrell approached the bartender and ordered two bottles of their best whisky to go. Once everything was placed inside the Marshal's office, a little celebration was in order.

These men had certainly earned it! "Justin," the Marshal said. "Since you and Wilbert are on duty and cannot take part in our celebrations, I wonder if you would mind taking Zeke here and go fetch Marshal Brewster. He needs to celebrate with these men." There was a loud vote of approval from the councilmen as the trio went to fetch the ex-Marshal. Leaving the office, it was Zeke who pointed out that the Marshal had finally called them by their first names. "Might be I could learn ta like that man after all!" Brewster was happy to be invited when he heard it was a celebration party. That night

Marshal Merrell changed his attitude completely. He was, also, now a respected man.

Smiley Lewis was one of the men who exited the bar as the Marshal's men entered. Smiley had proven that he had the brains to run a successful operation such as this, and now began to think ahead. *We've got to find and silence the carrier pigeon that Kruger received messages from. He could become a problem if law enforcement sobered him up enough to talk,* he thought. Pulling one of his thugs to the side, he gave him instructions and the man departed instantly. *Also, with the boss locked up, we had better call off the break-ins scheduled to take place*. Smiley entered the White Dog already knowing that the coins had been discovered and removed by the lawmen. Entering the office, he hesitated slightly then sat down at Kruger's desk. Smiley Lewis was now in charge and there was much to think about.

Chapter 34

The headlines of the Gas City Journal said it all: **Major Counterfeiting Ring Busted By Marshal's Office-Suspect Arrested.** Everyone who took part in the raid on the Kruger saloons was heralded as a local hero. Instantly it seemed that paper signs went up all over town stating all twenty-five cent pieces and silver dollars would be tested by the shop owner prior to acceptance. This practice also applied at the First National Bank. The Marshal's office urged anyone in possession of a counterfeit coin, either through making change or from questionable practices, needed to bite the bullet, so to say, and deposit them in the jar setting on the Marshal's desk. Arrangements would be made to turn these coins over to the Federal authorities, who had been made aware of the situation. Today was a great day to be in law enforcement with the fake coins stopped, and the presumed ring leader behind bars. Score it: Good Guys 2- Bad Guys 0.

Kruger remained mute and refused to answer any questions while his lawyer attempted to get bail posted. 'Squire Jones would have none of it, so Kruger remained a guest of the town. His lawyer was allowed to speak with his client but only through the cell bars. Gas City was just not equipped with better facilities - as the jail, after all, was inside a fire barn. Everything was not a bed of roses though, as the body of a man was found lying next to the Pan Handle Railroad tracks. It was Tommy Two-Fingers. Clearly, he was killed to prevent him from testifying against Kruger. The arms of this evil octopus extended far and wide, it seemed.

Kruger sat in his jail cell and contemplated his situation. All day an armed officer had remained inside the office to prevent any attempted jail breaks. *What do they have on me and how will they get me out of this?* He thought. He had little doubt that his friend Smiley Lewis was hard at work developing the perfect plan of action for his escape. All he could do now was sit back and wait for it to happen.

~~~~~~~~~~~~~~~~~~~~

Last evening had been quite an evening for ex-Marshal Brewster. Very surprised and a little on edge, Brewster was finally won over by the attempted kindness that the new Marshal was giving him by telling the reporter Jensen that it was Brewster's ideas that might eventually lead to the
~~~~~~~~~~~~~~~~~~~~

capture of the assassin. Brewster didn't see it that way, but every one of the councilmen as well as the mayor treated him with courtesy and respect. Last evening was a game changer for Brewster and he was now determined not to hide away on his front porch any longer, but to get out and be with people again. He was still the same man as before, only now he was confined to this wheelchair.

An early morning telegram arrived at the Marshal's office: *Department of Treasury Agents Wells and Gibson arriving your city today. stop. Your cooperation greatly appreciated. stop.* Marshal Merrell was happy at the thought of getting those beer kegs of counterfeit coins out of his office. The Treasury boys were more than welcome to them. All day long townspeople had entered his office rather sheepishly to deposit counterfeit coins they had received, and stressed their innocence in having them. Inwardly Merrell chuckled every time they went through the same sad story of now suffering great financial hardships. Maybe they thought he should make up their loss out of his own pocket?

Kruger continued to remain silent, but his day in court would be here tomorrow afternoon at 2 p.m. He said nothing when he was told of it but only smiled at Merrell. How strange, he didn't seem worried at all. Then in a loud voice Kruger addressed the Marshal. "If you think I'm going to remain quiet about your crooked brother's involvement in all of this you got another thing coming. He was the ring leader and we only took our orders from him. Just another crooked cop." Merrell knew he had to just let it go. Whatever was said about Cecil couldn't hurt him now, but inside he knew he might lose his own job if people began to wonder if he knew about his brother's involvement all along, but choose to do nothing about it.

Shortly after noon, the door to the Marshal's Office opened as two very well-dressed men entered. "Marshal Merrell? Agents Wells and Gibson from the Treasury Department," they said, as they flashed their badges for proper identification. The agents seemed quite startled by the amount of counterfeit coinage visible in the beer barrels. "I must congratulate you and your deputies, Marshal. This is a huge haul in coinage, far more that we can normally expect from a small town police force. No disrespect intended, sir." Merrell offered each man a seat but both preferred to stand. "We have arranged the use of the Pennsylvania railroad mail car to transport this evidence and the prisoner back to our office in Indianapolis." Pulling out an expensive looking pocket watch, Agent Wells continued, "If you can recommend a few good men to transport all of this to the awaiting car, we can catch the 2:45 southbound back today."

"Gentlemen, you are more than welcome to take all of these coins and those few in the glass jar that the public has returned, but you may not have my prisoner today. He goes before our local 'Squire tomorrow afternoon on three counts of murder and robbery charges."

The agents looked at one another. "We were not told of local charges pending, but I encourage you to allow the Federal Government first crack at the prisoner as our claim is stronger."

With a light shaking of his head, Merrell told them no. "You see gentlemen, this is a small community and this man is accused of inflicting death and terror upon it. Our people require some degree of closure as his victims were our citizens and neighbors. I suggest you stay overnight and speak with the 'Squire before tomorrow's trial." After a brief private discussion, Agent Wells announced that Agent Gibson would be returning today with the counterfeit coins and he would remain behind. "Is there a restaurant here you recommend for lunch? Also, I'll need to send a telegram to my supervisor for further instructions." Merrell quickly suggested the Mississinewa Hotel which was located just behind his office. "I highly recommend the pork chops. The Western Union is right down the street. I'll round up a few good men and a wagon, and have them here waiting upon your return. Enjoy your lunch." With that, both men departed towards the hotel.

Stepping out into the fire barn, Marshal Merrell noticed Zeke Miller tending to the fire horses with ex-Marshal Brewster watching from his wheelchair. Acknowledging

Brewster, Merrell spoke, “Zeke, are you interested in doing some patriotic work for your government?”

Zeke agreed, and knew where they could borrow a wagon for the less than one hour job. “I know a few fellers ta help out too,” he told Merrell.

“Good, that will solve that problem. Just have them hang out here while the agents eat their lunch.”

Across town, Justin Blake woke up hungry and decided to see what was on the menu at the Pan Handle Restaurant. Finding beef stew available, Justin devoured a large bowl of it before walking over to the post office to check his mail, but seeing that Postmaster Harris’ bicycle was not parked outside, knew he must return later. Feeling the stubbles upon his chin, he proceeded over to Matthew Brooks Barbershop for a much-needed haircut and shave. Brooks was one of the councilmen who took part in the raid and, being a barber, naturally felt he could share his adventures with each client who entered the barbershop. By now his own personal involvement in the story had grown to the point where Brooks single-handedly made the discovery, while each customer merely rolled his eyes with the tall tale. “Afternoon, Deputy Blake,” he said, “Any new police tasks you need accomplished? We haven’t chased any horse thief’s for quite some spell.” Brooks was a leading member in the Grant County Horse Thief Protection Association there in town. His group wore a special badge and returned most horses that were stolen to their rightful owners and the thieves to the Marshal's office.

"Nothing that I'm aware of, Matt," he replied.

"Then I'll be with you in a few minutes. So...where was I? Oh yea, so I figured the coins had to be inside of something sturdy..." Just then an out-of-wind man poked his head into the barbershop. "Pan Handle engine just hit a wagon with three people in it. This looks very bad." The man then rushed off to find the Marshal. Justin's first instinct was to rush to the scene, but on second thought felt he shouldn't interfere with Merrell. There would be enough there to assist, so he sat and waited his turn in the chair. The barber then changed his subject, "I keep telling folks somebody's gonna get killed at these unmarked railroad crossings while all along the railroads ignore the city council's ordinances..." The man in the chair responded, "This will allow the lawyers to circle like vultures."

Someone had gotten to Merrell first and he knew he had to go straight to the accident scene, so he asked Zeke to remain and take charge of the men for the loading of the coin barrels. Merrell was very hesitant on leaving his prisoner, unguarded, but sensing that, Brewster replied, "I'll guard your prisoner Marshal, go do your job. I got this covered." With a nod of thanks, Merrell departed for the accident scene. Once he arrived, the mangled bodies of the husband and a young boy were taken away to the undertaker while the wife was still alive and badly injured, but under Doc Baxter's treatment. The talk all over town was about the railroads ignoring the city ordinances to post warning flagmen at all crossings to warn of an approaching train. As tragic as this accident was, maybe it would finally awaken the railroads and force them into taking action. Only time would tell.

Zeke saw the two agents approaching and jumped into action. "We are ready ta haul dem barrels away for you ta the train," he said as the men began their loading under the watchful eyes of the agents. Of the original twenty barrels of coins that Smiley Lewis brought into town, nineteen appeared near full with a partial barrel remaining. Not bad, not bad at all. It was about 1:45 p.m. when the agents and the wagon team arrived at the Pennsylvania Railroad Depot. One of the agents remained in the wagon while the other went inside to speak with the stationmaster. Soon the mail car was opened up and the men began to load the coin barrels. "I'll be riding back here with them. See you tomorrow Bill," Agent Gibson stated. Soon the train was southbound for Indianapolis. Agent Wells walked up to Marshal Merrell. "Looks like you have your hands full, Marshal, with this accident, so I won't bother you for long. Agent Gibson has left with the coins. My supervisor wants me to remain here until after the trial and return with the prisoner then. I would like to speak with your magistrate this afternoon to explain our situation."

Merrell replied, "I'm pretty much finished here so I'll take you to meet him. I really need to get back to watching over our prisoner. I have a man in a wheelchair guarding him now." Agent Wells seemed surprised by that statement, so Merrell quickly added, "He's the town's ex-Marshal but he has my complete confidence. He's a scrapper and I would hate to see anyone try to mess with him."

"He sounds interesting, I wouldn't mind meeting him if you have the time," the agent replied.

"Not a problem. Is there anything else you require that we can help you with?"

"No," he said. "I always travel with a two-day stay of clothing just in case. I left my travel bag inside the office of the stationmaster, so I'll get it and we can be on our way."

"The Mississinewa Hotel is the best place to stay in town, and just across the street tonight at 8:00 p.m. is a Vaudeville show at the Lovett Opera House. Let me treat you to a ticket from one officer of the law to another." Stating that it sounded just fine, the men made plans to meet out front of the opera house on the sidewalk at 7:45. "You won't have any trouble seeing it, as the gas lights have everything well-lit."

~~~~~~~~~~~~~~~~~~~~~~

Earlier, ex-Marshal Brewster rolled his wheelchair into his old office and removed a 10 gauge shotgun from the
~~~~~~~~~~~~~~~~~~~~~~

rack, opened it to ensure both barrels were loaded, and laid it across his lap. Kruger was surprised he was now being guarded by Brewster. “Marshal,” Kruger spoke. “Nice to see you again. Since you aren’t wearing any stinking badge anymore I will tell you this, you were a good cop and we feared you would catch us sooner or later. My old boss, Big Jim Malone, always spoke your name with respect.” Brewster was surprised but pleased to hear this, but said nothing as Kruger continued. “This new guy can’t hold a candle to you, and wheelchair or no wheelchair, I would hate to tangle with you, so you can relax with that shotgun.” Brewster nodded and made an effort to show he was relaxing, only so Kruger might say something important. “Think the ‘Squire will hang me, Marshal?” Brewster was again surprised by his candid question.

“Well, I don’t know. Maybe that fancy lawyer of yours will get you off, but then you gotta go against the Federal boys. I’m guessing it won’t go easy for you, Kruger.” *Maybe now is the time to ask him a very important question*, Brewster wondered.

“Let me ask you something, just between us old street fighters... are you or your boys behind these random shootings taking place in town?”

Kruger was quick to answer, “No, Marshal, not me or any of my boys had anything to do with it. They have puzzled me too, and I even sent out feelers trying to find out who it was and why they were doing it. It just doesn't make any sense at all. The hardware store owner was a pretty nice guy. I can see shooting the whore, but why shoot old Smokey? He never done nuttin' wrong. I hope you do catch the guy behind all of it. Must be a psycho or something."

The door to the office opened, and Marshal Merrell and a man in a suit entered. Brewster, seeing he was no longer needed, wheeled his chair back over to the gun rack and returned the shotgun. "Marshal Brewster," Merrell announced. "I would like to introduce Agent Wells of the Treasury Department." As both men shook hands, Wells asked him, "Any relation to that Agent Brewster who stopped the Fishers, Indiana bank holdup in 1877?" A smile crept across Brewster's face that someone still remembered it. "You! You stopped those robbers in their tracks? It's a great honor to meet you, sir. Agents are still taught how you spotted the holdup in progress, and captured the three bandits before anyone was hurt." With a modest reply, Brewster said that was all ancient history and he was just at the right time at the right place that day. Marshal Merrell was clearly impressed, and realized that he had totally misjudged his predecessor. *Maybe we shouldn't judge a person so quickly.*

"Thank you again, Marshal Brewster, for your assistance in guarding my prisoner today. I guess I need another daytime deputy to help me," Merrell told him with a wave. "Glad to do it, Marshal, call upon me anytime," Brewster said, as he wheeled himself out of the office. Outside, Zeke had just returned the wagon to it's owner, and upon seeing Brewster, was determined to push him home. "Let's stop for a cup of coffee," Brewster requested. "I'm buying. It's a wonderful day to be alive." As they traveled down the new sidewalk, Zeke handed Brewster a paper. "Here take a look. The agent says we fill this out and send it in for our pay. You know I'm not able to read or write none." With a smile, Brewster said he would be glad to take care of it.

Despite his best efforts, Doctor Baxter was unable to save the woman as her injuries were too extensive. The family was identified as Robert and Nancy Long with their son Buck, local farmers in the area who were in town shopping for the day and were in route home when the train struck them. Being told that they had an older son at home, Marshal Merrell pointed the way to the 'Squire's office to the agent, then mounted up on a city-owned horse and proceeded to the farm with the tragic news. He would need a good comedy show tonight to get the taste of death out of his mouth.

Smiley Lewis knew that he, and he alone, needed to set this plan in motion for tonight. By early afternoon he had two sticks of dynamite wired together. These should easily do the trick. Now all that remained was the long wait until darkness fell. Then he would act.

Justin and Wilbert arrived to find Marshal Merrell waiting over to brief them. "Kruger's trial is set for tomorrow at 2 p.m. There's a Treasury Agent who has made arrangements with 'Squire Jones to transport Kruger to Indianapolis tomorrow should he be found not guilty, otherwise expect a public hanging to take place pretty quick. I'll be at the opera house tonight with the agent watching some Vaudeville comedy acts, if you need me. I suggest you two change out at two-hour intervals. Just don't let anybody in the office you don't know. See you."

Wilbert replied, "He sure has changed, hasn't he? Say, I have an idea, let's flip a coin to see who starts off the two-hour babysitting job?" Pulling a coin out of his pocket, he announced the rules, "Loser stays indoors first. Call it." "Heads," Justin announced. It came up heads. With a grin Justin waved to Wilbert on his way out the door.

"See you at nine. Don't fall asleep!" Wilbert picked up a newspaper on the desk and playfully threw it towards him. It would be a long and boring night for both deputies, or so they thought.

Marshal Merrell and Agent Wells were having a pretty good time at the comedy show. Granted, some skits were funnier than others but the crowd seemed to be enjoying the evening. And for the first time since this all began, Marshal Merrell began to relax. One way or another, all of this would be over tomorrow.

There are only so many times a fellow could read a newspaper over and over, and by eight Wilbert was starting to pace the floor. The prisoner in the cell had not uttered one word since he came on duty, and Wilbert took to day-dreaming to kill time. Then he heard an unusual noise, the sound of someone at the door. A strange shuffling sound. Wilbert placed his hand on his revolver, just to be safe, when the door opened and ex-Marshal Brewster rolled his wheelchair inside. “Thought you might like a little company tonight, Wilbert,” he said, knowing that he had just scared the living daylights out of the young man.

“Glad to see you, Marshal, come on in and rest a spell. You’re out kind of late tonight, aren’t you?” Brewster replied he just felt like getting out, and that the town was pretty dead with most of the people up watching the Vaudeville acts.

“I would have enjoyed watching too, but of course, there’s no way to drag this wheelchair up the stairs so you’re second best.”

“Glad to have the company”, a relieved Wilbert told him, “Justin and I are trading off every two hours, so you might as well stay a while and visit with him too. So how was your day?”

Justin found the town to be extremely quiet other than the typical noise coming from the lower end saloons. It was still early, and the serious problems there would normally begin after midnight. Both deputies had already agreed that tonight nobody would be brought into the jail cell unless it was absolutely required, and maybe then only to be cuffed to the exterior of the cell. Couldn't allow anything to happen to our special prisoner tonight. Looking at his pocket watch, he could see it was going on time to return and relieve Wilbert.

It was dark as Justin walked into the fire barn, and he was very pleased to see Marshal Brewster there visiting. "Looks like the Cavalry has arrived," Brewster joked.

"Everything's quiet out there, almost too quiet. Stay alert and be safe," Justin told Wilbert on his way out.

"Take care of that guy will you, Marshal?" Wilbert jokingly told Brewster as he left the building.

Watching from the outside, a pair of eyes waited until the deputy was now out of sight before he snuck around to the back side of the fire barn. Checking his weapon and taking another quick glance around to ensure he had nobody watching him, Smiley Lewis pulled out the double sticks of dynamite. He wedged them as deep as he could between an eye level side board he had managed to loosen with his knife. Removing a match from his pocket, he lit the double twisted fuse and jumped behind a small shed, as he waited for the inevitable to happen...

Chapter 35

The resulting explosion blew out the entire corner of the rear wall, sending debris everywhere, both inside and out. Justin, who was standing about four feet away from Brewster, was hit hard by a piece of the shrapnel on the side of his head and body, sending him to the ground. The impact flipped Brewster out of his chair against the office desk, as his wheelchair disappeared from immediate view. Many of the roof supports hung down at dangerous angles, indicating the entire structure might collapse at any moment. Complete darkness penetrated everywhere as Brewster's mind began to start clearing. "*Jail break*," he thought. Brewster found that he was not pinned down by the heap of broken lumber and began crawling, calling out Justin's name. Only an occasional grown indicated where to drag himself toward. The pain in his back was horrendous, feeling like his body had been twisted like a pretzel, and he could feel warm blood trickling down his neck and forehead, but finding Justin became far more important than his own pain. "Justin...

Justin, are you alright?" He asked, managing to slide along the floor a couple of inches at a time.

Kruger had been laying down in his cell bunk when the explosion occurred, with the bars of the cell holding back all but the smallest of pieces of wood. His ears were ringing loudly from the explosion, but his mind became clear quickly knowing that someone was here to bust him out of jail. A tall shadow emerged from the outside barely visible but stepping over and around the debris pile. "Boss, where are you?" Kruger instantly recognized the voice as Smiley Lewis.

"Here, Smiley, I'm over here. Get me out of this stinking cage," he shouted, as the figure approached closer and closer.

On the floor, Brewster was finally able to locate Justin through his occasional moans and slight movements. Justin was trying to get up and had managed to get on one knee, but continued to moan in confusion. Brewster began trying to push off the heavy timbers that were covering the young deputy marshal when he began hearing two people speaking. The voices were coming from over by the cell area and Brewster could see the glow of the gas street lights radiating inside. A lone figure was approaching the cell and the name Smiley was heard. *I know that name, it's Smiley Lewis*, he thought.

The loud explosion echoed throughout the opera house bringing the show to a momentary pause, before the stage actors returned to their lines. Marshal Merrell and Agent

Wells, on the other hand, realized something had just occurred and left their rear seats as a few startled townspeople watched them leave. Both men raced down the interior stairwell lit by natural gas lamps, arriving at the street level. A large cloud of dust and dirt hung over the fire barn. It's two swinging doors were standing open, blown open actually by the pressure of the explosion, and both fire horses were walking about the street. "Jail break," the Marshal uttered, as both men sprinted the short one block distance with their weapons drawn.

"Stand back while I shoot the lock open," Smiley commanded. "I knew you would come for me," a jubilant Kruger told him. Smiley fired two bullets into the lock, but the cell door wasn't budging. "Kick it open," he yelled. "We gotta get out of here pronto. I got two horses tied up and ready." Brewster's mind had cleared completely by now, and he knew he had to do something or the prisoner and Smiley would get away. Reaching over Justin's still semi-conscious body, Brewster removed the deputy's Remington 44-40 and searched for a target amid the smoke and dust. "Freeze, Smiley," he shouted. "I have you covered." Smiley dropped down behind some of the loose debris and pulled his own weapon. "It's the old Marshal," shouted Kruger. "He's in a wheelchair and not armed. Get me out of here now!"

Kruger was now frantic, more like a wild man, as he begged and pleaded but the cell door would not budge. Smiley now knew that his plan would not succeed and every second brought on the possibility of his own capture. Standing up to the cell door, Smiley looked very hard into the face of Kruger. “Sorry, boss, you know how it is. I can’t leave you here to identify me.” Kruger now noticed the pistol was being aimed in his direction. “Don’t, Smiley! You know I won’t talk. I’ll give everything I have to you, just let me live...” The last thing Kruger saw was something totally unbelievable... something he never saw before... a huge smile on the face of Smiley Lewis. A shot to the head then ended the life of the man known only as Kruger.

The gun flash allowed Brewster to locate the shooter easily, so the ex-Marshal got off two quick shots, with one striking Smiley in the leg. In response, Smiley blindly leveled his weapon and got off his two remaining shots towards Brewster. Now it was time to escape, so the wounded man limped out of the hole in the wall and toward the awaiting horses and.... escape from capture.

“Gunshots from within,” Merrell shouted as they ran past one of the fire horses. Suddenly a limping figure of a man appeared, while trying to stagger towards a pair of horses now visible about fifty feet away. The wounded man tried to fire his gun at the approaching officers but realized it was empty and threw it towards them, missing both. He frantically tried to grab onto an already frightened horse to make his escape, but was unable to muster the strength to mount it. Agent Wells shouted, “I have you covered. Make one move and I'll blow your ugly head off!" With that, Smiley Lewis sank onto the ground below.

Seeing that Wells had his man covered, Marshal Merrell charged inside what was left of the fire barn, calling out to his deputy, "Anyone here? It's Marshal Merrell, where are you?" The sound of gunfire helped clear Justin's foggy mind enough to groan, "Over here." By now Wilbert Vance had raced as hard as his legs could carry him, and he reached Justin just as the Marshal cleared his own pathway. Justin began to shout, "Marshal Brewster! Where's Marshal Brewster? Help me find him!" before he realized Brewster lay beside him with a bullet wound in his chest. It was clear to all that Brewster was dead, but Justin insisted Doc Baxter try to save him before he, too, realized his good friend was now gone.

It was a dark day in Gas City as ex-Marshal Kenneth Brewster was laid to rest. Almost the entire town, including the assassin, turned out as a sign of respect. Local businesses draped black cloth over their entrances as a sign of respect and deep mourning. Since Brewster didn't go to church, Justin took it upon himself to ask the Reverend Stokes to say a few words at the cemetery. Marshal Merrell, Justin, Wilbert, Zeke, Agent Wells, and 'Squire Jones served as pallbearers. As the men stood next to the grave and the wooden casket was being lowered, Justin remembered the final words Wilbert had told the Marshal before leaving for patrol, "Take care of that guy will you, Marshal? Brewster had done that," and now he was dead, and Justin was alive. The body of Kruger had been quietly buried earlier that morning. There had been no mourners in attendance as he was laid to rest in a pauper's grave.

The trial of Smiley Lewis was scheduled now for the following day. Agent Wells received permission from his superiors to remain another day, after the situation was explained. Smiley's leg wound was not serious but he cried and whimpered like a baby. This was the man who helped the criminals make a go of things, this was the man who ordered the death of others, and this was the man who now begged to tell everything he knew for a special plea deal and a lighter sentence. Smiley then sang like a bird, giving names and important information that brought closure to many outstanding cases. Inside his own saddle bag was a huge wad of cash that apparently was from the selling of stolen goods. Money was then distributed to the victims of his thefts for the replacement cost of their jewelry. The rest of the funds were given to the town to help in the construction of the new school currently under construction. "It will pay for many school desks the children will use for generations," the mayor had told them.

After the funeral, all of the officers, Zeke and Agent Wells met up in what was left of the Marshal's office. Zeke was in the act of making a pot of coffee when he noticed a large group of men and wagons approaching. Barber Matthew Brooks entered the office and spoke, "I have been asked to be our spokesman here today. A group of us businessmen felt it only right that we chip in and help repair the damage done to this fire barn. If you men would like to give us a hand, we would be mighty pleased for your help." Marshal Merrell wandered outside to see wagonloads of lumber, tools and equipment as well as happy men ready to make things right. Tears of joy filled his eyes as the men set about their work. "These are very special people, good people, and I realize I had totally misjudged them," he said quietly but loud enough to be heard. Everyone made a point of not noticing his tears and set about the work ahead of them. By evening the fire barn was as good as new, with some saying even better.

The trial of Smiley Lewis was held outside in the open park due to the huge turnout of townspeople, a first for 'Squire Jones. Security was very tight for fear that someone would shoot Lewis to prevent him from providing names but the word had somehow already gotten out. Over thirty rough looking men decided to permanently leave town early that morning for "health reasons." Good riddance to all of them, too. Smiley was found guilty of murdering the prisoner Kruger and sentenced by 'Squire Jones to be hanged in three day's time. Finally, justice would now be served.

As the men walked Agent Wells toward his awaiting train, Wells felt he needed to say something important to his new friends. "I know you all are in deep mourning over the loss of your friend, and I hope you won't mind an outsider saying this. But Marshal Brewster died the way he probably wanted to, in action until the very end. Once I tell the agents in my office about all of this, his legend will only enlarge. Fighting a jail break single-handedly like he did will be spoken about by our agents for years to come. Your friend died a hero. Please honor his memory, not with sadness but with pride. He wouldn't want to be remembered any other way. It was great working with all of you. Look me up if you ever make it down to Indianapolis. Good-by." Everyone waved as the train slowly pulled away from the depot and began its journey southward.

Three days later and the execution was now history. Smiley went to the gallows crying and begging for mercy. Thank God, that terrible ordeal was now over. That same evening Justin and Wilbert reported for duty, only to find Zeke and banker Howell waiting for them inside the Marshal's office. "Good evening, gentlemen. I have permission from your Marshal to meet with you privately here tonight for a short duration. The late Marshal Brewster had a safety deposit box in our bank and it was closed out early this morning after the public hanging. What I am about to tell you has already been shared with 'Squire Jones and meets with his full legal approval. You see, gentlemen, each of you were mentioned in a will we found inside Mr. Brewster's safety deposit box."

"Mr. Zeke Miller, you are to inherit the contents of Mr. Brewster's savings account which comes to $235.72. We can transfer the full amount into any account you would like to open with us, Mr. Miller, or issue you cash." Zeke could hardly believe it. "That's more than I ever has had in my whole life. Mighty nice of the Marshal to do that fer me."

The banker now continued, "Mr. Wilbert Vance, you have been left Mr. Brewster's weapon collection, which I am led to believe is quite nice." Zeke chimed in, "Yep. It's a dandy. Guns he got from folks he's arrested goin' way back."

And now the banker came to Justin. "Mr. Justin Blake, you are to have his house which is owned free and clear. Here is an extra key we found inside the deposit box. You need to go down to see the clerk and he will transfer it over into your name. Well, gentlemen, that's all I have and congratulations to all of you. Have a pleasant evening."

Nobody said a thing until Zeke finally spoke, "Don't trust no bank with my money, never have and ain't gonna start now."

~~~~~~~~~~~~~~~~~~~~

It felt very strange for Justin and Wilbert as they entered Justin's new house the following morning. "I feel like I'm breaking and entering," Justin told his friend. Together they searched every room and discovered the guns for Wilbert.
~~~~~~~~~~~~~~~~~~~~

"I'm not sure what I'll do with all of these," he stated, as he picked each up for examination.

"Any of them you want?" That was a very kind offer but Justin politely thanked him and said no. "What shall I do with all of Marshal Brewster's clothing?" he asked Wilbert. Inside the bedroom on top of the dresser lay Brewster's Marshal Badge. "If I ever get the chance to become Marshal one day, this is the badge I will wear." Wilbert placed his hand on Justin's shoulder saying, "He would like that." Justin felt funny opening drawers and closets, but knew somehow he would need to empty the existing contents and move his own in. That's the way Brewster wanted it. "Let's go eat breakfast and get some sleep. I don't have to be in a hurry to get all of this done today." Wilbert replied, "I'll pass on breakfast as I want to get these guns into my place and get some sleep. See you tonight."

With that, Justin locked the front door to his own home and left. After breakfast and a four-hour nap, Justin felt refreshed and came up with another idea. He would walk over to the Stokes family home and speak with the Reverend Stokes, as he might know of needy people who could use the clothing. Reverend Stokes was pleased to see him and said yes indeed there were people in need of the clothing, so Justin said he would box the stuff up.

"I got to tell you, Reverend, I don't feel comfortable having received his home."

With a light smile and a nod, he answered that he understood. “But you got to remember Justin, Marshal Brewster liked you enough to want to provide something permanent in your life. He probably hoped one day you would marry and raise your children there. He is with God now, but his gift is for your future. Don’t feel guilty, but proud to have known such a fine and kind-hearted man.”

Sensing there was more that was troubling this young man, he asked what was truly bothering him. Justin was surprised that this man of God could read him so well.

“Well, sir, remember when those gypsies came to town? One of them, a gypsy girl read my fortune. Something she said continues to haunt me. She said she could see I had lost a great love but would find love again in the arms of another. She then said, let me try to get her words spoken correctly, ‘I see danger...grave danger...I see...I see the death of a dear friend.’ Did she predict Marshal Brewster’s death and did I ignore her warnings?”

The Reverend Stokes paused briefly to compile his words. “My son, I know nothing of fortune-telling or hocus pocus, but I can tell you that you should have no guilt about your friend’s death. There is danger at times in everyone’s lives and we all lose those we love most dear. As for the statement about having loved and lost but will love again, well... that’s pretty easy. At your age, it was a pretty safe bet that you have loved at least once in your life. The fact that you wear no wedding ring says you will love again. These people are experts in reading the body mannerisms of people. The widening of the eyes or a slight smile tells them they are correct in their predictions. No, my son, you did not fail to warn your friend. The bullet that hit him could have easily hit you instead. This is all God's will, and while we cannot at times understand it, we must have faith that it's for a greater purpose. Leave any guilt you have here in this room and go in peace, my young friend." Thanking him for his time, Justin left with an entirely different attitude. When he opened the door to the house, he was now entering his own home. Thanks again, Marshal Brewster. God bless you, my dear friend.

~~~~~~~~~~~~~~~~~~~~~

The city council met that evening to a sparse crowd, no doubt due to the intense summer heat. The city attorney had two pieces of important information he wished to present to the council. He stated that a lawsuit was filed against those factories responsible for the heavy polluting of the Mississinewa River to force them to dispose of all waste products in other, safer methods. The second bit of information was a letter received from the Pan Handle Railroad stating that within two weeks they would begin complying with the city's ordinance to supply warning
~~~~~~~~~~~~~~~~~~~~~

flagmen at our railroad crossing. They also stated, no doubt as a swipe at the ordinance, that passenger fees for all arriving and departing passengers in Gas City would have their fares raised to cover this unnecessary financial expense. Most of the council members shook their head in utter disgust. One member even suggested a boycott by departing passengers might bring their fare prices back to normal. Still, everyone seemed pleased that the railroad had finally seen reason, and it was suggested that the "Penny" will most likely follow the lead of the Pan Handle.

At the conclusion of the meeting, Mayor Huffman asked all board members to remain behind, and also Marshal Merrell who was already halfway out the door. "Gentlemen, I have something I wish to show you. This arrived today in the mail." He then passed it over to the first councilman who, after reading it, produced a look of deep concern on his face as he passed it to the next man. Finally, it was handed to Marshal Merrell. The letter read:

I Won't Miss Next Time.

"I guess he's determined to shoot me and, frankly, I don't know what I can do about it. I can't crawl under my bed and hide." Councilman Davidson felt he had the answer, "Why don't you resign as mayor? Maybe then this person will leave you alone. We can appoint your replacement here and now."

With a look of annoyance, the mayor replied, "You, I suppose?" Putting his chin out in a show of authority, Councilman Davidson answered, "Why not, I'm just as qualified as the next man." Turning away from this discussion, Mayor Huffman sought Marshal Merrell's opinion. "The person tried to disguise his handwriting so we cannot determine who he is. The paper doesn't help. It's standard writing paper in hundreds of homes here in town. Looking at the envelope, he replied, "He printed every letter in your name and address. Other than giving you 24-hour police protection, I don't know what we can do. Sadly, we are no closer to catching this man than before. I urge you to remain at home as much as possible and don't expose yourself to any unnecessary risks."

Huffman tried his best to compose himself by saying, "Gentlemen, I will not resign and I won't hide like a scared rabbit." With that, the impromptu meeting ended. How would one stop a man determined to kill you anyway?

Chapter 36

Contractors worked feverishly to complete the final touches for the new school house. Located on the east end of town and only one block south of main street next to the Gas City Land Company, East Ward as it was being called, would solve the student displacement problems that currently existed. A formal grand opening was now scheduled for Saturday, with Mayor Huffman performing a ribbon cutting ceremony at 11 a.m. on the rear steps. That location would allow easier public viewing of the proceedings. Afterwards, the public would be invited to tour the new modern facility that would serve the community for generations to come, with classes beginning the following Monday morning.

The assassin read the headlines in the Journal newspaper and laughed to himself. This was the perfect opportunity to do away with Mayor Huffman, with a large crowd of people to witness his demise. The rear steps of the new school building where the ribbon ceremony would take place were high enough to allow a clear and precise shot above the heads of those assembled. Now to find the perfect sniper's location.

Tossing down the newspaper, Marshal Merrell stated, "I don't like this one bit. The Mayor is making himself a target for another assassination attempt. I can see three things happening Saturday: the assassin doesn't show; after all, the assassin shoots the Mayor; or we get lucky and prevent it from occurring in the first place."

Justin spoke up, "I see a fourth. We capture him and put an end to this madness once and for all." Taking out a sheet of paper, Justin began to sketch out an idea he had. "Here is the new school and the rear steps on the north side of the building where the Mayor will speak and cut the ribbon. The steps are elevated high enough to allow a clear shot. If a man with a sniper's rifle were to stalk him, he would have to be located somewhere north of Main Street either on a house rooftop or a second story window. He, also, has the ability to be anywhere within a quarter of a mile radius. Since little has been built beyond Fourth Street going east, we need to concentrate north to west," Justin said, as he moved his finger to illustrate. "I know Marshal Merrell here is one of the speaker's Saturday morning, so I propose that three deputies divide up and walk all areas in this vicinity to scour for any possible shooter. I figure he will be concentrating on his target and not paying all that much attention to men walking around the streets and alleyways."

Merrell liked the plan but pointed out there were only two of them. "Not if we use Zeke. Ask him to be a secret deputy again and I bet he will jump at the chance," Justin pointed out.

"Secret deputy?" Merrell asked.

"It's an old story, Marshal, but if you were to ask him, I'm betting he will jump at the chance." Realizing that Justin's plan did require more help, Merrell agreed to ask as he looked out in the fire barn for him. "He's not here, so if anybody spots him, please tell him I'm looking to speak with him," Merrell said. Now the officers had a plan, but nobody felt comfortable that the Mayor's life might be hanging in the balance.

The assassin located the best possible location from which to shoot. He would use the Holy Family Catholic Church's bell tower. Built last year in 1893, the wooden church provided daily Mass at 8 a.m., and confessions on Saturday evenings at 6:30 p.m. for it's members. With it's easy entry and a vertical wooden ladder to gain entry into the bell tower, it was the perfect choice to shoot from. After the Mayor had been killed, the assassin would remain hidden for two hours to allow the excitement to dwindle down before making his exit, before the priest's early afternoon arrival. That would work out just fine.

"You want ta see me, Marshal?" Zeke asked, as he entered the office.

"Yes, I do, Zeke, please pull up a chair." Zeke was slightly wary of doing that, but complied anyway. "Zeke, as you know, with the death of my brother, we are running short on manpower here and I have been given permission to hire another deputy marshal. I wanted to know if you might be interested in the job. It would be a nighttime position."

Zeke was set back on his heels with this news. "You talkin' about a secret deputy?" he asked.

"No, I'm referring to a full-time deputy position with uniform, badge and pay of $35 a month." Zeke sat there with his mouth open for a few seconds before he replied, "Gosh, Marshal... I guess you don't know I don't read or write well."

"Zeke, there's more to being a good deputy than just reading and writing. I have spoken to the mayor and he assured me he has total confidence in you and that, should I choose to hire you, the city council may just overlook the hiring ordinance it has on the books. If you choose to accept, I will team you up with one of the nighttime deputies and he can file the reports and log entries. As for handling drunks, I know you know about everyone in this town, and I figure you can use your own persuasive charms to talk your way out of any situation. If not, your partner can bash a skull or two. Why don't you do this, take a walk and think about the offer then get back with me later, alright?" Old timer Zeke Miller left the marshal's office with much to consider. *Maybe this new Marshal was alright after all?*

Zeke returned to the office thirty minutes before the marshal's shift was to end. "I have been a thinkin' hard on your offer and I will take it under one condition." Curious, the Marshal asked what it was.

"Well, sir, last summer 'efore you ever got here there was a hypno-man over at the opera house that turned me into a chicken. Folks laughed and called me chicken man for a long time. Hard ta live down, if you know what I mean and all. Well, sir, I'll be happy ta wear a badge and all, but I don't want ta wear no fancy uniform and start folks a-howlin' at me again."

Trying to hide his smile, Marshal Merrell said he thought something could be arranged. "Just do me a small favor...try to clean up a little, all right?" That was agreed upon. Then Zeke asked if he could wait and get sworn in official, like in front of his two friends. Shortly after 7 p.m., Zeke Miller officially became Deputy Marshal Zeke Miller. It was a proud day for everyone involved.

"Zeke, I only wish Marshal Brewster was here to witness this."

Zeke replied with tears in his eyes, "Maybe he is, Justin... maybe he is."

The men, then sat down and planned for tomorrow's event. "I know this is a lot of added work hours for you men," the Marshal stated, "I will try to get you time off, later on, to make up for it." Nobody had any squawks so the plans were laid out. “Whatever we do we must prevent another killing tomorrow. This assassin is only human... he will make mistakes and this may be our best chance to catch him, that is if he makes a try. The Mayor will not cancel his involvement so let’s do all we can to make it safe.” Opening his desk drawer, Merrell pulled out three police whistles. “I picked these up this morning thinking it will be hard communicating with the band playing and the noise of the crowd.” Each man pocketed the whistle and prayed he wouldn’t need to use it tomorrow.

After a middle of the night rain shower, Saturday morning was again bright, sunny, and hot. With the opening of the ceremonies starting at 11 a.m., many of the crowd began forming early so they could be close enough to hear the public speeches. After a brief three-hour morning nap, all three deputies were north of Main Street patrolling the streets and alleyways, watching for anything at all out of the ordinary. Each had discussed with the others to blow his whistle if he saw anything at all and the other two men would come a running. Caution was stressed, though, that should the assassin hear too many whistles, it would tip him off to added police patrols. Each deputy had also decided to wear normal every day clothing, so as to not stand out and to try to remain out of sight as much as possible. With the long range afforded to the Whitworth rifle, the shooter could be almost anywhere. By 10 a.m., everyone was in place with all eyes scanning their assigned target areas. Justin searched every home, business, church, shed, everything within his area from top to bottom with his sharp eyes over and over again, trying to drown out the band playing it's music. It was a festive occasion with children running and laughing, as parents tried to maintain order.

Luckily the band had stopped now, so if a whistle was blown, each man could hear it. With the playing now ended, that could only mean one thing, it was time for Marshal Merrell to address the assembled people and finally introduce Mayor Huffman. From his four block distance from the school, Justin could just make out the yellow ribbon stretched across the two rear doors. He continued now to move about quickly and scanned every door, bush, porch, rooftop, church, and shed again and again, and prayed that the assassin was home eating an early lunch rather than plotting another killing.

"...and so it is my honor to introduce to you our very own, Mayor Huffman." Applause rose from the assembled people as parents shushed their children's voices. "Thank you, Marshal Merrell, for your kind words. Early this spring, your city council presented a plan on building a new schoolhouse for our community..."

A flash of metal in the bright sunlight caught Justin's attention up ahead, as he focused upon the bell tower of the Holy Family Catholic Church. "... A much needed schoolhouse to help educate the over 600 students now residing within our community..."

Justin at first thought it was a simple sun reflection from perhaps the church bell itself, but to be sure he ran closer for a better examination. "Our productive community is thriving by leaps and bounds, as industry is bringing in better paying wages and offering a better way of life for our people..." Still two hundred feet from the church, Justin could finally make out a silver pipe now protruding between the wooden window slats. *It's a rifle barrel*, he realized. Grabbing his whistle, Justin began blowing it for all he was worth, as he reached for his holstered Remington 44-40 and got off two quick shots upward toward it. His bullets began striking the window frame as a second later the rifle discharged. Justin's firing had caused the momentarily startled shooter to raise slightly up as he fired. His bullet shattered the schoolhouse door glass above Mayor Huffman's head as the crowd of people screamed and ducked for cover. Justin had no idea if the shooter had found his mark or not, but one thing was for certain, he was now trapped inside the bell tower of the church. Justin continued to blow his whistle and saw the fellow officers fast approaching.

Zeke was the first to arrive as Justin shouted to watch the front door and bell tower, and he motioned Wilbert to follow him, "Take the back door, I'm going inside. We gotta prevent his escape." Charging inside the side door, Justin noticed a room off to the side where a wooden ladder was mounted vertically leading up into the bell tower. There was also a rope hanging down close by for the priest to manually ring the church bell. “You, up there, this is Deputy Justin Blake, come down with your hands up. We have you surrounded. Throw down your rifle and surrender.” Instead, the shooter began firing a pistol blindly downward. Realizing they now had a stand-off situation, Justin began racking his brain on what he could do to drive the shooter downward, when an idea struck him. The bell. Replacing his weapon back into it’s holster, Justin began pulling on the bell rope causing the bell to ring. Justin pulled as hard as he could continuously as the bell rang and rang. *It must be terribly loud up there*, he thought. *Good!* One thing the constant ringing of the bell did was to bring the assembled curious crowd to that location.

Zeke yelled for everyone to form a human chain around the church to prevent the shooter’s escape. The priest, Father Andrew, arrived and Wilbert asked him if there were any tunnels or means of escape out of the church. There were not, the Father replied. “Good, we have him trapped, so now it’s only a matter of time.” After fifteen minutes of constant ringing, Justin could feel pistol shots whizzing by him striking the floor near his feet. Justin thought he could hear the man shouting something, so he silenced the bells. “Toss your weapons down and you come down, or I’ll ring this bell all day.” Once the people had formed a protective ring around the church, Wilbert and Zeke had ventured inside and were standing next to Justin with their own weapons pulled.

Suddenly there was an object seen falling downwards and hitting the floor very hard. It was the shooter's rifle. "Toss down that pistol or I'll start ringing the bells again," Justin shouted. The pistol then fell to the floor. "Alright... slowly make your way down the ladder. Keep those hands where I can see them. We have you covered." From up above a voice pleaded, "Just don't ring that darn bell anymore! I'm coming down." Slowly a figure emerged and began descending the ladder. By now Marshal Merrell had joined his men inside and was trying his best to keep the curious onlookers outside. The figure paused halfway, and Justin wondered if he was contemplating going back up when he once again started his descent. The man finally reached the floor as all hands grabbed him and cuffed his wrists behind him. "I would never have guessed," Justin echoed what everyone else was thinking. The shooter was none other than 'Squire Jones.

"Just don't ring that bell anymore!" he pleaded, as he was escorted outside of the church.

There was a huge gasp from the crowd as they realized who the Marshals had just arrested. The last man many people expected to be the assassin. Now he would experience the other side of the justice system.

After an examination by Doctor Baxter, he ruled the prisoner's hearing would return to normal relatively soon. "I thought I knew Hiram Jones. I can't believe he was capable of this," Doc said, as he shook his head in amazement. Marshal Merrell telegraphed the Grant County Sheriff's Office to explain who he had locked up, and requested they arrive tomorrow by train to take him away. That delay might give them some time to discover some much-needed answers to their many questions.

By shift change, Marshal Merrell determined he would remain and try to obtain information from the non-talking prisoner. Finally, Justin felt he should make an effort, saying, 'Squire Jones, I always had nothing but the deepest respect and admiration for you. I just cannot believe a man of your high standing in life capable of such violence." Jones noted being referred to finally as 'Squire, having been called Jones and prisoner all day long, so he began to speak.

"Respect and admiration are important to me, deputy, and I appreciate your kindness. Respect is the one thing our Mayor failed to give me, insisting on calling me by my first name instead of the important title I held, a title I have earned in my service to this community." Justin was pleased he had him speaking, as he noticed everyone else was acting like they were not paying attention.

"Yes, sir, you passed judgment on many of those brought before you, and I never heard it said otherwise that you were not fair and correct in your rulings."

Nodding his head, Jones continued, “That is quite true young man, but many a man or woman brought before my court deserved a much harsher punishment than I was able to legally allow for their crimes and misdemeanors. That is why I have chosen this path.”

“I see,” Justin replied casually. “You are an expert shot. Were you a sniper during the war?”

Jones continued to talk as Justin brought him a cup of coffee, “Thank you for your kindness. No, I was not officially listed as such upon the rolls of the Kentucky regiment to which I belonged. I found the Whitworth lying beside the body of a Rebel sniper. I have never seen anything quite like it, so I kept it and occasionally used it. Then the war ended and I hid it inside a small cave I found close to where we were to be mustered out. I then returned and brought it home as a war trophy. Kentucky continued to have it’s problems, so I moved all of my belongings to Indiana and ended up here.”

“I see,” Justin replied. “Did you study the law before the war?”

“Yes to some degree,” replied Jones. “That’s why I was interested in the ‘Squire position, and I must say I feel I have served that role very well.”

“Why, sir, did you shoot Mr. Larson?”

“Jeb special ordered the .451 hexagon bullets from his contact in North Carolina. I could not allow him to later remember ordering them for me, so he had to perish before I could begin dealing out punishment to all transgressors."

Justin continued to sip his own coffee in a very casual manner, "But what of Mrs. Howell?"

Prisoner Jones puffed up at the mentioning of her name. "I have eaten many meals in their family home. I couldn't help but notice that when her husband James was out of the room, the woman openly flirted with me. After a few times of this, I thought I shall put her to the test and flirted back. She, in return, called me an old sick pervert. Then later, she took up with that piece of factory trash and left poor James a shambled wreck. She simply had to pay the price for her wickedness. No legal punishment would suffice."

With this information, and the correct assumption that poor old Smokey was shot by accident, his oral statements were written down for the Sheriff to have. The one thing that struck everyone was that Jones' demeanor had not changed one bit today since any other time they had worked with him in the past. One would fully expect 'Squire Jones to assume he would be sleeping peacefully in his own bed this evening. This, of course, would never happen again. Gas City was now in the need of another 'Squire. By early morning the sheriff and a deputy arrived to transport the prisoner to the city of Marion where his trial was soon scheduled to be conducted.

~~~~~~~~~~~~~~~~~~~~~~

The accolades came pouring into the marshal's office for successfully capturing the assassin. Marshal Merrell made it quite clear that Deputy Justin Blake was the real hero, as it was his plan and his efforts that brought the reign of terror finally to an end. The real shocker, though, came when Marshal Merrell submitted his letter of resignation to the city council. "I have the desire to travel out west and, frankly, things are a little bit boring around here now," he jokingly told them. He strongly urged that Justin Blake be chosen as his replacement. "The man is ready now and will do you proud," he told them. Two days later newly appointed Marshal Justin Blake and his two deputies walked the ex-Marshal to his awaiting train. Shaking hands with each man, Merrell expressed his satisfaction in knowing and working with each of them. Slowly, the train pulled away for destinations unknown. "Marshal Blake," Wilbert said. "That Marshal's badge looks great upon your vest." Glancing down upon it, he remarked with a bit of sadness, "It should... it once belonged to a fine lawman."

Later in the office, Justin found a little time to reflect. "After each of you returns from your richly deserved days off, I may take a couple of days of vacation for myself. Wilbert, do you remember what that beautiful gypsy girl told me during my fortune-telling session? She said I would
~~~~~~~~~~~~~~~~~~~~~~

one day obtain a promotion, I would lose a dear friend, and I would find love in the arms of another girl. Well, the first two have come and gone, so maybe I need to start working on the third part. I wonder what the lovely Marsha Weir is doing these days." His friends all laughed and wished him the best of luck in finding out.

Several months prior to his capture, 'Squire Jones had advised a badly shaken and distraught James Howell that if he himself ever required the use of an attorney, he would call upon the legal services of Mr. Hugh Williamson. As fate would have it, prisoner Jones called upon Mr. Williamson for his own personal counsel. Still, it had done him no good, as the past 'Squire of Gas City finally went to the gallows on March 25, 1895. May God have mercy upon his wicked soul.